Double-Edged Sword

A Novel of Reconstruction

J.D.R. Hawkins

Library of Congress Control Number: 2022932069

ISBN		
	Paperback	978-1-68536-316-1
	Hardback	978-1-68536-317-8
	eBook	978-1-68536-318-5

Westwood Books Publishing LLC
Atlanta Financial Center
3343 Peachtree Rd NE Ste 145-725
Atlanta, GA 30326

www.westwoodbookspublishing.com

Acknowledgments

I would like to thank the following people for their ongoing assistance and support. Without them, this book could not have been written.

John M. Coski, Historian and Director of Library & Research, The Museum of the Confederacy, Richmond, VA

Decatur Public Library, Decatur, AL

Joe Ewers, 2nd South Carolina String Band

Susan Forrey, genealogist, Dover, PA

Huntsville Depot and Museum, Huntsville, AL

My son, Jeremy, for assisting me with editing and coming up with the title for this book

John McClure, Virginia Historical Society

David Miller, Associate Curator, Military and Diplomatic History, National Museum of American History, Smithsonian Institution, Washington, D.C.

Mac Wyckoff, Chancellorsville/Spotsylvania National Military Park, VA

Chuck Yungkurth, Colorado Railroad Museum, Denver, CO

FOR JILL

Illis Victoriam
Non Immortatitatem Fata Negaverunt

Fates Which Refused Them Victory
Did Not Deny Them Immortality

Contents

"The government of the United States has in north Alabama any and all rights which they choose to enforce in war, to take their lives, their houses, their lands, their everything, because they cannot deny that war exists there, and war is simply power unrestrained by constitution or compact. If they want eternal warfare, well and good. We will accept the issue and dispossess them and put our friends in possession. To those who submit to the rightful law and authority all gentleness and forbearance, but to the petulant and persistent secessionists, why, death is mercy and the quicker he or she is disposed of the better. Satan and the rebellious saint of heaven were allowed a continuance of existence in hell merely to swell their just punishment. To such as would rebel against a Government so mild and just as ours was in peace, a punishment equal would not be unjustified ..."

- General William T. Sherman (1865)

Chapter One

The constant *ric-atata, ric-atata* of the wheels rolling against the rails lulled him. Sweat beaded on his forehead, and he found it difficult to breathe in the warm, humid, almost unbearable air. The soft whispering breeze of his wife's handheld fan gently whispered against his cheek. His mind eased. Voices seeped into his conscience, growing louder as they neared him.

"Over here!" a man yelled. "Bring that torch!"

A flame came into view. It quickly exploded into a fury of fire against the night sky. What appeared to be phantoms floated around burning buildings. The confusion escalated. Trees began to spark, glowing behind a dark swinging object hanging from one of the branches. A child frantically cried. Muffled banging noises, as if guns were being shot, could be heard in the distance. Someone ran out of the burning house. It was a woman. She screamed and kept on screaming; her screams grew louder and more blood-curdling.

David's heart leaped. He gasped as he jolted awake. Looking around, he remembered he was riding in a passenger car. The woman's screams turned into the locomotive's whistle, and the pistol shots became the train's churning wheels.

"We're in Richmond," Anna said to him.

He looked over at her, stunned at first.

"Are you all right?"

He drew a sigh of relief. "Yeah." He smiled, forcing himself to disregard the frightful nightmare. "I'm fine."

She smiled back at him, his new bride, the love of his life. Why she remained beside him on his journey home amazed him.

"Did we cross the river I told you about? The one they named after you?"

Anna chuckled. "You mean the North Anna? Not that I'm aware of, but I have to admit, I dosed off myself." She paused, contemplating.

"I think the first thing we should do is to go find the man we met in York who said he'd sell us a horse and carriage."

The train heaved and screeched to a stop. Passengers flowed out of the car onto the platform. David stood and held his hand out to her. She picked up the basket her aunt had given them before their trip, took his hand, and followed him outside.

"He's two cars down," he said, and led her through the throng.

Steam from the locomotive hissed out around their feet, rolling down the platform. The train's bell clanked rhythmically. A paunchy man with a stovepipe hat emerged from a passenger car.

"There he is! Mr. Tarver!" He let go of her hand and hurried ahead while Anna struggled to keep up. "Mr. Tarver!" David approached the man and extended his hand. "I'm the feller who spoke with you back in York." The man glared at him, so he continued, "About buyin' a horse and carriage?"

The man's blank expression turned to one of recognition. "Oh, yes! Mr. Summers, is it?"

"Yessir." He turned to Anna. "And this here's my wife."

"Mrs. Summers, pleased to make your acquaintance." Mr. Tarver tipped his hat.

Anna softly giggled. "The feeling's mutual," she said, returning the greeting.

"I have a driver waiting," the man said. "Why don't we walk over to my barouche and discuss the particulars."

"I need to fetch Renegade first," David explained. "I'll be right back!" He threw a glance at Anna before trotting off down the length of the resting train.

"We so appreciate your doing this for us, kind sir," she said with a smile. "We're newly married, and in need of transportation." She could tell by his expression that her glowing porcelain skin, and her aqua eyes sparkling from under her bonnet, caught him off guard for a moment.

"Why, I'm more than happy to assist, my dear," he stammered as he removed his hat.

Steam from the locomotive made the stifling August heat all the more noticeable.

Anna looked down the length of the train to see her husband approaching. He was leading a saddled piebald chestnut horse with a flaxen mane and tail and white patches on his underbelly: the magnificent little stallion she'd come to love. David grinned as he neared.

"That's a fine-looking animal," Mr. Tarver commented.

"Thank you, sir," he responded.

The man started for the parked coaches nearby, and the young couple followed. "Here we are," he said as he arrived at his barouche. "Now then, what was the price I quoted you?"

"One hundred dollars," David replied.

Mr. Tarver nodded. "Yes, well, I'm afraid the purchasing price has changed."

"What do you mean?" asked Anna.

"It means, my dear, that we are in the South now, and I must accept any opportunity as it arises."

David glanced at his wife. "How much?" he growled.

Anna could see his anger rising. His hazel eyes were darkening to umber, and his jaw clenched.

"Five hundred," Mr. Tarver replied.

"What!" David exploded. "Are you out of your cotton pickin' mind?"

Mr. Tarver laughed. His driver, a teenage boy, turned to sneer.

"We made a bargain!" David continued. "We shook on it!"

"Times are hard, Mr. Summers," the paunchy man explained.

David took a step toward him, but Anna blocked his path.

"Darling," she cooed, "why don't you go check on our trunk."

"I ain't leavin' you here with this ... this thief!" He glared at the man.

"Please darling."

The insistent tone of her voice was a warning. He realized he should cool down, so he stomped off.

"Now, Mr. Tarver," she said as she turned to face him. "Surely you're a man of reason. Can't we come to some kind of an agreement?"

Mr. Tarver snorted. "What do you have in mind, my dear?"

Anna glanced at the driver, then leaned in and whispered into the older man's ear. She stepped back. "And since both you and I are from Pennsylvania, I thought perhaps you might oblige."

"Well, I would certainly like to," he replied.

She could see he needed further persuasion. The thought had occurred to her on the train that this might happen, so she had mentally prepared herself. She retrieved a small purple velvet pouch from her reticule. "One hundred dollars ... and this." She dropped it into his outstretched palm.

He pried the pouch open and lifted out a pendant. Nodding as he beheld the sapphire, he said, "All right, Mrs. Summers, we have an agreement." He placed the necklace back inside, pulled the drawstring closed, and stuffed the pouch into his vest pocket. "Follow me."

Anna glanced up at the young driver, who raised a curious eyebrow at her as she walked away. They came to a baggage car where David was waiting.

"Your wife has persuaded me to honor our agreement," Mr. Tarver said.

He waved a finger through the air, motioning for the newlyweds to follow. David glared at Anna questioningly, but she only responded with a smile, and so he resigned to tagging along behind. They walked down the length of the train to a boxcar. The doors were opened. The strong, rancid smell of manure escaped the warm car and permeated the air. Anna began to gag. Quickly, she pulled a handkerchief from her purse and covered her nose. A ramp was placed in the boxcar's opening. Several black men emerged, each one leading an equine. David saw that some of the animals had been painted to disguise their age.

"Here is a good sturdy beast," Mr. Tarver said, taking the halter of a dark bay mule. "And it's all you can afford."

"A mule? It was my understandin' that we agreed on a workhorse," David protested.

"This little jennie is only four, and will give you plenty of years of devoted labor."

David scoffed. He looked the mule over. "Recently shod?" he asked.

"Just last week," the man replied.

"I don't know ... she looks older than four ..."

"Thank you, Mr. Tarver," Anna interjected. "She'll do just fine. Now about a carriage?"

"Ah, yes." He made his way past a few more cars to where men were unloading various vehicles and lining them alongside the road. Mr. Tarver walked up to a buckboard wagon. "You will be very comfortable in this, and it's ..."

4

"All we can afford," David finished for him. He removed his slouch hat and ran his hand through his dark brown collar-length hair in an effort to contain his composure.

"I'll even throw in the hitch and harness." Mr. Tarver grinned, exposing yellow tobacco-stained teeth.

"We're very grateful, sir," Anna said, taking her husband's arm.

David scowled. This wasn't at all what he had imagined. He had envisioned driving up to his family's farmstead in a bright, shiny carriage with his lovely new wife seated beside him. But it wasn't meant to be, and he knew he was better off to bite his tongue than to argue. Mr. Tarver obviously had the upper hand, and could back out if provoked. David also knew that, because the South was in disarray, his chances of finding anything cheaper were slim at best.

"Are you staying here in Richmond?" Mr. Tarver inquired.

David grunted. "No, sir. We're on our way to Alabama."

"Oh," said Mr. Tarver with a nod. "Then you'll be wanting to catch the train south to Petersburg, and it departs in two hours." He turned and pointed down the thoroughfare. "You'll have time to find yourselves something to eat, if you so desire. I'll have someone assist you with your bags." He motioned to one of the hands, who hitched the mule to the wagon and led it to the row of baggage cars. David found the trunk containing their personal effects waiting on the platform, so he pointed it out to the rail hand, who heaved it into the back of the wagon before walking off.

"That will be one hundred dollars," Mr. Tarver said.

David took out the greenback Anna's uncle had given him upon their departure and handed it to him.

Mr. Tarver withdrew a piece of paper from his vest. "And here, sir, is your bill of sale. Pleasure doing business with you." He smiled and turned to leave, but then remembered. "Go west a mile or two until you see the town. Can't miss it. Then be back here to catch the Petersburg train. Oh, and congratulations, you two!" He strolled to his waiting barouche, and climbed in with considerable effort. His driver tapped the reins before driving off.

"Why did he say that?" David asked aloud.

He sighed, wondering how a Yankee would know his way around Richmond so well, while he unburdened Renegade and threw the saddle into the wagon. After tying his horse to the back of the vehicle, he helped Anna climb in, stepped up, and sat beside her. He swatted the reins against the jennie's back, who turned her long head to get a good look at him.

"Damned mule!" he exclaimed, exasperated with his situation.

"Here, let me try." Anna took the reins from him. "Come on girl!" she coaxed, gently slapping the leather straps against the animal's withers.

The mule twitched her long ears and started forward. Anna handed the reins back to her frowning husband.

"All it takes is a little patience," she said with a smile.

They drove down the street in the direction indicated. David noticed all the Yankee uniforms about and gingerly pulled out his pistol, being careful not to draw the soldiers' attention.

"I'll take it," Anna said quietly. She set the handgun down in her lap, retrieved her handkerchief, tore it into long strips, and tied the weapon to her thigh before concealing it under her brown skirt.

The town was nearly deserted, vaguely resembling the bustling city that David and his best friend, Jake, had ridden through on their way to join J.E.B. Stuart's cavalry. Although it had been only two years since then, it seemed like a lifetime ago. The Southerners were impoverished now; it was evident by their shabby clothing and frayed hats. Although the hazy midday sun cast long shadows, there seemed to be a foreboding, dark shroud hanging over the city, and it wasn't long before David saw why. As they traveled along the riverfront, bombed out buildings rose up to meet them like ghostly skeletons, the remains of what was once the Confederacy's great capital. The Stars and Stripes waved atop flagpoles, only four months ago replacing the grand Blood-Stained Banner, a flagrant reminder of the recent victory won. Union soldiers paroled the streets.

"Dear God," David half whispered as he took in the horrendous sight. "What have they done?"

Southern women dressed in mourning black drifted like ashes.

"Lost souls for a lost cause," he muttered out loud to himself.

The women glanced up at the passing couple. David saw the empty expressions in their eyes, the overwhelming consummation of total loss. His heart grew heavier with each passing block. The South, he now realized, was left to cope with Sherman's destruction, Grant's depredation, and the Union's occupation.

Shelled out buildings lay in ruin, their open doorways and windows gaping to expose piles of rubble inside. They rose up like enormous jagged shards, splintered and broken. Chimneys within the buildings stood erect, which looked to David like long bony fingers extending up to the firmament. A few freed men stood idly on the street corners.

"It looks as though they're lost as well," Anna remarked.

David nodded. His imagination took over as he absorbed the sight. He visualized what it must have been like only a few months ago, when Sherman's army invaded and seized the city. *The poor people of Richmond*, he thought to himself. All he could do was slowly shake his head in disgust and despair.

As Mr. Tarver had directed, the city appeared, but nothing seemed to be open. David was more than eager to leave the destroyed city, so they returned to the depot, but no train was waiting for them. He parked the wagon, went inside, and learned that the train would be arriving within the hour, so he and Anna decided to sit down and finish what little food remained in their basket while they killed time.

A Union officer with a neatly trimmed beard approached them. "Are you planning on boarding the train?" he asked.

"Yessir," responded David as he stood. He already knew he didn't like the direction this conversation was going.

"No civilians allowed to board," the sergeant said. He turned and spit a long spray of tobacco juice, which made Anna wince with repulsion. "The trains are being used for military personnel only."

David glanced at his wife, who stood and said, "Sir, we would greatly appreciate it if you could make an allowance on our behalf."

The sergeant chuckled. "Now, missus, if I made an exception for you, I'd have to do it for everyone else who wants to ride the rails back home to Dixie." The tone in his voice changed to sarcasm. He glared at David, who returned the expression.

"Honey, would you excuse us for a moment?" She smiled at her husband. The shocked look on his face nearly made her falter, but she steadied herself.

He sauntered across the room and stood with his arms folded.

"Sir," Anna said, trying to bat her eyelashes, but not so much as to appear comical. "I'm in a predicament, and I desperately need your help. You see, I'm from Pennsylvania, and I ..." She glanced over at David, who stood scowling across the room.

"I'm sorry, ma'am, but I can't allow it," the sergeant said.

Anna spoke to him in a hushed voice. Suddenly, the sergeant looked over at David and grinned.

"All right, young lady, I'll see what I can do."

He walked out of the depot, and David returned to his bride.

A few minutes later, the sergeant reappeared, announcing that he was going to allow them to board after all. "And congratulations to the two of you," he said before walking off.

"What's goin' on?" David asked, confused by the sergeant's change in demeanor.

Anna merely smiled at him, just as the train arrived. He loaded their belongings into box and baggage cars after producing proof of his purchases and his discharge papers from prison.

The iron horse pulled away and chugged across a bridge spanning the James River. As it picked up speed, David glanced back at old Richmond, or what was left of it. The brick burned-out vestiges of structures stood along the riverbanks like crippled, withered soldiers, and wound around a curve until they were obscured from sight. The locomotive whistled and chugged south toward Petersburg. Debris along the tracks abandoned by both armies was still evident, and as the newlyweds approached Petersburg, trenches and fortifications became visible, remnants left over from a nearly year-long siege.

He stared out the window, unable to speak. It was all too terrible for him, how Dixie had been taken. Anna sensed his sorrow and took hold of his hand, but he couldn't look at her. It was all he could do to contain his emotions, to keep from getting choked up, and so he continued to stare out in disbelief as the train rolled past the ruins. He noticed a small sign that said "Crater" with an arrow pointing off to the east. Was it an indication that tourists and souvenir hunters were already descending on the relics? The thought made David uneasy. He hoped the same thing wasn't happening where Jake was buried. Farther down the line, he noticed several men walking out in a field with shouldered spades, and he wondered if they were gravediggers.

Soon, the locomotive reached the depot. His assumption proved accurate. Not far from the station was an embalming studio. The building was deserted. It had fulfilled its purpose, and stood lifeless, like the bodies that had come and gone from its hold.

The newlyweds changed trains once again, this time destined for Knoxville. Within a few hours, they were on their way, continuing their journey toward the Appalachian Mountains.

People on the train were very quiet, and it disturbed David even more. He knew what they were probably thinking, which was the same thing he was dwelling upon. How could such horror befall the South? All those lives wasted for naught, including those of his father and his best friend. He remembered his ride through these mountains with Jake, and suddenly, his heart hurt so badly that he thought it might burst. He would be home soon to confront his family with the awful loss. The pain it caused was inconceivable. He pushed the thought from his mind, glanced at Anna, who had now dozed off, and sadly smiled, relieved she was with him, and that she loved him. He remembered those long months spent in Elmira prison, where he wondered if she would receive him once he was set free. He thought of Stephen Montgomery, her proclaimed friend, and all the trouble he'd caused when he learned of Anna and David's secret marriage. Stephen's words to him before they left—a threat essentially—warned him that some fatal incident might happen to him, thus enabling Stephen to take Anna for his bride and combine their two farms into one enormous property. The recollection made David bristle, but then he chuckled to himself. Stephen would never follow them to Alabama. Anna would be safe.

The train barreled up into the mountains as the sun set. Not all the seats were filled in the darkened passenger car, which was dimly illuminated by kerosene lamps and decorated in plush red velvet. David and Anna managed to find enough room to spread out and sleep on the seats across from each other. In the morning, they were awakened by a conductor who asked if they would be partaking in breakfast. Since their victuals were gone, they made their way to the dining car, only to find the exorbitant prices were beyond their reach, so they settled for two cups of coffee, and split a biscuit between them.

With each passing day, the locomotive made frequent stops in route to refuel, giving the newlyweds an opportunity to check on their belongings and ensure their safety. They managed to obtain fruit and bread from vendors at various locations, and sustained until the train arrived in Knoxville. After David had exercised the animals, he and Anna waited patiently inside the depot. A regulator clock on the wall ticked loudly, and a calendar hanging beside it told them it was Thursday, August 10, 1865.

By mid-morning, another train arrived. The passengers were quickly boarded, and the locomotive departed toward Chattanooga. Another all-night ride ensued before the train finally arrived early the following morning.

"How long till the next train leaves for Huntsville?" David asked the conductor as they exited the car.

"Check inside," came the gruff reply.

David glanced at Anna, who looked haggard from the long trip. He smiled reassuringly, and led her into the depot, where he asked a man behind a dark-stained cherrywood counter.

"You have a few hours," the gray-bearded man answered without glancing up from his boarding schedule.

David directed Anna back outside. She stood waiting, brushing her long blonde hair from her face while he requested the assistance of a few rail hands to unload their wagon and mule. He led Renegade out himself. The stallion was his prized possession, and he would rather die than let harm come to the animal, or worse yet, have someone be harmed by the feisty steed. Anna could see why: the little horse definitely had a mind of his own. He was fast and sound, and as they had discussed on their long train ride, he might bring money by racing. She knew how much David cherished his horse, because his father had given it to him, and he had few reminders left of his father. Anna was endeared to the little horse too, and she had always been fascinated by the fact that David and his stallion had the same-colored eyes. He was the reason for David's entering her life in the first place, and Renegade had saved her from Stephen's savage attack. The thought made her shiver, even though she knew Stephen had not been himself when he'd learned that she was married to a Confederate, or in his eyes, a traitor.

"Let's go into town," David suggested as he led Renegade toward her.

She took the reins while he retrieved the mule and hitched her to the wagon, then walked the stallion around and tied him to the back. Union soldiers observed curiously as David heaved their heavy trunk onto the back of the wagon. One of them advanced.

"Sir, we need to check your luggage," he said with a sardonic grin, his ebony skin shining with sweat.

"What for?" asked David.

"We need to look for anything that might be considered a threat to the government. 'Specially firearms."

David scoffed, but after realizing the soldier wasn't going to back down, he glowered and opened the trunk, being careful to conceal the box of cartridges and his holster under his jacket as he did so. A few other black soldiers, attired in Union blue, drew closer out of curiosity. The first soldier stuck his hand into the trunk's contents and began rummaging through.

"Sir!" Anna exclaimed from the wagon seat. "Those are my personal effects! I insist you stop this instant!" She had wisely hidden the food they'd brought for her in-laws among her undergarments, and was startled with the revelation that they might be discovered.

The soldier looked up at her, realized her anger, gingerly withdrew his hand, and closed the trunk's lid. "Beggin' your pardon, ma'am. We meant no disrespect." He grinned to show striking white teeth from under his forage cap.

Anna held her penetrating gaze, and the soldiers backed away.

"H'ya!" David slapped the reins, prompting the jennie to trot, since he was eager to get away from the Federal soldiers. Once they had driven a few blocks, he said, "I want you to meet someone," as he directed the mule down the street.

"Is it the elderly woman you told me about?" Anna asked. She looked over at him, his handsome, tanned face shaded by the brim of his hat.

"Yeah, I hope she's still there. I reckon it was this way."

He turned and drove several blocks, trying to recall the direction of the house where he had stayed on his first night away from home. Everything appeared so disparate, and bluecoats were everywhere, swarming like flies. Down the street, a row of sutlers' shops had been erected for the benefit of the Union troops. The newlyweds turned a corner and continued on, past structures that were once beautiful homes, but now sat empty, the glass in their windows shattered, their walls crumbling. Tent cities and clapboard structures cluttered vacant lots. Some of the boards were still adorned with wallpaper, an obvious declaration that the walls had been torn from citizens' private dwellings. David recognized a two-story house, even though the paint was peeling around the window frames and the yard was filled with knee-high weeds.

"This is it?" Anna asked. "It isn't quite how you described it."

"It ain't how I remember it, either," he said.

He jumped down and tied the mule, then assisted his wife. They climbed the steps together. David tapped on the door. The brass knocker that had been there before was gone; holes from the bolts that had held it in place were all that remained. There came no response, so after a few moments, he tapped again.

"Last time I was here, she had a butler. Tall black feller, name of … Henry." David nodded as he recalled. "He didn't take to us much." He flashed Anna a grin.

"He's long gone by now, no doubt," she said.

David tapped once more, but still no response came, so he tried the knob. The door stuck in the jam at first, but then creaked loudly on its hinges.

"Do you think we should go in there?" asked Anna.

He stepped inside. The long hallway was as dark as he remembered, but the lavish paintings that had adorned the walls were missing. Anna followed him down the hall to a large room that was empty except for a solitary wooden stool that squatted in the center. The ornate draperies David remembered had been ripped down, and a transparent gauze sheet had been draped across the broken windows in an attempt to keep insects out. The fireplace stood dark and empty, and the tapestries David remembered seeing were all gone, along with the furniture and knick knacks.

"I don't think anyone's here," Anna whispered.

David walked to the window and looked outside. The back of the house was just as neglected as the front, and the stable doors yawned open with a passing breeze. There was nothing inside. He heard a thump and reeled around to see a small man standing behind Anna. She turned and gasped at the same time before rushing to her husband.

"Can I be of service to y'all?" the man asked feebly.

"Josiah?" David said, taking a step closer. "Is that you?"

The little man held his hand out to him. "That would be me. How may I help y'all?"

"Don't you remember me?" asked David, trying to keep his voice quiet. "I'm David Summers. I came here with my friend, Jake Kimball. We met on the train from Huntsville, remember?"

The man didn't seem to recall, so David went on.

"Your wife, Miss Martha, she had us stay the night. And her sister was here. Miss Mattie?"

"When did you say this was?" The old man shuffled to the wooden stool and sat down.

"It was in April of sixty-three. We were on our way to jine up with Jeb Stuart."

The words seemed to register. Josiah looked up and smiled. "Yes. Yes! I believe I do remember you!" He stood up and vigorously shook David's hand.

"This here's Anna, my wife," he introduced.

She stepped toward him. "Sir," she said, taking his bony little hand in both of hers.

"Where's Miss Martha? I'd surely like to see her." David chuckled. "She made me promise to stop by the next time I was in town."

The smile vanished from Josiah's furrowed face. Suddenly, he looked very old. "She's gone," he said flatly.

"Where did she go?" Anna inquired.

Josiah sank back down onto the stool. "She left me ... when the Yankees came. She got so upset with the occupation that one day, she ..." His voice trailed off.

David exchanged glances with his wife. "She what, Josiah?"

He looked up at them, his eyes filled with grief. "She took the pistol out from under the mattress ... and put it to her head."

"Dear God!" exclaimed David.

Anna gasped.

"It was more than the poor darlin' could bear, havin' Hooker's army come in here and take everything we owned. They took the nigger, they took the horses, they even took the rugs out from under our feet. Stripped clean, jist like a plague of locusts." He paused, the silence overwhelming, then said, "Wilst they were fightin', there was a lunar eclipse. Do you reckon it was some kind of omen?"

David gulped. "What happened to Miss Mattie?" he asked, afraid to hear the reply. "Where's Miss Martha's sister?"

"She's gone too. Ran off before they got here, and I haven't seen nor heard from her since."

"Do you know where she went?" Anna asked, taking her husband's arm to steady herself.

"No idea. I'm all alone here. Have been for quite some time now."

David was at a loss, not knowing what to say. "We could take you somewhere. So you ain't alone," he suggested.

"And where would that be?" Josiah stood, slowly straightening. "The whole of the South is like this now. And besides, this here's my home, and I'll be damned to leave it."

"Can we do anything for you?" Anna inquired.

"Jist leave me be, young'uns. I can fend for myself. Nice of y'all to stop by, though." He sashayed into the parlor, or what David remembered to be the parlor, and closed a dark oak door behind him.

"We should go," suggested Anna.

David glanced at her, unable to speak. He felt helpless, like he should do something, but was at a loss as to what. She took his hand and led him outside, where they boarded the wagon in silence and rode back to the depot. Chattanooga, David understood, had aged tremendously, just like Josiah. The town of two thousand was now overrun with bluecoats who seemed unconcerned with the annihilation they'd caused. What was once an elegant town was now demoralized by Yankees, and the whole city appeared beaten down and ancient.

The couple returned to the train station. As they sat on a bench inside, waiting for the train to Huntsville, Anna looked around, observing her surroundings. The long brick edifice had large domed picture windows lined down the perimeters, and at either end, two gigantic domed doorways allowed trains to enter and exit. The station was busy but not crowded, and like the rest of the town, was teeming with Union soldiers.

David's stomach growled. "I'm starvin'," he stated, but was unsure how to find any viands.

Anna leaned over and gave him a kiss. "How long will it take us, once we've left for Huntsville?"

"Well," he thought for a moment. "On the way here, it took about half a day on the train."

"And how far to your house?"

"Another half a day."

Anna sighed. "Oh." She was starting to wonder if they'd ever get there.

Laying her head against her husband's shoulder, he lovingly wrapped his arm around her.

Over an hour passed before the train to Huntsville arrived. Once the passengers were boarded, the train lurched out of the dark depot and into the bright sunlight. The humidity was nearly suffocating. Anna retrieved her fan from her reticule in a futile attempt to stay cool. She felt queasy, and started to wonder through her discomfort if coming down to Alabama was really such a good idea after all. She already missed her family, and it was the first time she'd ever been this far from home. What if David had been wrong about his mother and sisters? He had said they would love her as much as he did, but what if he was wrong? What if they resented her about the war, and for being a Northerner? All of a sudden, she felt very apprehensive, and wished for a way to turn back. But it was too late, and she knew she couldn't abandon her husband. She looked over to see him staring at her.

"Are you all right?" he asked, taking her hand.

She forced a smile. "I will be. When we get to Huntsville, though, I think I should eat something."

He kissed her forehead. "That sounds like a mighty fine notion. "I'm starvin'!"

Anna softly chuckled, and let out a sigh.

Like all the other train rides, this one, too, was nearly empty except for soldiers. Apparently, the Union army was in the process of building up the Southern railroads, or at least, so implied the soldiers with their talk of engineering, surveying, purchasing, and implementation. Some of the men even went into excited discussion about how friends of theirs, northern businessmen, saw Chattanooga as an opportunity for investment. David sighed, knowing the Yankees would probably be descending like vultures to take advantage of the weakened, vulnerable South. He hoped with all his heart that his home wasn't lost to them as well.

Glaring blankly out the window, he watched the empty fields roll by. It occurred to him that many farms were derelict, and the fields were dried up wastelands. Even the weeds had difficulty thriving. Lonesome chimneys jutted from the landscape; ravaged reminders of the horror his people had seen. Reaching to the sky like ominous tombstones in a graveyard, they were all that remained of farmhouses and villages.

By mid-afternoon, their train arrived at the Huntsville depot. After inquiring inside, David returned to Anna, who was waiting outside.

"The depot in Arab ain't open yet, since the Yankees tore up some of the tracks, so I reckon we'll have to drive from here."

"How far is it?" she asked.

"About two days away."

She nodded.

The newlyweds attained their equines and wagon. David loaded the trunk. As he did so, two Federal officers neared.

"We need to look in that trunk," one said curtly. He was heavyset with spectacles on his hairless face.

David hesitated. "Sir, we've already been searched at every train station we've been through."

"Then you should be accustomed to it by now," the other soldier said snidely. He was a tall black man with large brown eyes and a stolid expression.

David sighed and glanced at Anna. "Be my guest." He gestured sardonically, sweeping his arm out as an invitation for the intrusion.

"Do you have proof that you own these things?" the first soldier asked, so David obediently presented his bill of sale and discharge paper.

Anna walked over to the man rummaging through her trunk, and spoke softly to him, so quietly that David couldn't hear. He wondered what their dialogue consisted of, but was distracted by the first soldier.

"No proof for the horse, then," he said, and walked toward the back of the wagon.

"That's my horse, sir. I've owned him all his life."

The soldier simpered. "The army could use a fine animal like this."

He reached out to stroke the stallion's neck. Renegade snapped at him. The soldier yanked his hand back.

"Damn nag!" he exclaimed.

Anna and the black soldier stopped talking and gawked at him.

"All right, I believe you. On your way." He stomped off, obviously humiliated.

The other soldier nodded, tipped his kepi to Anna, and retreated behind his comrade.

David helped his wife up, climbed in, and started into town, anxious to get away from the brick three-story depot, and all the Federal jackals surrounding it.

"What were you and that Negro soldier conversin' about?" he inquired.

Anna chortled. "I merely appealed to his better interests, and told him that a lady has a right to her privacy, that's all."

David glanced at her out of the corner of his eye. Something told him she wasn't being completely truthful, but he had no reason to push the issue further. As they rode, they saw that the homes in Huntsville were intact, and in much better condition that those in Chattanooga. They drove past beautiful Italianate and Greek revival mansions, some with cast-iron fleur-de-lis fences. He remembered the hotel he and Jake had gone to for their final meal before they were mustered into the Confederate army, so he directed the jennie to that location. The public house was where he remembered it, on the corner of Madison Street, but the city looked different somehow: the bustling carefree happiness that had flourished before was now replaced with quiet remorse.

David helped Anna down after tying the mule, and followed her inside. A lanky man who stood behind a counter looked up from the hotel register as they entered. David nodded to the man, led Anna into the dining hall, and sat down beside her at a small round table. Like before, the room was nearly unoccupied. Three Union officers sat in the far corner, drinking whiskey and smoking cigars. Two men stood near the back of the room. One was playing a fiddle while the other attempted to sing a slow ballad in a low, baritone voice. The room was bright with sunlight, and lace curtains hung over the long windows. A thin, balding gentleman with an apron wrapped tightly around his waist appeared, pencil and paper poised in his hands.

"How do," he said softly. "What would y'all like to order?"

Anna smiled up at him, but he only stared back.

"Well," she began, "what is your specialty?"

"And more importantly, how much is it?" added David.

The waiter laughed. "More than you can afford, I'll wager!"

David chuckled. "We have two dollars. Bring us whatever that provides."

He glanced at his wife, who glared at him.

"It ain't Confederate currency, is it?" the man asked.

"Silver," responded David.

The waiter grinned and walked off into the kitchen.

Anna was still glaring. "The money you earned in prison?"

David nodded.

"You should hold on to that, sweetheart. We might need it for something important."

He smiled. "You're important," he answered. "You said you needed to eat, and I'm starvin'. What could be more important than that?"

The musicians began to play another melody, and the couple listened to the lyrics.

> "We shall meet but we shall miss him, there will be one vacant chair.
>
> We shall linger to caress him, while we breathe our ev'nin' prayer.
>
> When a year ago we gathered, joy was in his mild blue eye.
>
> But a golden cord is severed. And our hopes in ruin lie."

David couldn't help but think of the loss of his best friend. The lyrics saddened him deeply, searing his soul, rekindling the painful remembrance of discovering Jake's lifeless body on the battlefield. He drew a heavy sigh, and took his beloved's hand.

"It'll be all right," she comforted.

He nodded in confirmation, relieved when the song finally ended and the musicians broke into a lively tune.

After a few minutes, the waiter appeared with two plates, and set them in front of his customers. "Hope this will suffice," he said. "I'll come back in a minute to fill your glasses."

David watched him walk off, then glanced down at his plate. It contained a thin slab of meat and half of a small potato. "Ain't much to sustain on," he remarked before quickly devouring it.

Anna took a bite of hers. It was dry and chewy, repulsive except for the fact that she was famished as well. She forced herself to eat while the waiter returned to fill their glasses with water.

"Y'all from these parts?" he asked as he poured the glass pitcher.

"Yessir," David replied. "I'm from Morgan County. Jist got back from the war."

The waiter set the pitcher down on the table and rested his hand on his hip. "Well, bless you, sir!"

He jutted his hand in David's direction, who graciously took it, and the two men shook.

"We've had quite a time here for a while now. When did you jine up?"

"Spring of sixty-three," he answered.

The waiter nodded. "Not long after, that's when they came and occupied the town for good, and they're still here, as you've surely noticed." He threw a glance at the soldiers.

David grinned. "That we have."

"They've overstayed their welcome if you ask me," the waiter continued in a hushed voice. "Held parties and balls with their Yankee wives, jist to flaunt their authority. Done too many unChristian-like things to the townsfolk too."

"Such as what?" she asked shyly.

The waiter looked at her as if he knew she too was a Yankee wife. "Well Missus, anyone who resisted or revolted against them was shot. There were deserters hidin' up in the mountains, and every time they killed a bluecoat, the Feds burned down entire city blocks as reward, and hung the perpetrators in plain view to impress us into submission. They even used our churches as stables."

Anna gasped, placing her hand over her mouth.

"No!" David said, half grinning. He was skeptical as to whether these outrages actually took place.

"Oh, yessir," the waiter said, his face deadpan.

The grin faded from David's lips. He felt his revulsion roil up. "Right sorry to hear that," he stated.

"We're all under that Yankee General Pope's jurisdiction now, so it's a little better." The waiter nodded, and took the silver coins David laid out on the table. "I read recently that the state treasury has over seven hundred and ninety thousand dollars in it, but only about three hundred is in silver, and five hundred is gold. The rest is in Confederate currency, so it's worthless."

"That doesn't sound good at all," commented Anna.

"And rumor has it," the man went on, "that Atlanta has only a little over a dollar and a half left in the state's treasury, but it's all Confederate."

"Such a shame," Anna responded.

"Well, sir," David said, "thank you for the hospitality. We'd best be on our way now." He stood and took Anna's hand as she arose.

"Y'all have a pleasant day," the waiter said cordially before retreating into the kitchen.

David said little as he and Anna traveled down the thoroughfare. Everywhere he looked, there were more Union soldiers, and the odd thing was that most of them were black. They stared at him as though they knew he had fought for the Confederacy and had been incarcerated for it.

The couple rode past wooden structures. One had a signage attached to the front that read, "Freedmen's Bureau." Several black men loitered around the entrance, and ogled as they passed. The newlyweds found a telegraph office, went inside, and requested that the man at the counter send a telegram to Anna's family.

"Aunt Sarah, Uncle Bill, and sisters," the young man read back to them. "We have arrived safely in Huntsville, and are on our way to the Summers' residence. We miss y'all and hope to see you again soon. Love, Anna and David."

"That's mighty fine," David said. He handed the operator a silver coin before the couple walked out of the office and back to their parked wagon. "All right, my darlin'," David said as he helped Anna climb up. "We're almost there."

She could tell by the tone in his voice that he was excited about seeing his family. "Well, what are we waiting for?" she asked with a giggle.

He snickered and directed the mule out of town with Renegade trotting regally behind.

"And now we must decide on a name for our new little mule." She giggled again. "How do you like the name ...?"

"Ornery?" David suggested.

"No."

"Stubborn."

She shook her head.

"How 'bout muley cow."

Anna grunted. "I think we should name her Ginger."

David gave her a skeptical look, which caused her to chuckle. "Why Ginger?"

"Well, because I think it's a pretty name, don't you?"

He grinned. "I reckon she is full of spice. All right, darlin', whatever your heart desires."

She took hold of his arm and hugged it.

The couple rode across a bridge spanning the Tennessee River, along a winding road that meandered through the hills and past small villages. Each one appeared desolate, and the fields were wasted, which caused David some unease, but he shrugged it off, concerning himself only with his own homecoming. Then it struck him: this wasn't the homecoming he had envisioned at all. He had played the event out in his mind hundreds of times before Jake was killed, how they would ride home in glory as noble knights, victorious in the defense of their homeland. There should be celebrations, joy, champagne, laughter, dancing, and merriment. There should be speeches and ribbons and veneration. But he knew it would never be. There would be no Grand Review, like what the Yankees had received in Washington City. There would be no jubilation ... only desolation.

The hills darkened, and crickets began chirping in the ditches. Flashes of light shot across the sky as a meteor shower commenced. Anna's uneasiness heightened, so she scooted as close to her husband as she could. Although the road was dark, David knew the way, which comforted her.

"What if road agents jump out and assault us?" she whispered, shivering in the warm humidity.

"Don't fret, darlin'," he assured with a chuckle. "I'm your defender." He looked over and included, "As long as the witches don't git us."

"Witches?" she asked. "Oh, David, don't be silly. There's no such thing as ..."

"Oh, yes there is," he interrupted. "I seen one once."

Anna tsk-tsked. "Are you certain about that?"

He nodded, then retrieved the pocket watch she had given him. Clicking it open, he saw it was half past ten. Deciding they should stop to rest, he pulled the wagon over to the side of the road. They crawled into the back, wrapped themselves around each other, and finally fell asleep.

In the morning, they continued their journey, and rode all day. As dusk approached, David glanced again at his watch.

"The house is over this ridge," he said as he replaced it in his trouser pocket. "We're jist about there." He felt his heart leap with anticipation, and prodded Ginger to pick up her speed.

As night fell, the wagon came over a crest. In the valley sat a quaint wooden dogtrot house.

Observing that the windows were dark, David said, "Reckon they're all asleep." He pulled the mule to a halt in front of the saddlebag house. Nothing stirred. Helping Anna down, he took her hand and led her onto the front porch. He pushed on the door, but it wouldn't budge.

"It's bolted from inside," he informed, and enthusiastically pounded several times.

An owl hooted off in the distance. There came a rustling from within, and the bolt slid. The door slowly opened a crack. A girl peered out. She hesitated for a moment, then recognized her brother's grinning face, and threw the door wide. Anna saw she was dressed in a nightgown, her long dark brown hair hanging loose.

"David!" she squealed, throwing herself on him. "You're home! I can't believe it!"

The siblings embraced, laughing.

"Rena," he said after they'd held each other for a moment. "It's mighty good to see you." They hugged again, but then he remembered his manners. "Oh, this here's Anna!"

She immediately embraced her. "Anna, I'm right happy to know you!"

"I'm happy to meet you too," she replied, smiling.

Rena took hold of her hands and pulled her inside. I've so looked forward to this day!" David's younger sister said. She hugged him once more and gave him a kiss on the cheek, then took hold of his hands and led him into the front room. "Ma!" she cried over her shoulder. "Josie!"

David chuckled, ecstatic with the reunion. "You look beautiful," he remarked.

Rena snickered, suddenly conscious of her attire.

A door in the back room creaked. "What's goin' on out here? I thought I heard ..." The woman stopped and stared wide-eyed at the three figures standing in the dark. "David!" she wailed, and ran to him.

He enveloped her in his arms.

"Oh, praise be!" she began sobbing. "My boy has come home at last!"

David held her tightly, struggling to contain his emotions while Anna looked on, overcome with sentiment. Rena crossed the room and lit a few candles. Now the sight was even more profound, because the expression on their mother's face was heart-wrenching. Her eyes were pinched tight as tears streamed down her cheeks. He gave her a slight squeeze, released her, and saw that she seemed to have aged considerably since he last saw her.

"Rena! Go fetch your sister!" Caroline requested excitedly. "Oh, let me git a good look at you!" She stepped back, keeping her hands grasped tightly onto her son's arms, then pulled him close and kissed his cheeks. A younger girl with long auburn hair emerged through a side door with Rena following behind.

"David!" she shrieked. She threw herself into his waiting arms.

The two hugged like frolicking bruins.

"You're here! You're truly here!" She held onto him for a solid minute before his mother protested.

"Now, Josie, give him a chance to breathe!"

She released him, and he snickered.

"Why, take a gander at you, Josie! You ain't a li'l girl any longer. All of fifteen, now."

Josie nodded, a big grin on her face. "And you're an old feller, all of twenty!"

David laughed. "Reckon you have to beat the boys off with a stick!"

"No," said Josie solemnly. "There ain't too many boys my age left in these parts."

Rena stood beside Anna, absorbing the spectacle. She took her hand and smiled at her.

Anna couldn't help but smile back, even though she felt precarious and homesick.

"I've so much to tell you!" Josie exclaimed "We've so much to talk about!"

"First I want to introduce my bride," David said. "Ma, Josie, this here's Anna." He turned to her and held out his hand, prompting her to take it.

"Mrs. Summers," she said shyly, "Josie. I'm pleased to make your acquaintance."

David's mother looked at her for a moment, then smiled and embraced her. "Oh, my dear Anna." She released her. "It's right good to have you home."

Josie hugged her as well. Standing back, she exclaimed, "I have a new sister!"

Everyone chuckled.

David glanced around the room, which seemed to be missing a few pieces of furniture. He looked at the mantle, and saw the clock his father had given his mother as a wedding present, along with his father's portrait, but the photograph he'd had taken in Huntsville before he left for the army wasn't beside it. He was about to ask where it was when his mother grasped his hand.

"Come with me, David. We have somethin' to show you."

She led him out back, and the young ladies followed. Two dogs ran up to greet them, sniffing at Anna's skirts as she made her way through the unfamiliar dark. She knew they were the dogs David had told her about, Caleb and Si. The family trudged past neglected outbuildings. Chickens clucked inside the henhouse, alarmed by the invasion.

"Where are the pigs?" asked David.

"I'll explain all that later." Caroline led him up an incline to a little white cottage that was tucked before a thicket.

"Granny's old house?" he asked.

"We fixed it up for you!" Josie declared. "'Cause we knew you'd be comin'!"

The family entered the one-room dwelling, and Caroline lit a candle. In the glow, David saw a little table, two chairs, a five-drawer dresser with an attached mirror, and a double bed with a small nightstand beside it. Red-and-white checkered homespun curtains hung over each of the two windows.

Anna entered behind Rena and gasped. "You did all this for us?" she asked, her eyes welling up. She was far more exhausted than she had realized, and her emotions were soaring.

"We've been workin' on it for the past month," explained Josie.

Anna walked over and sat on the bed. It creaked in protest, but was firm, nevertheless. "I can't wait to try this out!" she exclaimed.

The girls giggled.

"Oh! I didn't mean ..." Anna blushed.

David gave her a crooked grin. "Ma," he said, turning toward her, "I know Joe Boy was stolen 'cause we got your letters."

"Yes, the soldiers took our horse, along with most of the livestock. It's a miracle our letters got through," Caroline stated. "A simple act of God, that's what I believe." She smiled. "And the postmaster, Mr. Ford, assisted, of course. Every time he saw a letter come from you, he stowed it so the Yankees wouldn't have a chance to confiscate it. And he made sure our letters got up to you, but since then, they've been watchin' us right close. How many did you receive?"

"Well, I got the one you sent to me in prison, and the one you mailed last summer, after I told you about my marriage to Anna. And I received one from Rena, and one from Josie while I was in prison."

Caroline nodded wisely, piecing it together. "Those first three letters were sent in February."

"They were? I didn't git them till spring."

"And I sent you cookies. Did you receive them?"

"No, ma'am. They were gone."

"That figures," Caroline grumbled. She threw a glance at Anna.

"What about Renegade?" Josie asked. "Did you bring him?"

"Sure did!" replied David with a grin. "Would you go fetch the wagon and take it around to the barn?"

His little sister nodded and ran out the door.

Rena stepped toward him and took his hand. "We're very proud of you," she spoke melodically.

His heart fluttered with the sound of her lilting voice.

The newlyweds proceeded to talk about their trip, and soon, Josie returned.

"They got us a mule!" she announced.

"We brought other items for you as well," informed Anna.

Caroline nodded, and discreetly covered a yawn, which sparked yawns from everyone else in the room. She smiled. "It seems we're all a bit tuckered out. Let us git some rest, and we'll talk further in the mornin'. There's food in the kitchen if y'all are hungry."

"Thanks, Ma," David replied.

Caroline and her daughters hugged him, and walked back to the house. He turned to face Anna after closing the door.

"Well, this is nice, ain't it?" He flashed a smile and sat down beside her. "And I can't wait to try out this bed, either." He wrapped his arms around her and kissed her tenderly.

They gazed into each other's eyes.

"So, this was your grandmother's cottage?" she asked.

"Yeah. She lived back here as long as I can remember. Jist her. Granddaddy died before I was born. She died here."

Anna cringed. "In this bed?"

"Uh huh. Oh," he said as he remembered. "I'd best go settle Renie and Ginger, and bring in the trunk. I'll fetch us some vittles too." He stood and strode toward the door. "I'll be right back," he promised as he went out, and closed the wooden slab door behind him.

Anna stood, brushed the wrinkles from her skirt, walked to the window, and peered out, watching her husband vanish into the darkness. She turned and absorbed the ambiance. *It is lovely*, she thought to herself, *the perfect honeymoon cottage.* She smiled, and investigated the tiny fireplace, running her hand across the roughhewn mantle, already making plans on how to decorate it.

She sank down onto the bed. Suddenly, she felt out of her element, and broke into a sweat. Could it be that David's family members were behaving the way they were for his benefit only? What if they weren't sincere, and considered her an intruder? Anna hoped with all her heart they would treasure her, but everything seemed so alien here. Perhaps, when they learned about another new family member they were about to acquire, they'd accept her. She lay back and placed her hand upon her stomach. David would need to know soon as well. This situation was only temporary; this was merely a visit. She would return home by year's end, even if she had to take him away from his family permanently. Somehow, she would make it happen.

"I am satisfied that the thinking men of the South accept the present condition of affairs in good faith. The questions that have heretofore divided the sentiment of the people of the two sections, slavery and state rights, or the right of a state to secede from the Union, they regard as having been settled by the highest tribunal – arms – that man can resort to."

- General Ulysses S. Grant (1865)

Chapter Two

Anna tossed and turned all night, too uncomfortable from the heat and humidity to sleep. She wondered how her husband could do it. Toward dawn, she finally dozed off, only to be awakened by the rooster's crow. Sleepily, David rolled over, opened his eyes, and seeing her beside him, smiled. He kissed her softly.

"Did you sleep well?" he asked, running his hand alongside her face.

"Somewhat," she replied. "It's a new bed."

"Don't fret, darlin', you'll git used to it."

She wondered if that was true. He suggested they arise and revisit the house, so she dressed and followed him down the incline. In the morning light, the farmstead was more vibrant, but flaws covered by darkness were now stark reminders of destitution brought on by the "War Between the States," as he called it. Several livestock enclosures had been dismantled, and the barn looked as though it might fall over if someone blew on it. She followed him through the open breezeway, and found his mother sitting in the front room.

"Well, there y'all are!" Caroline said as she set the Bible she was reading on a small table and stood. "I've been waitin' half the mornin' for y'all to git up!"

Anna felt like it was a criticism directed at her. Was she implying that Yankees were lazy?

David chuckled. "Ma, stop exaggeratin'."

He smiled at Anna, who forced one in return. She glanced around the room, noticing an oval raised portrait on the wall.

"Who's that?" she asked.

"That's my ma's ma," he replied.

"It's her cottage we're staying in?" Anna's eyes flitted around the room, taking in things she'd overlooked the night before: two floral paintings hanging on an adjacent wall, the stone fireplace, and the sparse rustic pine furniture.

"Yes, it is, dear," Caroline responded. "David, go fetch your sisters, and meet us in the kitchen."

He obeyed, and left Anna alone with her new mother-in-law.

"Anna, come with me, child."

She followed the older woman outside to the screened summer kitchen. They entered and sat at the table.

"There ain't much to sustain on at present," she stated. "But I'll make flapjacks when the young'uns arrive." She reached across the table and took Anna's hand. Gazing at her wedding band, the one she used to wear, Caroline said, "It's right lovely on your finger." She patted the back of Anna's hand and smiled.

For the first time, Anna looked at her, noticing her eyes were hazel like David's, and her dark brown hair had streaks of gray running through it.

"We brought some foodstuffs for you," she informed.

Caroline stared at her for a moment, as though she didn't want to take the charity, but said instead, "That's very thoughtful, dear. I'm sure we'll put it to use." She stood abruptly as her children entered. "Sit down and get reacquainted," she instructed. "I'll fix us up somethin' for breakfast."

Quickly, she lit the wood-burning stove, brought out a griddle, and produced corn flour, lard, and milk from the food safe, mixing them into batter in a large tin bowl. She ladled the concoction onto the sizzling griddle, and stood over the stove as her children conversed. The girls decided to assist their mother, so David moved over beside his wife.

He winked at her. "She's happy we're home."

"Are you certain?" Anna whispered. "I feel as though she doesn't really like me."

"Pshaw!" he exclaimed.

His sisters looked over at him.

"She jist don't know you, is all. Give her time."

Anna nodded.

The family sat down together, recited a short prayer of thanks, and proceeded to eat. The food was sparse, but the company warm. They talked for an hour before Josie was reminded that her chores were being neglected. David offered to assist her, so off they went. Caroline, after announcing she had clothes to wash, asked Anna and Rena to clean up the kitchen, and they graciously obliged.

As the two young women stood side by side over the dishwashing basin, they exchanged information, each one telling the other about their backgrounds, their families, and their aspirations. Anna was reminded that they were two and a half years apart in age, Rena being two years younger than her brother and Anna being half a year older than David. She told Rena about Pennsylvania and her farm, which her aunt and uncle were tending, about her sisters, and how she had lost both her parents: first her mother when her youngest sister, Abigail, was born, and then her father more recently to yellow fever.

Rena stated that they had lost their little brother, Elijah, to cholera. This Anna already knew, since David had informed her when they'd first met, and she described how she and her sisters found him nearly bleeding to death, nursed him and his horse back to health, and convinced him to stay in order to ward off Stephen's attempts to take the farm. She giggled as she explained how she manipulated David into pretending to be her cousin, and taught him to speak like a New Yorker.

During this time, Josie had returned, and sat listening in fascination. Anna described their courtship, secret wedding, his arrest, and their reunion after the war. She then offered to show them the photographs she'd brought along. They went to the cottage, where she produced numerous tintypes from her trunk: one each of her sisters, Maggie and Abigail, the little gems contained inside her locket and his pocket watch, and the wedding portrait they'd had taken. Josie insisted the photographs be shown to their mother, so the trio departed.

Meanwhile, David surveyed the farm, concluding that it would take him several months of hard labor to repair the damage caused. He checked the fence line, discovering several gaps, and struggled to place temporary obstructions by leveling saplings and dragging them across as barricades. Once he was satisfied, he let Ginger, Renegade, and the one remaining cow of the three they'd previously owned out to graze. He strolled to the house and found his mother setting the dining table.

"Ma, where's the rest of the furniture?" he asked. The rooms were missing chairs that had previously been there. "And where's my photo …"

He glanced at the mantle to see his tintype positioned beside his father's. "Oh," he said as he walked across the room and picked it up, "there it is. I didn't see it last night." He grinned at his likeness, impressed with the way he looked with his hat in one hand, his pistol in the other, poised across his chest, and a determined, yet apprehensive expression on his face.

"David, before you go findin' out for yourself, there are some things I need to tell you."

He set the tintype back on the mantle and turned to face her.

"Have a seat," she directed.

He did as she instructed.

They made themselves comfortable beside each other at the dining room table. "Last night I told you those letters we sent to you in prison were mailed in February, and praise the Lord you got them, even though it took a few months. But somethin' happened here last spring."

"What, Ma?" he asked, befuddled.

"I don't know if you heard, but Selma and Montgomery were attacked by a Yankee general named Wilson. The Huntsville Advocate was callin' it 'Wilson's Raid'. Anyways, they came through the state and destroyed the arsenals, the railroads, the mills, and people's homes. They even burned the University of Alabama down to the ground. General Forrest jist couldn't prevent it." She sighed, shaking her head. "Then they headed into Georgia, and even after the war was done, they ransacked that state too, and captured our beloved president, Jefferson Davis."

"Yeah, Ma. I know about ole Jeff Davis."

"Darlin', some of Wilson's soldiers came by our place, and took things that didn't belong to them."

"Like what?"

"Our china and silver. They would've taken that old clock on the mantle if I hadn't hid it in that cave yonder while they were pilferin'. They ran off with your books and guitar before I could hide them, though. I'm sorry, son." David's hurt showed on his face, as his mother could see, for she rarely referred to him as "son," and she knew he'd lost his most prized possessions. "I'm aware of how much those things meant to you, but they're only things, and you can git new ones someday when we're better off."

He looked down at the floor, disguising his disappointment by forcing a feeble smile. "Yes'm. Did they take the music box Pa made you?"

"Yes."

"And the furniture too?"

"They built a big bonfire up in the hills and used it for firewood."

"Damn!" he exclaimed, just as his wife and siblings made an entrance. "I mean, darn."

"What's wrong, David?" Rena asked.

He glanced at his wife. "Ma was jist tellin' me what happened last spring. About the Yankees stealin' our belongin's."

"What?" inquired Anna.

He only nodded in response, because his anger and repulsion were reborn.

Anna knew he was agitated, so she walked across the room and took his hand.

He forced himself to look at her, and seeing her concerned expression, displaced his anger for the moment. "Josie wrote that Kit Lawrence has been comin' around. Is he here now?"

"No. He's up in Tennessee at present, but said he'd be back directly." Caroline turned to Anna and explained, "Kit is a childhood friend of David's father."

"Yes, I know," she replied. "He told me of him."

"Oh?"

Anna felt compelled to confess. "He said he doesn't like him much."

Caroline sighed, glancing at her son. "Well, the man has a temper, there's no denyin' that. But the war changes people, and he's concerned about our welfare since Hiram died."

"Sure that's all it is, Ma?" asked David. "I ain't."

"The good book says it ain't our place to judge others, so don't be castin' judgment till you see him again."

"Yes, ma'am," he responded solemnly.

"Anna has some photographs to show you," Josie announced.

"And we brought along powdered milk, white sugar, coffee, and flour," said Anna. "I put the sugar away in the sugar chest, and stored the rest in the food safe in the kitchen."

"That's mighty fine, dear. The Northerners have plenty of food to eat, then. I appreciate your kind gesture."

She smiled up at her daughter-in-law, who was skeptical about her sincerity.

"Now," said Caroline, "let's have a look at those portraitures."

David spent the next few days making repairs on the farm and scrounging for rusty nails to reuse, while Anna tidied up their new little home. She gently extracted her cerulean gown from the trunk, and hung it from a peg on the wall, prominently displaying it as she dreamed of the day she would wear it. She would be like Cinderella at the ball, on the arm of her Prince Charming, and hopefully impress his friends and family with her sophistication and poise. After all, she was a Brady, and proud of it.

Once a week had passed, he decided to deliver Ginger and Renegade to the blacksmith's for inspection. To his relief, John Moss was still there, plying his trade. As David had suspected, John informed that the mule was older than four, and estimated her to be twice that age. After having a look at Renegade, he grinned through his bushy blond beard.

"He's held up purty good!" he proclaimed. "Not a flaw on him, far as I can tell. I'll change out his shoes, and he'll be good as new."

"Thanks, John."

David proceeded to answer questions the blacksmith threw at him, telling him about his adventures in the cavalry, and informing him that he was married. John educated him about Morgan County's experiences since he'd departed, including stories of some veterans' returns, and of other soldiers who hadn't. He complained about the Yankees, and then about the English and French, stating they should have come to the South's defense, to which David agreed. After he was finished shoeing, he wished David and his new bride well.

"It's a treacherous time, so be on your lookout," he said as a warning. "There've been quite a few incidences between free slaves and white folks, not to mention the Yankee soldiers patrollin' these parts."

"Do you think there'll be an insurrection?"

"Don't know. Best be prepared for the worst, though."

"I'll keep it in mind, John."

With that, David returned to the farm. He pastured Ginger, shared a small lunch with Anna, and then decided it was time to pay a visit to some of his neighbors. He had procrastinated long enough, and even though she offered to accompany him, he knew it was something he had to confront on his own. After kissing his wife and collecting Jake's pocket watch, he mounted Renegade and rode off.

His first stop was at the home of Bud Samuels, his father's comrade-in-arms. Bud was sitting in a rocker on the front porch, and recognized him immediately as he approached.

"Hey there, David!" he hollered, waving dramatically. "You've made it back after all!"

He rode up to the cabin and dismounted. "Bud," he said, grinning as he stepped up onto the porch and extended his hand.

The two men shook, and Bud patted his arm.

"Good to see you again."

"And you! Come on in."

David removed his hat and followed the older man, noticing his hobble. He greeted Bud's wife, who was sewing needlepoint in a wooden chair beside the unlit fireplace. She exchanged cordialities, commented on the scarcity of needles and thread, then excused herself, set the needlepoint down on the chair, and disappeared into a back room.

"Poor ole gal's feelin' out of sorts these days," Bud explained. "Been havin' heart palpitations lately."

"Sorry to hear that, Bud," David commiserated.

"Not me, though! I'm as spry as ever, even with this here wooden leg." He pulled his pant leg up to reveal a wooden appendage, and knocked on it like it was a door.

"What was it like in Tennessee? Last I heard, you were headed up that way."

Bud scratched his straggly graying beard and proceeded to describe the infantry battles he'd fought in: Chickamauga, Chattanooga, Nashville, Franklin, and Memphis, where he received his injury and was sent home to convalesce. "Funny thing too," he said, finishing his monologue. "One leg's shorter than the other one now, so when I walk, I have to limp, but it's better than the alternative." His expression changed dramatically. "Oh. Sorry, son," he muttered, suddenly remembering his fallen comrade.

"It's all right," David responded understandingly.

Bud sighed. "I'm afraid I never took note of where they laid your pa's remains," he remarked somberly, deliberately avoiding details of his friend's horrific death. He knew David would be unable to locate his father, because there had been nothing left to locate, but he could never confess what he'd witnessed.

"Reckon Pa's in an unmarked grave somewhere around Fredericksburg, but I never made it over there to talk to y'all's commanders. I know right where Jake's buried, though, and I intend to go retrieve him."

"Well, that's a noble notion, and I'm sure Jake's kin will appreciate havin' him home." Bud's continence grew misty for a moment. "I don't know if you were aware of this fact, since you were in prison and all. But the 4th Alabama, the regiment your pa and I fought with, was there at Lee's surrender."

"Is that a fact?" David asked, awestruck.

Bud slowly nodded. "Yep. The 4th was the first to fight and the last to leave, and never surrendered the colors. There were only eleven men of the 4th left at Appomattox. They're callin' us the 'Immortal Fourth'."

Deciding to change the subject, he went on to describe the poor condition of the crops, and probably would have talked well into the night, but David had other errands, so he dismissed himself graciously.

"Do you still have the Colt I gave you?" Bud asked as David mounted up, referring to the Colt .44 Army he'd given him before his enlistment.

"Yessir," David replied. "It saved me quite a few times." He chuckled. "Anna hid it under her skirts on the way down here, so the Federals wouldn't take it."

Bud nodded. "That was right smart of her. Make sure you keep it under wraps. The Yankees are taxin' us two dollars on every handgun, and their confiscatin' the larger firearms."

"I'll take your advice, Bud."

They exchanged farewells, and David rode on to his next destination. This time, it was Jake's parents he intended to see.

As he neared the house, he noticed it looked the same, with the exception of the peeling paint on the veranda. The property was strangely quiet; not even a bird chirped in the muggy summer heat. All the animals had taken cool refuge, and he wished he was one of them.

He tied Renegade, gave him a reassuring pat on the neck, mounted the steps, and tapped on the screened door several times. There was a long hesitation.

"Come in," a woman called from inside.

He circumspectly opened the door, removing his hat as he entered. The parlor was much as he remembered it, and Jake's tintype, the one he'd had taken after enlisting, was displayed on a wall. Awkwardly, David stood in the doorway.

"We've been expectin' you," Jake's mother softly said, startling him. She was sitting in an upholstered chair in the corner, clad in a black mourning dress. The sadness that had embraced her for the past two years was evident by the expression on her face. She arose and drifted out of the room, leaving him alone with his apprehension. Moments later, she reappeared with Mr. Kimball.

"David," he said, protruding his hand. The two shook.

"Mr. and Mrs. Kimball," he responded.

She motioned for him to take a seat. He did so, self-consciously.

"I wanted to come by, and express my condolences in person." He looked down at the worn tapestry rug on the floor. At a loss, he stated, "One of my messmates thought it best that I write you, instead of your hearin' it from a commandin' officer."

"Well, that was generous of you," Jake's mother said.

A long, uncomfortable silence followed. He gazed up at her. A faint smile crossed her lips, flickered, and was gone.

He turned his gaze to Jake's father. "Mr. Kimball, sir." He opened his mouth, but couldn't think of anything to say, so he closed it again.

Mr. Kimball merely nodded. He too was sorrow struck. "We understand what you've been through, and we want you to know that we don't blame you."

David squeezed his eyes shut. This was getting more painful by the minute. "I'm so sorry," he half whispered, choking back a sob. "I never meant for it to happen. I tried tellin' him he should buy a new horse, but he wouldn't listen. He wanted to fight, 'for Stonewall' he said. I should've stopped him." He stared back down at the rug.

Mrs. Kimball exchanged glances with her husband, and walked over to David. She knelt down and put her arm around him, which made it even more difficult to hold back the tears. "We don't accuse you."

He nodded in response. After expelling a deep sigh, he collected himself. "I'm fixin' to go up to Chancellorsville, and fetch him back." He looked over at Jake's father, who frowned.

"Do you recall where you buried him?"

"Yessir. I reckon I can find the place again."

Mr. Kimball scowled. "All right. We'll go find him then, soon as we can."

David slowly stood. "Have you talked to Miss Callie lately?"

"She's been anxious for your return. Jake's death shook her, but she's held out hope."

Grimacing, he said, "I'm married now."

"Yes," Mrs. Kimball acknowledged. "Your ma informed us. She asked that we let you tell the girl yourself."

"Yes'm. Well ... I'd best be callin' on her, then."

He started for the door, and as he walked outside, Mr. Kimball followed.

"David."

He turned to face him as he untied Renegade from the hitching post.

"I know you're fond of Percy. He's got his own place jist south of here."

He proceeded to give directions as David seated himself in the saddle.

"He and Isabelle have two young'uns now."

"I'll pay him a visit," David promised. He hesitated. "It's nice to see you again."

Jake's father stared at him for a moment. "You too," he finally uttered. "Tell your ma I said hello."

"I'll do that, sir."

Mr. Kimball turned and walked back toward the house. David watched, reminded of the man's limp. His injury had been caused while he was fighting in the Mexican War, and David thought somberly how so many more had come home maimed since then.

Placing his slouch hat on his head, he spurred his horse. Renegade cantered down the driveway to the road. Glancing over his shoulder, David saw that Mr. Kimball had retreated into the house. Prompting Renegade into a trot, he rode for half a mile until he was overcome with emotion. He pulled the stallion to a halt, and sat there for several minutes, looking out at an immense oak tree covered in Spanish moss in the middle of a pasture, recalling how he and his best friend had convened under it on many occasions, discussing their hopes and dreams, their ambitions and revelations. David had known Jake nearly all his life, and seeing these places where they'd shared their childhood tore at him like a sickle. Tears streamed down his face as he reminisced. Distraught with grief and guilt, he stepped down and walked to the edge of the ditch, staring at the ancient tree, remembering the conversations, and wishing with all of his being Jake was standing there with him now. After several minutes, he sighed, and wiped his face with the back of his hand. He patted Renegade on the shoulder.

"It's all right, ain't it, ole pard."

The stallion blew as if in response. David climbed back into the saddle, and cultivated the courage for his next encounter. He gently spurred his little stallion. As Renegade walked down the road, an uncanny breeze blew, and with it, David heard the sound of Jake's laughter float across the field.

He rode for nearly a mile, farther back into the hills, until he came to a bend. There before him sat Callie's farmstead. It also looked abandoned, but upon closer inspection, he saw clothes hanging on a line, rippling in the breeze. He stepped down and tied Renegade to a rail. Glancing around, he walked onto the front porch and tapped on the door. A moment passed, and then he heard footsteps. Callie appeared through the screen, recognized him, and hurled the door open.

"You've returned, I see," she said, her blue eyes twinkling as she faintly smiled.

"Miss Callie."

She took his hand and led him inside. As radiant as he remembered, she was dressed in a frayed cream-colored cotton dress with little pink roses sprinkled over it. A pink ribbon adorned her long blonde hair. She took him to the parlor, and sat down beside him on the loveseat. David saw the photograph he and Jake had taken together subsequent to their enlistment, perched above the fireplace.

"I've been wonderin' when you'd come a-courtin'." She took the hat from his hands and tossed it onto the coffee table. Drawing closer, she took hold of his arm, and gazed into his eyes. At first, he couldn't resist gazing back, but felt a twinge of shame, so he looked away.

"You got the letter I sent you … about Jake?" He looked over at her as she released him and stood.

"I did," she replied, slowly pacing the floor. "It took me this long to git over the loss. In fact, I don't know if I'll ever completely recover from it." She sat back down beside him, clamping onto his arm once again. "I sent you a letter? Did you receive it?"

He shook his head. "No."

"Well, ain't that a shame. I suppose I'll jist have to tell you what was in it, then."

She began to stroke the back of his hand as though it was a kitten. Moving closer still, he could feel her breath on his neck.

"It said that we share a common loss, and Jake would wish for us to be together in his absence." She slipped her hand up to his cheek and turned his face toward hers. "My folks have already consented, and I've been makin' plans for your return for nearly a year now."

Uneasy with the situation, he asked, "Where are your folks?" He wished they would walk in at any moment.

"They're out back, tendin' the garden."

She ran her hand through his hair, and gently pushed on the back of his neck, drawing his face closer to hers. He couldn't help it: he looked down at her mouth.

"Oh, David, how I've missed you so."

He wanted to let it happen. He could almost taste her lips. Suddenly, he remembered Anna, and bolted from the loveseat.

"That ain't why I'm here, Miss Callie." He sauntered to the window and stared out. Like all the other fields he'd recently seen, these too were mostly barren.

"Well, why then, darlin'?" She slid up to him from behind and wrapped her arms around him.

He turned, took hold of her hands to keep her at bay, and blurted, "I'm married."

Callie chuckled. "Why, whatever do you mean, married?"

"I mean … I'm wedded."

She snorted. "To who?"

"Her name is Anna."

Callie tore her hands from his grasp. She turned, took a few steps, then whirled back to face him. "Anna," she repeated snidely. "Well, sir, tell me all about this *Anna*." She made her way over to the loveseat and sat down, patting on the empty space beside her. He frowned and did as she requested.

"She's from Pennsylvania. A farm girl like you." He grinned, but saw it didn't soften her scowl, so he went on. "I was wounded at Gettysburg, and Renegade ran me to their farm. She saved my life."

Raising a skeptical eyebrow, Callie asked, "Jist because she saved your life, did you think you had to repay the favor by marryin' her?"

"No." He glanced at the back dining room, wishing someone would come in and relieve him of this interrogation. "It jist sort of happened that way. She wanted me to stay and protect her from her neighbor, who was tryin' to woo her into givin' up her land."

Callie smiled sardonically. She stood. "If you're married like you say, then where's the ring on your finger?"

"I ain't got one," he replied. "Anna couldn't afford one."

"Hmph!" she began pacing again. "Let me sort this through. You've been married for how long?"

"A year in November."

"And it jist *escaped* your mind not to tell me." She folded her arms across her chest.

"Well ..." Now she had him. He couldn't think of anything to say that wouldn't send her into a tizzy.

She stomped across the room, lashed out, and slapped him hard across the face, so hard that it nearly knocked him to the floor. "How dare you!" She raised her hand to hit him again, but hesitated, and let it fall to her side. "You promised me that if Jake didn't return home from the war, you would take his place. Do you recall?"

He rubbed his cheek, glowering. "As a friend, Miss Callie."

"A friend!" she exploded. "All this time I've been waitin' for you to come home, when I could've been pursuin' other ventures!"

"I know. I apologize. I didn't want to hurt you."

He continued to rub his cheek. She glared at him. He thought she might actually be able to bite his head off.

"It's jist that, things change. People change. I've changed." He stood, and took a step toward her.

41

Callie crossed her arms. "So what were you doin' to occupy yourself while you were in Pennsylvania? Besides courtin' Miss Anna, that is."

He shrugged. "Farmin' mostly."

She started to laugh, and her laughter grew more hysterical. He really wished someone would come to his rescue.

"You were farmin'. And I reckon you were sellin' crops to the Yankee troops too."

"That wasn't my decision to make."

Callie's mouth dropped open, and her eyes grew wide. "You're a traitor! That's what you are, Mr. Summers! A traitor! You're a … a coward … and a liar! And a traitor! Why, there's nothin' I can say that would be appropriate for a lady of my stature!"

He looked at her sadly, hearing each painful word as though she was spewing venom from her scorn. He wanted to run away, but just stood there, receiving the tongue-lashing, and knew he deserved every bit of it.

"… And I hope I never have to lay eyes on you again!" By now her voice had escalated to a scream. "Because, if I do, I will tell the entire county what you did, and what a coward you are! How you lied to me, and betrayed our beloved Dixie!" She gasped for air, her face as red as a burning flame. "I release you to your *Anna*," she growled. "Go and be with her, and I hope she never has to know the kind of man you truly are!" She turned her back on him.

"Miss Callie … I …"

His voice trailed off. There was nothing he could say. He withdrew Jake's pocket watch from his trouser pocket, and set it on the table.

"Jake had this on him when I found him. I thought you should have it."

Hesitating for a moment, waiting for her to respond, he got no acknowledgment, so he went out the front door and untied his stallion.

"That went well," he grumbled under his breath.

From inside, he heard Callie burst into sobs. He stepped into the saddle, riddled with remorse, wishing he would have done things differently, but it was too late. He prompted Renegade, and trotted away from the house, his head throbbing.

When he returned home, he found his mother in the kitchen. Wanting to make sure the womenfolk could adequately protect themselves in case trouble came knocking, as Bud envisioned, he asked, "Ma, do you still have the shotgun?"

She turned to face him and smiled, easing his tension. "Why, yes, of course. I sleep with it under my bed at night."

"Bud told me the Yankees are taxin' us and takin' all the big guns."

"Well, the Yankee rascals didn't find it."

He sighed, relieved. After excusing himself, he walked back to the cottage, but Anna wasn't there, so he went to the house, entered the breezeway, and heard voices coming from the other side of a door. She and Rena were in his old room, now Rena's, having a discussion. Instead of disturbing them, he decided to pester his little sister, and found her in the front room, drawing.

"Whatcha doin' li'l sister?" he asked with a smile.

She looked up from her paper to see him, and grinned. "I'm makin' plans on how to raise the barn before it topples over."

She turned the drawing toward him. On it was a penciled sketch of the lopsided barn, numerous stick figures standing around it, lines and arrows pointing in all directions, and what he thought represented a horse and mule pulling it up.

He gazed at it, trying to disguise his ambivalence. "Do you think Renie and Ginger can do that all by themselves?" he finally asked.

"I don't see why not. If we get the right suspension, and align the ropes jist right, it'll be easy." She smiled.

David shook his head in wonderment. She wasn't the little girl he'd left behind, that much was certain. "Reckon they've been teachin' you somethin' in school."

"We haven't had much schoolin' lately," Josie remarked flatly.

He sat down beside her, watching as she returned to her drawing. After listening to the pencil scratch on the paper for a minute, he said, "I went over to see Bud."

"How is he?" she asked without looking up.

"Fine. He seems to be gittin' around on his pretend leg all right." He paused, hearing the gentle tick of the mantle clock. "And then I went by the Kimball's."

This got Josie's attention. "Were they upset?"

He nodded. "They're woefully heartbroken. They said they don't blame me, though."

"That's good." She looked back down at her engineering project.

"I told Mr. Kimball I want to go up north and fetch Jake's body when the time is right."

Josie nodded, scratching away. "That would be mighty kind." She stopped for a moment and looked at him. "I ponder on Jake often. It's right strange to think I'll never see him again."

"Yeah," he agreed. It was all he could say. His throat tightened, and he had to wait for the feeling to subside before he could speak again. "Then I went over to see Miss Callie."

"I haven't seen her in quite a spell."

"Well, she ain't too happy with me."

"Why not?"

He sighed. "I told her before I left that I'd take Jake's place if he didn't come home."

Josie flashed an astonished look at him. "You said you'd marry her?"

"No." He shook his head. "She jist took it that way. I meant that I'd come back to take care of her, like any good friend would."

"Oh, David." Josie rolled her eyes. "You should've been more specific about your intentions."

"I know, but she backed me into a corner, and at the time, I didn't think ..." He sighed, glancing out the front window as a temperate breeze blew the lace curtain. "She called me a heap of bad names."

"Like what?"

He scoffed. "A traitor. A liar. A coward. She thinks I jist hid out up north to avoid the fight."

Josie set the pad on her lap, and looked at him harshly. "Why didn't you go back to fightin' after you were better?"

He forced a smile. "Well, 'cause I promised Anna, and Renie was lame. I would've had to leave him with her, and I knew if I walked back to the Mason-Dixie, they'd arrest me and have me thrown in prison, which happened anyways."

Josie resumed her drawing.

"The point bein' is that I never intentionally betrayed the Confederacy."

"I believe you," she responded indifferently. "But you might have to convince Ma."

He frowned. "What do you mean?"

"She had the same thoughts as Miss Callie. That's why she took your photograph down." Josie threw a glance at the mantle. "She was upset when she found out you married a Yankee."

David was stunned. This hurt more than any words Callie could cast at him. Josie looked up and saw his shocked expression.

"Don't fret, she likes Anna now. And your tintype is back on the mantle."

Her meager attempt to qualm his surprise disturbed him even more. He stood too quickly, and became lightheaded from the heat.

"Josie, I fought hard for this country. I nearly lost my life doin' it."

She shrugged. "You ain't got to explain it to me." She drew a few more lines, then added, "I'm jist glad the war's over."

He sighed. "Yeah, me too."

He walked back to the cottage, and sulked on the bed, reading *Kit Carson: The Prince of the Gold Hunters*, the "blood and thunder" novel Anna had purchased for him. Once she returned, he confided in her, and she consoled him, nearly convincing him he should have a chat with his mother. But he refused, stating he understood Caroline's feelings, and was afraid that if he did confront her, she would only confirm his doubts.

Several days later, David decided to ride over to another one of the neighbors to try and explain what had happened, and why he had left in the first place. As he approached the ramshackle Caldwell place, a dark, gloomy apprehension came over him. The last time he had been here, something terrible, incomprehensible had happened. Now it was time for him to face his fear.

He dismounted and stepped up onto the porch. The house was eerily still, but a few birds chirped in the trees. Taking a deep breath, he lightly rapped on the door. A rustling sound came from within the house, like a ghostly sigh. The roughhewn wooden door slowly creaked open on its hinges.

"Mrs. Caldwell? If I could please have a word with you, ma'am."

She glared at him for a moment. Her grayish blue eyes squinted at him. With a whisk of her bony hand, she motioned for him to enter, then swept back her white hair. She turned.

Removing his slouch hat, he followed her inside.

"I heard you was back," she said, seating herself in her wooden rocker. She motioned for him to take a seat in a tattered, stuffed chair, so he did so.

"Yes'm," he replied. "And I've been meanin' to git over this way to have a word with you. To tell you …"

She raised her hand, motioning him to be silent. "I know all about what happened," she said, glaring at him.

"I wanted to say how sorry I am …"

"Ain't no need. Callie Mae Copeland told us all about it."

"She did?"

Mrs. Caldwell nodded. "She said she was there when it happened, and she saw the whole thing. We confronted Tom's friends, Barney and Matthew, and they both 'fessed up as well. We would have told you we didn't blame you for Tom's death, but you ran off to jine the army before we had a chance."

"But Jake and I saw three men chasin' after us. We figured they were comin' after us for vengeance."

"That might have well been, but it was before Miss Callie explained the situation." She slowly shook her head, and looked out the window, as though looking back into the past. "Tom never should have blamed you for his father's death. His pa jined up, same as yours, and ain't no one to blame for his death but the Yankees. But what Tom did was wrong, and he paid for it with his life. It wasn't your fault the barn caught on fire, neither." She looked back at him.

He saw the deep, sorrowful pain in her eyes, now glossed over with tears. "I'm so very sorry for your loss, Mrs. Caldwell. For both your losses."

She nodded, and wiped a trickling tear from her cheek. "I know, David. And I appreciate you comin' by to tell me."

She slowly pushed herself up from her rocker. David noticed how aged and frail she had become in just two years' time. Following her lead, he rose, and followed her to the door.

"I ain't seen Matthew or Barney yet," he said, "but I'm fixin' to when I git a chance, to set everything straight."

"No need," she said. "They've both made amends. If you come across them, I'm sure they'll be nothin' but apologetic. Seems Tom was the instigator, and they jist went along. They didn't mean no harm to come to anyone, and once you left, they weren't sure they'd see you again anyway. So your returnin' home has got one up on them."

"What do you mean?" he asked.

"Means they'll likely do anything to avoid you, now that you've returned home a war hero. Makes them look like cowards."

"Oh." David stepped out onto the porch, placed his hat on his head, and turned to face her. "I reckon I never thought of it that way." He thought he detected a slight flicker of a smile cross her lips. "Well, I'd best take my leave. If there's anything you want or need, feel free to let us know. Ma would be most happy to stop by for a visit."

"I'll surely do that, young'un," she said. "Tell her I said hello."

"Will do, Mrs. Caldwell, and I'm very sorry ..."

She raised her hand again. "No need, child. No need." She closed the door.

David couldn't help himself. He drew another deep sigh before mounting Renegade and riding back home. On the way, he passed the place on the road where the barn had stood. There was nothing left, no reminder of what had taken place at all. It was reminiscent of the burned-out battlefields he'd seen, which had been covered over with newly-grown grass, erasing all remnants of death and brutality. He felt a distinct ache in his heart for everything that had transpired, and how they all could have turned out differently. Spurring Renegade, he galloped toward home.

A month went by, during which time the state of Alabama ratified the 13th Amendment to the Constitution, abolishing slavery. On September 18, Robert E. Lee accepted the presidency of Washington College in Lexington, Virginia, and on the following day, Anna turned twenty-one. Unable to afford a gift, David made her a card instead, which more closely resembled a valentine. He promised to buy her something special when he could, and she kissed him in return, stating he was with her, and that was all she wanted. Rena and Josie baked her a small cake with some of the flour she'd brought from Pennsylvania, and although Caroline disapproved, believing it was wasteful, since it could be used to sustain them through the winter, she smiled anyway, and expressed her opinion to her son later that evening as they sat outside on the front porch together.

"Ma, it's Anna's birthday, and she misses her family," he protested. "At least let her have this."

"I know, David, and I want her to feel welcome, but we have no idea how much food there'll be later on. The crops have done poorly due to the drought."

He nodded. "I know. If worse comes to worst, I reckon Anna's sisters can send us foodstuffs."

Caroline laughed. "What makes you think it will ever reach us? Everyone from here to Kentucky's likely starvin'."

He scowled. "Well, at least try to be nice to her. I know what you think of me, but at least pretend you like her."

"David!" Her mouth fell open. "How dare you say such nonsense to me! Of course, I like her. And as for what I think of you, I don't have the slightest notion what you mean." She withdrew a pipe from her pocket, filled it with tobacco, and lit it.

He cleared his throat. "Josie told me you took my photograph down when you learned I was married to a Yankee."

"Oh, she did, did she?" Caroline rocked slowly, puffing on her pipe.

"Yes'm. I reckon you think I deserted my country, but Ma, you have to understand ..." He went on to explain his position, just as he had to his little sister. "And if you don't think I suffered for the cause, then I have proof of it." He removed his shirt, and pointed out the scar near his left shoulder.

She frowned. "That's where you was shot?"

"Yes'm. And this." He turned to display the whiplash marks on his back.

"Dear Lord!"

Caroline broke at the sight, expelling a cry, which alarmed David immensely.

"They did that to you? Those ... those heathens!"

He pulled his shirt back on. "Ma, I'm sorry. I didn't mean to upset you." He fell from his chair to one knee, and took hold of her hand.

She gently pulled it away and wiped her tears. "David Ezekiel Summers! Don't you ever do that to me again!" she yelled.

He slinked back to his chair.

"Have you no idea what you're goin' off to the war did to me? To your sisters? The thought of your never comin' home again …"

"Forgive me, Ma."

"Of course, I forgive you, David. I was upset when I learned you'd married a Yankee, and God knows I had a right to be. I thought your father must've been turnin' in his grave. But the war's over now, and we have to learn to tolerate each other."

Her son gave her a questioning look.

"I'm very fond of Anna. She's a darlin', and she loves you. I can see that." She took another puff on her pipe, and rocked a few times. "I'm troubled about her, though. She seems right sickly."

He smiled. "She's fine. I reckon it's jist nerves, and tryin' to make a good impression."

"Well, she needn't fret about us. We're jist plain folks."

David nodded. "Ma, there's somethin' I've been meanin' to ask you, and I should've done it a long time ago, before I left for the war."

She looked over at him. "What's that?"

"I was wonderin' what the letter said. The one Bud gave to you when he came by here to tell us Pa had died."

"Oh, that." She rocked a few times, contemplating. "Your pa specified in it that I keep the deed to land in Texas he'd purchased from an Injun feller before the war. The same Injun who sold him Cotaco."

"We have land in Texas?"

"Sure do."

"What're you fixin' to do with it?"

"Don't rightly know. I reckon the opportunity will present itself when the good Lord sees fit."

He waited for a moment, then said, "I was hopin' we could have a weddin' ceremony here, since y'all didn't git to see me married off the first time."

She chuckled. "Why would you want that?"

"'Cause I want my family to bear witness."

"I don't see the need. You're already bound to each other in the name of the Lord. You did git married in a church, didn't you?"

"Yes'm."

"Then I don't see the need."

He felt the subject was moot, so he let it rest. But as the days passed, he continued to bring up the topic, even though he received protesting glares from his mother, and embarrassed glances from his wife. His persistence won out, however, and two weeks later after church, an intimate ceremony was held with only his family in attendance. He hoped Jake's parents, and possibly even Callie's family would be present, but they shunned the celebration. Still, it made David happy. Something that was missing before had been replaced, and he felt his vows were now complete.

One morning the following week, Anna woke early and walked down to the kitchen to find Caroline frying eggs.

"Good morning, Mrs. Summers," she greeted with a smile.

"Mornin', child. How did you sleep?"

"Fine, I guess." She set the table for her mother-in-law, then said, "May I help with anything else?"

"Only one thing." Caroline flung a glance over her shoulder. "That you refer to me as Mother Caroline, not Mrs. Summers." She snickered. "After all, you're Mrs. Summers too!"

The women chuckled. Anna drew close, but suddenly, clamped her hand over her mouth and nose, and ran outside. After a few moments, she returned, her face flushed.

"How many months is this?" Caroline asked.

Anna glared at her, amazed by her insight.

The door slammed, and Rena appeared. "Ma, need any help?" she asked, and smiled at her sister-in-law.

Josie approached the structure and entered. She glanced at Anna. "What's wrong?" she asked.

"Nothing," replied Anna. "Not a thing."

Caroline turned to face her. "I wouldn't necessarily say that." She nodded, prodding her to confess.

Anna merely smiled.

"Our Anna is expectin' a baby!" Caroline beamed, clasping her hands together.

Her daughters gaped at her wide-eyed, and enormous smiles consumed their faces.

Josie shrieked.

"When is the baby due?" Rena inquired.

"Well," replied Anna, brushing a strand of hair from her face. "I've estimated it to be in mid-March."

Josie jumped up and down, squealing, "I'll be an aunt! I'll be an aunt!"

The others laughed.

She settled down. "Where's David?" She gasped. "Does he know?"

Anna shook her head, provoking subtle chuckles from his clan. "He's absolutely clueless."

"That's 'cause he's a man," Rena interjected.

Josie giggled at the remark.

"I'd like to tell him myself," said Anna, "if it's all right."

Caroline walked over and hugged her tightly. "By all means, sweetheart." She smiled at her. "It's your privilege to tell him."

Anna was amazed. She had actually called her "sweetheart." She smiled back.

"Oh! Here he comes now!" Josie said excitedly in a hushed voice.

Her brother entered, looked around, and seeing the exaggerated smiles on their faces, raised an eyebrow and asked, "What's goin' on?"

"Oh, nothin'," replied Rena. "Take a seat. We're havin' eggs and cornbread."

He grimaced. "Again? Maybe I should mosey into town, and see if I can scrounge up some ..."

"Never mind that." Caroline cut him off. "Let us say grace. We've plenty to be thankful for."

Rena, Josie, and Anna exchanged glances as they sat down, and after reciting a short prayer, disguised their smiles by stuffing food into their mouths.

David quickly ate, stood, and said," I've got some chores to tend to."

As he left, Josie nearly protested, but Caroline stopped her by placing a hand on her arm. "Help clean up, darlin's."

Rena glanced at her sister-in-law.

Anna knew she wondered why nothing was revealed. "I'll tell him tonight," she explained with a smile.

She started to plot the scene out in her mind, and throughout the day, rehearsed how she would break the news. She couldn't wait, but wanted it to be so special that neither one of them would ever forget it. After all, how many times would she have the chance to tell her husband they were expecting their very first child?

Toward dusk, he returned to the house, dusty from digging in the fields all day, and disgusted with the dried up, fruitless crops. He inquired about supper, and Caroline informed him that Anna had prepared something for him in the cottage. Josie and Rena stifled snickers, which caught his attention. He turned to quizzically look at them, but they quickly retreated into Rena's bedroom.

"Why ain't we eatin' in here tonight?" he asked.

Caroline was silent for a moment, trying to come up with a viable excuse. "Anna jist wanted to have a quiet supper with you, but you need to go dust yourself off first, and make yourself presentable."

Still puzzled, he obeyed, went out back, and brushed off as much dust as he could from his clothes. He filled a bucket with water from the well, washed his face and hands, and walked up to the cottage. Candlelight flickered from inside the checkerboard curtains. He entered, and saw his bride sitting on the bed, writing in a journal.

"Evenin', honey," he greeted. "Ma said you have supper out here, and I'm starvin'!" He flashed a grin at her, sat at the table, and pulled off his boots, letting them clunk onto the floor.

She closed her journal and sat down next to him. "I hope you don't mind, but it's a cold supper." She lifted a pot cover to reveal two small fowl and a salad.

He scowled at it for a moment. "Is this it? Two li'l quail and raw greens?"

Anna nodded, slightly smiling.

"I don't reckon it'll be enough to fill me up," he stated blatantly. He propped his elbows on the table, folded his hands, and said, "Lord bless this food of which we are about to receive, Amen," as quickly as he could before snatching a quail from the plate and tearing into it with his teeth. He devoured it quickly, shoved the foliage into his mouth in three bites, and set his fork down. He looked at Anna, then at the remaining food on the table. "Ain't you eatin'?" he asked.

After watching the spectacle, she felt queasy. "I'm not very hungry," she replied. "Why don't you have it?"

He scratched the stubble on his face. His whole body was itchy from digging up weeds all day. "You need to eat somethin'," he observed.

"I will. I'll find something later." She pushed the plate toward him.

David shrugged. "Okay." He gobbled up the remaining food, chased it with a full glass of water, set the glass down, and uninhibitedly belched.

Anna winced.

"Oh, pardon me." He stood, walked to the bed, and sprawled out on top of it. "It don't look like we'll have much to sustain on this winter."

Anna let the comment slide, knowing she wouldn't be there to subject herself to starvation. She had more important things to discuss. After stacking the plates, she shuffled over to the bed and sat down beside him. With his eyes closed, he reached up and rubbed her back.

"Sweetie, there's something I need to tell you."

"What?" There was a long hesitation. He opened his eyes.

Anna reconsidered. "You look so tired," she said, stroking his cheek with the palm of her hand. *Perhaps the news can wait*, she thought.

"Anna?" He saw her apprehension, and propped himself up on one elbow. "Is everything all right?"

She smiled. "Yes, at least, I think it is." She glanced around the room, at the flickering candles she'd deliberately placed, the linen tablecloth she'd constructed just for the occasion, and the two strategically situated vases of flowers. She expelled a sigh.

"What is it?" He grew concerned. Frowning at her, he waited for a response.

Anna looked back at him, the candlelight dancing on his handsome face. "We're going to have a baby."

He stared at her for a moment, as though he hadn't heard her. "A baby," he repeated questioningly.

She grinned. "Yes. Isn't it wonderful?" She giggled.

"Are you sure?"

"Uh huh. We're going to be parents. I'm going to be a mother, and you're going to be a father!"

"Dear God." He sat up, slid his legs off the end of the bed, and rested his head in his hands. He glanced over his shoulder at her. "You're absolutely certain."

She nodded. "You don't seem very happy." She bit her lower lip.

He saw his reaction had upset her. "Oh. No, darlin', it ain't that." He swung around and put his arm across her shoulders. "It's jist amazin' news, is all." He kissed her forehead. "We're gonna have a baby," he said for her benefit.

They embraced, kissed sweetly, and hugged again, holding each other for several minutes. He released her, and took both her hands in his. She was so beautiful, he should be thrilled and honored. But instead, he was terrified. He hid his true feelings from her, telling her over and over again how happy he was. But the truth was, it didn't make him happy at all. It made him feel burdened and apprehensive.

"Are you certain you're happy about this?" she asked as they lay side by side.

"Of course. You jist caught me off guard is all. And I'll admit, I'm selfish. I wanted to have you all to myself for a spell before we started a family. But the good Lord has decided otherwise, so I reckon you're with child, then."

It wasn't exactly the answer she was looking for, but she reasoned with herself that, over time, he would adjust and be just as excited as she was. She sighed happily, and fell asleep in his arms.

After a few hours, he arose, took the dishes to the summer kitchen, and sat outside, patting his dogs until they grew tired and wandered off to sleep. He sat on a log, taking sips from the whiskey bottle Anna's neighbor, Patrick Mulligan, had given him upon their departure from Pennsylvania, and gazed up at the stars, noticing how every one of them twinkled in the night sky. He wondered, if he made a wish on each one, would they all come true? It would take that many to make his dreams a reality, and now with a baby on the way, his dreams were even more of a long shot. His disappointment grew, and he wished Jake was there for him to confide in.

The following morning, he stood by and observed as his family bestowed hugs, adoring kisses, and congratulations on his wife, with an occasional "you too, David," tossed in his direction for good measure. He lingered at the back of the group, realizing he was only an accessory, and after a few moments, scowled and ambled off.

Noticing his reaction, Rena asked, "Is David all right?"

Anna sadly smiled at her. "He will be. He didn't take the news as well as I'd hoped, but I think that, in time, he'll be thrilled about it."

Rena decided to follow her brother. She found him, and spied as he stood staring out at the fields. A dove hooted nearby. He cupped his hands, repeating the bird call their father had taught them. The mourning dove responded from a nearby oak tree, repeating the back-and-forth chant several times before David ceased, picked up a pitchfork, and began lifting hay into a trough.

Rena quietly approached him. "David," she said. "Ain't you happy about the baby?"

He stopped, stuck the pitchfork into the dirt, and balanced on it with one gloved hand while he wiped his brow from under his slouch hat with the other. "Yeah, I'm happy."

He went to stab at another forkful, but Rena prevented it by grabbing his arm. "You don't seem too excited."

Extracting a sigh, he frowned. "It's jist that, well, I was plannin' on attendin' Auburn someday. And now that I'm about to become a father, I'll have to support my family instead of goin' to school."

"Auburn's closed anyways. Has been for some time now."

"I know. But it'll open again. And now this ..." He gestured toward the house, and seeing Anna standing there, realized she'd heard the whole thing. She turned and ran.

"Anna!" he hollered.

She kept running.

"Damn it!"

He tossed the pitchfork and ran after her. She bolted into the woods, where he lost sight of her.

"Anna!"

Alarmed she might fall and hurt herself or the baby, he screamed her name again. He looked around in every direction, but didn't see her anywhere. Panic-stricken, he panted, catching his breath. He heard sobs coming from a short distance, and followed the sound to find her sitting on the ground, crying.

"Darlin'!" He knelt down and took her into his arms. "I'm so sorry. I didn't see you standin' there."

"That's obvious," she sniffed. "I regret this is ruining your plans."

"No, that ain't it." He refused to release her, and held her tighter. "I love you, Anna. Please don't run away from me again. We'll git through this."

She shoved him away. "You had something to do with this too, you know."

She wiped her eyes. He squeezed her hand. She looked up to see him grinning at her.

"Stop it!" she said, nudging his arm. She started to giggle, and they both laughed.

"We're havin' a baby," he said.

She nodded in response.

"They (African Americans) should be especially taught the utter absurdity of expecting or aspiring to a condition of social equality with the white race."

- Alabama Gov. Robert M. Patton
Address to State Legislature

This is a white man's government and a white man's state. We are opposed to any changes in the government except such as are necessary to get the state into the Union again."

- *Huntsville Advocate*

Chapter Three

By mid-October, it was evident to Morgan County's residents that the freed slaves were destitute. The *Montgomery Daily Advertiser* reported that the Negroes had nothing but the clothes on their backs, and were living in "deserted and ruined houses, in huts built with their hands with refuse lumber, under sheds and under bridges over creeks, ravines, and gutters and in caves in the back of rivers and ravines." At a housing settlement in Montgomery, referred to as "Hard Times," they "lived on the old fair grounds in shelters erected out of pine poles." Thousands were "living in shanties, old furnaces, boilers, and at the ruins of the arsenals' foundries, and under shelters on the banks of the river and other such places as they can squat upon and remain undisturbed. The manner in which they are living is calculated to arouse the sympathies of everyone."

David was no exception, and felt terrible for the poor souls thrown out of the only homes they'd ever known. All because the Yankee government dictated it, instead of paying the slave owners for their property, which would have enabled them to set their Negroes free. This, he believed, as did many of the locals he'd discussed the topic with, would have produced the best result, and the country could have avoided war. But now the South was left insolvent.

Each passing day grew increasingly colder, so he spent his time cutting wood and harvesting what little corn, oats, barley, and vegetables the nearly barren fields produced. One afternoon in late October, Anna came out to find him.

"David, I think a storm's coming," she called as he loaded wood into the back of the wagon.

He whirled around to see her approach. "What are you doin' here?" he asked upon seeing her.

"I wanted to make sure you were all right," she replied with a smile as she drew near, but stopped suddenly, seeing the panic on his face. "What's wrong?"

"Darlin', I told you not to come into these woods by yourself anytime, day or night." He glowered, took her hand, and hugged her. "I appreciate your concern, but I want you to stay where it's safe."

"It's perfectly safe here. I don't know what you're so afraid of. And I'm perfectly capable of taking care of myself."

"It ain't that."

He helped her climb up onto the seat, then positioned himself beside her and tapped Ginger's hindquarters with a stick. The mule lurched forward.

"What is it you're not telling me?" she inquired.

He glanced at her and grinned. "You'll jist think I'm bein' overprotective, but I have good reason to fret about you. And now with the baby comin', well, that's even more reason."

She grimaced at him, waiting for him to continue.

He only said, "I'll tell you when we get back inside the cottage where it's warm."

Once they had returned home, he made her promise to stay inside while he unloaded the wood, stacked it, and put Ginger in her stall. He entered the cottage to see her sitting on the bed, reading the book her sisters had given him, *Moby-Dick*.

She looked up as he entered. "All right, Mr. Summers, why don't you tell me what's on your mind."

Her warm, teasing smile radiated across the room, and drew him to her.

"You'll think I'm bein' silly, but I don't want you wanderin' around in the woods alone. There's a witch out yonder."

Anna stared at him, and suddenly burst into laughter. She caused him to frown. "Oh, sweetheart, you're absolutely right."

"I am?"

"You *are* being silly!"

He scowled.

She caught his hand and pulled him down beside her. "David, for once and for all, there's no such thing as ..."

"Yes, there is, Anna! I saw one when I was a youn'un. I wouldn't invent it."

Stifling a snicker, she asked, "What exactly did you see?"

"Well, it was a long time ago," he started out slowly. "I was up in the hills east of here with Jake, huntin' for squirrels, and that's when we saw her. She didn't see us, but we saw what she did."

This piqued Anna's curiosity. "What did she do?"

"There was this older woman, Mrs. Jenkins, whose husband had died. Anyways, she was about to give birth, and Jake suggested we go see how she was gettin' on. But when we got to the cabin, we saw the witch comin' out with the baby."

"What?" Anna wanted to laugh at the preposterousness of his story, but his serious demeanor prevented her.

"We saw her, Anna. She ran off into the woods with the infant. To eat it, I reckon. So, Jake and I, we went inside, and the widow Jenkins, she ... she was ..."

"Dead?"

He nodded sorrowfully. "We tried chasin' after the ole hag, but we lost her trail, and we got scared, 'cause it was gettin' dark. That's why I don't want you wanderin' around out in the woods by yourself."

Anna shuddered. He held her, and made her vow not to go into the forest alone. For the first time since her arrival, essentially all her life, she felt completely vulnerable.

A week later, David managed to obtain a current issue of the *Montgomery Daily Advertiser*, and read about the ex-slaves' continuing plight. In Columbus, Georgia, and Opelika, the police demolished over thirty shanties at local depots after requesting that the homeless Negroes remove themselves. Some landlords pursued exorbitant rents from the vagrants, who of course couldn't pay, and were thrown out in the cold to freeze to death. It was all too inhumane, so heartrending to read about, that David had to cease. He felt helpless to do anything, and providing for his own was such a deep concern that it overtook his thoughts and motivated him to keep foraging for as much food as he could before winter set in.

On October 31, he awoke with the sun, realizing it was All Hollows Eve, and recalled his celebration with Patrick a few years back. He chuckled to himself as he remembered Patrick's Irish spook story. Upon entering the house, he discovered his family seating themselves at the dining table, so he took his place. They held hands, said grace, and began to eat.

"There's an election today," Anna said indifferently. "I read it in the paper."

"Yeah, I know," David grumbled. "They won't let me vote though, 'cause I'm an 'ex-Confederate'. Why should it be a crime to defend your own country?"

"Don't feel bad," said Rena. "They won't let us vote, either."

The sisters chortled.

David scoffed. "Y'all shouldn't be allowed to vote any more than the niggers should."

Suddenly, it went deathly quiet. The ticking of the mantle clock grew louder. He glanced up from his plate to see his sisters and wife staring at him.

"David!" Anna hissed. "You know how I feel about that word!"

"Sorry," he muttered.

Caroline picked up the bowl of eggs and passed it to Josie. "I believe there's no need for us to vote, since we can do it through our husbands."

"But what if we don't have husbands?" Josie piped in.

"That's all the more reason why we should have the right!" exclaimed Rena.

"I completely agree," Anna said.

"I predict that in my lifetime, women *will* be allowed to vote," Josie proclaimed.

David raised a skeptical eyebrow at her. "Now you're startin' to sound like Miss Abigail," he commented, referring to Anna's clairvoyant sister.

He slowly shook his head, astounded by the absurdity, but noticed his wife was watching his behavior. Realizing he was outnumbered, he quickly ate before excusing himself. Perhaps soon, this whole mess would be over, and he could vote again, as was his God-given right. He sniggered as he walked to the barn. *Women vote?* he questioned to himself. *Wouldn't that be a hoot!*

Later that week, he made a trip to the mercantile for supplies. The one hundred dollars he and Anna had been given as a wedding gift was dwindling fast; he was down to sixty-five dollars and some odd cents. He entered the wooden structure, and propped himself against the counter, glancing around while he waited for Ben Johnson, the storekeeper, to fill his order. The two-story building had miraculously been spared from Yankee confiscation. Its wooden slat railings lined the upstairs perimeter, and every item above was visible from the main floor. Downstairs, glass cases displayed farming and household wares, as well as various necessities including clay pottery, sewing notions, and clothing. Ropes, halters, and spools of wire hung from the ceiling rafters. A few bolts of cloth lay heaped on a table in the corner. The entire medley of merchandise was coated with a thin layer of dust. The wooden floor creaked and complained as customers' boots clunked across it, and the smell of pungent cigar smoke lingered in the air. David leafed through several newspapers lying on the wooden counter. One story caught his eye, and as he read it, he fumed.

"Have you seen this?" he asked Ben.

The middle-aged gentleman glanced over from his hardware drawer. "Yup," he casually replied. "I don't know 'bout you, David, but it seems right strange to know many of our finest boys, such as yourself, ain't allowed to vote, and yet there are former slaves who've been elected as state officials. Ironic, that's what I say." He guffawed. "At least some of those bomb proofs, dead heads, featherbeds, and cripples Governor Parsons reappointed have been replaced. Can't run a state with a heap of ineffective old men. That's my take on it, anyway."

"Reckon I agree," David opined.

"And I don't know 'bout you, but I'm in support of President Johnson's policy, even if he is a Republican. The Radicals, tories, Unionists, and those fellers who are only interested in their own self-advancement, should our current government be overthrown ..."

"The papers are callin' them scalawags."

"Yessir. They're all hell bent on stirrin' up trouble."

David nodded in response.

"They all want to take control, and now the Radicals have succeeded in blockin' readmission of our southern states to Congress. It's a recipe for disaster, in my humble opinion."

"I can't agree with you more." David looked up from the printed page and asked, "Did you take the oath, Ben?"

"Yup. They came around the county in August and had us all take it."

"Hmm," David responded. "I've been readin' about Northerners comin' down to teach the freed slaves. Have you seen any?"

"No, can't say as I have. Not yet, anyway. Rumor has it they're buildin' schools in these parts though, and runnin' the Freedmen's Bureau. There's a big ole colony of freedmen right near here. Pitiful thing. Talk is thousands of the old and infirm have died from small pox. It's a damn shame." He shook his head remorsefully.

"I've a feelin' the Freedmen's Bureau is only cause for trouble."

"Along with the Yankee bluecoats. I read some black troops plundered and shot into white folks' houses in Decatur."

"That's appallin'," David retorted.

"Sure enough is. Last month, they combined Georgia and Alabama into one military province called the Department of the Gulf. Under a General Woods, I believe his name is. I don't know why they can't protect us from such outrages."

"Reckon they're main intention is to humiliate us," replied David.

Ben smiled ruefully. "Sorry I can't fill the whole order," he said as he placed several screws in a brown paper bag, "but we ain't received a new shipment in months. Don't know when we'll be seein' one, either."

"Much obliged, jist the same," David responded.

He took the bag Ben handed him. Exiting the building, he retrieved Renegade from a hitching post, mounted, and set off for the next destination he'd been anticipating for over a month. Riding south of the Kimball's farm, just as Jake's father had directed, he came to a ravine, and followed a path back from the main road over rolling hills until he saw a small cabin nestled in a glen with smoke billowing from its chimney. The smell of cooking food arrested his nostrils, making him salivate. He gave Renegade a slight kick. As he approached the structure, he saw a little boy emerge.

"Mama!" he hollered. "Dere a man here!" The toddler pointed his finger at David and grinned.

A woman followed him out onto the tiny porch. "Now what'd I tell you 'bout goin' outside all by yo' ..." She looked up, shading her eyes with her hand. "Well, Lordie be!" she said at last. "If it ain't Missa David!"

"Miss Isabelle," he greeted in return as he dismounted. "It's been a long time." He grinned as he tied his stallion to a shrub and withdrew his hat.

"Sho has!" she said with a bright smile. She was as handsome as he remembered, and her large brown eyes sparkled upon recognition. "Come inside!"

She waved him in and took hold of her toddler's hand. David followed them in.

"Jake's pa told me you had a place of your own," he commented, looking around the tiny, one-room dwelling.

The cabin was cozy and inviting, with a double bed draped in quilts against one wall, a pine table and two chairs against another, a small glowing fireplace with a steaming cast-iron pot hanging above it, and delicate embroidered curtains over three tiny windows. A pine cradle sat in the corner. He stepped toward it. "Is this the young'un Mr. Kimball told me about?"

"Yessir!" Issabelle beamed. "This here's Lincoln, name in honor of our emancipator. Ain't he a saint?"

David looked down at the slumbering, swaddled infant, his tiny pudgy face barely visible, and smiled. "He surely is." Turning toward the boy, he said, "And Tommy's grown considerably since I saw him last."

The little boy grinned and hid behind his mother's skirts. Isabelle chuckled.

"Now, if it's Percy you come to see, he's out yonder. Went off early this mornin', an' brought back some catfish fo' supper. He's out cleanin' them behind da shed." She gestured toward a small shack that more closely resembled an outhouse at the top of a knoll.

"I'll go fetch him," David offered.

He smiled, stepped outside, and walked to the shed. Whistling came from within, then a male voice burst into song.

> "Da mas'er runs, ha-ha! Da darky stays, ho-ho!
> It mus' be now da kingdom comin', an' da year of
> Jubilo!"

The whistling resumed. He realized the vocalist didn't know the verses' lyrics, but only the chorus, because when it came back around, the same lustrous voice sang out again. He walked behind the shed to see Percy whistling as he busily scraped scales off a fish.

"Percy?"

The man looked up, stopped momentarily, and smiled. He dropped the fish on top of several others lying on the ground. "Well, if it ain't Missa David!" he said, wiping his hands on his overalls. He thrust out his hand, and David took it. "Back from da war I see!"

David grinned. "It's good to see you again."

"An' you!" He nodded, still smiling. "Glad to see no harm came your way."

"Unlike Jake," David said contritely.

"Yessuh. Saddest day of my life, findin' out my boy had been killed." He shook his head slowly. "Have you seen my wife an' young'uns?"

"I have, and you should be right proud."

"That I am!" Percy exclaimed. "Remember our weddin' vows we took?"

"Uh, yeah, I somewhat do."

"We said till death or distance do us part, but now we ain't slaves no more, an' there ain't no threat of us bein' separated, unless Isabelle decides to run off. She ain't done it so far, though."

The two men chuckled.

"You've got a fine place here."

"Why, thank you kindly. Been workin' hard to keep it up, in between fishin' an' huntin', that is." Percy laughed. "I'm jist waitin' fo' da government to come through."

"With what?"

"With their promise! They says they're divvyin' up da plantations by Christmas, and us black folks'll all git our share. Forty acres an' a mule, that's what they say."

"Who told you that?"

"Why, da Freedmen's Bureau, of course. Some fellers have even staked out their land, waitin' for da day. An' I heard tell of a few who took over livestock they found on da land they claimed."

A lanky hound meandered around the corner. Percy bent down to pat it.

"This here's my huntin' dog. Got me a Spencer rifle too, for huntin'."

David remembered what Bud had told him, how larger armaments were being seized by the Yankees. Apparently, they were giving all the weapons to freed blacks. Percy's dog and rifle were his badges of freedom, and although David was happy for him, he felt a twinge of resentment as well.

"An' I opened an account with da Freedmen's Savin's an' Trust Company in Huntsville. Can you imagine that, Missa David? Me, with my own bankin' account!"

"That's mighty fine, Percy," he answered.

"I never thought I'd see this day come. It's a glorious country we live in!" He laughed heartily.

David forced a smile. He should be happy for this man he'd known since he was a child, but he felt envious instead, for his own privileges had been revoked. Irritated with himself, he pushed the feeling aside. "What else did the Freedman's Bureau tell you?"

"Well." The man rubbed his nearly bald head. "They said that our former massas should support us, that we ought not to work till we receive compensation, an' that we should be paid all wages owed us since January of sixty-three. I won't hold Massa Kimball to that, though. He was always right good to me an' my missus."

David frowned. "How are you fixin' to git money in the bank if you don't work?" he asked.

"Don't rightly know. Government'll take care of us, or if I have to, I'll scratch out a livin' as a farmer, same as you. Some freedmen is spillin' of the Gypsuns, but not me. No sir." Noticing David's blank expression, he clarified, "stealin' from the white folks."

"Oh." Deciding to change the subject, David proclaimed with a grin, "I got married."

"You did? Halleluiah!" Percy grasped his hand and shook it vigorously. "Is it Miss Callie?"

He chuckled. "No, it ain't Miss Callie. Her name's Anna. She's from Pennsylvania, and she's the purtiest gal you ever did see." He smiled happily.

"Well, ain't that grand!" He patted David's arm. "Come to da' house an' let's have us a celebration!"

Percy bent, retrieved the fish, and started for the cabin, his dog lagging behind. David followed. When Percy informed his wife of David's matrimony, Isabelle squealed.

"Dat won'erful news!" she said. "I've got jist da thing to rejoice with!" She retrieved two tin cups and a brown jug from a shelf. Motioning for the men to sit, she poured each of them a cupful.

"To Miss Anna!" Percy said, raising his cup. He sipped.

David took a drink and immediately felt a burn so profound he thought he'd swallowed liquid fire. He coughed.

Isabelle giggled.

Noticing a book on the table, he picked it up. "What's this?

"Oh, dat's my blue-black speller," said Percy. "Weze both learnin' to read."

David flipped through the primer's pages, observing the beginner lessons inside.

"Massa Kimball couldn't have us do no learnin'," Isabelle explained, "because it were illegal."

"Yeah," David nodded in acknowledgment. He set the book down. "Oh, I nearly forgot. We're havin' a baby too."

"Lordy be!" she exclaimed. "Weze havin' chil'ren all at once!"

Percy poured more sour mash into their cups. "Another toast, then, to da baby!"

They all partook.

"Will you take dinner with us?" Isabelle asked. "There's plenty."

David glanced at the little boy, who was playing with a large ball on the dirt floor. It seemed they barely had enough to feed themselves.

"No, thank you, Miss Isabelle. I'm sure Ma's got somethin' waitin' for me at home, so I'd best take my leave." He stood, propping his slouch hat on his head. "Percy, Isabelle, and Tommy. It's mighty good seein' y'all again."

"You too, Missa David," Isabelle replied. "Don't be a stranger, you hear?"

"I won't." He walked out and mounted his stallion.

"An' tell that wife of yours we said hello," Percy added.

"I'll do that." He smiled and turned his horse.

As he traveled back to the main road, he took into account what he'd just witnessed. Percy was obviously dazzled with his newfound freedom. He behaved like a man intoxicated, and understandably so, but David was wary about the whole situation. An insurrection was still a viable threat, and the thought made him nervous. Could he trust Percy when it came down to it? Or would the man find opportunity to retaliate for years spent in servitude? David was afraid of the answer.

He returned home, and walked into the house to see his sisters and Anna in Rena's room, so he rapped on the open door.

"Oh, you've returned!" Anna greeted upon seeing him. "We've been invited to a party!"

He glanced at his sisters, then noticed several dresses laid out on the bed.

"A party?" he questioned, wondering who in their right mind would have one now, when the county was suffering from poverty. "Who invited us?"

"Callie's folks," Rena replied. "They heard you were back, and wanted to invite some neighbors to welcome you. Ain't that nice?"

David raised a skeptical eyebrow. "Yeah, that's real nice." The party wasn't for him, he knew. Callie had told her parents about Anna, and they wanted to get a good look at her for themselves. "When is it?"

"Saturday night," responded Josie. "We have to fancy up our old dresses." She sighed. "They'll never look as beautiful as the one Anna has, though."

He gawked at his wife. "You're fixin' to go in that blue gown?"

"Of course!" She took his hands in hers. "That's why I brought it all the way down here. To make a good impression. And I want to wear it while it still fits." She gave him a quick kiss on the lips. "I'll have to wear it without hoops, though."

"All right, darlin'," he replied, disarmed by her affection. "I reckon you'll be the purtiest belle at the ball."

She smiled widely at his remark and turned to his sisters. The three young women giggled.

Two days later, as Anna primped, David lay on the bed observing her. She slithered into her gown, had him assist her in buttoning the back, and looked at herself in the mirror.

"How do I look?" she asked, glancing at him through the reflection.

"Breathtakin'." He hesitated. "Are you fixin' to wear that necklace Stephen gave you?"

"The sapphire? Yes, well, about that ..."

She proceeded to explain that she had used it for barter to obtain their mule and wagon. He didn't seem too disappointed, which came as no surprise.

"So I'll wear the locket you gave me, instead."

She retrieved it from the top dresser drawer, handed it to him, sat beside him, and lifted her hair. He fumbled with the clasp, finally pried it open, and managed to secure the chain around her neck. Anna let her blonde hair fall. She stood and gazed at herself again.

"All right," she stated, "I'm ready to meet Callie."

By the tone in her voice, he knew she was apprehensive. For some reason, she had built this up in her mind to be much bigger than it was. He followed her to the house. His mother and sisters were waiting in the front room, and stood as they appeared.

"The wagon's outside," he said. "Ladies."

He opened the door and held out his hand. They smiled as they filed past. Anna paused to give him a peck on the cheek before she boarded. She sat in the back with his sisters on blankets, and Caroline sat beside him on the seat. As they rode off, Renegade neighed in complaint for being left behind. They rode a few miles until they arrived at the Copeland residence, and saw four vehicles parked outside. David jumped down to assist his family. Caroline led the way and tapped on the door. Momentarily, a woman appeared to greet her.

"Hello, Fay, so good to see you again," Caroline replied as she went in, followed by Rena.

Josie glanced behind her. "Ain't you comin'?" she asked.

"We're right behind you," her brother responded.

As Josie proceeded inside, David held out his arm and smiled. Anna took it, returning the smile. They stepped up onto the porch and walked through the door. A small gathering was mingling inside, and turned to look as they entered. Suddenly, Callie swept in from out of nowhere, wearing the same dress she'd had on when David last saw her.

"Why, there you are! She took their wraps and handed them to a young Negro woman wearing a black dress and white apron who was standing nearby. Callie returned to David, took him by the arm, and pulled him away from his wife. "I've been wonderin' when y'all would git here." She reached up and stroked his cheek.

He grinned at her sheepishly, discomfited by the attention. "I thought you were riled with me, 'cause of the things you said before."

She laughed. "Why, I could never stay angry with you, darlin'," she cooed.

Anna's mouth dropped open with indignation. She quickly corrected herself, glanced around at the guests who were scrutinizing her, and realized she was exceptionally overdressed, as the others wore drab, ordinary clothing. The room grew quiet. People whispered to each other as they continued to stare. She looked for her husband. He was in the back dining room with Callie, who was conversing with another couple. She went to him, and took hold of his hand.

"David, please don't leave me alone with these people," she whispered.

Callie overheard and laughed. "Why, this must be your lovely bride." She smugly eyed Anna over from head to toe.

He remembered his manners. "Miss Callie, Anna. Anna, Miss Callie."

The two young women slightly bowed their heads to one another.

"I hope you don't mind, Miss Anna, but I need to borrow your husband for a moment."

She pulled him away again. He looked back at Anna with a bewildered expression on his face as they walked out the back door.

Anna's temper flared. This wasn't at all how she had envisioned it. She was supposed to have made a grand entrance, but instead, she'd been ignored and humiliated, and by her own husband, no less. She decided to follow them, but was intercepted by her sister-in-law.

"Where'd David go?" Rena asked.

"Callie took him outside," she responded, struggling to contain her frustration.

Rena scoffed. "Well, he should be the one doin' this, but I'll show you around." She took Anna by the arm, led her back to the parlor, and began introductions. "Mr. and Mrs. Draper, this here's David's new wife, Anna."

"Hello, dear," the woman said, who appeared to be in her thirties. "We all noticed you when you came in. My, but that's a lovely gown you have on."

"Thank you," she modestly replied.

"Anna's havin' a baby," Rena announced.

Mrs. Draper lit up. "You are? Well, congratulations!"

"Yes, yes. Best wishes to you and David, my dear," her husband added between cigar puffs.

Taking Anna by the arm, Rena led her to another couple. "Mr. and Mrs. Foreman." She introduced the same way, proclaiming Anna's pregnancy at the end of the avowal, and receiving a similar reaction.

Rena presented her to the rest of the group, which included Callie's parents and two other couples: the McAnnally's and the Skidmore's. When they had canvassed the room, she left her with her mother. Anna felt like a novelty. She was merely an ornament for David's arm, the proud Southern boy who'd come back from the war virtually unscathed. Callie's parents had undoubtedly informed them that she was a Yankee, as their loathsome stares indicated. The only reason they showed her any interest at all was because she was carrying his baby, as Rena had so blatantly pointed out to them. Anna knew it was her attempt to gain acceptance from their neighbors, but it stung, just the same.

"I think I'll go find David," she said to Caroline after a few moments.

His mother glanced around. "Where is that boy?"

"He went outside with Callie. I'll be right back."

Caroline looked perturbed. "Yes, darlin', you tell him he needs to git in here and show some respect." She began conversing with Mrs. Skidmore.

Anna walked through the house to the back door and went outside. The yard was lovely, even in November, filled with cypress, cedars, and what she imagined must be flowering shrubs, although they were dormant now. She walked along a stone path, under an arbor covered in dried vines, and heard their voices. Quietly, she approached to eavesdrop.

"I never meant to lead you on, Miss Callie," he was saying. "And I'm sorry I didn't write. Even if I had, you likely wouldn't have received my letters, anyways."

"I know," she replied, "and I only said those things because I was hurt. But I've had time to think, and I'm beyond it now."

Anna crept closer, and peered around the corner of the garden shed. They were facing each other, looking into each other's eyes. She seethed at the sight.

"I'm glad to hear that. I know you think I'm a hypocrite ..."

"Nonsense. I think any man in your position would have done the same."

"Is that a fact?"

"Yes, darlin'. It was a noble thing what you and Jake done, bearin' arms to defend our beloved Dixie."

"I wanted to avenge Pa, even though it might've been a bad reason to go."

Callie smiled. "Why, I don't see anything bad about it at all." She took his hand. "Your mother explained how you suffered for the cause, and it was wrong of me to assume otherwise."

"Ma was here?"

She nodded. "A few days ago. That's when my ma invited y'all over for a get-together."

He nodded. "I want to thank you for clearin' my name with Tom's ma."

"Of course! I was there and saw the whole thing. You were merely defendin' yourself, darlin.' Tom was in the wrong, and he paid for it with his life. You should've stayed to clear your own name, but I understand why you and Jake took off like you did."

"Miss Callie." He frowned, struggling to find the words. "I spoke out of turn when I made you that promise. I did it 'cause I loved you and Jake jist the same, and I thought it was the right thing to do at the time."

Callie stared into his eyes.

Anna bristled.

"But I couldn't replace him by marryin' you. It would have been unfair, a total farce, and neither one of us would've been happy. Surely, you must know you were holdin' out for somethin' neither one of us is capable of." He turned away. "Besides, I'm in love with my wife."

"I understand," she said, "and I'm grateful. If she hadn't found you when she did, you might well have ended up like Jake."

He turned back to face her.

"We understand each other, you and I," Callie continued. "Why, it's as though we're birds of a feather."

"Reckon so." He smiled.

"And we both miss him. It's been so hard without him, David," Callie whimpered. "I always gaze upon the photograph y'all had taken before runnin' off to Virginia, and I ... I ..." She threw herself on him, sobbing. He consoled her by wrapping his arms around her.

It was all Anna could take. She stomped toward them. "David, your mother requests your presence inside," she bellowed, louder than she intended.

They looked at her with surprise. He pulled away.

"She said to tell you it's rude to disregard the company who's here on your behalf," Anna went on.

"Oh, yeah," he uttered. "I'd best go inside, then." He walked to her, gave her a timid grin, and seeing her enraged reaction, ambled off.

She turned her scornful gaze to Callie, who looked like a sly fox that had just eaten the prize rooster.

"I realize you and David have been friends for a long time," Anna stated bluntly, "but he's my man."

Callie snickered. "I must go in and converse with our guests." She walked past, turned, and leered at her.

"Funny how someone so heartbroken cannot shed a single tear," Anna remarked.

Callie scowled. She spun around and tramped off, leaving Anna alone in the garden. She felt like breaking down, but restrained herself, for she would fight to the last breath if she had to. She and David would be leaving soon, anyway, returning to her home, thank God. She felt the baby kick, frowned, and strode back to the house.

David was standing beside his mother, talking with the guests. She walked over to him.

"Mr. and Mrs. Skidmore, this here's my wife, Anna."

"We've been introduced," the older, graying woman stated, "and Rena told us about the baby."

Callie overheard. "Baby?" she asked.

David turned to see her behind him. "I forgot to mention it," he muttered.

"That's right," Anna interjected, "we're having a baby." She stifled a sneer, expecting Callie to feign a faint, but she did nothing, showed no reaction whatsoever.

"How lovely," she said at last. "Why, I'll be jist like an aunt!"

The group chuckled.

Over my dead body, Anna thought. She looked at her husband. "David, darling, may I have a word with you?"

A sudden expression of alarm crossed his face. "Ma, Miss Callie, Mr. and Mrs. Skidmore. Pardon us."

Anna took him by the hand and led him outside.

"What is it, darlin'?" he asked.

"I want to go home," she said insistently.

His brow creased with concern. "Are you feelin' all right?"

"Yes. I mean, no. I felt the baby kick a few minutes ago."

"You did?" The inflection in his voice displayed his excitement.

She placed his hand on her stomach.

"I don't feel anything."

"Just wait."

They smiled at each other as they stood frozen, waiting for a sign. Suddenly, he detected a faint thump from within her belly. His eyes grew wide, darkening from hazel to brown.

"I felt it!" he exclaimed as he hugged her. "There really *is* somebody in there!"

She giggled, and gave him a playful nudge on the arm. "I feel very awkward here," she said, her smile fading. "May we go please?"

"Of course. Let's jist say our goodbyes, and we'll be on our way."

"Thank you." She held his hand as they walked inside.

For nearly an hour, they intermingled with the guests before David's family was finally ready to leave. On the ride home, Anna said very little, listening while Rena and Josie discussed their neighbors. It seemed all had lost loved ones to the war, or personally knew someone who had. There was a shortage of virile young men. Anna was thankful she'd found one; her soulmate at that. Unavoidably, she thought of him and Callie together, and her uneasiness resurfaced. He was allowing Callie to manipulate him, which infuriated her.

When they were back inside their cottage, he lit a fire, then lay on the bed, reading a newspaper Callie's father had given him. She disrobed, hung the gown on a post, slid into her nightgown, and sat down beside him.

"We need to talk."

He glanced up from the newspaper he was reading. "About what?"

"You and Callie. I overheard you talking in her garden."

"Oh?" he asked innocently.

"Yes, and I didn't especially like what I heard."

He laid the paper on the bed and sat up. "Callie was jist teasin' is all. She always does that."

"With everyone, or do you receive special attention?"

"With everyone." Amused, he snickered. "You're jealous."

She stood with a huff. "No. I'm looking out for your wellbeing. I know your neighbors don't like me, but you *are* a married man, and I'm certain they'll judge you for being flirtatious with another woman."

He glared at her questioningly. "I wasn't flirtin'."

"Well, she was." Anna folded her arms across her chest. "I don't like her, David, and I don't trust her."

"Oh, Anna, Miss Callie ain't a threat to you."

She scowled at him. Suddenly, she began to sob. "I don't think I've ever been so humiliated in my whole life!"

"Anna, darlin'," he tried to comfort as he stood and reached out to her.

She pushed him away. "I shouldn't have worn that gown. It was a mistake."

"Honey, it's all right."

"Now everyone thinks I'm a selfish, brazen, Yankee ..."

He reached out again, but she backed away, tears rolling down her blushed cheeks.

"No one thinks that," he assured her.

"You saw the way they looked at me." She turned away, and sorrowfully gazed at her beautiful cerulean gown. "They hate me."

He tried to protest, but she wasn't listening.

"I never should have worn that dress. I never should have come down here at all." She whirled to face him. "David, I want to go home to Pennsylvania."

"I know you do, sweetheart."

"I want us to leave right away, so that we're home by Thanksgiving."

He winced. "I don't reckon that's possible."

She stared at him.

"Darlin', the money we brought down, well, I had to spend some of it."

She hesitated, but he needed prompting. "How much?"

"We have about fifty dollars left."

Anna started to sniffle. "That was money for our train tickets back!"

"I know, but I had to purchase food, and things for the farm." He retrieved a piece of paper from the top of the dresser. "I've been keepin' a runnin' total of all my expenditures."

She glanced over the list he gave her and handed it back.

"I told you about this before."

"Yes, but I didn't realize how much you'd spent," she whined.

"Money goes fast," he tried to explain. "Everything's expensive."

"How am I supposed to get home?" She walked past him and sank down on the bed. "I don't want to give birth here."

He gawked at her. "Anna, it ain't the end of the world."

"It is for me!" she snapped. "I think you should go."

"What?"

"Go away! Just leave me alone!" She threw herself down on the bed, weeping.

At a loss, David stood watching her for a moment, retrieved his hat, coat, and whiskey bottle, and went outside. He walked to the barn.

"Hey Renie," he greeted his horse. "Sorry to wake you."

He stood beside his stallion, who softly nickered at his presence. David pulled the bottle from his coat and took a deep swig.

"Women," he mumbled.

Renegade nosed him, so he gently rubbed his muzzle.

"Who can figure them out."

He took a sip, wishing he knew what to say to her, wishing he had the money to take her home. He knew he couldn't leave his family though, what with all the turmoil occurring in the county. Things were dismal, no question about that. Completely torn, he took another swig. After a while, he returned to the cottage to find her motionless under the covers. He quietly pulled off his boots, stripped, and crawled into bed.

She lay there until she finally heard his deep, rhythmic breathing. Never before had she felt so isolated. This day had been a nightmare, a disgrace so cruel that she hoped she would never see any of those people again. But now, it appeared she would have to, since her future had become suddenly murky. She didn't even know how to get a letter to her sisters. Consumed with foreboding and heartache, she quietly sobbed herself to sleep.

"I daily part with my raiment for food. We find no one who will exchange eatables for Confederate money. So we are devouring our clothes."

- Mary Chesnut

Chapter Four

David spent the next few days busying himself with winter preparations: chopping wood, repairing fence rails, and hunting for what little game he managed to bag. To his disillusionment, Anna had become increasingly moody. With no better explanation, he chalked it up to female unpredictability ... and her pregnancy.

On November 15, he rode to John Moss' blacksmith shop, and heard about the hanging of Captain Henry Wirz from some of the locals. Wirz, who had been commandant of Camp Sumter near Andersonville, Georgia, was hung five days previously at the Capitol Prison in Washington. He was buried in the yard of the Washington Arsenal alongside four conspirators who had been put to death earlier in the year for rolls they'd played in President Lincoln's assassination. The Yankees referred to him as "the Andersonville Savage," even though Wirz claimed he had merely followed orders. The night before his execution, he rejected an offer of pardon by refusing to testify against Jefferson Davis, stating he would not base his freedom on a lie, since the president wasn't responsible for purposefully ordering atrocities against the inmates. According to reports, the audience chanted "Remember Andersonville" as Wirz ascended the stairs to the gallows. Robert E. Lee was quoted as saying his execution was "a judicial murder." It was the Northerners' revenge, their reward for winning the war, and retaliation for their prisoners of war.

Wirtz had been made a scapegoat. David understood the circumstances surrounding Andersonville were unavoidable, because the South had been disabled by enormous inflation, along with lack of food and medical supplies. Union forces had effectively closed off shipping lanes and railroads in their effort to cripple the Confederacy. Grant had murdered his own by putting an end to prisoner exchange. David sadly remembered the months he'd suffered in prison, and wondered if justice would come to Elmira's commanders for the horrors he'd witnessed, and all the deaths that were caused by their intentional negligence. He doubted it, seeing as Colonel Tracy had been promoted, and Colonel Hoffman had returned all of $58,151.54 to the U.S. government, money he'd saved back from the prison fund which should have been spent to provide prisoners with adequate food, clothing, and shelter. David shuddered as he recalled the things he'd seen, and forced them out of his mind. It was something he rarely allowed himself to dwell upon, and never discussed. He'd just as soon forget it ever happened.

He also heard about Frank Gurley, who was recently elected sheriff of Madison County. Gurley fought under Nathan Bedford Forrest, and had been wrongly accused of killing a Union officer in cold blood during the war. Like David, he had been incarcerated. Once the war ended, northern outrage prevented Gurley from returning home, due to pressure asserted by Judge Advocate General Holt, the same man who insisted on hanging Mrs. Mary Surratt merely because she ran the boarding house where John Wilkes Booth conspired to assassinate Lincoln. Fortunately for Gurley, he had many friends in high places, and although Holt tried to claim his supporters were ex-Rebels, Gurley was finally freed.

Caroline kept her son well-informed with what the Yankees were doing to Jefferson Davis, "our beloved President," as she called him. He was imprisoned in Fortress Monroe, Virginia, bound in shackles, and disallowed the benefit of visitors or sunlight. The Pope had even sent him a crown of thorns, created by the Pontiff himself. Davis had been the most wanted man in America, as the Yankees believed he had ordered Lincoln's assassination. Northern publications were having a heyday by exaggerating his predicament, and committing libel by bragging that he'd been camouflaged in his wife's petticoats upon arrest. The Yankees had even written a satirical song about the event: "We'll Hang Jeff Davis from a Sour Apple Tree." David's anger rose as he thought of it. *This is their idea of justice? There's no justice in it at all, at least not for the South.*

One thing he found strange was the disappearance of the gold from the Confederate Treasury. According to what he'd been told, President Davis left with it when he escaped Richmond. But when he was captured in Georgia, there was no sign of the gold. Where it went to, nobody knew.

With each passing week, winter became more prevalent as the weather grew harsher. David and Anna celebrated their one-year wedding anniversary on November 19 with a dance by candlelight alone in their cottage. He softly sang, and assured her of better things to come. Thanksgiving Day came and went with barely a mention, for the people of the South had no intention of observing a Yankee holiday. Christmas drew nearer, and with it, the prospect that no one would be celebrating that holiday, either, since there wasn't money to purchase gifts or materials to make them.

David did his best to whittle gifts for his family, but because he was responsible for most of the heavy chores, his spare time was limited. Lack of food was a constant concern, not only for his loved ones, but for the livestock as well, and he struggled with their upkeep, along with chopping sufficient firewood.

Late one afternoon, two weeks prior to Christmas, he walked toward the barn, and looked up the lane to see a rider approach. He squinted, trying to figure out who it was. The rider wore a wide-brimmed hat, which made it difficult to distinguish his face. He rode up and stopped. Removing his hat, David immediately recognized him.

"Tailor?" he asked.

The man jumped down off his steed.

"It *is* you!"

"Summers!"

The two shook and embraced, patting each other heartily on the back.

"You survived too, I see!"

They laughed.

"What are you doin' here?" David asked.

"I told you I had relations in these parts, remember? They heard from the Draper's that you'd returned home."

David grinned. "Well, you damned Rebel, it's mighty fine to see you again! And all in one piece!" He patted his friend on the arm. "Come inside!"

They walked to the house and entered the front room.

"Ma, Anna, this here's Michael Tailor!" he exclaimed.

His mother stood and extended her hand. Michael kissed the back of it.

"Sir, how do we owe you this pleasure?" she inquired.

"Tailor and I were in the cavalry together!" David explained excitedly. "Up until Gettysburg."

"Oh, that's right," Caroline said. "I remember your tellin' us about him."

Michael smiled as though he was famous. "I'm stayin' with my cousins, the Ryan's," he said. "My kin are still back in Savannah, but since that devil Sherman marched through Georgia, the state is near ruin, so I figured I'd be better off here."

Caroline nodded with a smile. "Well, I'm right pleased to make your acquaintance."

David walked over to his bride. "This here's my wife, Anna."

"Why, Summers, you ole rascal!" Michael approached her, took her hand, and kissed it. He winked at his comrade.

Anna noticed that, by his demeanor, he was every bit a dandy. She blushed, which caused David to snicker.

"Thank you, Mr. Tailor," she politely replied. "I've heard all about you."

Michael raised an eyebrow. "Only good things, I hope." He smiled. "From the sound of your voice, I'd say you're a Yankee."

"Yes sir, that's correct," she replied, smiling. "I don't know if David told you, but we're expecting a baby."

Michael's eyes grew wide, along with the grin on his face. "Summers, you *have* been busy!"

The two chuckled like school boys. At that moment, Rena and Josie walked in. Michael turned to see them enter. "Who do we have here?' he asked.

"These are my sisters, Josie and Rena," David introduced.

His friend bowed to each one and kissed the backs of their hands. He looked intensely at Rena as he straightened. "Miss Rena," he half-whispered, "you have a lovely name."

"Thank you, sir," she replied.

The two smiled at each other. Rena broke his gaze by glancing at her mother.

"I'm here to speak with your brother," Michael said, "but when we're done conversin', I'd like to have a moment with you ... if'n that's all right."

Rena softly snickered. "Yes."

She clutched onto Josie's hand and dragged her off to her bedroom. Muffled laughter escaped from behind the closed door.

Michael turned back to face his friend. "Shall we?"

"Ma, Anna, pardon us." David excused.

The two men walked outside and back to the cottage. David pulled open the checkerboard curtains, allowing daylight to filter into the chilly room as he retrieved his whiskey bottle. They made themselves comfortable at the table.

"Summers, your sister is a breath of fresh air," Michael gushed, and took a sip from the bottle.

"You've taken a likin' to her!"

They chuckled. "And your wife is a beauty," he went on. "Where did you find her?"

"Near Gettysburg." David described the story of their encounter and proceeding events. When he had finished, they took another drink.

"That's amazin'," remarked Michael. "You even saw ole Abe Lincoln."

"That I did. It's a damned shame how he met his demise."

Michael nodded. "After Gettysburg, I decided it was time to head on home," he stated matter-of-factly.

"So you flanked the sentinel, then?"

"Reckon you did too!" he chortled.

David shrugged with a grin. "I didn't mean to at the time, but Renie had different intentions for me."

"How is that feisty critter of yours?"

"Jist fine. He's all of five now. And yours?"

"Died on the way home. I ended up havin' to walk for quite a spell." Michael took a drink. "I wonder how John Chase is doin'," he said.

David frowned as he recalled the last time he'd seen his other messmate. "I'm afraid Chase didn't make it. At least, I don't see how he could have."

Michael glared at him.

"He lost both his legs from a shell, and the last time I saw him, he was unconscious in a barn they were usin' for a hospital."

Slowly shaking his head, Michael said in a low voice, "That's too bad. Right sad to lose such a good man."

David felt compelled to take a drink. "We're in for happier times now, though. To happier times!"

He took a swig and handed it to his friend, who did the same.

After nearly an hour had passed, Michael asked to speak to Rena, so the two walked back to the house. They found the ladies setting the table.

"Would you like to take supper with us, Mr. Tailor?" Caroline asked.

"Oh, no ma'am. I reckon I'm expected back. I jist wanted to have a word with your daughter for a moment, if'n you'll permit it."

Caroline glanced at Rena and smiled. "Anna, Josie, please assist me in the kitchen."

"I'd best be gettin' back to my chores," David said, taking his cue.

He went about his farm duties, fed the livestock, secured them in their pens for the night, and tended to his dogs. When he had finished, he checked the kitchen to find it empty, so he returned to the house. The womenfolk were peeking through the cracked door, eavesdropping on Rena and Michael, who were seated in the front room.

"What y'all doin'?" he asked loudly.

They turned on him at once. "Shhh!"

He looked in over their heads. Michael was nervously rubbing his knee, but his eyes were fixed on Rena. She reached over and laid her hand on his wrist, causing him to stop.

David softly said to his wife, "This reminds me of the time your sisters ..."

Anna whirled around and placed her index finger on his lips. "Quiet!" she harshly whispered. She leaned in toward Josie and asked, "What are they saying?"

"I think he's askin' her if he can come courtin' again."

Caroline smiled at her son, then walked off to the kitchen.

He couldn't help himself: he peered in with his wife and sister. "Now what're they sayin'?"

"Rena said she would like him to," reported Josie, "and Michael said he finds her very attractive."

"Well, he ain't wastin' no time." David slid his hands along Anna's hips.

She glanced over her shoulder at him and smiled. He gave her a gentle kiss on the neck.

"Would you two stop it!" hissed Josie. "I want to hear what they're sayin'!"

Michael stood. "I'll see you Saturday at eight, then." Taking her hand as she arose, he bowed and kissed it.

Rena giggled. "I'm lookin' forward to it."

They started for the door. Josie quickly scurried into her room, leaving Anna and David exposed as the door swung open.

Embarrassed by the discovery, David blurted, "Let me walk you out," in an attempt to dislodge the awkwardness.

He and Michael strolled through the yard to his horse.

As he mounted, he said, "Well, Summers, it's been a pleasure seein' you again."

"And you," David agreed.

"We'll have to make a habit of it."

"I'm all for that." He grinned up at his long-lost friend.

"I'll be by on Saturday evenin'. We can talk more then."

He spurred his horse and rode off down the lane. David returned to the house to find the ladies preparing to dine.

Rena seated herself, and after the family had given grace, she teased, "I hope y'all heard everything that was said." She glanced around at their mock stunned faces and grinned.

"Jist about," replied Josie. "but we missed the first part. Could you enlighten us?"

Rena rolled her eyes. "Very funny!"

Josie giggled, causing David to chuckle. He looked over at his wife, smiled, and took her hand. She smiled back at him.

The week dragged by until Saturday night arrived, and with it, so did Michael Tailor, just as he'd promised. He politely conversed with Caroline while he waited nervously in the front room for Rena to present herself. Josie, who had been waiting impatiently, ran to the cottage to inform her brother that he'd arrived. She dragged him back with her, and as he walked into the front room, he stifled a chuckle. Michael was pale as a ghost. His dark eyes were dilated, making them look black as coal.

"Tailor!" he greeted, and shook his comrade's hand. "Good to see you again."

"And you, Summers," Michael exchanged. He posed a grin at Caroline as she left the room, but then his expression changed to dread. "Tell me more about your sister. What am I gettin' myself into?"

He laughed. "You had some time to think!"

Michael frowned.

"Once you see her, you'll remember why you came."

As he said it, Rena entered, dressed in Anna's cerulean gown. David gaped at her. She gave him a quick wink.

"My dear," said Michael. He took her hand, bowed, and kissed it. "You look positively ravishin'!"

Rena and her brother exchanged glances.

"Mr. Tailor, right nice to see you again." She gestured toward the two chairs David had constructed for his mother. "Shall we?"

"Certainly."

They made their way across the room and seated themselves. Rena glared at her brother, waiting for him to leave.

He snickered. "Well, I'd best be gettin' on to my wife," he declared. "Tailor, I'll talk with you later. Rena, that sure is a mighty fine dress you have on."

She grinned at him.

He turned and walked out to the kitchen, where his mother was preparing hot tea. He opened the screened door and offered, "Ma, need any help?"

"No, dear. I'll keep an eye on those two." Caroline picked up the tray and carried it toward the door as David held it open for her. "I'm quite certain your li'l sister is takin' care of that for me while I'm preoccupied." She smiled widely, displaying a few missing molars.

"I'm goin' to bed, then."

He walked up the slope to the little whitewashed, clapboard cottage and went inside. Anna was busy writing something in her journal.

"Whatcha writin'?" he asked. He'd been curious for some time, but with her mood swings, was afraid to ask.

"It's my account of the baby," she enlightened. "I want to record everything I think and feel, so I can share it with Maggie and Abigail when I return home."

He gave her a compassionate grin. "Oh."

Slowly, he sank down on the chair next to her. For a few moments, she continued scratching with the ink pen, but then felt him watching her, so she put the pen aside. "What is it you'd like for Christmas?" she asked.

He snorted. "Oh, I don't know. There ain't nothin' we can afford. And don't you be gettin' me anything, either."

"I'm giving you this, in here."

She pointed to her stomach, which made him smile.

"I mean, if you could wish for anything, what would it be?"

"I already have everything I want."

He leaned over and kissed her. She gazed at him, waiting for an answer.

"All right. If I could have anything in the whole world, I reckon I'd want my old guitar back, seein's how my pa made it and all."

"Oh. He did?"

David sorrowfully nodded.

"Well, I'm sure Abigail will return the one you gave her when she hears what happened."

He shrugged. "I told her she could have it."

"She'll understand."

"No," he said, shaking his head, "I ain't an Indian giver."

Anna snickered.

He smiled at her reaction, and took her hand. "I love you."

"I love you," she echoed.

"I'm sorry I can't git you home to your kinfolk right now." Reaching over to her, he gently touched her cheek.

"I know. Christmas will be very difficult without them." Anna struggled to contain her tears.

David stood. "Darlin', I promise I'll take you home jist as soon as I can." He took both her hands as she arose. "When I git the money ..."

She stepped toward him and kissed him. They wrapped their arms around each other.

"You don't need to say another word."

They kissed again, more passionately this time. She took his hand and led him to the bed. He sat beside her and embraced her. They lay back, caressing each other. Anna stood, disrobed in the firelight, and allowed him to pull her back to him. She unbuttoned his clothing and slid them from his taut body. Quietly, gently, they became one and made love in harmonious elation. For several minutes afterward, they lay side by side, basking in the afterglow.

As he softly slid his fingertips over her bulging belly, she asked, "Are you more comfortable with the idea of becoming a father?"

"I'm gettin' used to the fact," he admitted with a grin. They kissed sweetly. "Anna, I'll do anything to make you happy. If you give birth here, well, Ma will help you, 'cause she's been through it before …"

She chuckled.

"And my sisters will be here. It wouldn't be so terrible bad, would it?"

She ran her fingers through his hair. "By the time spring arrives, so will the baby. I don't relish the idea of riding on a train for hours in my condition."

"I'll take care of you, sweetheart." He tenderly stroked the side of her head. "I'll see to it that no harm comes to you, or our baby."

Anna smiled at his words. She hugged him tightly. "I'm sorry I've been so quarrelsome with you. I know you can't help what's happening, any more than I can. Perhaps it's God's design that we're here, instead of at home."

He withdrew his hand. *You are home, Anna*, he felt like saying. "Jist try to make the best of it, and in a few months, I should have enough money."

She kissed him deeply, cuddled into him, and fell asleep. He lay there with his eyes closed, listening to her softly breathe as the fire died down. *Why do I keep doin' this?* he asked himself. *I don't know if I can keep that promise.* Assured that she loved him regardless, he gradually dozed off.

Over the course of the week, he worked diligently to finish his family's gifts, and smiled to himself as he envisioned what Anna's reaction would be. Her present was the largest and most difficult, however, and he struggled from lack of appropriate tools. In the evenings, he read the book his sisters-in-law had given him, *Moby-Dick*. He equated the story to his current situation: in his mind, Moby Dick represented the North, bearing down on the conquered South, which was portrayed by the Pequod. He could picture himself as Ishmael, and various other characters took on recognizable forms to him as well. He wished his country wouldn't suffer the same ending, and vanish into the sea of obscurity. Although the beaten Confederates were ready to accept defeat, come back into the Union, and get on with their lives, David wondered if Yankee tyranny would prevail. He hoped the white whale wouldn't consume them whole.

On Christmas Eve, he walked out to the woods and found what he considered to be the perfect tree, so he chopped it down and hurled it onto the back of the mule. As he took hold of the reins, an eerie feeling came over him, like someone was watching him. He looked around. A slight breeze stirred, but besides a few dead, rustling leaves, it was quiet. He shivered, thinking about the witch, and quickly led Ginger to the house.

That evening, the family gathered together to sing carols, hang darned stockings over the fireplace, and decorate the tree with strands of berries and a few homemade ornaments Caroline had saved over the years and managed to hide from marauding Yankees. They reminisced about Christmases past, and about Hiram, who had been deceased for two years. As they sat around the blazing fireplace, Anna listened to their stories with fascination, learning about the father-in-law she would never meet.

In the morning, they enjoyed breakfast, which consisted of corn muffins, milk, eggs, and coffee, and then went into the front room, where David presented his creations to each one: a set of wooden candlestick holders for his mother and fans for his sisters. He made hair combs for all of them, and promised that he would carve intricate details into their gifts once he had more time. They thanked him graciously before presenting him with their gifts: socks, a scarf, and a set of handkerchiefs made from old worn-out dresses.

David glanced at his wife. "I'll be right back!"

He sprang from his seat and went outside while the ladies exchanged their gifts of reconstructed garments. Anna, who had previously penned promissory notes for her new family members, bashfully distributed one to each recipient.

Rena opened hers. "I owe you a specially cooked dinner for you and a guest." She blushed, knowing Anna was referring to Michael. "Thank you," she beamed.

Josie unfolded her note. "Mine says, I owe you a shoppin' trip after the baby's born." She grinned widely, indulging her. "That sounds like fun!"

Anna smiled, waiting for Caroline to open hers. She did so, and read, "I owe you anything your heart desires, because you gave me David." Her eyes welled up. "Oh, darlin'!" She arose from her seat, walked over, and hugged Anna. "You've already given me what my heart desires."

"But I want to do something more," she said, "I want to give you something special."

"You jist deliver my grandchild safely, and that'll be gift enough."

They turned to see David enter. He was carrying a large wooden object that resembled a box on legs.

"What is that?" Anna asked.

He grinned. "Well, it ain't finished yet 'cause I ran out of time, but this here's a cradle I've started. For the baby."

"Oh!" Anna rushed to him and wrapped her arms around his neck. "Thank you!"

"Yeah, well, like I said, it ain't finished yet ..." he stammered.

"It's a right nice gesture," remarked Caroline. "We truly are blessed, all of us. We've got our David back, and Anna to boot. And now there's a baby on the way!" She laughed, and looked at her son. "Oh, my word, I nearly forgot!" She scampered off to her bedroom. Shortly, she reappeared with a guitar in her hand.

"Ma?" His eyes grew wide with excitement.

She smiled and handed it to him.

"Where did you git this?" he asked.

"I searched high and low, and had everyone in the county out lookin' for me," she explained, "but at long last, Mr. Blevins found one."

David sat down and propped the guitar on his knee. Plucking it gently, he realized it was slightly out of tune, so he turned the pegs. He began picking the strings, his voice rising with his accompaniment.

"Oh, holy night, the stars are brightly shinin', it is the night of our dear savior's birth."

He sang through the entire song, pleased with himself that he'd remembered the lyrics, and humbly accepted their tearful praise when he'd finished. "I can't believe you got me this, Ma!" He stood, hugged her, and kissed her cheek.

"Guitars are hard to come by in these parts," Caroline stated. "We found fiddles, banjos, and a bass fiddle, but no guitars. Finally, Mr. Blevins met a man who's recently come down from Massachusetts, and he sold him his."

David frowned. "How much did you spend?"

She smiled. "Not much. I made a barter, so this spring, we'll be owin' the Blevins several pies and candies."

They chuckled. David ran his hand over the strings. "I wanted to make one myself, but I couldn't figure out how."

"Well, now you don't have to fret about it," Anna said.

He grinned at her. "You knew about this all along, didn't you?"

She nodded, smiling.

"Anna had us out lookin' two months ago!" Josie proclaimed.

"She asked me a while back what I wanted, and I told her a guitar, but I didn't think I'd really git one."

"Well, this here's a mighty happy Christmas, indeed," declared Rena.

That evening at supper, Caroline led the family in prayer, repeating her thanks, and asking God to watch over them in the coming year. David knew there'd be hardships ahead, because he'd been the one to harvest the poor crops. He squeezed Anna's hand as his mother poured her heart out to the Lord, then all said "Amen." They passed around dishes containing a roasted chicken, smashed sweet potatoes, corn, and biscuits. For dessert, his mother had created a cake containing dried apples and black walnuts. This was the most food they'd had at one sitting for quite some time, but it was a special occasion, so therefore, justified. The family lingered after the dishes had been cleaned while Caroline read the story of Jesus' birth from the Book of Matthew. They played a game of charades before retiring, then exchanged wishes of thanks, a merry Christmas, and pleasant sleep.

David escorted his wife back to the cottage. He closed the door behind them, and embraced her for several minutes in the dark, warmed by her body heat, until he released her and lit a fire. Exhaustion set in, and soon after they'd climbed into bed, Anna was asleep in his arms. He sighed, thinking of his father, of Jake, and this year's Christmas. It was a damn sight better than last year, when he'd been held captive in that rancid prison. He kissed his slumbering wife softly on her forehead, and drifted into contented sleep.

He was standing in a barren field, looking around at the depressingly gray desolate surroundings, when suddenly, an ebony horse with a rider dressed in black approached from out of nowhere. As they came nearer, he waved in recognition. The rider stopped in front of him.

"You've got to be on your lookout, Zeke," he said, and smiled. "Them darkies'll take advantage of you every time." He vanished into thin air.

David awoke with a start. He had broken into a cold sweat, and gasped as he realized the dream he'd just had, the omen he'd just experienced. Jake had given him another warning, and it scared the living daylights out of him.

A few days later, Michael returned, exchanged cordialities, and proceeded to quiz him.

"Did she say what she thinks of me?" he eagerly inquired.

David couldn't help but chuckle. "Friend, I reckon you've got it bad!" He grinned as Michael waited for an answer. "Yes, she said she's fond of you."

His eyes lit up. "Fond of me?"

"She said you're a superb specimen of the male gender, and she thought you'd make a fine husband."

"She said all that? We hardly got a chance to talk at all!"

David snickered, remembering how Josie had made a point of spying on them, "for Rena's protection," she reasoned.

"Could I possibly see her now?"

"Unannounced? That might seem too forward."

Michael thought for a moment. "Yeah, reckon you're right. That ain't why I came by, anyways."

"Oh?"

He motioned for David to follow him. They left the cottage and walked up into the woods. "I've been thinkin' about ways we could come up with some money. Bein's Christmas was scanty at our house ..."

"Ours too," agreed David, deliberately failing to mention his gifted guitar.

"... And prosperity don't seem too probable," said Michael.

"Poverty is more likely. What do you have in mind? Are we gonna rob a bank?"

Michael burst out laughing. He stopped, thought about it, and shook his head. "No, we ain't robbin' a bank. That would be too risky. What I have in mind is a whole lot easier." He commenced explaining his plan, and the two decided it was feasible, so they scoured the nearby hills until they found an appropriate location on Cotaco Creek.

"I've been scroungin' around my cousins' place. My aunt's got a copper kettle we can use, and I can round up a coil," Michael said. "You come up with the ingredients."

"What do we need?"

"Corn meal, sugar, yeast, and malt."

"Okay, I'll git right on it."

After considerable effort, David did as instructed. In a matter of days, their corn whiskey still was up and running. They created several batches, adding a slight variation to each one by incorporating balsam cucumber, dogwood, poplar, and rolled cherry bark, and invented a name for their recipe: "ruckus juice."

"Soon as we git a good batch, I'll have a talk with that Yankee officer who's been patrollin' 'round my cousin's place, and see if'n he'll buy some."

David nodded as he stirred the heating mash. Once the concoction vaporized, Michael transferred it into a smaller container. The resulting condensation thus became moonshine.

"The way I see it," Michael said, "this here still should provide us with food, money, anything we need."

They greedily grinned at each other. Both were starving, so the notion sounded immensely attractive.

"Why ain't your cousins goin' along with this scheme?" David asked wryly.

"Well, it's like I said before, there's eight of them, and only one of me. Even though it's my idea, they'd want to split the profits, which wouldn't amount to a hill of beans. I'll git them food with what we sell. That should qualm their curiosity." He grinned slyly, and took a swig, but quickly spat it out. "Needs more time," he croaked.

David laughed.

By week's end, the temperature had dropped significantly. David mumbled complaints to himself while he hitched Ginger to the wagon. His mother and Josie boarded, reminding him they would return before nightfall after visiting Jake's folks. Concerned the Kimball's were still in mourning after all this time, Caroline had baked them a Christmas cake, and was determined to console them. Josie was only escaping her cabin fever. They set off as David led his stallion out of the barn and hitched him to a cart he'd assembled. Shaggy with his winter coat, Renegade protested slightly, but after being promised an apple for his trouble, he submitted. David led him up into the woods and tied him to a sapling.

Forced to confront the task at hand, he began chopping trees for firewood. A crow cawed from atop a nearby oak. Thinking he felt drizzle, David only stopped momentarily to readjust his slouch hat before continuing on with his chore. He cut down half a dozen small cedars, and started on another, his axe whacking into the green tree trunk with sharp cracks that resonated against the hills. Caleb and Si started barking off in the distance. *Must've found a badger or somethin'*, he reasoned to himself. Another crow cawed relentlessly. Suddenly, he understood the caws were actually screams, and looked up to see Anna running toward him through the underbrush.

"David!" she shrieked. "David!"

He dropped the axe and ran to her. "Anna, what is it?"

She was shaking like a leaf. He held her hand as she gasped for air.

"You have to save her! You have to save Rena!"

His eyes grew wide with terror. "Stay here with Renegade. If anything happens, ride him out of here!"

He bolted through the scrubs toward the farm, panting as he yelled. "Rena!"

He broke into the farm's clearing, and hollered her name again. A black man appeared from out of the henhouse, holding two flapping, cackling hens by their feet. He turned and ran just as David pulled his pistol and fired. The man cried out in agony. He clutched his thigh and dropped the chickens, which fluttered off as he limped down the lane. David heard his dogs bark from inside the barn. His sister screamed his name, jolting him with panic. He ran to the barn. Rena was holding her attackers at bay with a pitchfork. Caleb and Si were on either side of her, baying frantically.

"David!" she screeched again.

He aimed just as the two black men scurried past him. He fired. They ducked as the bullet whizzed by. One fell, but scrambled to his feet. Stopping at the door, David looked at his sister, who was leaning against the wall.

He started back toward her. "Rena?"

She began to cry. "Git them!" She wailed.

He ran out and took aim, but they had retrieved their horses, escaping in a thunder of dust down the lane. He returned to his sister, and knelt beside her.

"Are you all right?"

She cried harder, clasping onto him. "They were tryin' to take the cow." Her speech was broken through anguished sobs. "They wanted to hurt Anna, so I ..."

"Did they do anything to you?" He helped her to her feet. "Rena, did they violate you?"

She sniffled. "No, but they tried to. They said some terrible things to me. I got hold of the pitchfork ..."

"Damn it!" he spat with loathing. He looked up to see Anna at the barn door. "Stay here."

He ran into the house, retrieved the shotgun, and returned to the barn. He handed the weapon to his wife, then quickly unhitched Renegade.

"Take her inside, Anna," he requested.

He sprang onto the horse's back, and galloped off. Thankful for his stallion's speed, David pulled his pistol in preparation. He rode around a curve, up hills and down slopes as the road winded ahead. Suddenly, he came to a crossroads. The dust had settled; there was no sign of them.

He spun Renegade around, trying to decide on the correct direction, but realized he'd lost them. Exasperated, he slid the pistol back into its holster, and spurred Renegade home.

"Did you find them?" Anna asked as he entered the front room. She was kneeling beside his sister, who held a handkerchief in her quivering hand.

"They got away," he muttered, livid with himself for letting it happen. He walked across the room and knelt down in front of Rena, who took his hand. "I'm sorry."

"Don't be." She let out a little gasp. "It ain't your fault."

He kissed the back of her hand. "Next time they come back here, I won't miss." He stood. "Better yet, I'll hunt them down myself."

"David," Anna said, attempting to soothe him, "they won't return, because they know it's too dangerous." She straightened. "They were most likely freedmen who are starving. I rather pity the poor souls."

He glared at her. "Then they should pay a visit to their Freedmen's Bureau if they're lookin' for a hand out, instead of stealin' from honest folks like us." A heavy sigh escaped him. "I'll round up those two chickens they tried to run off with."

Glancing at his sister, he tromped out the door. He led Renegade back to his stall, and walked out to the barnyard in search of the missing hens. They were nowhere to be found. He called his dogs, which assisted in the search, but still, the poultry came up missing. All that remained were a few scattered feathers that flitted across the yard. David cursed under his breath. Now they were down to two hens and one rooster. Between the freedmen and the Yankees, he wondered if they'd have any livestock left by spring. He called his dogs back, latched the door to the chicken coop, and went to the barn. As he brushed down his stallion, he tried to remember if he saw the bandits make off with the chickens. It occurred to him that they might have come back for them, which enraged him even more. Somehow, he'd find out who they were.

His mother and Josie returned. Once they'd learned of the assault, they comforted Rena, covered her with a quilt, and filled her with warm sarsaparilla tea. David noticed she had stopped shaking, which was a relief, but still, it fueled his fury to know he couldn't prevent what had happened to her. He wished he would've been able to defend her when it happened, so that he'd had the opportunity to shoot all three of them right between the eyes. And then, the realization hit him. *Dear God*, he thought to himself. *It's really happenin'. They're risin' up to kill us all, and take our land.*

Law and order needed to be maintained: the Yankees were responsible for this. He knew they were few and far between in the hills, but even so, it was their responsibility, now that they had taken over, forcing themselves on the South. They had sent their Union League down, but had failed to protect Southerners. Somehow, someone had to be held accountable for this outrage. David vowed to find the attackers and avenge his sister. God help them when he did.

"We have already lost all but our honor by the last war, and I must say, that in order to be men we must protect our honor at all hazards and we must also protect our wives, our homes and our families."

- Nathan Bedford Forrest

Chapter Five

Kit Lawrence made his appearance on New Year's Day. At over six and a half feet tall, he was as big as his ego, and twice as ominous. David recognized his gruff voice, stopped mucking, and looked out from the barn door to see a wagon approach. Kit expelled a long line of expletives directed at his shaggy draft horse. He pulled the vehicle to a stop in front of the house. David let out a sigh. This was the moment he'd been dreading, because he knew what was about to transpire. Summoning his courage, he walked out as Kit jumped down from the driver's seat.

"Mr. Lawrence." He extended his hand, and the lanky, middle-aged man took it. "Right good to see you again."

"And you, young Summers," the man replied. To David's surprise, he smiled at him, exposing long tobacco-stained teeth. "You've been expectin' me, I reckon."

"Yessir, Ma said you'd be comin' by this way."

"How's your ma holdin' up?"

David grinned. "She's fine. Everyone's fine." He started feeling awkward, as the man's steely gray eyes glared unblinkingly at him, boring into his soul.

"When did you git back from the war?"

"Last August."

"Your ma said you was in prison."

"Yessir." He was beginning to feel ill at ease with the man's interrogation, and knew by his series of questions that he would soon discover David's situation.

"She said you married a Yankee gal. Is that right?"

Kit walked toward his wagon. He motioned to David, and they threw back the tarpaulin to reveal two wooden slat cages. One crate contained a squealing hog. In the other was packed a dozen cackling chickens. Kit requested David's assistance. They lifted the swine's cage with great effort and placed it on the ground, then set the chickens' cage down beside it.

"You didn't answer my question," Kit growled. He spat a long strand of tobacco juice.

"Yessir, I married a Yankee gal. Her name's Anna."

Kit grunted. "This here sow is full of litter. Should provide y'all with several piglets come spring."

David smiled. "Why, that's mighty nice of you, Mr. Lawrence. Ma will surely appreciate it."

Kit stroked his chin, which was covered with gray stubble. "Looks like your barn's about to topple over." He pointed a bony finger in that direction. "We'll have to take care of it while I'm here. In fact, my son will be arrivin' in a day or so." He retrieved an axe from the wagon. "I've been hankerin' for some fried chicken," he announced as he returned to the crates. He pulled two birds out by their feet.

"How long are you fixin' to stay?" David asked, but his question fell on deaf ears.

Kit raised the axe and easily chopped off the chickens' heads. The decapitated bodies ran and tumbled around the yard, catching Caleb and Si's attention. The canines loped over to sniff at the heads, whose eyes still blinked and beaks still moved silently. Each dog snatched one head up in its jowls and trotted off.

"Clean those chickens up for dinner, boy. Put that sow in the sty, and take care of my horse." Kit ambled toward the house, removing his slouch hat to reveal collar-length, salt and pepper hair. He entered without knocking.

David scowled, but complied, and dutifully defeathered the poultry, unhitched Kit's horse, and stabled him next to Ginger. He managed to get a rope around the sow's thick neck, and prodded her with a stick, directing her into the dilapidated pigpen. He then pulled the chickens from their crate, carried them to the henhouse, and released them. When he had finished his chores, he took the bald chickens to the kitchen, scrubbed the dried blood and pinfeathers from his hands and lower arms, then went to the house to find Kit and Caroline in the front sitting room.

"I put the chickens in the kitchen," he announced, taking a seat across from her.

"Your ma told me how you hid out up north, pretendin' to be a damn Yankee." Kit stared at him, making him shrink. "You done deserted the army, didn't you, boy."

"No sir, it wasn't like that." He looked to his mother for support, but Caroline only smiled at him. "I was shot, and Anna found me, took me in, and nursed me back to health."

Kit scoffed. "Sure you weren't jist bein' a coward?"

David frowned at him, but was reluctant to stand his ground. He didn't appreciate Kit's mordant teasing, if in fact, that's what it was. "No, I wasn't bein' a coward."

"She also told me what happened last week with your sister."

Clenching his teeth, David struggled to contain his anger with the subject change. He flashed a glance at Caroline again, whose smile had faded to angst.

"It ain't nothin' I can't take care of." David stood, attempting to make himself feel larger.

The man chuckled. "Fightin' for the cause got you all fired up, huh, son."

He flinched. Even though Kit and his father had been friends since before he'd been born, it didn't give him entitlement to call him "son." Lost for words, he gazed at his mother. This time, she finally spoke.

"Mr. Lawrence has had a long trip." She stood, and Kit followed her lead by rising to his feet as well. "Go fetch your sisters. I need some help fixin' dinner."

"Yes'm," David muttered. He briskly walked out of the room, and tapped on Josie's bedroom door before opening it. "Ma needs your help with dinner," he informed. "Kit Lawrence is here."

"He is?" Josie sprang from her desk and smoothed the ruffles from her skirt. "Where's Rena?"

"I don't know. I thought she was in here with you."

"She's probably up at Granny's cottage with Anna."

She whooshed past him and started for the kitchen. David followed. He felt his face flushing, but managed to contain his annoyance. Josie glanced over her shoulder, reading his expression as she walked.

"So Kit Lawrence is the same ole charmer he always was!" She giggled.

"It ain't funny, Josie," he grumbled.

"What did he say?"

David shook his head. "He's jist the same ole Kit is all. He said Tucker'll be here in a day or so."

Josie snickered and went into the kitchen as David continued up the slope to his cottage. He entered to find Rena and Anna drinking tea at the table. "Kit Lawrence is here," he announced dryly.

The young women glared at him.

He looked at Rena. "Ma wants you to help with dinner."

Rena arose and obediently started for the door.

"She told him what happened last week."

She stopped. "I really wish she hadn't done that."

"It's nothing to be ashamed of, Rena," said Anna. "It wasn't your fault."

"Maybe she thinks he can help track them fellers down," added David.

"I hope not. I don't ever want to lay eyes on them again." Rena opened the door and departed.

"You're not pleased that he's here," Anna stated. She stood and took his hand. "Is everything all right?"

"He brought a sow and some chickens, which was right thoughtful, but I'm sure he'll want repayment for them." David shrugged. "He jist rubs me the wrong way is all. And his son is no exception, either. Reckon the apple don't fall far from the tree. At least Tucker won't be here for a day or two."

She smiled. "They can't be that bad."

David snorted. "You haven't met them yet." He kissed her. "Come on. Might as well make your acquaintance."

He led her to the house, and reluctantly introduced her to Kit, who behaved amiably. When he was informed that she was expecting a child, he seemed genuinely happy, to David's amazement.

The family gathered around the dinner table, gave a prayer of thanks, and partook in a midday meal of fried chicken, creamed corn, mashed potatoes, and gravy. David observed as Kit inhaled his portion, barely stopping to take a breath between mouthfuls. He considered that the sow and her master had much in common.

As Caroline passed around sweet potato pie, Kit described his various exploits since his departure last summer. David knew he was a widower with two children, a boy and a girl. The girl, Georgina, had married some time ago and moved to Kentucky. Kit's son, Tucker, was more of a wanderer. David hadn't seen him in ages, and wasn't sure if he'd recognize him when he did see him again. Since the start of the war, Kit informed that he had kept himself occupied with various business ventures. His home in Tennessee was about thirty miles north of Huntsville, and he'd resided there for the past six years, persuaded to leave Alabama by his brother. However, their business endeavors were continually failing, so Kit maintained his livelihood with barter and betting as well. David listened as he and his mother reminisced, but soon found himself daydreaming as Kit droned on about the economy, the war, the plight of the plantation owners, and his latest investment schemes.

"The free coloreds remind me of the tories," Kit was saying as he helped himself to seconds. "The way they've been terrorizin' honest Southrons devoted to the cause."

Leaning in to her husband, Anna whispered, "What's a torie?"

"A Unionist," he explained as Kit went on talking. "A loyalist."

"Oh," she replied.

"They called themselves the 'destroyin' angels'," Kit said to her. "Most were deserters, and some disguised themselves as Union soldiers. They went around the countryside settin' fires, murderin', and theivin'."

"Are they still about?" inquired Anna.

"Most got chased out, shot, or hung when our boys came home on furlough," Kit explained. "The tories jined up with the Peace Party and the Union League, but then the war ended, so I don't reckon they have much potency now." He turned to Caroline. "There's talk about lettin' the Sambos vote," he said casually. "The 'nigger teachers' with the American Missionary Association are comin' down here, wantin' to educate them. Makes me wonder what this country's comin' to."

David somewhat agreed with Kit's philosophy, because he'd heard that plantation owners considered learned Negroes to be a threat. In his mind, however, Percy was an exception.

"I don't see anything wrong with enabling them to vote," Anna blurted, immediately regretting her statement.

Kit stared her down, then smiled snidely. "You have a lot to learn about the ways of the South, li'l missy," he growled. He turned his gaze to David, who scowled at him. "Tomorrow you and me will pull the barn back up. You got that sow penned?"

David hesitated, tempted to defend his wife, but withered instead. "Yessir," he meekly replied. "The sty needs some repairs, though."

"Hmph." He arose, wiped his mouth with a napkin, and threw it on the table. "Let's git started then."

"I have somethin' to tend to first."

David stood and quickly departed before Kit had a chance to riddle him with questions. Quickly, he saddled Renegade, collected a few scraps from the kitchen, and galloped off. He made his way past the Kimball's farm, considered stopping, but decided it would be too awkward, so he continued on into the hills. Soon, he saw the familiar cabin, dismounted, and tapped on the door. Percy answered.

"Well, Missa David! Come on in!" The man took him by the arm and gently tugged, prompting him to enter.

"Hello, Percy. Happy New Year!" He set the knapsack full of foodstuffs on the table. "Where's Isabelle and your young'uns?"

"They went fishin'. Should be back directly." He motioned for David to sit, and retrieved his jug of moonshine. Pouring the contents into cups, he placed them on the table, then took his seat.

"Weze celebratin' the jubilation," Percy proclaimed with such conviction that he reminded David of a preacher. "Three years ago today our emancipator set us free!"

They toasted, and both sipped from their cups. David winced uncontrollably, causing Percy to chuckle.

"I brought some victuals." David unfolded the cloth knapsack to reveal a small bag of cornmeal, some chicken scraps, and a sweet potato pie he had requested from his mother. "The last time I was here, it looked like y'all didn't have much to sustain on, and Ma wanted to help you out some," he explained.

"Why, dat's mighty generous," Percy said, mist forming in his large brown eyes. "You tell your ma I said thanks."

"I surely will." The two clanked their tin cups together and took another sip. "I've been missin' Jake a lot recently," David admitted.

Percy smiled solemnly. "He always liked dis time a year."

"I haven't talked to his kinfolk lately, nor Miss Callie either, for that matter."

"Seems like you got your hands full jist keepin' your farm goin'. How is Miss Anna?"

David graciously grinned. "She's fine. The baby's about three months away."

Percy nodded. "Dat's mighty fine," he thoughtfully said.

"Kit Lawrence showed up earlier today with a pregnant sow and some pullets."

"Oh, he did, did he? How y'all takin' to that?"

David grunted. "I've already had my fill of him."

The men chuckled. They heard voices outside. In burst Tommy, followed by Isabelle, who was carrying baby Lincoln.

"Missa David! I didn't spect to see you here!"

"How do, Miss Isabelle." David stood. "I brought y'all somethin' to eat."

She glared at him for a moment. "We ain't lookin' for no charity." She set the baby in his crib.

David glanced at Percy, who said, "Mrs. Summers thought it would be a kind gesture to bring us somethin', bein's it's New Year's."

Isabelle folded her arms, and broke into a grin. "Well, you tell her we 'preciate it, and we'll do somethin' in turn when the crops are in."

"I'll do that, Miss Isabelle." He returned to his seat. "Kit Lawrence showed up at our place today."

She glowered at him. "I never did like that man."

"I don't reckon anyone does," David sympathized. "I'm hopin' he won't stay for long."

"He brought some livestock," Percy informed his wife.

"I'll be happy to deliver one of the piglets after it's weaned," David offered.

Isabelle smiled widely at this. "That would be right kind a you, Missa David." She walked to the cupboard and retrieved a glass jar. "You give these here preserves to your ma with my gratitude."

"Yes'm." David took the jar and stood. "Well, Kit's puttin' me to work, so I'd best take my leave."

He started for the door, but Tommy jumped out at him and grabbed hold of his leg. David reached down to tickle him. The little boy giggled as he backed away, then clamped onto David's leg again. The game continued until David dragged the boy, still attached, across the room.

Isabelle exploded with laughter. "Tommy! Leave him be!"

She pried her son off and took hold of his hand. David chuckled as he untied his stallion and mounted up.

"Take care." Percy offered his hand, and the two shook.

"You too, Percy."

David turned Renegade and rode toward home. On the way, he passed by the Ryan farm, and decided to go in. As soon as he rode up, he was surrounded by children, dogs, and goats.

"Hey, Mr. Summers!" one of the girls greeted him. She stroked Renegade's muzzle, who tried to shy away, but her siblings kept hold of his halter.

"Jessica," David said with a smile as he dismounted. "I'm here lookin' for your cousin, Michael. Is he here?"

"Yessir!" said another girl, Jane. "I'll go fetch him!" She ran off, her long blonde hair flowing out behind her.

"What's your horse's name again?" one of the boys asked.

David remembered his name to be Jordan.

"Renegade," he responded.

"How come he's all covered with spots?"

"Jist 'cause. Y'all havin' a good New Year's?"

"We sure are, mister!" Jessica beamed, her blue eyes shining. "We went crawdad fishin' this mornin', and Pa says he'll take us for a hayride later on!"

"That sounds like fun," replied David.

He reached down to rub one of the goats on the head, but the animal butted, and he dodged its curled horns. The children roared with laughter.

"Watch out for that one, Mr. Summers!" the other boy, Jack, warned. "He'll eat the clothes right off your back!"

Jane ran back to join her siblings, giggling as David continued to avoid the carnivorous goat.

"Summers! What're you doin' to that goat!" Michael approached with a wide grin on his face.

"It's what the goat's tryin' to do to me!"

The children laughed hysterically.

"Y'all watch Renie for me," he requested, and walked off with his comrade.

"What brings you by?" Michael inquired.

David proceeded to tell him about the thieves that had attacked Rena. Michael's face reddened as his friend described the event.

"Do you know who they were?"

"No, but Kit Lawrence is here, and he aims on findin' out." He went on to remind his comrade what he had told him about Kit, and then asked for Michael's assistance in raising the barn the following morn.

"I'll be there soon as chores is done," he promised.

David thanked him, mounted Renegade, and rode back home to find Kit already making alterations on the pigsty's lean-to shed. He complied to Kit's commands by hammering nails into the small wooden structure, then walked around the perimeter of the pen to ensure its security. He filled a trough with dinner scraps, and another with water, letting the sow have her fill. When he had completed his tasks, he endured Kit's criticism about his lack of responsibility, and shirking his duties by taking a pleasure ride when there was work to be done. So frustrated that he thought he might burst, David sought refuge in his cottage with Anna, and avoided the man for the remainder of the evening.

Michael arrived in the morning to see David's family standing in the yard, staring up at the barn. Ginger, Kit's horse, the cow, and Renegade were grazing in the pasture, and the barn's contents had been set outside in case the building collapsed. He dismounted and joined the little group.

"You're jist a dumb li'l ole gal!" Kit was saying to Josie, who held her drawing pad. "That won't work!" He guffawed.

"My dear Mr. Lawrence, I've surveyed the barn myself, and I reckon my plans are accurate." She sounded snooty, intentional or not.

Caroline smiled at her youngest daughter. "It can't hurt to try."

"Well, yeah it can," Kit quipped, "'cause the damn thing might fall over."

David glanced at Michael, then Josie. "I'm all for tryin' Josie's idea," he said supportively, and gave her a wink.

Kit spat. "Okay, it's your barn. But if it falls over, don't say I didn't tell you so."

Michael snickered, but Kit glared at him, so he quickly stifled. "What would you like me to do?" he asked, looking to Josie.

She immediately took charge, barking orders as the three men obliged her. They gathered Ginger, Kit's horse, Michael's mount, and Renegade, tied ropes to the beasts, and aligned ropes and pulleys according to her specifications within the barn's rafters. Josie counted to three. Like expecting a dynamite explosion, they prepared for the worst. The men provoked the equines into action; they tugged against their enormous obstacle. As they strained, the barn creaked, groaned, and slowly leaned to its upright position. Anna, Rena, and Caroline held the animals as the men rushed to the back side of the barn and angled logs against it to support the weakened side.

"It worked, Josie!" Caroline exclaimed. "Your plan is a success!"

Josie smiled. "Thanks, Ma." She glanced at the men as they approached her.

David picked her up and spun her around. "Good job, sis!" he said, and gave her a peck on the cheek.

"And we didn't even have to wait for Tucker to git here," said Caroline.

David grinned at her. He'd never expected Kit's son to arrive in time, anyway.

Michael walked over to Rena as Josie glanced at Kit, who raised an eyebrow at her.

"I reckon your idea was a good one at that," he admitted, "but don't git too cocky." He sauntered over to his horse, untying him as Josie grinned at her brother.

The barn was now stable enough, but the men set to work anyway, securing it by replacing joists and sideboards that had deteriorated over the course of nearly three year's neglect. As they worked, Kit questioned them about their exploits with Jeb Stuart's cavalry, how they had met the grand Robert E. Lee, and insisted that they describe their battlefield experiences. David explained how he had discovered Jake's body after Chancellorsville, had helped bury him, and intended to retrieve him. After a while, the topic turned to Michael's attraction to Rena, and the men who had attacked her.

"You know," Kit said, stopping to wipe the sweat from his brow. "Up in Pulaski, they've been havin' the same problem, so they started up their own militia to keep the freed niggers from attackin' the whites. They call themselves 'the organization'."

David and Michael looked at each other. "Do they have the darkies arrested?" asked Michael.

"No. They jist give them a warnin', and the sumbitches back off their lootin'." He grinned sadistically.

"I think I know who was here last week." Michael's admission startled David, who glared at him. "Or at least, my uncle does."

He went on to explain what he'd been told by Johnny Ryan, how a family of squatters was up in the hills not far from his place. Mr. Ryan claimed to have evidence, stating that his youngest son had spied them riding down the road with two chickens, which occurred at approximately the same time as Rena's assault.

Kit decided it was proof enough for him. "I want to talk with some local fellers about the situation at hand," he said bluntly. "We'll discuss this further then."

He walked off to the house for refreshment, leaving David and Michael to ponder his statement.

Two weeks dragged by and winter grew even colder. Still, David was glad to be home, for it was far better than the place he'd been a year ago. Anna, on the other hand, was suffering miserably, longing for her home and sisters. She occupied her time by writing to them, letters she had David deliver to the post, albeit in vain. She doubted very much if her sisters would ever receive them, and waited hopefully for one to arrive for her, but it didn't come. Although her husband tried his best to make her feel loved, he couldn't fill the hole in her heart. She felt isolated.

David knew Kit was staying at a local tavern, and he learned Tucker had arrived to the area as well. He also discovered that Kit was riding out nearly every night after dark, and David wondered what he was up to. He asked, but Kit only replied he was attending meetings "of great importance."

One evening in late January, he requested that David accompany him, so the two men rode off into the night. They stopped at the Ryan farm to collect Michael, then continued down the dark dirt road until they came to what appeared to be a deserted farmstead. They dismounted. Kit knocked on the door. Slowly, it creaked open, and a scraggly boy sporting several pistols answered. He recognized Kit, pulled the door back, and allowed them to enter. As he closed the door behind them, David saw several men sitting around a large table. Candles flickered from sideboards, and a warm fire glowed in the fireplace. The windows were covered with quilts, prohibiting light from seeping through to the outside. One man arose. David recognized him as Louis Banes, whom he hadn't seen since before his father had left for the war.

"David Summers," he said, extending a hand of welcome. "And this must be Michael Tailor."

They shook.

"These are the two I told you about," Kit said, a serious expression on his already stern face. "They're both good Rebel boys."

Louis smiled. "We're right proud. Here, let me introduce y'all." He motioned to each man at the table, stating their names. David knew two of them: Ben Johnson, the storekeeper, and Mr. Ford, the postmaster. There were a few younger men as well: ones he vaguely recognized and a few he'd gone to school with.

"And you remember my son, Tucker," Kit said.

David acknowledged him, but Tucker only glared.

"You boys have a seat," Louis requested, so they took their places. "As y'all are aware, we've been presented with a dilemma that requires our immediate attention."

The men nodded.

"Mr. Summers here can attest to the fact, since his sister was brutally attacked last month."

David frowned. He didn't want to be singled out or reminded of the incident. He merely wanted retribution.

"We've been made aware of the situation that's escallatin'," Louis stated, "and it's time we take action."

"Here! Here!" Some of the men stood with passion at this.

"It is our duty as Southerners to uphold our God given right," continued Louis, taking up a Bible, "as it is written that the Caucasian race is superior to all others. We are the only race that has achieved endurin' civilization. What man tries to destroy, God will rectify, for it is the great law of nature, jist as God intended."

David began to withdraw from the man's dynamics. He was convincing, however, and the others in the room obviously agreed with his viewpoint.

"We are proud of our heritage, and we'll defend it to the end!" Louis exclaimed.

The entire fraternity stood, applauding Mr. Banes. He started singing "Dixie," and the congregation contributed their deep voices. David glanced at Michael, who was singing along with the rest. Regardless of his doubts, his patriotism swelled, and he joined in as well.

Once the song ended, Louis said, "Mr. Summers and Mr. Tailor, we want you to become members of the den encompassin' your homes, and ask that you patrol the area on a regular basis to keep order in our state. Do you agree to this?"

"Yessir," the two young men replied in unison.

"Then take the oath."

Louis retrieved a piece of paper from the pocket of his waistcoat. The men took their seats as Kit motioned for David and Michael to stand at the head of the table. He sat down while Louis began reading.

"This creed acknowledges the supremacy of the Divine Bein'." He paused to clear his throat. "Do you vow to uphold the laws of the United States of America?"

"Yes," Michael and David responded.

"Do you vow to uphold the beliefs of this den with loyalty, obedience, and above all, secrecy?"

The young veterans agreed.

"Do either of you belong to the Union League, the Grand Army of the Republic, the Radical party, or the Federal army?"

"No sir."

"Are you opposed to the principles of these organizations?"

"Yessir."

"Are you opposed to Negro equality, both political and social?"

"Yes," Michael responded, but David hesitated.

Louis glared at him. "Think of your sister, son," he reminded.

Scowling at the remembrance, David said, "I am."

Louis nodded. "Are y'all in favor of a government run strictly by white men, of constitutional liberty, and equitable laws?"

Unsure as to what that meant exactly, David agreed along with his comrade anyway.

"Will you protect the weak, the innocent, and the defenseless against those who commit wrongdoin's, outrages, and indignities?"

"Yessir," Michael stated.

"We will," David acknowledged.

"Do you vow to uphold the law, to police with authority in bringin' to justice the lawless, the violent, and the brutal? To succor the sufferin' and the unfortunate?"

The young men started to answer, but Louis interrupted, for he was on a roll with his proclamation.

"Are you both in favor of reinfrancisin' the emancipation of southern whites, and of restorin' southern people's property, civil, and political rights?"

Again, David was a bit confused by this question, but agreed to it, nevertheless, feeling pressure from his peers to do so.

"Are you in favor of maintainin' the constitutional rights of the South?"

"Yes."

"Do you both believe in the unalienable rights of the southern people's self-preservation against the exercise of unlicensed and arbitrary power?"

"We do," they said together.

"It is my duty to inform you that you are hereby sworn in, this twenty-ninth day of January, 1866, to uphold the challenges set before you." Louis turned, and threw the paper into the fireplace. "David Summers and Michael Tailor, you are hereby presented as members of this den, which is known as the Knights of Peace."

The men stood and immediately started applauding. David and Michael glanced at each other and grinned, amused by their sudden celebrity.

Kit arose and shook their hands. He stood back as the remainder of the crowd congratulated the young men, and shared introductions, discussing battles they'd experienced, generals, and units they'd fought under. The men shared jokes, antidotes, and familiar remembrances until Louis caught their attention by blowing a whistle. He handed it to Michael, then pulled another from his pocket and gave it to David.

"These whistles will be used to communicate when you're out in the field. Mr. Lawrence will instruct you about what shall transpire within the next few days."

He shook Michael's hand, then David's, and the meeting dispersed.

"I'll be back in a spell," Kit said to Tucker as he walked out the door with David and Michael.

As the threesome rode off into the night, Kit explained further.

"There are several troublemakers in the area that we know of," he said. "Come Friday evenin', they'll feel our wrath."

"Are we gonna kill them?" asked Michael.

Kit laughed. "No. We could git hung for murdererin'. But we are fixin' to teach them cuffies a lesson, so they quit stealin' from us."

"Over the past week, we lost four chickens," David stated. "They jist disappeared."

"Lucky they didn't git hold of that hog yet." Kit spat.

"They will if'n they can," replied Michael. "And all our livestock too. They set the Draper's corncrib on fire last Tuesday."

"That's why we have to put a stop to it," responded Kit.

"I think some of them might be stealin' for a deadfall store," Michael said.

"What's that?" asked David.

"It's when the whites git the blacks to steal farm produce," Kit interjected, "so's they can trade it for whiskey, candy, jewelry, whatever."

David glanced at Kit, whose face was shielded from view by his hat.

"The country's becomin' one big raidin' party," Kit mumbled under his breath.

They reached the Ryan farm. Michael promised to meet them at a crossroads Friday night, and set off for home. As they rode, Kit described what he thought would transpire, sparing no curse words or defamations as he did so.

"That li'l wife of yours will protest to our way of doin' things," he said, "but up north, they don't understand. We've been left to fend for ourselves. The Yankees stripped us of our victory, and now they're tryin' to humiliate us into submission. They let all the niggers go free, but they don't do nothin' to assist or protect us, so we've got to do it for ourselves."

"I know," David replied. "Anna won't find out."

"Good."

The next day, David rode to the mercantile, being especially careful to honor his vow of secrecy by not giving his oath away to anyone else who might be in the store.

"David," Ben greeted. "What can I do for you?"

"I need some wire and a bag of nails," he replied.

The man nodded. "How's your kinfolk?"

"They're all doin' fine. Rena too."

"Glad to hear it."

He went about his tasks while David stood at the counter, looking over a recent newspaper. He came to a story that made his heart leap.

"Have you read this?"

"Yessir. The Radical press is makin' up stories. I don't see how honest white folks could do what they're sayin'."

David quickly scanned the article, which told about several "outrages" committed by southern whites against the "innocent" Negro population. He shook his head in disgust.

"How can they be afforded to print such lies?" he asked out loud to himself.

"It's those damned Radical Republicans," stated Ben. "They've been comin' into the state, workin' to demoralize upstandin' Democratic folk such as ourselves, and tellin' lies to sway the voters. It worked to a degree too. Some of them got elected."

"It's appallin', that's what it is," David grumbled.

Two days later, Caroline invited several neighbor ladies over for a quilting bee. While they stitched together old clothing scraps, Anna listened to their gossip. David entered as the women were departing. When they had gone, she informed her husband what she'd learned.

"Mrs. Skidmore said that the carpet bag men are arriving in droves. Men from the Pittsburgh Relief Association."

"Reckon I've heard that too," he replied. "They're all jist Radicals, tryin' to force us to change. Them and the American Missionary Association. The northern missionaries are religious extremists, in my opinion."

"Speakin' of missionaries, Mrs. Collier says northern churches are sendin' down charitable food shipments," Caroline said. "So if we have to …"

"We ain't takin' the damn Yankees' charity, Ma!" he exclaimed, but then glanced at Anna. Reading her hurt expression, he corrected himself. "What I mean is, we're gettin' by jist fine without it."

"Yes, but if we need it later on …" Rena's voice trailed off.

"Let's fret about that only if we have to," said Caroline, flashing a reassuring smile at her son.

"The livestock ain't doin' well," Rena remarked. "We're runnin' out of fodder, and we only have a few chickens left."

David sank down into a chair. "I'm well aware, Rena," he sighed. "If need be, we'll butcher the sow."

"But we need to protect her so that she may have her piglets," Anna insisted.

He balanced his elbows on his knees, cupping his face in his hands. "Then nothin'll happen to her."

"The Freedmen's Bureau set up a school nearby," she informed, "and I was thinking I'd like to teach there, at least until the baby's born."

David glared at her. His mouth dropped open. "It … it's only two months away," he stammered.

"Perhaps I can teach after the baby's born too, until we return home." She smiled at him.

He stood, looked at his mother and sister as they exchanged disapproving glances, and took her hand. "Anna, darlin'," he said slowly, "I know you mean well, and you want to help them, but it ain't safe."

She frowned. "Why not?"

"Anna, jist take me on my word. I forbid you to teach those people."

She scowled at him, immediately making him wish he hadn't said that. "How dare you, David Summers!" she exclaimed. "I will not allow you to tell me what to do!"

She stormed past him, but he caught her arm.

"I didn't mean it the way it sounded," he uttered. "I only meant that I'm concerned for your safety. Right, Ma?"

Caroline snickered. "Don't git me involved in this."

He let out a moan. "Bud told me about a white schoolmarm up in Murfreesboro who got dragged off and murdered."

Anna gasped.

"No!" cried Rena.

"It's the godforsaken truth," he declared. "I've never known Bud to lie."

Rena gave her sister-in-law a hug. "I agree with David, Anna. It ain't safe right now." She smiled and went to her room.

Caroline followed her out.

Anna sniffled. "I was so looking forward to it!" Suddenly, she burst into tears.

"Oh, darlin', don't cry." He embraced her. "You'll have plenty to do in a couple of months."

She looked up at him as tears spilled from her eyes. Wiping them away, she said, "It's just that, I miss my family, and I thought, if I could keep myself occupied ..."

He kissed her. "I know, honey. It'll be all right." He took her by the hand, and led her to the cottage.

On Friday, David waited until the women were asleep, then stole away into the night. He met up with Michael, Kit, and five other Knights of Peace, the younger members who were approximately David's age. Upon Kit's directions, they went to a nearby barn where white sheets had been stashed. They placed sheets over their horses, securing them on with ropes and saddles. Kit handed them each a robe and mask constructed of white cloth.

"Put these on," he commanded. "We don't want to be recognized."

The young men obeyed his request, pulled on their robes, pistoled to the hilt underneath them, and cut eye, nose, and mouth holes into the masks.

"We look like ghosts!" one young man, Henry Cook, exclaimed idiotically.

"That's the idea," Kit said. "We're fixin' to play on their superstitious nature."

He placed a tall, white cardboard, funnel-shaped hat upon his head, which was adorned with gold stars, reminding David of a wizard's hat. He mounted up.

"Follow me, boys."

He rode out of the barn, and the other seven followed. They traveled silently so as not to alert their intended victims, and arrived at a shanty set back in the woods. Smoke billowed from the chimney, but other than that, it was dark and quiet. The men dismounted and went inside. Kit motioned for them to enter a back room, where they discovered three black men sleeping. They encircled the bed. Kit kicked the bed frame. The Negroes sat up, bewildered. When they realized they were surrounded by strange beings, they drew back in horror.

"We are the spirits of the Confederate dead," Kit growled in a low, menacing voice.

The black men quivered with fright.

"Men you have formally known."

He stepped closer to the bed. The Negroes cowered toward the corner.

"We died at Shiloh," another man in white, Charlie Abbott, said ominously. He rattled some bones that he had concealed under his robe.

The Negroes cried out in fear.

"And at Chickamauga," said Michael surrealistically. "We haven't been able to rest in our graves, because of your misdeeds."

"We have scratched through from the depths of Hell to warn you about the consequences of your misconduct," said another Knight of Peace, Wes McGrath.

"What do you want with us?" one terrified black man asked.

David thought he might drop dead of heart failure before his very eyes.

"It's dry down in Hell," said Robert Powell, disguised in white. "We need water."

One of the squatters sprang from the bed and went outside to the well, returning shortly with a tin cup. Robert took it from his quivering hand. The man had obviously seen their ethereal horses outside. Robert poured the water into a concealed leather pouch. It sizzled and expelled steam. He returned the cup to the man, who stood paralyzed with fear for a moment, dropped the receptacle, and ran back to the bed. The tin cup clanked as it rolled across the floorboards.

"We know what you've been up to," said another Knight, Levy Murphy. "We've seen you stealin'."

"We only did it cuz weze starvin'!" one of the black men exclaimed.

"You must stay at home," Kit said in a sepulchral voice, "instead of preyin' on the innocent."

"But what are we gonna eat?" one of them boldly inquired.

"Silence!" Kit roared.

He raised his hand, making himself appear even taller and more portentous. The black men shivered with fright.

"You will do as we tell you!"

They stared up at him, their eyes wide, too terrified to speak. Kit turned on his heels and exited the shanty, followed by his faction. They mounted and rode off into the night, waiting until they were at a safe distance before they began laughing and whooping it up. David was too angry to laugh. He had recognized two of the three Negroes in the shanty. They were indeed the men who had stolen from him, and had tried to assault his sister. He hoped they'd learned their lesson and would stay away, because next time, their encounter wouldn't be so pleasant.

"I don't reckon we'll have any more trouble with those fellers," Kit said.

He spurred his horse, and the ghostly group galloped off to their next destination. They intimidated their intended targets similarly, coming up with clever lines to tell the terrified believers. Once their incursion was done, the raiders returned to the barn. As they hid their garb behind hay bales, Kit did most of the talking, blaming the Yankees, cursing the "niggers," and justifying their retaliation. David listened without comment. An inexplicable wave of guilt washed over him, even though he rationalized to himself that the black men had deserved their attacks. The Knights of Peace bid each other good night and went their separate ways.

Once he arrived home, David unsaddled his mount, and retrieved the last of Patrick's whiskey. He sat outside, stargazing as he sipped it. Although their excursion had been amusing, it was ornery, nonetheless; downright mean. He wished for another way to solve the problem, but knew the Union soldiers were too incompetent to protect them, so it seemed like the only solution.

During the following week, the Knights of Peace raided two more residences in the area, and subsequently, the thievery ceased. Happy with the results of their foray, David and Michael decided to celebrate with some "ruckus juice" they'd created from their still. They invited Kit to try some, and stood staring at the stubble-faced man as he took a sip, then gulped down the entire cupful.

"Ain't too bad," he commented. "It's a far cry better than what the Watson boys are makin' in their gum log still downstream. Might want to cut back on the yeast, though." He poured himself another cup. "Mind if I take some of this with me when I go?"

"Oh, you leavin'?" asked David. He had secretly been waiting for the day.

"Not for a while yet. But I know some people up in Tennessee who'd like a taste of this." He swigged down his liquor. "In fact, I've been givin' some away to the locals in exchange for favors."

Michael and David glared at him. "You knew this still was here?" Michael quizzed.

"Yup. I know everything that goes on in these parts." He pulled a plug of tobacco from his coat pocket and stuck it between his gum and cheek.

"I ain't sure if I like you jist helpin' yourself ..." David started out, but was interrupted as Kit raised his hand in protest.

"Where do you think I got the money for you to buy that hardware last week?"

He glared at David, making him waver.

"And repairs for the wagons, and extra hay for the loft? It ain't like I'd go robbin' a bank in broad daylight, like what happened in Liberty, Missouri last week."

"I ... I jist thought you'd tell me if you were usin' whiskey from our still to do it, is all."

Kit spat a long brown strand of tobacco juice into the dead grass. "Well, I didn't. You don't need to know everything I do, boy." He flashed an ugly grin at him.

David frowned.

"I've been sellin' some to a Yankee officer who patrols by my uncle's place," said Michael, attempting to dislodge the tension in the air. "He's payin' me ten dollars for every gallon. I figure it's justified, bein's the Yankees are taxin' a whoppin' twenty-five percent on every bale of cotton."

The men delved into discussion about the situation of the state. According to Kit, United States Treasury agents were regulating all trade, and deducting up to fifty percent of the cotton value before it could be sent north. Cotton, he informed, was selling for as high as five hundred dollars a bale. Michael shared how he'd learned that some thieving Southerners were in cahoots with the treasury agents, and the Freedmen's Bureau was being supported solely by the sale of confiscated property, which the government had unrightfully taken from ex-Confederates. David stated that they were being taxed more than what the federal government was giving back to their state in relief for the destitute, both white and black. All three agreed the Yankees were vindictive in nature, punishing them when there was no threat of revolt. Their revenge was corruptly unjust, since no other part of the country was being taxed. Alabamians were sinking further into poverty because they were making less than what they were being taxed.

"Ten dollars for a gallon of moonshine seems fair enough," remarked Kit, referring to the previous subject. "What're you fixin' to do with the money?"

Michael grinned. "We're savin' it up."

"Where y'all keepin' it?"

Before David could protest, Michael blurted, "Miss Anna's got it." He noticed his comrade's expression, and quickly clamped his mouth shut.

"You boys keep on with what y'all are doin'."

As Kit walked off, David immediately felt concern for Anna's safety. "What the hell did you tell him that for?" he snarled.

Michael's eyes grew wide. "He won't do nothin' 'bout it, will he?"

"I don't know." David sighed. "I don't trust him. I think he's hidin' somethin'."

"What?"

"I ain't certain. It's jist a feelin' I have. Come on, let's git on back."

They climbed up a hill to find the dogtrot house nestled in a valley on the other side.

"I surely hope I didn't cause you trouble," Michael apologized. He excused himself, and went to find Rena.

David panicked. He ran to the cottage, only to find it empty. Knowing where Anna kept the money, he checked inside her pillowcase to find it, and decided to conceal it under a floorboard, so he struggled to pry one up, then stuffed the currency into the small abscess. After stomping the board back into place, he returned to the house, where he found his siblings, wife, and Michael in the front room.

"Anna, I need to have a word with you," he said, startling Rena and Josie.

"What is it?" she asked as she stood with much difficulty, her belly protruding from under her skirt. She placed her hand on her stomach in discomfort.

He realized he'd overreacted. The last thing he wanted to do was upset her. "I … was jist wonderin' where Ma is."

"She's out milkin' the cow," Josie notified him.

David turned and strode to the barn, leaving his wife and sisters bemused over his demeanor.

He entered the building and started to speak, but the sight beholding him caught in his throat. His mother and Kit were embracing. David backed out of the barn, struggling to contain his composure as he leaned against the sidewall. His assumptions had been accurate after all. The letter he'd received from Josie while he was in prison, telling him of Kit's unexpected visits, gave him suspicions that he now found true. This man was out to obtain his farm! David's anger flared. He didn't care how his mother felt. He knew she was lonely, but Kit was definitely not the right man for her. His intentions were misdirected, self-absorbed, and although he'd been a family friend for years, it wasn't all that long since Hiram had died. How could Kit disrespect his friend's memory in such a morbid manner? David grimaced: the pain was all too real. His father must be raging in his unmarked grave, wherever it might be.

Tempted to make a confrontation, he ran into the pasture instead. Renegade looked at him as he approached. He patted his stallion on the side, and sprang up onto his back. Without a command, the horse understood, bolted across the field, and jumped over the rail fence. David provoked his steed to go faster. There was only one person who could appropriately console him, who completely understood his plight. She would know what to do.

(About Andersonville)
"There are deeds, crimes that may be forgiven but this is not among them. It steeps its perpetrators in blackest, escapeless, endless damnation."

- Walt Whitman

Chapter Six

Prompting his little stallion onward, David rode through the backwoods, the vision of what he'd just witnessed still too vivid. The sight of his mother and Kit embracing enraged him acutely. He fought to keep his anger at bay, but the dilemma had presented itself, and he was forced to deal with it.

He came upon the familiar farmhouse, slid from his saddle, and stepped up onto the porch. It was unseasonably warm for mid-February. Sweat trickled down his temples as he rapped on the screen door. Removing his slouch hat, he wiped his forehead with the back of his hand, waiting for a response. A middle-aged woman appeared, smiled, and invited him in.

"What brings you by, David?" Fay asked.

"Mrs. Copeland," he acknowledged. "Is Miss Callie here?"

"No, she ain't." She stared at him momentarily. "Oh, you have no idea, do you?"

"Ma'am?"

She smiled. "My dear, Callie's on her honeymoon."

David gaped at her, stunned. The whiskey he'd indulged in earlier made his head spin. "What?" he asked, stupefied.

Mrs. Copeland nodded. "She's married now. I thought you might've heard."

He scowled. "No ma'am." He looked over her shoulder, struggling to grasp what he'd just learned. "Why wouldn't she tell me herself?"

"I do believe she wanted to avoid it." She patted his arm assuredly. "Why?"

"Because she had high hopes that the two of you would become, shall we say, romantically involved. When she learned you were married, she was devastated."

"Dreadful sorry," he mumbled. "I didn't intend to hurt her."

"Yes, well, she ran off with the first feller who would have her. He ain't so bad, really, 'cept that he's nearly twice her age. You might know him. The name's Mumford, from up near Murfreesboro. He's originally from Boston."

He shook his head slowly. "No, ma'am. Don't reckon I do."

"He's a fine man. Into politics. He says there's a future for those who'll abide by the Yankee government."

David snorted. He was all too familiar with the Yankees' way of governing. Six months in Elmira Prison had taught him that. "So she's up in Tennessee now?"

Strangely, Mrs. Copeland laughed, surprising him with her outburst. "My dear boy, we both know our Callie. She wants the best of both worlds, I'm certain of that. She vows to return in two weeks' time, after which she intends to arrange social events in the county, and travel to and fro to see her new groom. There's no love shared between them, you know."

His head reeled. He could feel his cheeks flushing. "Well, I'd best git back. Please tell her I stopped by." He took Fay's hand and gently kissed the back of it.

"I surely will do that. Tell your young bride I said hello."

"Yes'm, and give my regards to Mr. Copeland."

He strode outside and mounted. With barely a signal, Renegade trotted the way he'd come. As he rode home, David could only imagine what had provoked Callie to do something so rash, but he knew he was the cause of it. His ire blended with guilt, and he struggled to contain it lest it explode open once he reached home. Somehow, he had to find a way to get rid of Kit on his own.

As dusk set in, he arrived. After leading his horse to a stall and unsaddling him, David walked toward the cottage. A light flickered from inside. He knew Anna was waiting for him, but he wasn't ready to encounter her yet. Instead, he returned to the still, pulled the corncob cork from a bottle with his teeth, and took sips to sample while he sat contemplating the quandary. His thoughts consumed him as time slipped by. Suddenly, he realized it was nightfall, so clumsily, he made his way home in the dark. The light that had flickered invitingly before was extinguished. He entered the small structure, grimaced as the door squeaked on its hinges, bolted it shut, shed his clothes, and climbed in beside her. Relieved he'd snuck in without waking her, he sighed.

"David."

Her voice punctuated the quiet. She rolled over to face him. "Where were you?"

"Jist … out for a ride." He didn't want to alarm her with his circumstance. His emotions were too confusing; he couldn't begin to convey them to her.

"I was worried." She reached out, stroked his cheek, and gently kissed it. "You've been drinking."

"Anna," he growled. He flopped over on his side to avoid her. "Go to sleep, darlin'."

He felt her stare at him, but she obliged, her soft breathing soon becoming deep and rhythmic. He despised himself for lying to her, but he'd needed a friend to talk to, someone who understood his mother, someone distanced enough to see what was happening without being drawn in, someone with a woman's perspective. Afraid to tell Anna the truth, he thought she would turn it into something it wasn't, fully aware of how she felt about Callie. Overwrought with guilt and shame, he lay awake for hours. The conclusion came to him: he wasn't the man she deserved at all.

In the morning, he awoke with a stiff neck and a profound headache, blaming himself for his agony. Anna was gone. He struggled to dress, then walked down to the house. His mother was there, all smiles, pretending like everything was fine, when he knew it wasn't. He couldn't find words to express his feelings, so he swallowed them, along with his pride, and went back outside to complete his chores. As he finished, he saw Kit ride up, dismount, and go into the barn. He decided to confront the source of his troubles, so he followed Kit into the barn, and found him repairing a harness.

"Kit," he barked, commanding his own courage more than the man before him.

Kit continued his work with no acknowledgment.

"I saw you and my ma in here yesterday."

He spat. "Your ma's a grown woman. She can figure out what she wants."

David's anger roiled. "No one invited you here. I think it's time you left."

Kit slowly stood on his long, gangly legs. "Your ma don't feel that way. And so far, I haven't heard a complaint from her."

"It's my responsibility to take care of the farm," he bluntly stated.

"And your ma, is she your responsibility, too, boy? What about her needs?" He stepped closer. "I can tend to those needs in a way you can't." He grinned and took a step backward, staring hard at David with steely gray eyes. "You're the one who left her here to fend for herself."

"I went to fight! For Dixie! For ..." he paused. "For Pa."

Kit scoffed. "You left her here, regardless, and your sisters too. It's a wonder nothin' bad happened while you were off playin' soldier, glorifyin' yourself with honor and duty, findin' yourself a purty li'l Yankee gal to bed."

Unable to contain his rage, David lunged at the man.

Kit dodged his charge with a chuckle. "You can't keep up with me, boy," he teased.

David attacked again, but Kit ducked his punch.

"You best be gettin' on to that young wife of yours. She'll have you, but I don't reckon the rest of us will."

"What the hell is that supposed to mean?" David roared as he clenched his fists.

"Your ma's been tryin' to keep it from you, but everyone here knows how you deserted to be with that Yankee gal."

"That ain't what happened!"

"Oh, it ain't? Anna's itchin' to go back up north, and you'll be taggin' along behind her like a damned puppy with its tail 'tween its legs. Where's that leave your ma, boy? Have you thought of that?"

"You're twistin' the truth," he blurted, unable to think of adequate, combative words.

Kit laughed. "Go on back to your pregnant wife. I'll take care of things here." He swaggered past David, chortling loudly as he walked to the house.

David's temper overpowered him. He glanced at the sickle hanging on the wall, considered going after Kit with it, but struggled to regain his composure. After several minutes, he tromped to the cottage, which he presumed to be empty. But upon entering, he saw Anna sitting at the table, writing a letter. She looked up and saw the angst in his large dark brown eyes.

"David?" she asked as she stood. "What is it?"

He gritted his teeth before forcing a smile. "Nothin', honey. I'm jist tired is all." He walked to the bed, pulled off his boots, lay back, and squeezed his eyes shut.

Anna sat down beside him. "I know something's bothering you." She gently laid her hand on his forearm, but he kept his eyes closed. "Please tell me."

"It's nothin', like I said," he grumbled.

Her grasp grew tighter. "I won't relent until you confess."

He opened his eyes and looked at her, melting at the sight of her radiance. Aware that she meant it, he sighed. "It's Kit. He's out for the farm, like I thought."

"Why would he want this place?"

"Reckon he ain't got the money to buy his own, but that's beside the point." David pried himself up on his elbows. "I saw him and Ma huggin' in the barn yesterday."

She showed no expression, which amazed him. Slowly, she reached over to the nightstand and withdrew the Bible that had been gifted to them by Pastor Tully upon their marriage. "I've chosen some scripture that I thought you might find healing." She fingered through the gold leaf-edged pages. "God is our refuge and strength, a very present help in trouble. Therefore, we will not fear though the earth should change, though the mountains shake in the heart of the sea; though its waters roar and foam, though the mountains tremble with its tumult."

"What are you doin'?" he asked sarcastically.

She cleared her throat to continue as she found another selected passage. "He who hates, dissembles with his lips and harbors deceit in his heart; when he speaks graciously, believe him not, for there are seven abominations in his heart; though his hatred be covered with guile, his wickedness will be exposed in the assembly." She grinned. "Remind you of anyone?"

"Are you referrin' to Kit?"

Anna smiled, and flipped to another page. "For if you forgive men their trespasses, your heavenly Father also will forgive you; but if you do not forgive men their trespasses, neither will your Father forgive your trespasses."

"Now you mean me." He frowned.

"Darling, I know you don't like him, but look to yourself. You're a better man than he is. Don't you see that?"

"I'm a coward," he muttered.

"What? Whatever gave you that idea?"

He gazed at her for a moment, then sat up and embraced her. "I should jist kick his ass right out of here, but I can't, 'cause he's attached himself to Ma, and she'd resent me for it."

"David, your mother is an intelligent woman. I know that if you discuss this with her ..." Anna's voice trailed off as he shook his head. "What do you plan on doing, then?"

"I don't know. He's fixin' to find a way to take the money we've earned from the still. I hid it under that floorboard." He pointed at the safehold indicated. "He wasn't this diabolical when Pa was alive, but it's like Ma said. War changes people."

She kissed him softly. "I'll discuss it with her if you'd prefer."

"No, I feel awkward bringin' it up at all. We should wait a few days. See what happens." He gazed into her eyes. "I love you, Anna. I want to be a good father, and a good husband. I want to make you proud. But sometimes, I can't help myself. I jist feel like killin' ..."

"Stop!" Placing her fingertips on his lips, she silenced him. "Or I'll make you suffer through more scripture readings!"

He snickered. Nothing Kit could say could harm this. David's love for her was monumental, and he knew she felt the same way toward him. He kissed her deeply.

"I do wish he would leave, though," Anna said. "He makes me feel somewhat self-conscious."

"Why?"

She pulled away and shrugged. "Things he says. The way he behaves. The way he looks at me." She fell against him, allowing herself to be swallowed up in his embrace. "Your sisters have expressed the same sentiment."

"Dear God," he whispered.

The man he was dealing with was the devil in flesh.

Two weeks of tension ensued. David participated in a few night rides, keeping his distance from Kit as much as possible while he performed his duty of patrolling the nearby roads. Kit seemed to have forgotten about their encounter, for he didn't mention it, and remarkably, didn't send jabs in David's direction about his time in the army or his choice of wife. His mother behaved as if nothing had happened, which shocked him, but he was relieved he didn't have to admit to her his acquired knowledge of the past event.

He occupied himself by concentrating on the situation at hand, struggling to remedy it as best he could, but the long cold winter was made more evident by lack of food. Starving horses in the area peeled bark from the trees, and livestock continued to disappear. David knew Ginger and Renegade were both too stubborn to allow thieves to steal them. Though the winter was extremely harsh, his family was faring better than their neighbors, who were forced to submit by begging for charity from the Freedmen's Bureau. They were provided with bare essentials: wheat flour, salt, and white sugar. David knew that, if worse came to worst, he could obtain food for his family there, but the idea repulsed him tremendously. Like him, many southern whites were too proud to accept charity, and these "refugees" starved because of it. He'd read how one woman walked seventeen miles to obtain corn meal, but died on the way home.

The Bureau allowed freed blacks to idly loiter at their offices instead of providing them with livelihoods. Negroes were dying by the thousands from small pox, and the Yankee occupation did nothing to prevent it. He was furious with the U.S. government for allowing the South to be treated so badly as retribution, both blacks and whites alike. His fellow Knights expressed their repulsion about the Bureau as well, declaring that it was an unnecessary institution, feeding the starving and needy when the state of Alabama was capable of providing food with less demoralization. At the same time, the Bureau was convincing freedmen that the southern whites were their natural enemies, thus managing to break up the labor system, which had been reestablished the previous year.

With the advent of March 1866, Kit made his departure, vowing to return from Tennessee when the weather warmed. He left the sow, nearly ready to litter, and the chickens, but took his draft horse, wagon, and five gallons of ruckus juice. David was happy to see him go. A few days later, however, he remembered, and checked the floorboard where he'd hidden his profits from selling moonshine. To no surprise, it was gone, all $150 of it. Tempted to ride after the hooligan, he decided he was needed more at home, so he stayed put, fuming.

He learned U.S. military operations ended at Elmira as all Union soldiers had been mustered out. Barracks #3, where he'd suffered so profoundly and where other Rebel soldiers had expired, was dismantled, with the materials auctioned off to the highest bidder. The only reminder left of that terrible site was the cemetery, where nearly three thousand Confederates were buried. David's misery would forever be scored into his memory and heart, but the physical truth was little more than the fading whiplash scars on his back.

Anna was nearly due, her belly swollen so immensely that she hadn't been able to see her feet in weeks, and now she couldn't lace up her shoes, either. Frustrated with her plight, she tore her cerulean gown into shreds, then stitched the pieces back together, creating blankets and clothing for the newborn. She tried her best not to complain, but she was despondent. More than anything, she wished to receive a letter from her sisters. She missed them terribly, especially since she was almost ready to give birth, which scared her to death, and although David's mother and sisters tried to comfort her, they couldn't possibly understand how she felt. Her husband did to an extent, because he'd been a stranger in a foreign land when he was abandoned in Pennsylvania by the Army of Northern Virginia. Still, he wasn't with child, like her. She was absorbed in self-pity, and although she appreciated the back rubs he gave her, they didn't come close to easing her discomfort.

He understood how much she missed her family, but couldn't comply by returning her home. Kit had made his intentions clear; there was too much at stake for David to leave. Although he conveyed this to Anna, he knew she still felt homesick. He watched in amazement as her body changed, the baby inside becoming more active, and observed in awe as she sang quietly to the unborn child while she sewed clothing for it. Their lives were about to change forever, which thrilled and terrified him at once. Taking her example, he sang lullabies and "Mary Had a Little Lamb" to the babe as his wife dozed off to sleep, his hand gently lying on her rounded stomach. The little person responded, so he knew it could hear his voice. The entire process was remarkable to him.

By mid-March, the sow had given birth to a litter of nine black and brown piglets that David helped deliver. He was thankful the weather had broken, as the harsh frigidness had now softened to temperatures above freezing. The little pigs were an amusement, and the entire family took turns watching over them. Even Michael and some of the neighbors participated.

Another week went by: Anna was overdue. He sympathized for her, the way she must be tormented, but he was otherwise helpless, and could only give her reassuring comments. She was obsessed with her pregnancy, and only discussed that topic, usually with his mother and sisters, since he didn't have much to contribute. When she brought up the subject of choosing names, nothing was agreed upon. He felt like there was a wedge between them, and although unintentional, in the back of his mind, he blamed the baby.

On the afternoon of the 25th, Mr. Kimball rode up to the house, spoke cordially for a moment with Caroline, and went to find David upon her direction, who was in the woodlot cutting cords.

"David?" he said as he approached.

The younger man stood, recognized his visitor, and extended his hand. "Mr. Kimball!"

"We didn't see y'all in church this mornin'. Everything all right?"

"Yessir," David replied. "Anna's nearly ready, so we thought it best to stay close to home. What brings you by?"

"I have somethin' I want you to see," he said with a grin. "Saddle Renegade and come with me. We'll be back right quick."

David obeyed. As the two men rode out, he asked, "What is it you'd like me to see?"

Jake's father cracked a wide smile and chuckled. It occurred to David that it was probably the first time he'd smiled in a long time.

"It'll be worth the wait," Mr. Kimball said. "We're ridin' over to the Skidmore farm."

Once the men arrived, they dismounted. The day had warmed considerably, and trees were beginning to bud. As David looked around, he noticed the farmhouse had recently been whitewashed, and the barn was immaculate. This surprised him, since none of Morgan County's other residences seemed to be in such fine condition. Mr. Skidmore, he knew, had made his fortune before the war without the dependence of slave labor, and obviously, had managed to maintain his lifestyle because of it. The man relied on horse breeding and basic crop cultivation, and he also dabbled in the railroad. It was an exceptionally intelligent thing to do, David considered. Mr. Skidmore had wisely avoided growing cotton, the recent downfall of most predominant plantations. Three well-fed terriers ran up to greet them, bouncing against their legs and yapping until they attracted attention.

"In here!" a woman's voice called out from inside the stable.

The two men walked into the barn to find Mr. and Mrs. Skidmore admiring a sleek bay mare in one of the stalls. Upon closer examination, a newly-born foal was with her. The young filly stood on wobbly legs before teetering over to her mother's udder.

"I'll be damned!" David said under his breath.

"It's a sight, ain't it?" remarked Mr. Skidmore.

"Like father, like son," Mr. Kimball observed.

To their amazement, the foal looked identical to Renegade. David could only stand there, shaking his head in disbelief.

"What do you mean by that?" asked Mrs. Skidmore.

David took the opportunity to explain. "My pa brought an Injun pony back with him from Texas before the war, but the stallion got out and bred with the Collier's thoroughbred mare, resultin' in ole Renie." He motioned outside toward his stallion.

"And it looks like the same thing's happened to your mare!" Mr. Kimball guffawed.

Mr. Skidmore appeared displeased. "I expect some kind of compensation for this, Mr. Summers," he groused.

David reacted by raising an eyebrow. "Now Mr. Skidmore, I'll be happy to take the filly off your hands for you, but I've a feelin' you'll be wantin' to keep her."

"Oh? And why is that?"

"'Cause if she's anything like her sire, she'll be the fastest racehorse in the county!" He grinned in an effort to dislodge the tension.

"I'm not interested in a racehorse," he moaned, "but I will consider a trade."

"What do you have in mind?" David asked.

"Three of those piglets I heard about."

David grimaced. He glanced at Jake's father, who sniggered. Forced to agree to the barter, he relented. "All right, Mr. Skidmore. Soon as they're weaned, I'll bring them by."

The portly man nodded in agreement.

"Well," David said, "I'd best be gettin' on. My wife'll wonder where I went off to."

"Is she still waitin' on that baby?" Mrs. Skidmore asked with a smile.

"Yes'm. Gettin' right antsy about it too."

The middle-aged woman brushed her hand over her graying temple. "Well, you tell her we're prayin' for her."

"Thank you, ma'am. I'll do that."

He glanced at Mr. Kimball, and the two men departed.

On the way home, David pondered out loud. "I sure would like to know how Renie got with that mare."

"You must not have latched the barn door tight enough," Mr. Kimball remarked.

David shook his head. He reached down and patted his stallion on the neck. "I'm sure I secured him, 'cause of all the trouble we've been havin' with vandals and such."

The older man chuckled. "Then I reckon it'll be a mystery forever."

They rode into the yard. As David dismounted, Josie ran out of the house.

"David!" she squealed.

He spun around to look at her.

"Why didn't you tell someone you left? Anna's havin' the baby!"

David's mouth dropped open. His eyes grew wide. "What?"

"She started havin' pains!"

"Where is she?"

"Up at the cottage. Ma and Rena are with her."

Seeing the panic on the young man's face, Mr. Kimball said, "I'll go fetch Mrs. Kimball and bring her back here. Y'all can use the help." He spurred his mount and cantered down the lane.

"Take Renie for me, Josie!" He handed her the reins. "I've got to git up there."

"No, you can't!"

He stopped and glared at her. "Why not?"

"'Cause you're a man!" She giggled.

"I'm her husband too, damn it. I'm goin' up there."

Josie shrugged. "All right, but you'll jist git kicked out."

She clucked to the stallion and prompted him to follow her to the barn while David ran up the incline to the cottage. As he burst through the door, he saw his mother and sister beside his bed-stricken wife. Anna let out a shriek so terrible it made his blood curdle.

"David! Git out of here!" Caroline bellowed.

He was stunned, and could only stare at his wife, whose face was ashen.

She looked up at him. "Where have you been?" she asked, her pain expressed in the sound of her voice.

"Anna, darlin'."

He started toward her, but Rena stood and intercepted. "David, Ma said you should leave."

"But, I ..."

"Right now, David!" insisted Caroline.

She frowned at him, making him wither. Slowly, he slinked from the cottage, and sank down on the wooden bench outside the front door. Anna shrieked again, which made his heart ache. He propped his elbows on his thighs and cupped his head in his hands. After a few minutes, his mother emerged.

He sprang to his feet. "Ma, is she all right?"

His mother wiped her hands on her apron. "Go down to the house and fetch some towels and hot water. See if you can scrounge up some red oak bark and black haw root too. I reckon we're in for a long evenin'." She stroked her son's arm, then returned inside.

At a loss, he did as instructed, wishing he had some male company to ease his anguish. Josie was a step ahead of him, already heating water on the stove, and she assisted him in finding the other requested items. They walked up to the cottage. Josie took the towels, water, and herbs inside, leaving him alone with his trepidation. Anna's screams subsided. He stood and rapped on the door. Rena peered out.

"Is she okay?" he asked, his voice cracking. "I don't hear ..."

"She's fine, David." He tried to see past her, but she prevented it. "Go fetch somethin' to eat," she suggested before closing the door.

He scowled, wanting to help his wife through her agony, but not wanting to be there to watch her suffer. He went to the kitchen, found some leftover biscuits, and munched slowly, not tasting anything. Anna let out another howl, which nearly caused him to drop his biscuit. He set it on the table, looked up, and saw a wagon approach, so he sauntered into the yard.

"Whoa!" Mr. Kimball said, pulling back on the reins.

"Mr. and Mrs. Kimball, so glad you could come to assist," he greeted.

Mrs. Kimball sympathetically smiled, noticing his nervous demeanor as her husband helped her down.

"They're up yonder in Granny's old cottage," he informed.

She nodded, slightly lifted her skirt, and started across the yard toward the incline.

Mr. Kimball patted him on the back. He extracted two stogies from his pocket. "Reckon it's time we fire these up." He handed one to David, and lit them both.

David inhaled, but expelled the smoke with uncontrollable coughing. "I reckon I'll save this for later," he croaked, crushing the glowing ember into the dead earth near his feet.

Mr. Kimball grinned. "How's she doin'?"

"I don't know. Ma won't let me anywhere near her."

"Well, you don't want to be there anyway, do you?"

"No. Not really. Anna would like me to be, though."

"She told you that?"

"Yessir."

The older man puffed thoughtfully. "I'll wager she's changed her mind right about now."

A muffled scream could be heard, and both men looked off in that direction.

Mr. Kimball extinguished his cigar. "Come on. Let's go play a game of chuck-or-luck while the ladies tend to their womanly duties."

David glanced over his shoulder as Mr. Kimball limped to the house, but knew he was right, so he reluctantly followed.

After a few hours, they had exhausted every entertaining prospect they could imagine, and sat idly, looking at the mantle clock as it slowly ticked, each minute longer than the last.

Finally, David broke the silence. "Maybe I should mosey up there and see how she's doin'."

"No, I wouldn't recommend it. If somethin's happened, you'll be the first to know."

David expelled a heavy sigh. He rose to his feet. "Well, I can't jist sit here. The wait is drivin' me crazy!"

Mr. Kimball chuckled. "I recall thinkin' the same thing when I was waitin' for Jake to be born." He looked up at David and grinned.

Returning the gesture, David retook his seat. "Not with Jenny?"

He shook his head. "Nope. Even though she was the first, it was different with her. She came into the world easier. She was always easier."

David smiled kindheartedly. "I hope you don't mean this one will be difficult!"

"No, that ain't what I mean. Some things in life jist stick in your mind better, like flies to honey. Some git stuck in it, some don't."

David laughed. "That reminds me of somethin' Jake used to say. 'When spider's webs in the air do fly, the spell will soon be very dry'."

Smiling, Mr. Kimball remarked, "He always did come up with some amusin' notions."

"Cobwebs on the grass are a sign of fair weather," David stated, repeating his friend. "If you kill a black snake and hang it on a ladder, it'll rain before sundown. Oh, and if you see a cat sharpenin' his claws, the way he's facin' will be the way the wind'll blow the next day."

Mr. Kimball chortled. His smile faded as bittersweet remembrances swept over him. "I still miss him somethin' fierce."

David nodded. "Me too."

Jake's father paused, deep in thought for a moment, then said, "Tell me about when you found him."

"Oh, Mr. Kimball, I can't do that."

"I jist want to know … did he suffer?"

"No, sir, I don't reckon he did."

He hesitated, but Mr. Kimball stared at him, waiting for him to elaborate, so reluctantly, he did. He proceeded to explain the course of events, how Jake's mare, Stella, had suddenly died, how he'd delivered him to the infantry and had visited him there, how he could hear the battle raging miles away at Chancellorsville. He told him how he'd gone looking for his best friend, risking court-martial, and finally succeeded in finding him. The horrible sight would be a haunting memory forever. Jake's eyes were closed, as if in peaceful repose, long-dried blood sticking to the side of his face, trickled down from the bullet hole in his right temple. He was sure Jake had died quickly, possibly hadn't even seen his Yankee attacker. When David was done pouring his heart out, he stopped, the memories too painful to continue.

"Sometimes ... I hear his voice," he admitted. "He visits me in my dreams."

Mr. Kimball smiled sullenly. "I reckon that's a common occurrence when folks lose their loved ones." He sat for several minutes, contemplating. The mantle clock chimed: it was now eleven o'clock. "Sure you know where he's buried, son?"

"Reckon so. I made a headboard, but I doubt it's still there, bein's the Battle of the Wilderness took place there afterward." He swallowed hard, forcing down his sorrow. "I paced it off from the turnpike, and I believe I can recognize trees and land formations by it."

Jake's father sighed. "After the babe is born, once things have settled down, we'll go fetch him."

"Yessir." David nodded in agreement. "I'd like to search out my pa too, if there's time."

They heard a door open, and turned to see Josie enter. Her face was flushed, and her hair hung down in strands. "Anna stopped havin' pains," she announced. "I'm goin' to bed."

She turned to leave, but David stopped her.

"Wait, Josie! What do you mean, her pains stopped?"

"Jist what I said. She ain't havin' the baby tonight."

She departed as David and Mr. Kimball rose to their feet. They walked outside to see Mrs. Kimball and Rena approach.

"Mother," Mr. Kimball said to his wife.

She shook her head sadly. "There ain't nothin' we can do for her." She looked at David. "I'm afraid you won't be a father jist yet."

He glanced at his sister, who gave him a reassuring smile before brushing past. She entered the house as Mr. Kimball escorted his wife to their wagon. After helping her in, he climbed up beside her, the leg brace he wore doing little to hinder his movement.

David stood dumbfounded. This wasn't the outcome he'd expected at all.

Mrs. Kimball sensed his confusion, and said, "Don't fret, David. I'll come by in the mornin'. See how she's gettin' on."

"Yes'm," was all he could murmur.

The wagon rumbled off down the lane, ingested by darkness as its sound grew fainter. He made his way to the cottage and opened the door to find his mother dabbing Anna's forehead with a towel. Flickering candlelight cast eerie, long shadows across the room.

"Ma?" he asked quietly after closing the door. "How is she?"

Caroline stood. He saw that Anna was asleep, and thought she resembled a fairytale princess. He drew closer.

"She's havin' a pause," his mother said in a hushed tone. "Where did you ride off to earlier?"

"You won't believe it," he said softly. "The Skidmore's mare foaled, and the filly looks jist like Renegade."

"What're you sayin'? That he's the sire?"

"Reckon so, I don't know how he managed it, though."

"How'd Mr. Skidmore take it?"

He shook his head. "Not too well. Said he'd trade for three pigs."

Caroline frowned. "Oh, David, we don't need that right now."

"I know, Ma. I'm sorry."

She sighed. "We'll discuss it further tomorrow." She glanced down at her daughter-in-law. "You stay with her tonight, but if her pains start up again, come fetch me, you here?"

He nodded. She kissed his cheek, smiled, and left. He sat down beside his wife. Somehow, he knew her discontinued labor wasn't a good sign. He blew out the candle and lay down beside her, fully clothed, his arm vigilantly draped across her body.

"David."

He felt a nudge, which awoke him. Realizing it was Anna, he bolted awake. Early dawn's light filtered in through the drawn curtains.

"What is it? Are they startin' again?"

She nodded.

He jumped to his feet, but regretted it, for he immediately grew lightheaded. "You stay here, darlin'!" he said, rushing to the door. "I'll fetch Ma!"

"Don't leave me!" Anna's eyes grew wide.

He hesitated, taken aback by her behavior.

"I'm frightened," she stated, and started to sob.

He came to her, sweeping her into his arms. "Sweetheart, everything'll be all right."

She sniffed. "My mother died in childbirth. You know that. What if the same thing happens to me?"

David winced, unable to bear the thought. "It won't happen to you."

"David, please. Something's terribly wrong." She let out a soft moan, and grasped her belly.

"I'll be right back, I promise." He left her and sprinted to the house as quickly as his feet would carry him. Stumbling, nearly falling, he caught himself and ran inside. He pounded on his mother's bedroom door. "Ma!" he shrieked. "Ma!"

The door opened. "David, quit bangin' on the door," she growled.

"Hurry, Ma!"

"All right, dear, settle down. Go wake your sisters, and start boilin' some water."

"Yes'm!"

He rushed across the breezeway to his sister's doors, knocked loudly on each one until they answered, hurried to the kitchen, and started some water. Too anxious to stand there waiting for it to boil, he ran back up to the cottage. Anna was sitting up, her legs draped over the side of the bed.

"Darlin'? Why ain't you lyin' down?"

"I need to get up."

"What for?"

"David, don't argue." She stood, supporting her enormous belly with her hand.

His mother and sisters arrived just as Anna had a severe contraction, buckling her in agony. David caught her and helped her back to bed.

"Anna, you'll be jist fine," Caroline comforted. She sat down on the edge of the bed. Throwing a glance at her son, she said, "Saddle Renegade so's Josie can ride over to fetch Mrs. Kimball."

He dashed to the barn and quickly saddled his horse, ran back to the cottage, and burst through the door. "He's ready!" he panted.

Josie took her cue and started to leave.

"Darlin', tell Mrs. Kimball we need a midwife here," Caroline instructed her daughter. "Soon as possible. She knows of one over in Marshall County. Renegade's fast, so you can likely fetch her quicker. Then hurry back."

Anna squeezed her eyes shut and let out a shriek of pain so unnerving that her husband thought he'd been inflicted as well. Rena exchanged fleeting looks with her mother. A serious expression crossed Caroline's face as she slowly shook her head.

"Ma?" David asked, terrified.

"Go out and tend to your chores," she ordered.

He stood, numbly watching Anna groan in pain. With no other recourse, he walked down to the barn. *Dear Lord*, he prayed to himself as a feeling of dread swept over him. *Please don't let anything bad happen to her. Please don't let any harm come to her ... or the baby. Dear God, I can't live without her. Please! Please ... oh, please.* Fighting to control his panic, he rubbed his hand over his face several times, and forced himself to do his farm duties.

An hour passed, then two. David found himself pacing between the barn and the house, the house and the kitchen, wearing a triangular path into the dirt. A rider approached. He ran to the front of the house to see that it was Josie. She jumped off Renegade as the horse slowed to a halt.

"How is she?" his sister gasped, handing him the reins.

"I don't know. I haven't heard anything for quite some time now."

"Mrs. Kimball's on her way."

"What about the midwife?"

Josie started for the cottage. "She is too." She disappeared over the knoll.

Moments later, the Kimball's wagon approached. This time, only Mrs. Kimball arrived. David helped her down, and she also hurried to the cottage. Alone once more, he led the Kimball's horse toward the barn for some fodder. As he stood patting the animal on the neck, he saw a mule coming down the lane. The rider was swathed in a black cloak. Mrs. Kimball reappeared long enough to wave at the rider, who slid from the mule like a strange silhouette and disappeared through the trees. David stared, wondering if he'd actually seen what he thought he'd seen, and decided to investigate further. He walked past the white-faced mule, up the incline, and neared the cottage. He heard whimpering, and women's voices speaking in calming tones. As he was about to reach for the doorknob, Rena emerged.

"David, go back down," she half-whispered.

"What's goin' on? Who's that woman?"

"She's the midwife, from Marshall County."

Rena motioned for David to leave by whisking her hand at him, but just as he turned to leave, the door creaked open. The midwife emerged, flashed a hideous scowl at him, and swept down the hillock. David stared after her, stunned; the stark appearance of the intruder with large dark eyes shocked him. He considered Anna's safety, and stood looking at the budding trees through which the stranger had disappeared until Rena broke his train of thought.

"Go, David. We're takin' care of her." She smiled and closed the door.

He was afraid to go toward the midwife, who reminded him of someone. Slowly, he sank down onto the bench. Where had he seen her before? He struggled to recall, so hard that it made his temples throb. Suddenly, he remembered. It was the woman he and Jake had seen, leaving a cabin with a baby so many years earlier. The witch! He jumped to his feet, whirled and pounded on the door with his fist.

Caroline answered. "David! I thought we told you ..."

"You can't let her back in here, Ma!"

"Who?"

"That woman!"

"What?"

"You can't Ma! She ain't who she pretends to be!"

Caroline glared at him.

"She's a witch!"

She scoffed. "Don't be ridiculous," she said, shaking her head in disapproval.

Anna wailed.

"David," Caroline scolded, "I've got more important things to tend to than your absurd notions." She started to close the door, but he prevented it.

"Ma, please!"

"I don't know what you're talkin' about." She opened the door wider for the midwife, who had appeared from behind David out of nowhere. The woman wafted past him, and the door closed in his face.

His imagination soared. He could picture the witch sneaking out after Anna had given birth, into the woods with the baby in her arms. His baby! He considered knocking again, but knew it was futile. He recalled something Percy had told him many years previously, when David had confided in him.

"You know how to keep dem witches away, don'tcha?"

David had shaken his head, wide-eyed.

The man said, "Git yourself some mustard seed."

Deciding he'd give it a try, he trotted to the house, where he found a jar of seed in his mother's cupboard. He went back to the cottage and spread the seeds around the outside. Determined to keep an eagle eye out for the hag, he made himself comfortable a few feet out from the cottage, sitting on the dead grass, his back against a hickory stump. Another hour passed. The witch hadn't been expelled. His apprehension escalated as he imagined her conjuring up evil potions to force on Anna. His mind flashed back to something Jake had told him.

"If you want to kill a witch, put her clothing on a frame and stab it in the heart with pure silver."

He knew that was an impossibility, however, since the Yankees had stolen his family's silverware.

Incessantly, his stomach growled, but he resisted. Finally, he could tolerate it no further, so he went to the kitchen, found a piece of cornbread left over from the previous day, and crammed it into his mouth.

Sure could go for a cup of coffee with this, he thought wearily. The bread was so dry he could barely chew it. He walked to the well and withdrew a bucketful, then gulped down several swallows of water. His head started whirling from lack of sleep. He drew a labored sigh, wishing for some word. Again, the terrible thought crossed his mind: he could lose her, and there was nothing he could do to prevent it. The idea made him heartsick. It was the same dreadful feeling he'd experienced when his father had died, and when he'd found Jake. He shuddered uncontrollably; the possibility was too horrendous. After gasping a few times, he forced the contemplation from his mind and returned to his post. Soon, his head grew heavy. He lay down in the dead grass, and within moments, dozed off.

The braying of a mule startled him awake. Disoriented, he sat up. The air was dead still. Alarmed, he arose and started for the cottage. He thought he could hear weeping, which stopped him in his tracks. He stood staring at the door, unsure of what to do next. Each second was an eternity. The door opened, and his mother emerged. A somber expression covered her face. She motioned for him to enter. Afraid of what awaited him, he reluctantly went inside. The females were standing around the bed. They turned to see him. His sisters noticed him and moved aside. Mrs. Kimball did as well. The midwife stared up at him from her seat beside the bed. She flashed a withering smirk at him, stood, and stepped back. He looked down at his wife as she looked up at him, and the swaddled babe cooed in her arms.

"Anna."

He came closer, and fell to his knees beside the bed. She smiled, so radiantly that he thought her angelic.

"Darling, meet your new daughter," she softly said.

He gazed upon the tiny face of their swathed babe, and a joy so profound came over him that he grinned widely. "Why, she's amazin'," he whispered.

"I think she looks like you," Anna said.

"Oh." He chuckled embarrassingly. He tenderly kissed his wife, the mother of his child. "She's beautiful. You're beautiful." He kissed her again, and took her hand.

"We'll leave you two for a moment," said Caroline.

The women departed.

David looked deeply into his wife's eyes, and back at the baby. "It truly is a miracle," he declared. "Are you feelin' all right?"

She nodded with a smile. "I'm fine. We both are."

He released a sigh of relief and sat beside her on the bed. "I wish your kinfolk were here to see this."

143

"I'm sure my parents are." She lovingly stroked the top of her baby's blonde head, and lightly kissed it. "She's absolutely adorable, don't you agree?"

"That I do." He paused, taking in the sight. "In fact, I think that's a right fittin' name."

"What is?"

"Why, she's so adorable, let's name her Adora."

She smiled. "I like that. We'll call her Dorie for short."

He stroked the back of Anna's hand, smiling.

"But what for a middle name?" she asked.

"I've been givin' that some thought, and since we can't agree on which of our relations we should name her after, I'd like to name her Lee, after our general."

Her smile faded, a quizzical continence crossing her face. She reflected for a moment. "All right. Adora Lee, it is."

He beamed.

A faint tap came at the door, and Caroline entered.

"Ma, we've decided on a name," he informed. "Adora Lee."

Nodding in acknowledgment, she cracked a smile. "That's lovely. Right fittin' for my new granddaughter." A chuckle escaped her. "Son, come on with me now, and let your wife git some rest."

David stood. "I love you, Anna," he said happily.

"I love you too," she replied.

He followed his mother outside.

"She'll need a lot of rest," Caroline remarked. "She's lost a lot of blood. The baby was breech."

"Oh." He frowned at the thought of what his beloved had suffered. "I'll do what I can," he added.

"For starters, you need to apologize to Mrs. Winifred."

"Who?"

"The midwife."

"What for?"

"For callin' her a witch."

"She heard me?"

Caroline scowled.

He raised an eyebrow at her, but obeyed her command, and found the woman in the yard astride her mule.

"Mrs. Winifred, thank you," he said diffidently.

She pulled the hood of her cloak down to reveal long black and gray streaked hair. In the midday sun, she wasn't nearly as daunting. "Glad I could help," she grunted.

"I'm sorry if you overheard what I called you."

"Why would you do that, David?" Mrs. Kimball asked.

"Because." He stopped, searching for delicate words, but none came, so he blurted, "Jake and I saw you leave a dead widow's house with her baby."

"Jake and you? When was this?" inquired Mrs. Kimball.

"A long time ago."

Mrs. Winifred studied his face. "I believe I know what he's talkin' about." Looking straight through him, she stated, "After Mrs. Jenkins died, I took the baby boy to her cousins', and informed them of her passin'. She's buried in the Faith Baptist Church cemetery."

Stupefied, he uttered, "Oh."

"Is this Lucas Jenkins we're discussin'?" asked Rena.

"It is," replied Mrs. Winifred.

She snorted. "David, he's a pupil in my Sunday school class. If you'd come to church once in a while, you'd know that."

He glared at her. "How was I supposed to ..."

"That's enough jumpin' to conclusions," interjected Caroline. She held her hand up to the midwife, who took it. "Thank you for bein' here," she said.

"I'm honored to assist." Mrs. Winifred shot a disapproving glance at David while pulling the hood back up over her head. "Let me know if I can do anything further." She kicked her mule and rode off down the lane.

Mrs. Kimball glanced at him and faintly smiled. He knew she had experienced his and Jake's overactive imaginations many times before, so the revelation came as no surprise to her.

"You know, David, that she's a distant relative of Jake's."

"No ma'am. I wasn't aware."

Mrs. Kimball nodded. "Her grandfather was a renowned medicine man in these parts."

"She's an Injun?" David blurted without thinking.

"Part Cherokee. A distant cousin of Jake's pa."

"Oh." He glanced at his mother, who shook her head at him.

Mrs. Kimball yawned. "Oh, my, pardon me. It's been a long mornin'. I'd best take my leave."

David helped her onto her seat, thanking her before she drove off.

"Let's go see the baby!" Rena suggested to her sister.

"I can't believe we're aunts!" exclaimed Josie.

They started for the cottage, but Caroline protested. "You two tend to dinner. Let Anna git her rest."

Humbly, they conceded, and walked off toward the kitchen. Caroline turned to face him. She scowled, shook her head, and snickered, then followed her daughters.

He clambered up the incline and entered. His wife was asleep, as was their new baby. He quietly pulled a chair from the table and set it bedside. As he sat beside his family, gazing lovingly at them both, he realized.

"I'm a father," he whispered out loud to himself as it finally sank in. "I'm a father, and I have a daughter." Overwhelmed, he made a solemn vow.

"I'll be the best pa you could ever wish for, my li'l Adora. I'll be there to protect you, and to guide you, and to teach you right from wrong. 'Cause you're the apple of my eye, and your ma's too." He leaned over, and sweetly kissed her little forehead.

"The Radical party are likely to do a great deal of harm, for we wish now for good feelings to grow up between North and South, and the President, Mr. Johnson, has been doing much to strengthen the feeling in favor of the Union among us. The relations between the negroes and the whites were friendly formerly, and would remain so if legislation be not passed in favor of the blacks, in a way that will only do them harm."

- Robert E. Lee, May, 1866

Chapter Seven

"Lookit what jist pulled up!"

Jessica Ryan's shrill voice caught the men's attention. They turned from the mercantile counter to look outside through the plated-glass windows. An elaborate horse-drawn coach, complete with driver and footman, had come to a halt in front of the store. As they watched, a pudgy man in a black waistcoat and top hat emerged.

"Who's that?" asked David as he squinted at the newcomer.

"Darned if'n I know," replied Michael.

Without acknowledging the footman, the obese visitor waddled up the steps and entered through the paned-glass door as the bell above it tinkled.

"Good day, gentlemen!" he bellowed, his ridiculously long black moustache fluttering as he spoke.

He removed his hat to reveal a large bald spot covering the crown of his head. His thin black hair curled around his collar, which David reckoned was to make up for the lack of locks on top.

"I'd like to make a purchase, and invite you to a town hall meeting tonight at the Calvary Baptist Church at precisely eight o'clock."

Pulling back his breast coat, he withdrew several silver coins from his vest pocket, exposing solid brass buttons and a heavy watch chain complete with golden seals. Michael glanced over his shoulder at David, who raised a skeptical eyebrow at him.

"If you please, my good man, I would like two dozen of your finest candles, and four candelabrums, if available."

"We have candles, made special by this feller's wife, here," Ben Johnson said as he picked the coins from the counter. He motioned toward Bud, who stood on the other side of David. "But since most of the silver was taken by the Yankees, all I can provide you with are tin candlesticks."

The man grunted. "That will suffice," he grumbled.

"New to these parts?" inquired Bud.

"That I am, my fine fellow. I've recently acquired a wife. In fact, you might know her."

"Oh?" Johnny Ryan took hold of his daughter's hand and walked toward the man.

Voices could be heard outside. The chubby middle-aged man turned to see. "There's my lovely bride now."

David's mouth dropped open as Callie stepped down from the carriage and walked up the steps to the mercantile. Upon entering, she saw him at once.

"Why, hello, Mr. Summers," she cooed. "I see you've met my husband."

He was flabbergasted. With all his imagination, he couldn't have dreamt up a man like this for her. "In a manner of speakin'," he stammered.

"Ambrose Mumford, I'd like for you to meet David Summers. He's a childhood friend of mine."

The man jutted his hand out, and David felt obliged to take it.

"Pleased to meet you," Ambrose proclaimed.

"And who might this be?" Callie stepped close to Michael, whose face broadened into an immense grin at the onset of her attention.

"Miss Callie, this here's Michael Tailor. We were in the war together."

Callie slid her arm around Michael's and smiled up at him. "Why, a purty man such as yourself could give cause for a girl like me to swoon."

"He's courtin' Rena."

She scowled and retracted her arm. "Oh. I see." She flashed a sneer at Michael, then turned back to David. "Ma told me you'd been by. How's your … wife? Miss Anna, is it?"

David gulped. "She's fine. We had a baby two weeks ago."

Callie's eyes grew wide. A spurious smile consumed her face. "A baby. How nice." She turned to her husband and took his arm.

The oversized man smiled at her.

"Boy or girl?" she asked.

"A girl," he replied. "We named her Adora Lee."

"Hmm." Callie looked away. "Oh, Ambrose, darlin', I would like some of those lovely linens in the corner." She took several steps toward the table displaying cloth bolts, the heels of her laced shoes clunking on the hardwood floor. She stopped, glanced over her shoulder, remarked decorously, "So nice to see you again," and clomped off.

Michael nudged David's elbow, bringing him back. "We should be takin' our leave too," he said with a nod.

"I look forward to seeing you tonight, Mr. Summers. Mr. Tailor," Ambrose insisted gruffly.

The two young men went outside and mounted their horses. As they rode off, David glanced over his shoulder at the gilded carriage, ornately out of place in front of the rustic, wooden two-story mercantile.

"Miss Callie, huh? Reckon she's a man-eater," Michael commented.

David snorted. "She's been known to have her way with a few. She and Jake were engaged."

"Oh. That's the one." Michael grinned. "She had her sights on you, ain't that right?"

He didn't respond, which answered Michael's question.

"Well, it ain't no wonder what she sees in Ambrose, there. I'd like to attend tonight, jist to see what that ole feller has to say."

Reluctantly, David agreed.

That evening, the two rode to the designated church, where a male congregation had already assembled. They entered the building and took a seat in the last pew as Callie's husband spewed from the pulpit.

"It is in our best interest to conform to the wishes of Washington by accepting the form of government they are proposing," he read, and extending a finger into the air, exclaimed, "by cooperating with the Freedmen's Bureau and the Republicans, we will have a stronger nation! The time of the Negro is upon us, and equality is an inexorable issue!"

The men hollered in objection.

"The Radicals in Congress only want to take away what little freedom's we have left!" bellowed Levy Murphy.

"We ain't allowed to vote!" shouted Johnny Ryan. "And the Freedmen's Bureau ain't helpin' us out any, neither!"

"They're the ones takin' away our rights!" Wes McGrath yelled.

The men jumped to their feet, complaining in protest.

"My dear fellows!" Ambrose's voice rose above the din. "Please, sirs! Your attention, please!"

The men settled down.

"As I'm sure you're well aware, President Johnson vetoed the Freedmen's Bureau Bill last month, and now he's vetoed the Civil Rights Act as well. In my humble opinion, he's made a grave error."

"Johnson only wants what's best for us Southrons!" cried out Robert Powell.

"The President is therefore enforcing his negative associations with Congress," responded Ambrose.

"What do you know about our way of life, Yankee!" roared Louis Banes.

The men jumped to their feet, yelling and screaming at once.

"You're jist like one of them!" Ben Johnson shouted. "A damned Radical Republican!"

The men started toward Ambrose, who backed away. David and Michael glared at each other in shock. Without thinking, David bounded to the pulpit.

"Calm down, y'all!" he yelled. "This man is only tryin' to help us!"

"Help us how?" Billy Ryan, Johnny's brother, inquired.

David recognized him as a store owner in Apple Grove.

"By tellin' us we don't have any rights?"

"What're you doin' up there with him, Summers?" asked Henry Cook balefully. "Defendin' him?"

The men bantered amongst themselves.

"No!" David's anger flared. "We should behave like civilized folks is all!"

The group grew louder and more agitated. Suddenly, a loud pop exploded at the back of the room. The men quieted, and turned to see Kit standing in the doorway, holding a pistol aimed to the sky.

"Reckon this meetin's over," he said in a low, threatening voice. He stepped aside as the men filed out past him, some glaring angrily at him as they did so.

"Thank you, my dear boy," Ambrose said to David, taking his hand and shaking it vigorously, "for coming to my defense." He flashed a grin from beneath his dangly moustache and shuffled out.

Kit slid his firearm into the holster on his hip. "Good thing I showed up when I did to save your sorry hide!"

David scowled. "You took our money!" he exclaimed.

"Now, now." Kit gestured by moving his hand in a downward sweep. Before y'all git your gizzards in an uproar, hear me out."

Michael frowned, crossed his arms, and looked at David.

"Better yet, meet me back at the house and I'll show you."

He left the two young men bewildered, but after exiting to find the yard empty, they decided to comply. Once they arrived at the farm, they saw Kit struggling with a large crate. He carried it inside.

"Caroline!" he hollered.

His mother and sisters entered the front room.

"Look what the cat dragged in," she said with a smile.

"I brung you somethin'." He glanced over his shoulder, making sure David and Michael were witnessing, then pried open the crate. Inside was a green silk gown.

"This is for you, my darlin'. To match your purty eyes," he said as he stepped back.

Caroline's mouth dropped open. "Oh, my Lord." She bent down and pulled the dress from the box. "This is absolutely stunnin'. But you spent too much."

"Naw." Kit chuckled as he threw a glance at David, who frowned at him. "I brought some things for you girls too." He went outside, quickly returning with three hatboxes. The girls opened their boxes and pulled out colorful satin ribboned bonnets. After oohing, aahing, and thanking him, they tried on their new accessories.

"Where'd you git these things?" David asked.

"My brother made a trip to St. Louis," Kit replied. He handed David a hatbox. "This one's for Miss Anna. Hope you don't mind."

"As a matter of fact, I —"

"David," his mother interrupted. "Mr. Lawrence did a right nice gesture, and we are all appreciative of it. Why don't you go fetch your wife and baby? I'm sure he'd like to meet my new grandchild." She smiled at the man, who winked at her.

The sight made David cringe. He stomped off to the cottage, and entered to see Anna sitting in a chair, gently rocking the roughhewn cradle he'd made for her, the gauze coverlet sealed around it.

"Oh, you're home," she commented with a smile.

"Kit Lawrence is back," he announced unhappily, handing her the box. "He brought you a present, and wants to see the baby, or at least, Ma wants him to."

"Oh?" Anna rose, took the hatbox, and set it on the table unopened. As she gently lifted the infant and cradled her in her arm, she asked, "Did he purchase it with the money he took from you?"

"Yeah, but don't let on to Ma. I never told her."

Anna took his hand and followed him down to the house. Upon entering, she saw Kit, and immediately remembered why she disliked him. He was too uncouth for her taste, but she played along, nevertheless.

"Mr. Lawrence," she greeted unenthusiastically, "nice to see you again. Thank you for the gift."

"You're welcome, my dear. Well, now, let's have a look," he said, peering in at the swaddled baby's face.

"This is our new daughter, Adora Lee," introduced Anna. She couldn't help but beam at her newborn.

"A girl." Kit smugly smiled. "Couldn't produce a boy, eh, David?"

Caroline laughed, but David didn't think it was funny.

"No girl can carry on the family name," Kit went on. "You need to think about that. It's what your pa would've wanted."

David's blood started to boil.

Michael sensed his ire, and said, "It's been right quiet 'round here lately. No thievin' or outrages of any kind."

"Glad to hear it," Kit said. "You two come on out to the wagon."

Michael followed the lanky, bristle-faced man out, and unwillingly, so did David. They walked to the wagon, where Kit unfurled a tarpaulin from the back.

"I bought some feed for the livestock, and somethin' for you." He glanced at David out of the corner of his eye. Handing him a long wooden box, he said, "Here."

David forced his scowl away. He pried open the box to discover a rifle inside. "Oh," he stammered. "I don't know what to say."

"Thanks would be fine," Kit quipped.

David stared at it, stunned. He hadn't expected to receive a gift, especially from this man.

"It's a Henry. A belated birthday present. Your birthday was a week ago last Monday, right?"

David nodded, too astounded to speak, since he never expected Kit to remember.

"Now you're all of twenty-one, and a father to boot. Reckon it's about time you learned how to act like a man."

David's frown inevitably returned.

"Tomorrow mornin', the two of us is goin' huntin' so's we can try out that rifle. Times is changin', you know. Could be, some buckra'll come up on you when you least expect it, wantin' to make off with your goods ... or your wife. A repeatin' rifle will take care of him, jist in case you miss on the first shot."

David glanced at Michael, who nodded thoughtfully.

"I wouldn't miss. I mean, yessir. Thank you."

"My pleasure." Kit turned and began to unharness his draft horse.

"So is that everything then?" asked David.

Kit laughed. "You expectin' more, boy?"

"No. I jist meant, did you spend all the $150 we had saved up?"

"Sure did. No need in your goin' up north, anyway. There's too much at stake down here. We've got a job to do, and that's to protect the kinfolk."

David winced at the reference, disturbed that Kit considered himself to be a part of his family.

"How's that sow gettin' on?"

"Jist fine. She had nine piglets," Michael informed.

"Good! They're all here and accounted for?"

David glanced at Michael. "Well, come to find out Renegade sired a filly nearby, and the owner wants to trade for three of them."

"Son of a bitch!" Kit spat. "Your damned horse is as unreliable as you are!" He walked back to the house, leaving David smoldering.

Early the next morning, the two men set out in search of game. As they trudged into the forest, a light drizzle began to fall, sometimes exploding into steady rain. David felt miserable, but his discomfort was just beginning.

"Did you have a chance to look at that rifle last night?" Kit asked as they made themselves as comfortable as they could, squatting near a deer trail.

"Only long enough to load it. The baby was cryin' most of the night, so I helped out."

Kit scoffed. "Who's the mama, you or your wife?"

David refused to dignify Kit's dig with an answer. "I appreciate that you got me this rifle. When I was in the war, we called it 'that damned Yankee rifle that they load on Sunday and shoot all week'."

"Sometimes I wish I would've gone."

Kit sighed, but David knew he was lying. Kit was a schemer, not a soldier.

"You'd think the glorious U.S. government would reward those of us who didn't heed the call to arms against them," he went on. "But I've yet to git mine." He snorted. "I got you that gun 'cause I left on a bad note, and I wanted to make it up to you." He quickly grinned at David. "Your ma and me are gettin' mighty serious."

"Oh?" He quietly coughed, wishing to change the subject.

"You don't like it, do you, boy?"

David stifled his anger. "I don't like you callin' me 'boy'."

Kit chortled. "But you're like a son to me."

Unable to hide his disbelief, David said, "I'm sorry, Kit, but you can't replace my pa."

"I wouldn't want to do any sich thing," he said smoothly. "Your pa was a good man, and a good friend. I know you think I'm courtin' your ma jist to git at your farm, but that ain't so."

"It ain't?"

"Hell no! I got my own problems up in Tennessee."

"I thought your brother took control of all your land ownerships."

Kit smirked. "He'd like to, but I won't let him. As a matter of fact, that reminds me ..." He withdrew a handful of folded papers from his knapsack. "I was wonderin' if you could read this for me." He handed the papers to David, who unfolded them, discovering that it was an attorney's contract.

"You still haven't learned to read?" David couldn't resist making the jab, since it was only fair treatment.

"No, I haven't learned to read," Kit mocked him. "I wasn't fortunate enough to have a grand pappy who was a preacher," he added, referring to David's paternal grandfather.

"Says here you've been served with these papers, gives the date," he pointed out, "and that you relinquish all land rights owned in partnership with said Marcus Lawrence."

"Damn him!" Kit threw a punch into the dirt. "I knew he'd pull somethin' like this!"

David hesitated. "Kit, whose mark is this?" He pointed to the letter X beside the word "signed."

"Mine," he growled. "I signed it." Kit rose to his feet.

"Why did you do that? Without havin' someone read it for you?"

Kit turned on him and snarled, "Because I didn't want them to know I can't read. My brother lied to me. He said we was to split everything fifty-fifty." He pulled out his bowie knife and began sharpening it against a tree trunk.

David sighed. "I'm sorry," he said softly.

The older man showed no reaction, which David found odd.

As the hours dragged by, he grew tired of Kit's constant ridicule. He knew it was the gangly man's way of getting back at his brother by using David as a target. Still, it was the longest morning of his life, even longer than when he was in the cavalry, waiting for battles to commence. The situation was intolerable, he decided, and finally, he'd had enough. He stood and started picking up his gear.

Kit wheeled on him, holding his index finger to his lips. He jerked his head to the side, provoking David to look in that direction. A young buck had emerged, gingerly nosing newly formed shoots. Kit motioned for David to ready his rifle. He did so, and as Kit held up first one finger, then two, then three, David took aim and fired. He dropped the deer on the first shot. A crow cawed in surprise from the gunfire.

"Hit him again!" Kit exclaimed.

"I already did," David responded.

"There's fifteen more shots in that damn thing. Fire it in the trees, then! I want to see it in action!"

David glared unbelievingly at the scruffy man for a moment, but obliged, and fired off the remaining rounds into the blossoming foliage.

That evening after supper, he and Anna retired to their cottage. The day had worn him out completely, and he fell onto the bed with his boots on, unable to move. She pulled off his boots as she pinched her nose, causing them both to chuckle, and sank down beside him. Within moments, the baby fussed, but as tired as he was, David arose and picked up his guitar, because he'd discovered his daughter was a music lover. His newborn child was a wonder to him, and every day, she became more alert and responsive. He altered the lyrics to a familiar song; one he'd sung to himself while on picket duty ... to pacify his fears. He recalled the melody, and the words formed easily on his lips:

> "In thy blush the rose was born, music when you spake,
> Through thine azure eyes, the moon, sparkling seemed to break.
> Dorie Lee, Dorie Lee, birds of crimson wing,
> Never song have sung to me, in that night, sweet spring."

He set his guitar in the corner and glanced at his beautiful wife, who had fallen asleep. Carefully, he picked the babe up in his arms, lay her beside her mother, then stretched out beside her. "Sweet li'l angel," he whispered, smiling. He gently kissed her tiny cheek before falling asleep.

At least twice a week, he made a point of visiting the mercantile so he could keep current on events and enrich his mind. He read that on April 10, the American Society for the Prevention of Cruelty to Animals was incorporated. He decided it was most likely due to the war: he'd seen far too many horses and mules die with their masters, and knew how badly some animals had been treated. A similar gesture of caring was instituted for soldiers who had suffered, as Congress authorized national soldiers' homes. Two weeks later, he read that, on April 25, a group of women in Columbus, Mississippi decorated graves of the fallen, both Union and Confederate alike, not only to honor the dead, but to remind those who provoked war that it was a futile endeavor.

Frank Gurley, the previous sheriff of Madison County, had been arrested and sent to be executed for murdering a Union officer. However, Huntsville civilians threatened to resume killing Yankees if the execution took place, so President Johnson issued a stay of execution, and General Grant dropped the case after Hurley signed an oath of loyalty to the United States.

April gave way to May, and as the month went by, the humidity increased. On the 11th, the South breathed a sigh of relief as their beloved President Davis was finally set free after two years of imprisonment. Anna was learning what life in the South consisted of, which wasn't much different from Dover, except there was more heat and less prosperity. The farms slowly began to revitalize, but still, vagrancy was commonplace, as well as thievery. Two piglets from the litter disappeared overnight, sending Kit on a rampage. He hunted the Negro brigands down, called on them at night, and although the pigs were long consumed, stuck his pistol in the robbers' faces, making them swear never to steal again while the Knights of Peace stood witness.

When June arrived, summer had already commenced. Every night was aglitter with fireflies, and deafening with the songs of crickets, frogs, toads, and cicadas. Their orchestration was so loud that Anna had difficulty falling asleep, and usually walked down to the creek for reprieve before bedtime, even though the creek bed was but a trickle. One night in mid-June, she burst into the cottage as David sat in a rocking chair he'd created for her, quietly soothing the baby.

"Oh, you're here," she said, panting as she closed the door behind her.

He chuckled. "Where'd you think I'd be?"

Suddenly, a terrified continence swept over her face.

"Darlin'? What is it?"

"I thought it was you down there." She wrapped her arms around herself.

David quizzically stared at her. "I've been here since you left." He raised an eyebrow. "Was someone down there?"

"I think it was Kit. He was probably at the still. It was dark, and he was too far away to see, but someone was standing on the other side of the bank, watching me." She rushed over and took the baby in her arms, caressing Dorie to calm herself.

"Did he say anything to you?"

"No. That's just it. I called your name, but you didn't answer, and I got anxious, so I came back home." She frowned and sank onto the bed.

"Maybe he jist didn't want to startle you," David reasoned.

She sniffed. "I feel very awkward with him around, David. It's as though he's always watching me. Watching us all."

"Well, he says he wants to protect y'all."

She shook her head. "No. I've a feeling there's more to it than that." She hugged the baby, who giggled.

David's anger sparked, but he knew if he confronted the man, Kit would only deny it. Somehow, he had to catch him in the act, which he knew was nearly impossible.

"And another thing. I know you've been out patrolling at night, but it's scary alone up here."

"Ma's jist down the hill."

"It's not the same, sweetie. I feel safer when you're beside me."

He sighed, searching for comforting words. "First thing tomorrow, darlin', I'll show you how to use my pistol."

She scoffed. "Your Colt? That thing's far too ungainly."

"Well, I'll look into gettin' you somethin' more ladylike, then."

"You'd want me to use it? If the opportunity arose?"

"I want you to be able to protect yourself."

Leery of his offer, she accepted it anyway.

By late June, the summer drought was already apparent. Most of the Union soldiers who had occupied the state were gone, except for a few who patrolled the railway stations. Congress bypassed President Johnson's veto, and sent the Civil Rights Bill to the states, which gave blacks the same rights as whites, but stopped short of guaranteeing their right to vote.

Although young people had picked up and moved on with their lives, trying to forget about the terrible war by marrying and starting families, the old were heartbroken from their losses, and the newspaper was filled with their obituaries. Sadness still strangled the South, its sorrowful grasp so tight, it seemed happiness and prosperity were but pipedreams for those crippled by never-ending, dreary existence. The blacks who had determinedly loitered around the Freedmen's Bureau's doors were now ordered by the government to go to work or thereby be arrested and thrown in jail. It was reported some of the Bureau's agents had sold supplies that should have been distributed to the needy. Those who had starved to death in fortitude had done so in vain while the gluttonous prospered.

When the Fourth of July arrived, Callie decided to throw a garden party, to which she invited all her neighbors. David heard many a complaint about her timing, since the South refused to celebrate such an objectionable holiday. After all, it was only a reminder of the terrible atrocities they'd suffered at the hands of the Yankees at Gettysburg and Vicksburg. Still, the neighbors justified it as their opportunity to get to know Mr. Mumford better, and although David wanted nothing to do with the man, upon his family's insistence, he attended.

With the girls and Anna adorned in their new bonnets, the family arrived to see several vehicles parked outside Callie's parents' house. To David's relief, no Stars and Stripes were on display. A string quartet quietly bowed their instruments in a corner of the yard. The scene reminded him of a similar gathering he'd attended a few years prior in Pennsylvania, before he had proposed to Anna. It was the place where he'd let his feelings be known to her; where she had rejected him. He smiled as he thought of all that had happened since, happy that he'd won her heart after all. Instead of going inside, they went around the house to the garden, which was in full bloom with purple-blue hydrangeas, fragrant gardenias, wisterias, roses, and lilies. A swine hung from a spit over a barbeque pit, and people milled about with crystal glasses in their hands. Mr. Mumford's money was in full play.

"Why, the state of things hasn't affected my cousins, the Lynn's, at all," Callie was saying. "They still have Negroes workin' for them, and continue to prosper." She glanced over, noticed their entrance, and walked over to greet them.

"Hello, Mrs. Summers, Miss Rena, Miss Josephine. What a pleasure it is seein' y'all! Please feel free to join in our li'l soirée. There's wine and ginger beer over yonder, and Ma's made up a mess of peas, taters, grits, and greens to go with the pork."

She smiled as she gestured with an outward sweep, so the family made themselves comfortable and started to mingle.

Callie turned her gaze to David, and noticing Anna with the babe in her arms, said, "My dear, sweet Anna. May I see?"

"Of course." Anna moved closer, allowing Callie to peer down at the child.

"Why, she's adorable! Looks jist like her daddy!"

"Really?" David reacted.

Callie snickered. Taking David by the arm, she said, "Miss Anna, please allow yourself to join the others. I'd like a word with your husband."

Anna stared at her, then awkwardly walked off.

"Miss Callie." He smiled. "You look lovely."

Her blue eyes glittered. "Thank you, kind sir."

"Where's your husband?"

"Over yonder." She threw her head in the general direction without looking. "I wanted to discuss somethin' with you."

"Oh?"

"There's a young man down the road, a darkie, who's been makin' advances toward me, and I want it to stop."

David stifled a chuckle. "Are you certain?"

"Of course, I am! Now, it's my understandin' that you and several other fellers from around here have been makin' night visitations."

She stared into David's eyes, so deeply that he had to look away.

"Miss Callie, what're you sayin'?"

"I'm sayin' that I'd like for you to call on him, and convince him to stop. I can't bear the thought of ... one of those ... findin' me attractive."

He smirked. "I'll see what I can do," he replied.

She nodded, and pulled him back toward the crowd. "Ain't it funny how we both ended up marryin' Yankees!" she laughed loudly, making sure Anna heard.

Callie released him, so he walked across the yard to his wife, but she turned her back to him. Not noticing her shun, he ambled over to where the men had congregated. Heady tobacco fumes encircled the group, who were boisterously discussing politics. They took turns congratulating the new father and offered him a cigar, which he declined.

Mr. Kimball approached him and said, "David, do you recall the discussion we had the night before your baby was born?"

"Yessir," he responded.

"I've been givin' it some thought, and I've talked to Jake's ma about it. What do you say we go up to Chancellorsville in two weeks' time, and see if we can find him?"

"I'd like that," replied David.

He and Jake's father exchanged smiles.

"The station in Arab still ain't open," said Mr. Kimball, "so we'll have to ride up to Huntsville."

David nodded in acknowledgment.

As the afternoon progressed, the men grew louder; the wine was taking effect.

Anna found her husband and pulled him aside. "How long are we staying?" she asked, a twinge of anxiety in her voice. "Dorie's getting quite fussy."

"We can go anytime you want, darlin'." He smiled happily at her. "Mr. Kimball and I have decided to go up to Virginia in two weeks."

"Then I'm going with you." She handed him the baby. "And I'd like to see my sisters. Perhaps for an extended stay."

"Anna, I don't see how that's possible."

He cradled the infant, whose fussiness had escalated to full-blown bawling. The guests took notice and turned to see.

"I'm not staying here by myself." She stomped her foot like a little girl.

Caroline came to her son's aid. Taking the baby, she said, "The heat is startin' to wither us all. Perhaps it's time we went home." She smiled knowingly at Anna, and walked off toward Callie's mother.

"Reckon we'll discuss it later then, when there ain't so many folks around to hear us." David slightly scowled, and followed his mother.

"Anna, we don't want you to leave." Josie came up from behind her and took her arm. "We so enjoy havin' you here with the baby."

Rena came to stand beside her. "We know how you miss your own, but we love you too."

Anna wilted. The humidity fogged her mind. She smiled at her sisters-in-law, and the three walked through the garden toward the gate.

When they arrived home, David unhitched the jenny. He walked up to the cottage to find his young wife weeping, and came to her side.

"I miss my sisters terribly," she sobbed, wiping her eyes.

"I know, darlin'." He gently embraced her.

"Your mother spoke with me on the way home, and informed me that it's a 'Southern wife's proper place to remain with her husband'." She added a drawl for effect.

He grinned. "She needs you here. We all do. And I can't leave right now. The crops are comin' in, and Kit comes and goes with the weather. If we ever git a bumper year, it'll be easier, but for now, we have to stay." He released her and looked intensely into her aqua eyes. "I need you to do this for me, darlin'. Please don't let me down." He kissed her on the cheek.

She frowned. "I've been writing letters to them, but I don't think any have gotten through."

He smiled sympathetically.

"Will you deliver them to the post up north? I believe they might make their destination if they're mailed above the Mason-Dixon Line."

"Of course, I will, honey. You write your li'l ole heart out. As a matter of fact, we'll send a photograph of the baby too."

Her eyes lit up. "Yes! Let's do that!" She giggled.

He smiled, and kissed her lovingly.

The following week, David took his wife and daughter to a photographer in Lacey's Spring, where the three of them posed for a portrait. Dorie tired of behaving quickly, and because she was teething, decided she'd had enough after only two attempts. Still, one tintype was acceptable, so he paid the man. As they rode back home, the baby began to babble.

"Did you hear that?" he exclaimed with excitement, pulling the wagon to a halt in the middle of the road.

"Hear what? David, all I hear is poor Dorie being miserable."

"I know! I mean, she said her first word. Dada!"

Anna chuckled and shook her head. Dorie continued to repeat "dadada" in an attempt to ease her soreness.

"Yes, that's what it sounds like to me." She kissed her baby's forehead.

David slapped the reins on Ginger's withers, and an enormous grin spread across his face.

On July 16, a second Freedmen's Bureau Bill was passed over Johnson's veto, causing an uproar amongst the county's residents, most of which were against Negro suffrage. Three days later, on the eve of his departure, David packed a knapsack on the bed while Anna sat quietly rocking the infant, her little finger in Dorie's mouth for the baby to teethe on. Too distraught to speak, she wanted with all her heart to accompany her husband.

"Are you sure you won't reconsider?" she asked.

Even though a slight breeze blew in through the open windows, the cottage was stifling. He straightened to face her. "Anna, it's best if you stay here with li'l Dorie right now. It'll be a sad state of affairs, and I don't want you to have to bear witness to it. We wouldn't have time to go visit your sisters, and we already discussed our stayin' up there. Mr. Kimball and I shouldn't be gone more than two weeks at most, anyways." He returned to his packing.

She stood and set the baby in her cradle. "It won't be long before she's outgrown this thing," she remarked. "David."

He looked at her, and their eyes captured each other's. In an instant, they were wrapped around each other in an emotional embrace.

He kissed her. "I swear to God, Anna. I'll come back to you soon as I can."

"You promised you'd never leave me again."

He sighed. "Yeah, but you understand the circumstances."

She nodded, forcing a smile. "I'll anxiously await your return. We both will."

David glanced at the baby, who peered through the bars of her cradle with big round blue eyes. He smiled. The little girl smiled back before letting out a squeal.

"I'll miss y'all immensely."

She pulled away, withdrew the tintype and letters she'd written from the nightstand, and handed them to him. He slipped them inside his knapsack, then held her tightly.

At daybreak, he sat on the front porch of the saddlebag house. He'd made a point to bring along his Testament, the one that had carried him through many battles, but opted to keep the bookmark Josie had sewn for him at home. She'd given it to him just before he had gone off to Virginia. It was an embroidered replica of the Southern Cross, the Confederate battle flag. He held the Testament gently, rubbing his thumb across the cover. Renegade stood beside him, dozing. Soon, Mr. Kimball rode up the lane. David recalled the morning he and his best friend had gone off to join the cavalry, how Jake had ridden up the same way. A lump caught in his throat as he remembered. The two men briefly greeted each other before continuing in silence for nearly an hour until they stopped to gulp down a few swallows from their canteens. Morning dew cast a thick mist in the valleys, and the stillness made it spookier. David found the scenario too unsettling, so he decided to break the silence.

"Reckon we'll rent a wagon when we git there?" he asked, already knowing the answer.

"Spades. And a pine box too," came the answer.

He clenched his teeth. Unable to think of a reply, he kept his mouth shut, and rode beside his best friend's father. When nightfall came, they made a makeshift shelter and dined on salt pork and beans. Arising early the next morning, they rode until they reached Huntsville. A few women in well-worn dresses walked down the street, but other than several wayward travelers, the thoroughfare was quiet. They rode to the familiar train depot, where Mr. Kimball purchased their tickets. David's mind flashed back to the day he and Jake had gone off to Virginia. They went in search of adventure, but instead, Jake had found a bullet. The thought made David sob, but he quickly suppressed it. He knew it was only the beginning of what heartache was in store.

The men waited for nearly an hour. Finally, a train pulled in, gushing steam and expelling groans. They boarded their horses and found their seats. A conductor came down the aisle, requesting to see their tickets. The ride was long, but not nearly as tedious as when David had enlisted with Jake. He reasoned it was because the war was over, the rails were fixed, and the army wasn't tying them up any longer. The iron horse made a brief stop in Chattanooga, where the passengers were besieged by crackers, white folks who were down on their luck, forced to beg and migrate for work. David thought of Josiah, and pondered on his well-being, but was secretly glad there wasn't enough time to find out, since he was afraid of what he might ascertain if he searched the old man out.

The locomotive continued on, chugging over the Appalachian Mountains: along the Great Smoky, Cumberland, Allegheny, and Blue Ridge. In route, larger towns seemed to be restoring, but even more homesteads appeared deserted than when David and Anna had come down nearly a year ago. He and Mr. Kimball conversed along the way, with David talking about his baby daughter, his wife, the still, and Kit, and Mr. Kimball informing him that his daughter, Jenny, and her husband, Nate, had come home for a spell. Times were hard for his son-in-law, as he had been an overseer on a plantation near Montgomery, but since the slaves were set free, the master couldn't afford him on his payroll, so he'd been let go. Nate was in the process of securing employment in Huntsville, but so far, was unsuccessful.

Within three days' time, the ride ended midday in Baltimore aboard the B & O Railroad. The cars were disconnected from the engine, hitched to horses, and pulled through the city. Once again in Yankee land, David saw how the war had benefited the north: prosperity and good fortune abounded. Coaches and carriages were shiny and new. The horses were sleek and well-fed, as were the citizens, their attire consisting of fine silk hats, wool suits, and summer dresses. Tall storied brick buildings lined the streets, including an enormous block-long department store, banks, hotels, and municipal buildings.

The men retrieved their horses and cantered through town until they found a wagon repository and went inside. Mr. Kimball requested the use of a flatbed. The proprietor distinguished his Southern inflection and, after learning of the wagon's intended purpose, accepted his offer of three dollars a day, and allowed him to borrow a harness. David supposed the man felt sorry for them, but the proprietor's pity only riled his pride.

Mr. Kimball hitched his large brown Morgan gelding, and David tied Renegade to the back. They proceeded to the undertakers', where Jake's father solemnly purchased a plain pine coffin. Jake's measurements were irrelevant: his father knew there wouldn't be much of his son left to bring home, if they were lucky enough to find him at all. Therefore, they wouldn't need to pack the body in coal and salt, either. Mr. Kimball paid the man, who assisted him in sliding the small box onto the flatbed while David looked on helplessly, fully aware that this trip was most likely costing Mr. Kimball whatever savings he had left. After purchasing spades from the general store and victuals from a vendor, they set off toward their morose destination. By nightfall, they had reached Fredericksburg, and slept out on the open flatbed with the pine box between them. At one point, David thought he could hear Jake's father sobbing. He bit his lip to keep himself from doing likewise, and rolled over on his side.

He was in a valley, sitting on the bank of a pond. A familiar voice called from behind him.

"I've been waitin' for you!"

He turned to see Jake, and felt himself smile at his most loved friend, who smiled back at him, his brown eyes twinkling. Out of nowhere, he produced a twig and line, and cast in. Within moments, Jake got a bite. Laughing hysterically, and in one jerk, he expelled the enormous catfish onto the bank. The flopping, whiskered fish was the biggest David had ever seen.

"Let's go home!" Jake said with a grin.

Startled, David sat up. It was pitch black out: a few crickets chirped nearby, but other than that, it was quiet. Mr. Kimball, who had apparently been roused by his abrupt awakening, stirred, snorted, and rolled over. David frowned. He withdrew the pocket watch Anna had given him from his trouser pocket, clicked it open, and squinted to see that it was nearly three-thirty. Lying back upon the hardwood, he counted three hours till dawn, and lay there, pondering his dream, wishing for sleep, and terribly missing his best friend.

In the morning, the men set out for the battlefield. Mugginess already suffocated them. The overcast sky threatened to rain, and insects became a nuisance. David had awoken at dawn, trying to recall anything he could about Jake's location. He remembered it was behind a church, where the Orange Plank Road met the Orange Turnpike. They rode through the lush green rolling countryside covered with knee-high grass. It was hard to imagine such terrible fighting had taken place here. The landscape had returned to its previous appearance, and few reminders lingered, except for scattered wooden markers where graves still existed, as well as the burned-out remnant of what was once the Chancellor estate. In several locations, weed-covered holes gaped where soldiers' remains had been exhumed. Some local families had taken their sons home, and so the Confederate cemeteries in Fredericksburg and Spotsylvania continued to cultivate.

They arrived at the Wilderness Church. Because it was Monday, the house of worship was deserted. A small graveyard sat beside it with stone markers depicting the residents.

"I reckon it was back up this way," David said, pointing to a hillock behind the church.

Mr. Kimball prompted the Morgan, and steered the wagon along a back road until David asked him to stop. The two men clambered down. David walked into the field, searching desperately for the headboard he'd carved, but to no avail. As the day went on, a few passersby stopped to take notice. One asked if they were looking for a soldier, and offered his advice before driving on.

The temperature continued to climb. David wiped sweat from his forehead with his shirt sleeve while he stumbled around, trying to recollect his location on that horrific day. It was difficult to tell, since the terrain was covered with underbrush. Frustrated, he sat on a log and threw down his hat.

"Pshaw!" he cried, exasperated. "I can't remember!"

"Now, don't fret, David." Mr. Kimball stood over him. He clicked open his watch. "It's nearly four. Why don't we head back to town, git a good night's rest, and try again in the mornin'."

David scoffed, annoyed with himself. "How many days did you want to spend out here?"

The older man shook his head. Lines on his face seemed to have deepened within a week's time. "If we don't find him in the next two days, we'll have to go back without him."

David glared at him.

"He's already with our Lord. I don't want you blamin' yourself if we can't find him."

He turned and walked back to the Turnpike, but as David followed, he did blame himself. Tremendously.

Once they returned to town, David requested that he and Mr. Kimball visit the cemetery. He had hoped to investigate the location of his father's grave, but without a clue of where to begin, he started by roaming the cemetery aimlessly, gazing at headstones; hoping for a familiar name. There were too many marked "Unknown," and in his heart, David knew his father occupied one of them. Still, he persisted, until nightfall forced his retirement.

After dining at a hotel, the two repeated their sleeping arrangement from the previous evening, out in the open air atop the flatbed. David lay awake for hours, straining to recall anything he might have forgotten. His head throbbed from the effort, and his heart ached for his lack of competence. He sighed heavily, wishing he could find his friend, as well as his father, and he missed his wife and daughter. Silently, he prayed for God to help him in his search as he grasped tightly to his Testament for solace.

The next day proceeded much the same way, except David noticed details at the battlefield he'd missed the day before, such as bullet holes in tree trunks, craters where shells had exploded, and a few charred areas left from the fires that had raged. As far as he could tell, there were no souvenirs left. He thought he came upon the place where he'd found Jake, and wrestled with his memory to relive the horrific event: how he'd helped the undertakers load Jake's body, followed the wagon full of dead soldiers, and assisted the gravediggers in burying him. After a few hours of shoveling and coming up empty, he sat down on the flatbed and let Renegade graze while Mr. Kimball carried on a discussion nearby with one of the locals. *It has to be here*, he thought to himself. *The Army wouldn't dig him up and not tell his folks. But where the hell is his grave?* He shook his head in frustration. His mind drifted back to times spent with Jake, things they'd done together, things they'd said. A few more of Jake's superstitions came to mind, causing David to chuckle.

"When you bump your elbow, if you don't rub it on wood or someone else, you'll have bad luck," he could hear Jake say, and "If you git hair in your mouth, you're gonna kiss a fool." Another axiom sprang to mind: "If you're walkin' down the road on a dark night by yourself, just look over your left shoulder, and whatever you see will disappear. You have nothin' to fret about, so jist keep on goin'." David snickered to himself, trying not to become saddened, but then recalled another adage: "If you hear a voice and there ain't no human near, then either God or the devil is tryin' to talk to you." This one made him shudder. He could have sworn it was Jake's voice he'd heard floating across that field. Another of his friend's maxims sprang to mind: "If you have a bruised spot on yourself, it's where a ghost has touched you while you were sleepin'." David glanced down. He pulled up his sleeves, but saw no visible bruises. With a scoff, he looked up, and noticed Renegade nosing toward a red-leafed sapling. The sight momentarily struck him as odd, because the tree stood in the middle of the field by itself. He slid off the flatbed and walked to where Mr. Kimball was standing with another man.

"David, this here's Alexander Hawkins," he introduced.

"Havin' any luck?" the middle-aged gentleman asked.

"No sir."

"Sorry to hear that." Mr. Hawkins gave a sympathetic smile.

"And I ain't had any luck findin' my pa, either," David remarked.

Mr. Hawkins glanced quizzically at Mr. Kimball.

"His pa died at Fredericksburg in sixty-two," explained Mr. Kimball.

Mr. Hawkins nodded in response. "Did you try askin' Colonel Smith's office in town?"

David shook his head. "No sir. Where would I find it?" he asked.

Mr. Hawkins proceeded to chart directions.

"Well, reckon we'd best git on back to town then," Mr. Kimball said slowly.

The three men shook hands. On the return trip, David mumbled curses at himself, aggravated that he'd been unsuccessful in locating Jake yet again.

"We'll give it one more day," Mr. Kimball stated, "but if we don't find him tomorrow, we'll bid our farewells here."

The thought filled David's heart with sorrow. When they returned to the town of Fredericksburg, he searched out the man Mr. Hawkins had recommended. Fortunately, the colonel was still in his office. Upon David's request, the elderly, graying gentleman in a formal Yankee uniform produced a file from one of the wooden cabinets lining the walls of his musty office, withdrew several sheets, and ran his finger down each one as he scanned the listings.

"I'm sorry, young man," he finally said in a low voice. "There is no mention of your father's name here. He's undoubtedly been laid to rest in an unmarked grave." He gazed at David with grayish blue eyes, the sadness of his many years of personal suffering evident in them.

David grimaced. He knew the man would utter those words, even though he'd held out hope as the colonel flipped through the pages. "Thank you kindly, sir," he replied, and quickly departed the office, with Mr. Kimball following behind. Struggling to hold back his sorrow, frustration, and disappointment, he said nothing to Jake's father as they returned to the hotel.

Later that night, he lay awake once more, too distraught with the thought of leaving his friend in an unmarked grave forever, just like his father was. He tossed and turned, and in the morning, his head groggy, he began rehashing the preceding day. Suddenly, a revelation came to him.

"Mr. Kimball, I think I know where Jake is," he announced.

The men set off for their grim location. David directed Jake's father, sprang from the wagon seat, retrieved a shovel, and began digging. Within moments, he discovered that his presumptions were true.

"I found him!" he exclaimed, carefully scraping the dirt away.

"How did you know?" Mr. Kimball inquired.

"This saplin' here. It's a buckeye. I buried Jake with the buckeye you gave him when we left for the war."

He dug up the tree, and below it, found the bones of what once was his friend. Carefully, they excavated the site, trying to stay detached from what was really happening, and retrieved what they could, most of which had been eaten away except for partially decomposed brogans and clothing. A few strands of hair still clung to the skull, the same dark brown hair as Jake's, and a bullet hole gaped from the skull's right temple. David knew, without a doubt, it was him. Gently, they pried the remains from the makeshift grave, encased them in the pine box, and returned it to the flatbed. David brushed the light brown dirt from his hands and trousers, then sighed with relief and exhaustion combined. Mr. Kimball opted to keep the tree, and set it in the back of the wagon beside Jake's coffin.

The men returned to Baltimore and relinquished their rentals. Mr. Kimball purchased a small cart, as well as burlap to wrap the tree's root ball, and David asked the wagon repository's proprietor to mail the letters Anna had given him. They rode to the depot, arranged train fare, and departed that evening for home.

On July 28, they arrived back, their sullen journey lasting over a week. It was Saturday night, and after David assisted placing the small coffin and tree in Mr. Kimball's barn, he rode home, dusty and tired, where he was embraced affectionately by his wife. A week away from her was like a week without sunshine, and he swore to himself he would never leave her again. At least they hadn't returned empty-handed, and in church the following morning, Mr. Kimball made arrangements with the pastor to perform a funeral service on Tuesday afternoon.

A small service was held in Jake's honor, with many local people in attendance. The pastor said a few words, then motioned to Mr. Kimball. With barely a limp, the stoic man stepped up to the pulpit, acknowledged his son's bravery and daring, wished for his family's peace of mind, and finished by saying he had no regrets in his only son's enlistment in the war. He gave a slight nod to David, and stepped back to his pew, seating himself beside his wife as David approached the pulpit. He had hastily prepared a speech, but as he glanced around the room, seeing all the familiar faces, his written words vanished from his thoughts.

"As most of y'all know, Jake and I were friends since we were young'uns." He sighed, his lower lip quivering as he looked into the faces of those who had known Jake so well. "We were like brothers, and I never regretted bein' his friend. Not for one day." He looked at Jake's mother, who, like the other women, was dressed in black crinoline. "When the war broke out, we didn't much notice, but then my pa died. Jake and I decided to go fight, and he left behind his ma and pa, his sister, Miss Jenny, and his fiancé, Miss Callie." He paused, glanced at the faces of his own mother and sisters, and looked at Anna, who flashed him a slight smile of encouragement. "Jake was the finest person I've ever come to know," he said, his voice cracking under the strain of his heartache. "He was honorable, respectable, decent, kind, and carin'. He was noble. He would do anything you asked of him with a smile on his face." David forced back tears. "I've lost the finest friend I've ever had, and he can never be replaced."

Callie whimpered.

"His life was cut short far too soon, but he'll live on … in all of us."

He stepped away from the pulpit as the women dabbed their eyes with their dainty handkerchiefs. Upon the pastor's direction, the congregation hung their heads in prayer, then departed for the plot beside the church. A grave had already been dug and a carved headstone had been erected, one that Mr. Kimball had purchased specially.

Standing beside his family, David glanced at the sepulchral gathering. Bud and his wife were there, as was Jenny and Nate, Percy and Isabelle, and Callie and her husband. Levy Murphy and Wes McGrath, who he and Jake had attended school with, were there, as were some of Rena and Josie's friends, Johnny Ryan and his wife, a few other neighbors, and Ben Johnson. Michael Tailor also stood present. He had been a comrade of Jake's for a short time before Jake's horse, Stella, had died, compelling Jake to leave the cavalry and fight in the army. As the group gathered in the unbearable humidity, clouds began to thicken above.

"Gone to dust as flesh must, to be restored by the Savior's return," the pastor was saying.

But David was too distracted by raindrops that had started to fall. They thumped on the top of Jake's pine coffin.

"So loved in life, Jacob Arthur Kimball shall be in death, for he is with our Father in Heaven."

The rain started coming down harder. Apparently, no one was prepared, because no umbrellas were produced.

"Come to me, all who labor and are heavy laden, and I will give you rest," the pastor went on. "Take my yoke upon you, and learn from me, for I am gentle and lowly in heart, and you will find rest for your souls. For my yoke is easy, and my burden is light."

Rain fell steadily, but the mourners remained undeterred.

"Our Father, who art in Heaven …"

The crowd chanted along, and after a sorrowful "Amen," they quickly retired into the church. There was a downpour for several minutes before the storm passed and it turned humid once again.

"I knew it would rain," David muttered to his wife. "It always rains when there's a funeral."

She smiled at him and took his hand.

"Not enough to ward off the drought, I don't reckon," Bud commented.

The congregation returned outside, surrounding the pine coffin as "Taps" was played. After bidding David their condolences, along with Jake's family, the funeral party departed for the Kimball's, where a wake was to take place.

"I nearly forgot," David said to Bud. "I wanted to put somethin' inside."

Bud nodded, retrieved a hammer to pry out the nails, and cracked open the lid. David pulled his Testament from his breast pocket. He gazed down at the worn black cover for a moment, kissed it, and set it inside. As he watched Bud reattach the lid, he stifled a sob. He assisted Percy, Bud, and Nate in settling the coffin and shoveling it over. When the sad task was completed, he rode back to the Kimball residence with the men who'd been chosen as pall bearers.

David sat beside Percy on the driver's seat while Nate and Bud rode behind on their horses. The wagon rattled, rolled, and groaned in the heavy afternoon air. He wished it would rain again, if only to relieve his discomfort.

"It was right nice," Percy said as he tapped a stick to Ginger's rump.

"What was?"

"What you said. It was right nice."

The two men rode on for a distance without speaking. Suddenly overcome with emotion, David squinted as a sob escaped him.

"There, there, Missa David." Percy reached over, his dark brown hand upon David's tanned one. "He's in a better place. We both know dat."

He sniffed with a nod. "When we left to go fight, I never thought I'd have to bury him. And twice, at that." He bit his lip as he stared down at the wood beneath his feet.

"I know it's hard, but you'll see him again, when you git to de Promise Land." Percy lightly patted David's hand before taking his away. He shook his head remorsefully, and said, "He was a fine boy. Always a fine, fine boy."

It was then that David understood. Jake had been like a brother to Percy too.

When they arrived at the Kimball's, David conversed very little, and ate even less. He stood in the parlor corner, observing other mourners give their commiseration. Anna found him, attempted to offer comfort, but knew she'd be better equipped when they returned home. He noticed Callie from across the room, who didn't appear sorry at all, for she had moved on with her new, rich, Yankee husband. He went outside and sat alone on the veranda steps, seeing that Mr. Kimball had planted the buckeye sapling in his front yard. Momentarily, Mrs. Kimball joined him.

"There you are," she said with a smile, the first one he'd seen grace her face since he'd arrived home from the war. She sat down beside him. "I want you to know, my dear, that Jake's father and I appreciate you."

"Ma'am?"

"We understand how difficult it was for you to go fetch him and bring him back here. And to speak of him in church today."

David looked down at his dusty boots, twirling his slouch hat in his hands. "It was the least I could do," he finally uttered. "If it weren't for me …" He squeezed his eyes shut with self-blame.

"We love you, David. We'll all git through this together." She patted his arm, arose, and went inside.

Once his family had returned to their farm, David occupied himself with chores until after dusk. He brushed down his stallion, all the while telling Renegade of the day's events, then patted both his dogs. He bid goodnight to his mother and sisters, conversed briefly with his wife, walked to the creek, and sat alone by the still, swallowing his sorrow with sips of ruckus juice. Sadly, he gazed up at the night sky, watching as a flurry of shooting stars streaked across in the darkness, and wondered if it was meant as some kind of message or omen for him. After sobbing uncontrollably for what seemed like hours, he gathered himself and walked back to the cottage. Quietly, he opened the door to see Anna and Dorie asleep. He silently pulled off his boots, disrobed, and gingerly climbed into bed. His eyes burned, so he clamped them shut. His heart ached, but he knew it would eventually subside. Without intention, he sadly sighed, knowing his unfinished business was completed at long last. Faintly, off in the distance, a whip-poor-will chanted. David lay awake, wishing for sleep, and wishing to see Jake again, although he knew his best friend wouldn't be visiting him in his dreams anymore. Jake was finally where he was meant to be: he was finally home.

"...We owe the negro no grudge; he has done nothing to provoke our hostility; freedom was forced upon him. He may have been the companion of your boyhood; he may be older than you, and perhaps carried you in his arms when an infant. You may be bound to him by a thousand ties which only a southern man knows, and which he alone can feel in all their force. It may be that when, only a few years ago, you girded on your cartridge box and shouldered your trusty rifle to go to meet the invaders of your country, you committed to his care your home and your loved ones; and when you were far away upon the weary march, upon the dreadful battle-field, in the trenches, and on the picket line, many and many a time you thought of that faithful old negro, and your heart warmed toward him."

- Judge Henry D. Clayton, charge to the grand jury of Pike County, Sept. 9, 1866

Chapter Eight

David learned that while he and Mr. Kimball were in Virginia searching for Jake, Michael had gone back to Georgia to see his family. He hadn't stayed long, and said he'd returned with a family secret. What it was, he wouldn't say, not even to Rena. David also learned Tennessee had been readmitted to the Union. To his irritation, Kit didn't seem swayed by the fact either way, since he was more concerned with Caroline and the farm. The following day, July 25, Ulysses S. Grant was named General of the Army, the first officer to ever hold that rank. David sarcastically thought it was grand for him, considering all the Southern bloodshed and suffering he'd caused to attain the appointment. Even more infliction was put upon the South, with the increase of the cotton tax from 2 ½ cents to 3 cents, or $12.50 to $15.00 per bale.

Meanwhile, the summer heat ignited fighting out west as Sioux Indians waged war at the Powder River in Montana. They were obviously revolting against wayward expansion, and much was due to prospectors who invaded their land. David wondered what it must be like to be a miner and to strike it rich, and his imagination soared. He envisioned himself finding a gold nugget the size of a rooster, lugging it to the assay office, and discovering it was worth millions. He caught himself grinning at the thought, and recalled how he and Patrick Mulligan had discussed traveling west. The idea still appealed to him, but for now, he was stuck where he was.

He read about how a skull believed to be from the Pliocene age was discovered in a mine in California, and they were referring to it as "The Calaveras Skull." Perhaps he could make a unique find while mining, and get his name in the history books. After some consideration, however, he decided he'd rather find a gold nugget.

The week after Jake's funeral, on August 11, President Johnson formally declared the war to be officially over, even though fighting had ceased for months. The weeks dragged by gradually, and the heat was unbearable. Dried-up creek beds bore evidence to the lack of precipitation. David and Michael found it increasingly difficult to produce whiskey from their still because of it, and resorted to hauling in water from whatever other sources they could find.

When September arrived, so did reports that Frederick Douglas had been appointed as the first U.S. black delegate to the National Convention, and the news caused a stir amongst David's fellow Knights of Peace. They raucously expressed their disdain for black suffrage of any sort, and although David didn't agree, he didn't verbalize it, either.

Anna celebrated her twenty-second birthday on September 19. Fashion designers had abandoned the corset, for which she was ecstatic. Uncomfortable in the heat, she complained about not being afforded the privilege to wear trousers, like she did back home, for fear of offending her new family. Incessantly waiting for word from her sisters, she continued to write, hoping to receive a response, but still, none came.

As the month came to a close, Kit departed, taking one of the pigs with him, and left David with all the harvesting. Like he'd promised, David delivered a pig to Percy, traded Mr. Skidmore three pigs for the filly, slaughtered the two remaining pigs, and hung their carcasses in the smokehouse to ripen. The family would have to wait for meat and sustain on wild game, if any could be found, since David was trying to keep the three remaining chickens alive for procreation. He had enough feed to last the livestock through January, but then he would have to trade hams for fodder. Peas, corn, and wheat didn't amount to more than a few bushels, and he'd dug about five bushels of sweet and Irish potatoes. The garden also did poorly, but the apple orchard had produced fairly well, of which he accumulated nearly fifty bushels.

As October pressed on, David found himself idle; his meager crops had already been harvested. Union officers who had reveled in purchasing southern land to grow cotton were now finding it a nearly impossible venture, so many gave up and returned north.

He regularly visited the mercantile to stay abreast of the latest gossip and catch up on world events. On the 6th, a clan called the "Reno Brothers" committed the country's first train robbery near Seymore, Indiana, netting ten thousand dollars, and on the 30th, Jesse James' gang robbed a bank in Lexington, Missouri, nabbing two thousand dollars. David couldn't begin to envision the kind of life these outlaws had carved out for themselves, living constantly on the run with the Pinkertons in hot pursuit. Although he was impoverished as never before, his conscience would not allow him to steal from innocent folks, even if they were Yankees.

On November 1, 1866, the first Civil Rights Bill was passed. Alabama, however, refused to ratify it, and was therefore held under military rule. People in North Alabama couldn't see their way past allowing Negroes to vote, let alone hold elected positions of authority.

"It is one thing to be oppressed, wronged, and outraged by overwhelming forces," The editor of the *Mobile Register*, John Forsyth, wrote in regard to adopting the Fourteenth Amendment. "It is quite another to submit to voluntary abasement."

The U.S. government had disallowed fifteen thousand Confederate officials and senior officers the privilege of voting, and the recent election had placed the Radicals in control of Congress, so they now had the majority rule. President Johnson reversed his stance on freedmen by stating: "The better class of them will go to work and sustain themselves, and that class ought to be allowed to vote, on the ground that a loyal Negro is more worthy than a disloyal white."

On a Tuesday in late November, Anna decided to accompany her husband to the mercantile, and left Dorie with her grandmother. She rode beside her husband on the wagon seat, listening as he talked on about the South's suffering, and how this winter would undoubtedly be as bad, if not worse, than the previous one. All she could think about was her baby's good health and her family up north. She had tried to bury her emotions for months, but it was resurfacing ever stronger. Even though she knew he adored her, Anna's resentment toward her husband grew.

Within an hour's time, they arrived at the two-story building, noticing a few horses tied to the outside rail. He helped her down, took her hand with a grin on his face, and led her inside.

"How do, Ben!" he greeted the shopkeeper happily. "You remember my wife, Anna."

The clean-shaven, middle-aged man looked over his shoulder from stocking the drawers, smiled as he turned, and extended his hand. "Well,

Miss Anna. We've all been wonderin' when you might be by here!" He chuckled.

"I've been meaning to stop by," she said cheerfully. "But with the baby, I've been quite busy, as you can imagine."

"How is that li'l gal of yours, Dorie?" Ben asked.

"She's fine. Growing like a weed," Anna responded as she glanced around the store's interior, taking in the merchandise and the customers. "But surely David's kept you well-informed." She giggled.

Ben glanced at David and grinned wryly. "Every now and again he remembers to mention her."

He let out a guffaw while David protested.

Anna realized her presence was causing the men to perform on her behalf. "Darling, I'd like to have a look around, if you don't mind," she said, relieving him of his peril as she walked off.

She meandered around the enormous room, observing commodities displayed on tables. As she neared a cabinet full of hair ornaments, she overheard the two men standing beside it converse. One was dressed in Union blue, the color faded from his uniform like he'd been wearing it for too long. The other, an Indian with shortly-cropped black hair, was dressed formally in a black suit and stovepipe hat reminiscent of the late president's attire.

"I might procure this one for my wife," the soldier was saying. "I'm not sure she'd like it, though."

"Why don't we ask this young lady?" the Indian suggested as he gazed at Anna, compelling her to approach.

"Sir?" she inquired cordially.

"Missus, this gentleman would like your feminine opinion," the Indian costumed as Lincoln said.

Somewhat taken aback by his eloquent speech, Anna smiled at him. She glanced at the soldier, who struck her as handsome, although his face was disguised by a trimmed brown beard and moustache. His blue eyes glimmered merrily, she assumed because he was so near someone of the opposite sex.

"Ma'am, I was considering this one here." He turned and pointed through the top of the glass case.

She glanced at the tortoiseshell hairpin he indicated. "Why, that's lovely," she remarked. "I'm quite certain your wife will appreciate it."

"Thank you," the soldier said shyly. "Oh, my manners. I'm Corporal Hathaway. This is Adahay, but he goes by Ad."

"Pleased to make your acquaintance," replied Anna.

"It's nice to finally meet someone else from the north. Someone who isn't hostile." He grinned genially. "Say, you wouldn't know where we could get some good grub around here, would you?" The corporal took on the appearance of a begging dog for a moment. "I've been assigned to these parts for nearly a month, and I believe I've lost twenty pounds!"

He burst into laughter, and she chuckled along.

"Well, sir, I'd be willing to provide you with certain amenities. That is, for a price."

"Amenities?" he asked, raising an eyebrow.

Anna blushed. "What I mean is, I'd be willing to sell you pies. Our apple harvest did quite well this year, and we could by all means use the money."

"Why, it's making my mouth water just thinking about it," the soldier said, causing the Indian to snigger. "If you'd like, we could set up a prosperous business together. I know several other fellows who would enjoy some homemade apple pies."

Anna clasped her hands together. Smiling, she said, "That sounds like a wondrous idea! I'll get started right away!" She took the soldier's hand in both of hers, but realizing her overt gesture, quickly released him. "I'm very happy to meet you, sir," she said, suddenly flustered. "I'll return to your outpost in three days' time with five pies."

"Splendid!" the soldier exclaimed.

Anna returned to the counter and stood beside her husband as he and Ben immersed themselves in discussion about current prices. Ad and the corporal approached the counter, whereby the soldier paid for his trinket.

"This here's one Mrs. Forman is sellin' on consignment," Ben commented as he placed the hair bauble into a small paper bag. "Seems like all the womenfolk in these parts are sellin' their belongin's or creations jist to make ends meet." He smiled at the corporal, but a glimmer in his eye indicated to Anna that he blamed him for the women's misfortune.

"Thank you very much," Corporal Hathaway muttered. He turned to leave, tapping his index finger to the brim of his kepi at Anna as he did so. "Ma'am." He departed, with Ad following.

On the way home, Anna considered telling her husband about her new venture, but decided to keep it to herself in case she should fail. She knew David was too proud to allow her to work, and he thought it was his manly duty to support his family, so she would surprise him. Surely, he would be proud of her once he realized her potential as a contributor.

Over the course of the next three days, she busied herself with paring apples, preparing crusts, and baking square pies. She then rode to the Union army post with Caroline, and found Corporal Hathaway. Eager to eat the pies, he graciously paid her, then requested a dozen more. Caroline and Anna looked at each other, their eyes wide in disbelief. This was a much bigger undertaking than they had envisioned, but they were excited about the prospect, nevertheless.

Anna returned a few days later with the requested confections. She went into the army post building and asked to speak with the corporal. After a messenger departed to search him out, Corporal Hathaway returned and greeted her kindly. As he assisted her in transporting the pies from the wagon, they discussed what had brought them both to Alabama, and she described how she'd met David. Before long, the subject of Thanksgiving came up.

"We didn't celebrate this year," she stated. "They don't celebrate it down here."

"Well, I don't suppose they have much to be thankful for," said the corporal compassionately.

"Now with Christmas only a few weeks away, I'll have money to purchase gifts for my in-laws, and for my baby," she informed.

"Oh, you have a child?" he asked.

She nodded. "A girl. Her name is Dorie. And you?"

"The missus is busy at home in Ohio with our three boys," Corporal Hathaway said with a gigantic smile.

Anna could see how proud he was of his brood. "I was hoping I'd be home in Pennsylvania by now, but alas, it isn't to be."

"Sorry you're missing yours, Mrs. Summers. I certainly can relate to your plight."

"I've been trying to contact them by letter, but I don't know that any have gotten through, because I haven't received a reply in over a year."

"I might be able to assist you with that." The corporal picked up one of the baskets and carried it inside as Anna followed with hers.

They set the pies on the front desk, and soon other soldiers appeared, attracted like flies.

"None of you boys get a pie unless you paid me in advance!" the corporal proclaimed.

Several men produced currency, saying, "I'd like a pie!" as they handed bills to the corporal.

He begged Anna's pardon, scribbled down each man's name along with the number of pies he requested, and collected their money.

As he wrote, she asked, "That Indian who was with you at the mercantile, Ad. How do you know him?"

"He's been associated with us for a while now. He wants to be military but he doesn't want to be a soldier, if that makes any sense. So we send him on errands and such. When he was ten, his family came through on the Trail of Tears. The Indians called it 'Nunna Daul Tsunny'."

"Oh," Anna remarked, impressed by the corporal's knowledge of the Cherokee language.

"Ad ended up here, because he lost track of his parents, so he ran away and hid. Some local farmer found him, and instead of turning him in, felt sorry for him. The man was a teacher, so that's how Ad can talk so well."

"I see."

Turning back to face her, he said, "Mrs. Summers, if it's no trouble, we would like fifteen more pies."

Anna was stunned. "It's no trouble!" she exclaimed. She took the money he offered her for the pies she'd delivered and stuffed it into her drawstring reticule.

"If we had the facilities, we could set up business for the entire state!" Corporal Hathaway said, laughing. "Too bad General Swayne can't taste one of these!"

Anna recalled how David had cursed the man, Swayne, who was in charge of overseeing military rule throughout the state. He was happy the man "reigned," as he called it, from Montgomery, which was far enough away so he couldn't be a real threat. Swayne had elected northerners of questionable integrity to hold state and federal offices, who in turn organized the freedmen for their own gain. The Bureau was being manipulated as a political machine, and taxpayers' money and property were being used to obtain it.

"Now then, Corporal Hathaway, you were saying ..."

The sudden onslaught of soldiers had distracted him. "I was saying?"

"About delivering the letters."

"Ah, yes! I can make sure those letters arrive at their intended destination, and it shouldn't take more than two weeks." He bent down to inhale the aroma of the pies.

"I would appreciate that!" Anna removed the pies from their baskets, and set them on the table. Taking her baskets in hand, she said, "I have a friend in the military. His name is Stephen Montgomery. He's a sergeant-major, stationed in Washington."

The corporal scratched his head. "I'll send him word too, if you'd like."

"Thank you, Corporal."

He smiled politely at her, then glanced at the table. Anna knew he couldn't wait to indulge upon her departure, so she bid him farewell until the following week.

With the advent of Christmas, Kit reappeared, but this time, showed up empty-handed. He was his usual self: obnoxious and overbearing to everyone but Caroline, whom he coddled. David half-heartedly carved a walking stick for his Christmas gift, since time and ambition wouldn't allow for much else. The stick twisted around itself, which to David, resembled a snake, making it a fitting gift for Kit.

On December 21, an enormous, bright full moon appeared. A few days later, David read about how Sioux Indians, led by Red Cloud and Crazy Horse, had attacked and killed eighty soldiers at Fort Phil Kearny on that very day. The Indians called it "the night when deer shed their horns," but he thought a more appropriate name would have been "the night when soldiers shed their blood."

The day before Christmas, Kit went out to the woodlot and cut a tree, which David thought was the ugliest thing he'd ever seen. Caroline and the girls decorated it while Kit stood by, leering at them. Anna became increasingly uncomfortable around him, but she tolerated him in good Christian faith.

Michael surprised everyone by proposing to Rena, and she naturally accepted. That evening, after the family had gathered to sing Christmas carols, they announced their engagement. Tentatively, their wedding was set to take place in the spring.

Anna and Caroline had earned enough money selling pies to purchase small gifts for the entire family, making their holiday exceptional in comparison to their neighbors'. When David asked how the gifts were afforded, the women confessed about their business, but made a point of not telling him they were selling pies to Union soldiers. Upon Caroline's insistence, Anna kept a portion of the earnings for herself to purchase train tickets for their passage to Pennsylvania when the time was right. She intended it as a surprise, because she knew David was worried about money, and would want to spend it on pressing necessities instead. Therefore, she kept it a secret from him.

On Christmas night, David presented Anna with a special gift he'd been saving up for, and wanted to give to her in private. She opened the box to discover a new 1866 Derringer inside. The tiny silver handgun had double barrels and black grips. For Dorie, he constructed a larger crib, since she had long outgrown the cradle, and had been sleeping between her parents. She protested by whining most of Christmas night. Although they were exhausted and were tempted to give in, they resisted bringing her to bed with them.

Dorie was learning how to walk, so everything in her path went directly into her mouth. She kept her parents occupied, laughing as they constantly chased after her. David wondered if she found amusement in challenging them, and realized his beautiful baby daughter had an ornery streak.

Kit only stayed as long as the holiday before he was gone again. His son, Tucker, showed up a few days later, but once he was told Kit had left, he quickly vanished.

January 1867 was cold and bitter. The demand for pies had slowed somewhat, but Anna still managed to do a brisk business. She rode to the outpost once a week, hoping for word from home, and finally, it came. She raced back to the cottage, tore open the envelope, and read the contents.

> *My dear sister,*
> *We were so happy to learn that we are aunts! How exciting for you and David. We received the photograph you sent us, and look forward to the day we will be reunited again. Abigail has written to you several times, but we learned that our letters have failed to reach you. Aunt Sarah and Uncle Bill have remained here indefinitely. He sold his portion of his farm to his brother. I met a nice fellow at church, but I'm afraid he's more serious than I. His name is Kenton Price. He fought for a year under our beloved General Grant, and is now living with his cousins, the Dalton's. I hope you are doing well in the South, my dear sister. We miss you terribly and pray for your safe return very soon. Please give David and the baby our love, and hurry home.*
>
> *Love and embraces,*
> *Maggie*

The following week, she received a letter from Stephen.

> *My darling Anna,*
> *I have been worried sick about you down there with those southern degenerates. I was afraid you had ceased communications with me because of my outburst and irresponsible behavior before you departed. Believe me, Anna, I am more sorry than you will ever know. I understand that you thought my motives were selfish, but they were not. I only have your welfare in mind. During your absence this past year, I have come to realize that your heart truly belongs to another, painful as that is to admit. However, you will always have my utmost devotion and admiration. I was pleased to learn that you are content with your husband and new infant, but I certainly understand your longing for home. Just remember, my dear, that I will forever remain your humble servant. If you wish me to come for you, I will.*
>
> *All my love,*
> *Stephen*

Anna shared the letter from Maggie with David, but kept Stephen's from him, and burned it in the fireplace. She couldn't bring herself to tell him that she and Stephen were corresponding, yet she continued to do so, wishing secretly he would come to take her away from her miserable existence.

The days were cold and frosty, the nights were frigid, and food was running out. Somehow, someone had stolen a side of pork from the smokehouse, leaving less for the family. David managed to shoot a gamecock occasionally, but there wasn't much game, and ice fishing produced no results. What little money they'd had dwindled, and was used to purchase hay for the cow and equines instead of food for themselves.

One afternoon as he sat on the edge of the bed, wishing for the icy rain to stop, he noticed a cockroach slowly make its way across the floor. Instead of being repulsed, he pondered the creature's appearance. Even cockroaches were having trouble finding food. There was none inside the cottage; the bug would find no relief here. He frowned, his growling stomach angering him to the point where he blamed the cockroach for his despair. He arose and crushed it under his boot heel, wanting to crush his hunger along with it. When would the dismal days of winter end, allowing the South to finally heal? As their poverty increased, their spirits decreased, but still they persisted, some perishing in the process. His muse distressed and disturbed him deeply.

Anna received a letter from Abigail with a copy of a Pennsylvania election poster enclosed, which pictured a Negro lazing on his back while a white man beside him chopped wood. It was in protest to the Freedmen's Bureau and President Johnson. Anna had heard of freedmen breaking their contracts with plantation owners, claiming to be lashed or not paid, which caused their employers to be arrested and unjustly convicted. The Bureau always took the Negro's word, and some accusations were so trivial they involved less than a dollar. While the employers were detained, the freedmen were taken to "home colonies," where hundreds died of disease.

In February, Josie contracted croup. She was so ill that she was unable to eat, drink, or talk. For fear she might expire at only sixteen years of age, the womenfolk took turns at her bedside, forcing fluids into her. David promised her she could have the filly, but she had to get well first. Through her agony, Josie expressed her excitement, and made him vow to let her name the foal. Finally, after two weeks, and to her loved ones' relief, she recovered.

Rena notified her brother that Auburn University, the school he had wanted to attend before the war broke out, was reopened. Because of the Morrill Act, she informed, sons of farmers could attend for free. David was at first overjoyed, although it was bittersweet. He wished his father was still alive to see him graduate magna cum laude with a degree in journalism. But upon further investigation, he found out he was disqualified, because Alabama had not been readmitted to the Union. He knew he couldn't afford school himself, and his duties as farmhand, son, husband, and father were too overbearing to allow him to enroll. Frustrated and hurt, he resigned to daily farm chores, all the while despising his life, and wishing for a better one.

In March, the Reconstruction Act was passed, granting citizenship and protecting the civil liberties of everyone born in the United States, excluding Indians. It guaranteed the federal war debt, and promised the Confederate debt would never be paid. President Johnson vetoed the bill, but Congress passed it again on the same day. General Grant issued the order to overturn the civil government established by the president. Therefore, the South was divided into five military districts, and General John Pope commanded over Alabama. Pope was given authority to supervise elections and provide assistance for constituting new governments. The southern states would be readmitted to the Union, and thus allowed representation in Congress, only after they ratified the Fourteenth Amendment.

Ad and Corporal Hathaway told Anna that General Grant was in favor of reconstruction because, without it, the old officials would prevail unless they were kept disenfranchised. In Grant's opinion, the leading Rebels should be forced to leave the country for good, and it was better to have incompetent loyalists in office than Rebels with ability. The corporal told her that administrators were instructed not to give any advice unless it was in favor of reconstruction, and Grant had the authority to remove those who didn't follow orders. Pope had already removed some civil officials and reappointed new ones. Civilian meetings outside after nightfall were prohibited, and indoor ones had to be approved in advance, thus allowing sufficient military force to attend in order to quash any would-be revolts.

Anna had run out of apples, so her pie business floundered. Even so, she rode to the army post weekly to see if any letters arrived for her. Corporal Hathaway was transferred out, which caused her great concern. However, Ad assured that he would continue channeling her letters through the post. Most grateful, she promised to repay him, but he refused her offer, stating that their weekly discussions were payment enough.

While the South suffered, engulfed in poverty, the world changed and prospered. It was reported that one-fifth of Mississippi's state revenue had been spent the previous year on artificial arms and legs for veterans. Jefferson Davis' plantation had been turned into a home for freed slaves. The first ship passed through the Suez Canal, Nebraska was admitted as the 37th state, and Alaska was purchased by Secretary of State William H. Seward, who had been attacked in his home the same night Lincoln was shot at Ford's Theatre. Seward bought the land for $7.2 million from Alexander II of Russia, and the news media had a field day, referring to it as "Seward's Folly."

Once spring finally arrived, David busied himself with planting. The creek had thawed, enabling him to ferment more whiskey. With the proceeds he received, he purchased a few chickens and pigs, and spent his free time running the filly on a line. Josie had fallen in love with her. She decided on a name: Belle, after the famous Confederate spy, Belle Boyd. Spending hours stroking the little filly's muzzle, she was anxious to be able to ride her, but knew she'd have to wait at least another year.

One afternoon, Rena came out to the fields to find her brother, and the two sat under a persimmon tree for a picnic lunch.

"So, how are the weddin' plans comin' along?" David asked between bites from his sandwich.

"Fine," she replied with a radiant smile.

He couldn't resist smiling back.

"David, I want to talk with you about somethin'."

The serious tone in her voice alarmed him. "Okay," he replied.

"First off, Michael has been hidin' a secret, but he shared it with me."

"What is it?"

"I can't rightly say at present. Jist know that, if any Yankees go sniffin' around the Ryan place, you should be prepared to take up arms to protect it."

David frowned. "Okay, but why would the Yankees ..."

"Jist be prepared," she said ominously. "And there's one more thing."

"What's that?"

"Michael and I are fixin' to go north after the weddin'. His cousin in Virginia has offered to let us stay for a spell."

David remembered Michael's cousin, Thomas Jefferson Little, whom he'd met in the cavalry. "You're leavin'?" he asked, suddenly grief-stricken.

Rena nodded. "Things are gettin' mighty tense here, and we'd like to start our new life up in New York."

He gave her a quizzical look. "New York? Why the hell would y'all want to go there?" David's heart ached as he recalled how he'd suffered there in prison.

"Well, you know how I've always wanted to sing, and I want to audition for the opera in New York City." She enthusiastically grabbed his lower arm. "Ain't it excitin'? Goin' to the big city with all its hustle and bustle!"

"Did you tell Ma?"

She nodded. "I'm gonna miss our home somethin' fierce, but it's for the best. New York City! I jist can't wait!" She let out a giggle.

"That's right fine, sis," he said, forcing a smile. "When we get up to Pennsylvania, we'll come see y'all."

"Dandy!" She kissed him on the cheek before departing.

Watching her walk away, David felt a twinge of jealousy. He wanted to be able to escape as well.

In May, a wedding took place at a little Baptist church in a nearby glen. Before the nuptials commenced, Michael presented David with his cavalry saber.

"I want you to have this," he said as he handed it to his comrade.

David withdrew the weapon from its sheath, and stared down at the shiny metal sword with its distinctive, swirling brass quillon, recalling how he'd wielded one identical to it in battle. "Your ole wrist breaker? Are you sure?" he asked.

"Rena don't want me takin' it up to New York, and I don't want to leave it with my uncle," Michael explained. "I know you'll take good care of it, 'cause it means as much to you as it does to me."

David smiled. "This means more to me than you'll ever know," he said.

"And I want you to have this too." Michael produced an artillery sword with both edges sharpened. "I found this on the battlefield as I was leavin' Gettysburg."

Looking the weapon over, David said, "Thanks Tailor. I'll cherish them always."

The men shook hands, and fondly embraced.

"I expect you'll take good care of my sister."

Michael snickered. "I'll treat her like a queen. Hell, it won't be long afore she'll be queen of the opera, anyways!"

David nodded. He gave the two swords to Anna, and took his place at the front of the church next to Michael. Within moments, the procession started. Josie came down the aisle first, all smiles. Rena appeared, breathtaking in her mother's beige gown. She was escorted down the aisle on Bud's arm. Michael nervously shifted his weight from one foot to the other. David stood beside him, stifling chuckles, because Michael's reaction reminded him too much of his own wedding. "Uncle" Billy Ryan officiated as Justice of the Peace, and his wife provided appropriate hymns on the church's old box piano.

Afterward, the newlyweds spent a few hours celebrating with guests outside the church beneath flowering magnolia trees before riding off in a rented carriage. Their departure was painfully happy for the Summers, who knew their darling daughter and sister was gone, probably never to return. David was sorry to see Michael go as well, because they had grown quite close, but he kept his hope alive, promising Anna they would go to New York once things settled down. With a scoff, she said nothing, since she was seriously starting to doubt him.

In Mobile, Judge "Pig Iron" Kelly from Pennsylvania spoke to a large audience of one hundred whites and two thousand Negroes, the latter being armed with unloaded firearms. He riled the crowd by violently insulting and accusing the whites. A riot ensued, the result of which left one Negro and several white men dead.

Through the summer, Kit came and went as he pleased, and Tucker randomly appeared and disappeared. Their actions provoked Anna's curiosity. She asked David where he thought Kit went, to which he replied Tennessee, tending to business with his brother. Still, Anna was suspicious. She knew Kit had signed away his half of the farm to his brother, so why would he keep going up there? David had no answer.

She continued corresponding with her sisters and Stephen. He wrote to tell her that, if she desired it, he would pursue a transfer to Alabama, but she avoided responding to his request. Maggie wrote that she was still being courted by Kenton Price, but only on her terms, and only on Sundays. Abigail, at age twelve, was expanding her clairvoyant abilities, performing readings to the neighbors without her aunt and uncle's knowledge. Maggie thought it amusing, but was skeptical as to her authenticity. In a later letter, however, she swore by her younger sister's talent, for she had seen their father in a séance. The notion struck Anna as strange, and she was glad she wasn't present for the ceremony. What would her father think if he knew she was living in the south with a baby and a husband who had fought against his brethren? The idea made her shiver.

On August 12, President Johnson sparked a move to impeach Secretary of War Edwin M. Stanton, defying Congress by suspending him. David was happy about the removal of Stanton, whom he disliked immensely, especially while he'd suffered at Elmira. For the president, however, he sympathized. He knew if the Radicals had their way, Johnson would be gone by year's end.

One morning, David ran across Percy on his way from the mercantile. Exuberant to see him after so long, he sprang from Renegade's back and enthusiastically shook the man's hand.

"Percy! Good to see you again!" he said with a smile.

"You too, Missa David. How's da family?"

"Jist fine. Dorie's 'bout seventeen months now. And your young'uns?"

"Mighty fine, indeed. My, my. How time flies." He flashed a big smile at the young man.

David noticed a painted stick Percy was holding. "What's that for?" he asked.

"Dis here's a striped stick I got from a nice feller by da name of Mr. Whittaker. If I place it on a white man's land, I git da land fo' myself. He even give me dis here deed." He pulled a folded piece of paper from his shirt pocket and handed it to David.

As he skimmed over the words, he couldn't believe what he was reading, and made a point not to read it aloud:

Know all men by these presents, that a naught is a naught, and a figure is a figure; all for the white man, and none for the nigger. And whereas Moses lifted up the serpent in the wilderness, so also have I lifted this damned old nigger out of four dollars and six bits. Amen. Selah!

He looked up at the man, who was still smiling. "Percy, this ain't a deed."

"Why, sho it is, Missa David. Says right here."

David bit his lip. Apparently, Percy hadn't been very successful at teaching himself how to read. He wanted to tell his friend he'd been taken, but decided to leave it for another day. Instead, he offered his congratulations. Quickly changing the subject, he asked, "Have you and Isabelle enough to eat?"

"I reckon we do," Percy responded. "But we can always use mo'. Dose two scamps are eatin' mo' every day!"

David laughed. "In a few months, I'll be butcherin', and we'll have some hams y'all are welcome to. I'll bring two of them by when they're ready."

"Much obliged, Missa David!" Percy beamed.

David nodded with a grin, happy he could help his neighbors in need.

With autumn, so too, came the crops. At long last, after years of suffering, the bounty was fair. Apples were harvested by the bushel, as were corn, peas, beans, wheat, oats, potatoes, barley, and sorghum. The family enjoyed wild raspberries and collected black walnuts. While David toiled in the fields, the women made preserves, canning their produce for winter.

Because of Anna's ingenuity selling pies, they had enough money to purchase much needed clothing, hardware, and farm machinery. Without telling David, she relinquished some of the earnings she'd been saving to do so, for her conscience wouldn't allow otherwise. As much as she dreamed of going home for Christmas, she knew it wouldn't be a reality.

Others were struggling, due to the fact that taxes were quadrupled to pay for railroad bonds and school costs. Many were bitter, because the schools were teaching their ex-slaves. The cotton tax, however, was restored to 2 ½ cents, or $12.50, a bale. Plantation owners believed their overpaid taxes would be reimbursed. David was glad Anna had dropped the notion about teaching Negro children. She was too busy with Dorie, which to him, was a blessing, and a battle he wouldn't have to fight.

In November, freedmen were entitled to vote for the very first time. It reignited hostilities, and ex-Confederates had a heyday with the Negroes, playing on their superstitions by becoming more threatening and outrageous. The Knights of Peace were no exception. They gave the Negroes a "gentle reminder" by wrapping bedsheets around themselves and perching atop tombstones in graveyards they knew freedmen would have to pass by on their way to meet with Union League officials. The officials emphasized that the blacks affiliate themselves as Republicans, and assisted them in registering to vote. The freedmen had no idea who was committing outrages against them. They were harassed when they attended Loyal League meetings, and the poor souls were nearly scared to death in the dark of night. One Knight would sit on the shoulders of another, both covered with a sheet, and follow the Negroes down the road, horrifying them with their enormous height, all the while moaning and rattling chains. They told their frightened victims that Hell had frozen over to permit the passage of their spirits to return to earth. They terrorized with silent parades, and drilled in town and country as visual reminders to all. However, even with all the intimidation, and against all odds, the Negro men voted.

David thought it was necessary to instill fear into the freedmen, even though he felt reprehensible for it. After a while, he decided not to participate, for in his heart, he knew it was wrong. Kit coerced him into going on night rides, however, calling him a traitor and a coward if he didn't, which infuriated him. He mentioned to Anna how Kit irritated him to the boiling point, and she responded by reading him a scripture.

"Do not grumble, brethren, against one another, that you may not be judged; behold, the Judge is standing at the doors."

He scowled at her. The message didn't ease his anger. It only fueled it.

Following the elections, Governor Patton appointed John H. Rapier, Sr. as notary public, and James T. Rapier as political appointee. They were the first colored men to take office in the state of Alabama. After expressing his disgust about "niggers gettin' elected," Kit departed for the holidays. David, Anna, and Josie breathed a sigh of relief when he was gone.

On Christmas Eve morning, Caroline received a letter from her younger brother in Tuscaloosa, notifying her that his wife of twenty years had passed away. He was struggling to keep his plantation, but all seemed bleak, as his ex-slaves refused to stay on. His four children were motherless, and he conveyed in his letter that he was fighting to keep up their spirits. Caroline wrote back, and had David deliver the letter to the post, but she wouldn't mention what she'd written.

After Christmas, General Pope was replaced by General Meade. To David, he was no improvement. They were still both Yankee generals, imposing their hostile beliefs upon the ragged South.

On February 13, William Hugh Smith became Alabama's first Republican governor. President Johnson escaped impeachment, only to be impeached again in March.

The men in white sheets who roamed the countryside grew increasingly agitated, and their attacks were more frequent. Negroes who aired their opinions about equality attracted the Knight's attention. Upon Kit's return, the Knights of Peace met for the first time under the umbrella of the secret order known as the Ku Klux Klan. The Klan had reorganized itself to include all dens in North Alabama, and titles were given to their chosen officers, names David thought were ridiculous, but humorous, nevertheless. The Grand Wizard reigned supreme. Below him, the Grand Dragon, Grand Titan, Grand Cyclops, and Grand Giant reigned down the line, the smallest area being a county. Each leader had several staff officers, known as Genii, Hydras, Furies, Goblins, and Night Hawks. There was also a Grand Turk and his legion of Ghouls.

Over a short amount of time, the Klan expanded their scope of attack to include lazy men, thieves, and drunkards, regardless of color. Other bands in the area wreaked havoc on the freedmen's schools, setting them on fire and chasing out teachers. They set churches ablaze where they knew Union League meetings were held. If they heard of a black man sleeping with a white woman, they lynched him, and if a black woman slept with a white man, they beat her. The Klan posted warnings to anyone they regarded offensive, intentionally disguising their handwriting and misspelling words. David learned that Callie's husband had received such a letter, because he had also become a target. The man showed him his letter of threat one day at the mercantile.

Mr. Mumford,

You had better leave. You are a thief and you know it. If you don't leave in ten days, we will cut your throte. We aint after the negroes; but we intend for you damn carpet bag men to go back to your homes. You are steeling everything you can find. We mean what we say. Get away! We aint no cu-cluxes but if you don't go we will make you.

Ambrose was visibly shaken, and decided to leave the area, at least for the time being, while Callie remained behind.

Orders of the Klan were printed in local newspapers, one of which read:

KKK

Hell-a-Bulloo Hole – Den of Skulls.
Bloody Bones, Headquarters of the
Great Ku Klux Klan, No. 1000
Windy Month – New Moon.
Cloudy Night – Thirteenth Hour.

General Orders No. 2
Clansmen – meet at the Trysting Spot when Orion kisses the Zenith. The wolf is on his walk – the serpent coils to strike. The second hobgoblin will be there, a mighty Ghost of valor. His eyes of fire, his voice of thunder! Clean the streets – clean the serpents' dens. Meet at once – the den of Snakes – the Giant's jungles – the hole of Hell!

Be ready! Crawl slowly! Strike hard!
Fire around the pot!
Action! Action!! Action!!!
The Great High Priest Cyclops! C.J.F.Y.
The fifth Ghost sounds his trumpet!
The mighty Genii wants two black wethers!
Make them, make them, make them! Presto!
By order of the Great
BLUFUSTIN,
G.S. K.K.K.
A true copy,
Peterloo.
P.S.   K.K.K.

The editor of the *Tuscaloosa Independent Monitor* summed it up this way: "The very night of the day on which said notices made their appearance, three notably offensive negro men were dragged out of their beds, escorted to the old boneyard and thrashed in the regular ante-bellum style, until their unnatural nigger pride had a tumble, and humblences to the white man reigned supreme."

As Kit and David rode alongside each other on horseback to a Klan meeting one evening in mid-March, Kit said, "I wonder why that ma of yours hasn't re-wed."

David glared at him in shock, causing Kit to chuckle at his horrified expression. "Why?" he asked, dumbfounded.

"Same reason everybody gits married."

David gritted his teeth. The thought of this tyrant marrying his mother disgusted him to his core. "Reckon you haven't heard."

"Heard what?" Kit sneered at him, making David wish he could punch him in the face.

"Women have the right to keep their own land now, whether they're widowed, divorced, or single, and if they marry, the husband doesn't git their land."

Kit's smile vanished. "When did this come about?"

"Last fall, while you were up in Tennessee."

"Well, why the hell didn't somebody tell me?"

He spat, and David could see his face turn red. Amused with Kit's discomfort, he hoped the news would be enough to send him packing.

After a few minutes, Kit started singing.

"Pretty Polly, Pretty Polly, would you take me unkind,
Let me set beside you and tell you my mind.
Well my mind is to marry and never to part,
The first time I saw you it wounded my heart.
Oh Polly, Pretty Polly, come go along with me.
Before we get married some pleasures to see.
He led her over mountains and valleys so deep.
Pretty Polly mistrusted and then began to weep.
Oh Willie, Oh Willie, I'm afraid of your ways,
The way you've been ramblin' you'll lead me astray.
Oh Polly, Pretty Polly, your guess is about right.
I dug on your grave the biggest part of last night.
Oh she knelt down before him a-pleadin' for her life,
Let me be a single girl if I can't be your wife.

Oh Polly, Pretty Polly that never can be,
Your past recitation's been trouble to me.
Oh went down to the jailhouse and what did he say,
I've killed Pretty Polly and tryin' to get away."

David rode in silence, contemplating the message. Was Kit threatening to kill his mother if he didn't get his way? Was Caroline in real danger? His heart ignited with fury, but he kept silent.

The following morning, he delivered two hams to Percy as promised. When he returned home, he found Anna in the front room, waiting for his mother. She was engaged in lively discussion with Josie.

"I hope he does get impeached," Anna proclaimed, referring to President Johnson as she bounced two-year-old Dorie on her knee. "He's nothing but a bigot. He thinks coloreds should return to their plantations with no land of their own, and no homes, and that they should accept subordination to the whites."

"Don't git so riled, darlin'," David requested.

She rose to her feet, set Dorie down, and paced the floor. "What is taking your mother so long?"

"I'll go fetch her," offered Josie. She rolled her eyes at David on the way out. He knew what it meant: Anna was on her Yankee bandwagon again.

"Anna, honey, calm down."

"No, David, I won't calm down. I've had it with this place! I want to go home!" She folded her arms across her chest and stamped her foot down for emphasis.

He sighed. "We've had this discussion."

She whirled on him. "And every time, you say we'll go when things are better. They're better now, aren't they?"

"Well ... yeah. But I'm still needed here."

He knew that, if he left, Caroline and Josie would be unprotected from whatever Kit had in store for them. He hadn't gotten a chance to tell Anna about the previous evening, and didn't dare bring it up at the risk of being overheard.

"David Summers, I hate you!"

She picked up Dorie and stormed out, leaving him stunned. She had never spoken such harsh words to him before. The revelation hit him. He hadn't fulfilled his promise to her. Two and a half years later, they were still in Alabama. Although it was her wifely duty to stay by his side, he wanted more than anything to make her happy, but he knew she was slipping away from him. Somehow, he had to make things right between them again. She was his foundation.

That evening, he tried to explain the circumstances to her, but his plea fell on deaf ears. Anna was tired of it all, and rightfully so. Suddenly, a knock came at the cottage door. David answered to see Kit standing on the other side.

"Git your horse," he commanded before tramping off.

David glanced at Anna over his shoulder. She had turned her back to him.

"I'm goin' out patrollin'," he said, but got no response.

She hadn't asked what he was up to late at night, and he didn't tell. He walked across the room, kissed Dorie on the forehead, went outside, and retrieved Renegade.

"There's a commotion down a ways," Kit growled.

He rode off at a gallop. David prompted his stallion after him.

The dark night was illuminated by a full moon rising, which glowed with enough brightness to cast eerie shadows across the road. Kit's horse cantered ahead, but Renegade easily caught up to him. They rode along familiar back roads, over hills and through valleys, and past the Kimball's farmstead. Kit pulled back on his draft horse. He dismounted, retrieved a white sheet from his saddlebag, instructed David to cover his horse, then ordered him to disguise himself as well. Kit covered his head with a white mask, and placed a cardboard hat upon his head. He kicked his horse, screaming, "Hya!" as he bolted away. Renegade thundered after him. They rounded a bend, crossed a ravine, and started down a path. Suddenly, David realized their direction, and just as it dawned on him, he saw flames licking up from beyond the dark trees.

"What the hell!" he shrieked.

He followed Kit into the clearing. Klansmen surrounded the little shanty, which was billowing with smoke and fire. A body hung from the end of a rope, swaying slightly from a tall tree's branch. The fire threw flickering, demonic shadows over the entire scene. Two Klansmen emerged from the cabin, dragging Isabelle out with them.

"No!" she screamed, so horribly that David's heart leaped from the shrill sound and the sight of her. "No!" She fell to the ground.

David leaned forward, preparing to jump off his horse, but Kit held him back with the barrel of his shotgun. The masked men dragged her off to the barn. Three other members ran around the buildings, setting more fires as they hollered directions at each other.

"What is this?" David half-whispered.

Kit overheard. "This here's what happens when you git caught stealin'."

"What?" he glared at the man through his cutout eye holes.

"He was caught red-handed with two stolen hams."

David stared at him in shock. "Dear God," he groaned. He looked back up at the tree, at Percy's lifeless body dangling from the rope. "I gave those to him."

Kit scoffed. "Well, you should've told me so," he flippantly stated.

Suddenly, David remembered. "There's two young'uns in there!" He quickly dismounted, but a familiar click caught his attention. He turned to see Kit holding his shotgun on him.

"If you go in there, I'll shoot you in the back," he growled. "And I'll find pleasure in doin' it."

David stood frozen for a moment, but complied. He slowly remounted. He heard a child cry, and turned to see Tommy standing behind some bushes with his brother, Lincoln. "Thank God," he whispered to himself.

The Klansmen who had dragged Isabelle off reappeared. "Reckon we took care of that nigger wench right good!" one said.

"Oh, wait," said the other, "here she comes back for more!"

The men burst into sickening laughter. Isabelle stumbled into the gathering, holding her dress where it had been torn at the sleeve. Tears of torment streamed down her face. Her expression distressed David so badly that he considered gallantly grabbing her and galloping away, but he knew Kit would gladly uphold his promise.

"How could you!" she screamed. "How could you do dis to me? To my Percy!" She looked around at the men, who had fallen silent.

"Mama!" Tommy screeched.

He ran out from his hiding place, leading his little brother by the hand, which spooked the horses. As he and Lincoln were embraced by their mother, Kit's gelding backed into Renegade, who reared and whinnied. He bolted, and his sheet caught on the underbrush, tearing it off to reveal his recognizable coat.

Isabelle immediately saw. She rushed over, her dress falling from her shoulder, and caught Renegade by the bridle.

"You!" she screamed.

Renegade shied at the sound of her voice, pulling away from her grasp.

"How could you?" she cried. Her anguish overtook her; she collapsed to the ground in a heap, keening.

The men mounted, turned their horses, and rode away from their destruction. Kit motioned for David to follow. Unavoidably, he glanced back. Isabelle was lying on the ground, wailing, while Percy's body swung above her.

As they rode home, he fought to keep his outrage at bay. Finally, he said, "You knew he was a family friend."

"I don't give a damn if he was the King of England," Kit quipped. "He was fixin' to cause trouble, and now we've sent a message out to the entire county." He looked over to see David glaring hatefully at him in the moonlight. "If it's an apology you want, don't hold your breath." He kicked his workhorse and trotted ahead.

Once David arrived home, he led Renegade into the barn, unsaddled and curried him, and wondered how his mother would take the news. Jake's ma and pa would likely be crushed too. The whole episode left his head spinning. He went down to the still and swigged down several cups of ruckus juice, staring up at the clouds as they floated into bizarre shapes before the full moon. He imagined seeing a skull, with the moon shining in one eye socket. The image became a dog, a hellhound he reckoned, which seemed to turn and look straight down at him with one shining, creepy eye. It startled him, sending a cold shiver up his spine. He meandered back to the cottage in the dark. After he'd crawled into bed, his mind started to play back the horrible event. All of a sudden, he remembered the dream he'd had after the war, on the train home as he and Anna rode into Richmond. It had been a premonition, and he'd ignored it. He prayed silently for God to forgive him. If only he'd paid attention to the dream, Percy might still be alive.

Three days later, after returning from church, David sat in the dining room with his family and Kit as they gathered for dinner. He said very little, avoiding eye contact with Kit as much as possible.

Anna noticed his sour mood, and asked, "David, you're not very talkative. Are you feeling all right?"

He smiled, nodded, and took her hand under the table.

"I'm jist thankful we're all here together on this glorious day, that we're all healthful and happy," Caroline chirped.

As she passed bowls of food around, a loud pounding came at the door.

"I'll git that." Kit got up, walked through the front room to the door, and opened it.

In burst Isabelle. David looked up to see her, and stood as she stomped across the room to him. She reached out and ruthlessly struck him across the face. He stumbled back in surprise, putting his hand to his cheek.

"What is goin' on here?" Caroline exclaimed as she stood and started toward Isabelle.

David stopped her. "Ma, it's all right. I had it comin'."

Kit walked into the dining room as Isabelle glared spitefully at David. "I knowd it was you," she spewed venomously. "You was part of it! That vile horse of yours was there!"

"What's she talkin' about?" asked Josie, rising to her feet.

"Beggin' your pardon, Missus," Isabelle said to Caroline, suddenly becoming subservient. "My Percy was hung up on Thursday last, and your son here had somethin' to do with it."

She pointed an accusing finger at David, whose eyes had turned from hazel to dark brown.

"We heard about your loss, Miss Isabelle," Caroline said, trying to comfort her. "But what makes you think David had anything to do with it?"

"Because I seen him. He was dressed up like one o' dem Ku Kluxes, and he was on dat painted horse o' his." She stared at him, her large brown eyes so intense that he felt himself cower under her penetrating gaze.

"Ma, it ain't what you think …"

Anna let out a whimper. "David," she half-whispered mournfully. Her pained expression cut into his heart like a knife. "What did you do?"

He glanced at Kit, who shook his head at him scornfully. He knew if he revealed "the secret," all the Klan would be after him, and he didn't want to be the next one doing a dance at the end of a rope.

"Don't you deny it, Missa David! You be lyin' to the Lord if you do!"

Isabelle grasped hold of his arm, so tightly that the pain made him wince.

"I jist wanta know how you could let it happen."

He said nothing, but looked at Kit. Isabelle's expression changed from pain to anger. She released him.

"Oh. It's as I thought."

She spun around and started toward Kit, but the man withdrew his sidearm and pointed it at her.

"I reckon it's time you left now, missy," he growled like a rabid dog. "You've disrupted our dinner long enough."

Isabelle stopped, looked around at their faces, expelled a sobbing whimper, and ran out the door. Kit sauntered across the room and closed it behind her.

"Crazy as a loon," he retorted, shaking his head. As he reentered the dining room, he shot a threatening glance at David.

Anna rose from her seat, stunned. She had watched the entire incident play out in front of her, and comprehended what her husband was capable of. She picked Dorie up and started for the door.

"Anna, where are you goin'?" he asked, afraid to hear the answer.

She turned. Her countenance expressed her repulsion. "David ... how could you?" A tear trickled down her cheek. She hugged Dorie, threw a scowl at Kit, and walked outside.

The look on her face cut into David's heart, causing more damage than any pain Isabelle could inflict, although he felt she was entitled to do just that.

"Anna!"

He started after her, but Kit stepped in his path.

"Let her dwell on it a spell," he said. He took his place at the table, motioning for Caroline and Josie to do the same.

David had lost his appetite. "Ma, may I please be excused," he muttered.

She nodded in response, her eyes filled with tears.

He strode to the door and stepped out into the breezeway. The spring sun shone upon his face, making it burn, so he rubbed his hand on the cheek Isabelle had slapped. He ambled to the barn, retrieved a bridle, hurried to the pasture, put his thumb and forefinger in his mouth, and shrilly whistled. Renegade responded by trotting up to him, expecting his usual treat. David threw himself onto the animal's back and started down the lane. He rode for nearly an hour until he felt he was far enough away, slid off, and tied Renegade to a tree, allowing him to graze. Sitting beside him in the new spring grass, he was afraid to go back home. *This'll surely be the straw that broke the camel's back*, he thought. *Anna won't have me now, not after all this.*

He pulled a blade of grass out by the root and stuck it in his mouth. Soon, he became drowsy and reclined back onto the cool grass. Things had gotten out of control, that much was certain. He had to find a way to get rid of Kit once and for all. That rascal was the source of all his troubles. Still, he had gone along with it, and because he'd been a coward in the worst way by allowing it to happen, his wife, Isabelle, and nearly everyone else hated him. He blamed himself for not communicating with Kit, for not standing up to him, and he wanted to leave so badly it hurt, but there was no way out. Loathing himself, consumed with hatred and resentment, he sighed, surrendering himself to his predicament. His eyelids grew heavy, and he dozed off into a fitful slumber.

"The origin of Ku Klux Klan is in the galling despotism that broods like a nightmare over these southern states, - a fungus growth of military tyranny superinduced by the fostering of Loyal Leagues, the abrogation of our civil laws, the habitual violation of our national constitution, and a persistent prostitution of all government, all resources, and all powers, to degrade the white man by the establishment of negro supremacy."

- *Tuscaloosa Independent Monitor*, April 14, 1868

Chapter Nine

David awoke to discover twilight was ascending. He quickly sat up, and to his relief, saw Renegade standing patiently beside him. Slowly, he rose to his feet and mounted his horse. Once he reached home, he found Anna in the cottage. She looked as if she'd been crying all afternoon.

"Anna," he said softly as he entered.

"We need to talk."

She walked from the table to the bed and sat down. He sat beside her.

"Please tell me this wasn't your fault," she said.

He proceeded to tell her the course of events: how he'd promised Percy two hams, had delivered them to Percy that morning, and how Kit had blamed Percy for thievery and had ordered his murder. He claimed innocence, although he knew he was as culpable as the rest, and told her if she breathed a word of his involvement with the Klan, he could be hung for treason. When he'd finished spilling his heart out, he sighed heavily, and reached for her hand. She allowed him to take it.

"Never in my wildest dreams would I have imagined this happening," she said, slightly shaking her head. She looked over at him. "What are we going to do?"

He shrugged. "I have to find a way to git rid of Kit. I know that, if I leave now, he'll jist come back once I'm gone, and who knows what he might do to git what he wants." He gently squeezed her hand. "I'm sorry, darlin', so very sorry."

Dorie let out a squeal, which caused them both to chuckle.

"We'll get through this together," she replied, astonishing him. Tenderly, she kissed him on the cheek Isabelle had slapped.

The following afternoon, a funeral was held for Percy Kimball. Although David wanted more than anything to attend, he felt unwelcome, and stayed behind as his wife, mother, and sisters attended. He spent the afternoon enjoying his daughter, which he rarely had the opportunity to do, and thought constantly about Isabelle and her two boys. If only there was some way to turn back time, he would gladly do it so as to warn Percy. Damn Kit! He wanted to shoot him stone cold, but his mother would likely disown him. As Dorie napped in the new trundle bed he'd made for her, he lay sprawled across the big bed, dreaming up ways to eradicate Kit. All of his ideas, however, ended the same, with him being tried, convicted, and strung up for murder. He even invented ways to kill Kit off by making it look accidental, but his eyes were drawn to the Bible on the nightstand, and his guilt simmered up. Several hours later, his family returned from the sad ceremony, and described the event to him.

"What's to become of poor Isabelle?" he asked his mother as the family gathered for supper.

"She'll be stayin' with the Kimball's for now. But those folks don't have the money to support her and her young'uns." Caroline shook her head in remorseful disgust. "It's a sad state of affairs, I do declare."

David and Anna looked at each other, their sorrow expressed in each other's eyes. When they were alone in the cottage, she requested that he cease making night rides, but he refused.

"I can't make that promise," he stated simply.

"Even after everything that's happened?" She stared at him in disbelief.

"It's my duty to protect the community. What happened to Percy was wrong, but it don't mean it'll happen again."

He went out to the still, leaving Anna with her resentment and antipathy.

Early the next morning, she walked outside and down the slope to see Kit loading up his wagon. She approached him.

"Where are you going?" she asked, forcing a genial smile.

"On up to Tennessee," he replied wryly. "I'll be back around in a month or so."

Anna waited for him to leave, then jumped on Renegade's back and ran him to the army post. Inside, she found Ad, whereby she requested that he follow Kit, enlisting him as her personal spy. Ad consented, happy to help a damsel in distress. He went outside, loaded up his pack mule, tied the mule to his saddle horse, and mounted.

"I'll find out for you, Miss Anna," he said with a grin as he tipped his stovepipe hat. "I do relish a good chase!"

She stood watching him ride off down the road, wondering what he might discover. If her suspicions were correct, Kit was up to no good, and this time, she would catch him at his own game.

Over the course of the next week, the family celebrated Dorie's second birthday on David's twenty-third. Their birthdays were exactly one week apart, and it was obvious to all that they were cut from the same cloth. Dorie mimicked her father at every opportunity, for she obviously adored him.

As April progressed, David struggled to keep up with his increasing responsibilities. The sow gave birth to a litter of ten healthy piglets, which he had to oversee, the fields had to be dug, and seeds needed to be prepared for planting. He spent many lonely afternoons in the barn, sifting through seeds and readying himself for the upcoming spring. He continually fantasized of faraway places, and wished for a better life. Somehow, someday, he would have enough money to take Anna to places she'd always hoped to see. He'd also make sure Dorie had the opportunity to experience wonders he never could, and that she would grow up happy and well provided for. He began to wonder if his dreams would ever come true.

To break up the monotony, he rode to the mercantile, just as his neighbors did, to discuss current affairs. He heard about the release of Clement C. Clay, a former Alabama senator who was implicated in Lincoln's assassination as a co-conspirator. After the war, Clay went to Canada, where he remained for more than a year, devising a plan for negotiated peace. When that strategy failed, he returned home and turned himself in. Because no arrest was made, the $10,000 reward was never paid. After serving a year in prison without a trial, Clay was released.

David learned of the rumor that a man by the name of McCoy had mysteriously appeared in Huntsville, but the locals believed him to really be "Bloody" Bill Quantrill, the notorious Confederate guerilla who had murdered Union soldiers in cold blood with the help of Frank and Jesse James in Missouri. Quantrill had supposedly been murdered in 1864, but had he really? The citizens claimed they'd seen Quantrill's tattoo of an Indian maiden on one arm, and said that the first joint of his little finger was missing. McCoy was a circuit rider for the Methodist church, traveling to country churches to minister. The rumor escalated when McCoy, after much persuasion, displayed his sharp shooting abilities at a local Methodist church picnic. The mystery intrigued David immensely, but he understood. If this man really was Quantrill, it only seemed reasonable that he would become a minister in repentance for the sins he'd committed. He wondered if becoming a man of the cloth would help him shed some of his wrongdoings as well, but shook off the notion. He would go west and strike it rich, instead.

The following week, Anna rode to the outpost to deliver apple fritters she'd fried that morning. Ad was there, waiting for her. With a smirk on his weathered face, he described what he'd discovered, to which she squealed in response with elation. She hugged him, apologized for her outward behavior, and left him smiling as she hurried home to tell David. Once he'd heard, his eyes grew wide with surprise.

"Do you reckon we should tell Ma?" he asked, awestruck.

Anna shook her head. "No. I think we should reveal it when the time is right, when we can embarrass Kit into leaving."

With that, David agreed.

Several rainy weeks went by, and toward the end of April, David grew anxious from being confined, so he ventured out in the drizzle. He decided to make a visit to the Kimball's, hoping that, by some fluke, Isabelle would hear him out and forgive him. He stepped down from Renegade, tied him, climbed onto the veranda, and tapped on the door. Jake's sister answered.

"Why, Miss Jenny!" he exclaimed. "I didn't expect to see you here!"

"Hello, my David," she purred with a smile. "Please do come in and git out of the rain!"

He returned the smile, removed his slouch hat, and stepped inside. To his amazement, the house looked clean and bright. Even the chandelier above the dining room table sparkled. "You've been busy," he remarked.

"Ma and I decided the ole place needed a good sprucin' up."

"Why, it looks like a palace in here! In fact, I'm envious. Our li'l ole 'stead would never measure up."

She nudged him on the arm. "Don't despair, darlin'. You have a very nice home."

He shrugged with a grin.

"What brings you by?"

David expelled an uncomfortable sigh. "Well, I was hopin' to have a word with Miss Isabelle. Is she here?"

Jenny's smile vanished. Her big brown eyes grew even larger. "No, sir, she ain't."

He stood by, waiting for her to elaborate.

"She's gone away."

David frowned. "What do you mean?" he glanced around the parlor for a sign of Lincoln or Tommy, but found none. "Where are your folks?"

"They're upstairs. Do you want me to fetch them?" she started away, but he stopped her.

"No, no. Don't disturb them." He brushed his damp, long brown hair away from his face. "Where's she off to?"

"She couldn't stand the thought of stayin' here when we can't afford her, so she went on down to Cullman County to find work as a field hand."

He scowled. "She don't have experience workin' in the field."

Jenny forlornly shook her head. "I know, but she insisted. Said it was her duty to support her own young'uns, and off she went."

"Do you know where in Cullman County?"

"Sure do." She walked into the dining room, scribbled on a piece of paper, and handed it to him. "It's about half a day's ride from here."

David glanced down to see the map she'd drawn. "Thank you, kindly, Miss Jenny. I'm much obliged." He slightly smiled, took her hand, and kissed the back of it. "It's always an honor seein' you."

"Oh, David, you make me blush!" She giggled. "Reckon that rascally brother of mine taught you a few things."

"Like how to woo the ladies?" he asked. "I could never compare to him!"

They laughed together, and it felt good. It was the first time they'd shared laughter since Jake's death.

"Well, I'd best be on my way," David said. Placing his hat upon his head, he asked, "Where's Nate?"

"Up in Huntsville. He found a job workin' on the railroad line, and comes home every weekend. We ain't thrilled about the situation, but we're hopin' it's only temporary."

David nodded compassionately. "At least he's found work, and that's a start."

She smiled. Reaching around him, she gave him a hug. "Tell your kinfolk I said hello."

"Yes'm, Miss Jenny, I will indeed." He tipped his hat, climbed onto his steed, and rode out toward home.

"Try to stay dry!" he heard her holler after him.

He clucked to Renegade, and the horse broke into a trot, kicking up clumps of mud behind him.

Two more weeks of soggy, dreary weather ensued. Dorie grew bored and restless with her surroundings, so David entertained her by holding her while sitting atop his stallion inside the musty barn. Renegade glanced back at them curiously, as if wondering why they didn't go anywhere. The toddler loved holding the reins. She exclaimed "Giddyap!" and giggled every time. David cherished her dearly, and fondly embraced his time with her, knowing her childhood would be fleeting.

Late one evening, on the 30th of April, Kit returned. He behaved as cunningly as ever, repulsing David to the point where he wanted to do away with him on the spot. But Anna insisted, so he waited for the "perfect time," as she called it, to expose him. Meanwhile, Caroline embraced Kit with open arms, referring to him as her "good Christian friend." David could only shake his head in disbelief. If only she knew.

Two weeks later, after discussing his plans with Anna, he departed for Cullman County. The rains had stopped the previous week, and the 14th of May, a Thursday, was sunny and warm. He was glad to have chosen such a lovely day to travel. The air was heavy with the fragrance of blooming oak leaf hydrangeas, and birds twittered above as they flitted in the trees draping over the road. Upon Jenny's directions, he rode for several hours until he found the plantation he was searching for. He dismounted, gazing up at the enormous, white three-story antebellum house, which was in disrepair. The white portico, even with its peeling paint, complete with carved embellishments on its columns, and ironworks adorning its corners, exuded elegance. He imagined many genteel parties taking place there, and considered walking up to peer inside the front paned windows, but decided against it, lest he be discovered. He led Renegade around the weathered building, where he saw two men standing near a flowering cotton field. Farther off, he distinguished people out among the young plants.

The men gaped at him as he approached.

"Sir?" one asked. "What can we do for you?"

"I'm lookin' for someone," he stated. "She's new here. Her name's Isabelle Kimball."

One of the men, who was paunchy and middle-aged, slid his hat off his head and wiped his brow with the back of his hand. "You know of anyone by that name, Hubert?"

"Can't say as I do," the younger man with the bull-whip said. He grinned, displaying yellowed teeth, evidence that he indulged frequently in tobacco.

David frowned. "I rode over three hours to git here." He hesitated, then slowly removed a few silver coins from his trouser pocket. "Sure you don't know of her?"

The younger man held out his hand, to which David deposited the coins.

"She's down yonder," Hubert said. He motioned in the general direction.

"Thanks, sir." David led his horse out several yards to the field, tied him to a nearby shrub, and started down a row. The midday sun was hotter than he realized: he removed his slouch hat and kept on walking. After fifteen minutes, he reached the group of field hands. He sauntered over to an elderly Negro who was working the light brown soil with a hoe.

"Pardon me, sir?"

The man looked up at him and slowly straightened, putting his hand to his lower lumbar.

"I'm lookin' for a young lady, name of Isabelle Kimball. Would you know where I might find her?"

The man glared at David as though he was speaking a foreign language, but then said, "Why, yes. Yes, I do. She's right ober dare."

"Much obliged." David started across the field, and finally saw her. He waited until he was close before he called, "Miss Isabelle!"

She turned to see his approach. "Oh, no. I ain't got nothin' say to you, Missa David. You keep away, you here? Keep away!"

"Miss Isabelle, please. Here me out."

She thrust her hands to her hips and glared at him as he drew closer.

Once he reached her, he said, "I came here so you could know the truth."

Circles under her eyes bore evidence to the trauma she'd recently experienced. "Oh, I know da truth!" she snarled. "Truth is, you can't stand up to dat Kit Lawrence. You let him walk all ober you!"

He grunted. "I didn't know till I got to your place what happened to Percy, and then it was too late. Miss Isabelle, you've got to believe me."

Slowly, she eased her defiant stance and dropped her arms. "It don't matter now. Percy's gone, and I got to keep on."

David stared at her, not knowing what to say. It was obvious he wasn't going to receive forgiveness. "Where are your youn'uns?"

Isabelle's expression changed from anger to sheer sadness. "Dey took 'em away."

"What?"

"You heard me. Dey took my two boys away. Chances are, I likely won't see dem again."

"They can't do that!"

Isabelle laughed, finding humor in his naivety. "Dey can do whatever dey please, Missa David. For all I know, dey's been sent off to da orphan's asylum. It ain't no different than when we was slaves." She withdrew a wrinkled piece of paper from her dress pocket. "Here's my contract. I keep it on me always."

She handed the paper to David, whereby he read:

> *State of Alabama, Cullman County April 20, 1868. This shows that Isabelle Kimball (freedman) for herself and children, namely Tommy and Lincoln, agrees to do all reasonable work or service required of them on, or for the farm, or interest, or benefit of Captain Joseph Miles and family during this year respectively obeying his or his agent's orders and not to leave the premises without permit; for and in consideration of two hundred and sixty dollars to be paid by C.J. Miles at the end of said term of service, to said Joseph Miles, and eight dollars per month for Tommy. And quarters, and food, and cotton, and cards, wheels, loom, and leather to be furnished for their two suits of clothes and shoes during this year: And their*

Doctors bill, which with all other things furnished them not afore mentioned is to be deducted from their pay. All lost time for sickness or otherwise to be deducted from their pay. Therefrom also shall be deducted all burial expense.

"Dey says weze free, but we ain't really, 'cause of da black codes," Isabelle was saying. "We have to sign five-year contracts, an' can't leave without permission, 'cause if we do, we git arrested an' sent back. The goods they sell out of da plantation commissary are so high priced that we all be in debt forever."

David looked at her, frowning.

"You know what they call us, Missa David? Peons. So's dey can pee on us."

"Miss Isabelle, you know how sorry I am. Is there anything I can do?"

Her continence softened. "Dere is one thing."

"Anything. Jist name it."

"Percy had a bank account in Huntsville. See if you can git me dat money."

"Yes. I surely will."

She turned to walk away, but pivoted suddenly. "Oh, an' one mo' thing."

"Ma'am?"

"I don't know if it's possible, but see if you can find my boys. Make sure dey's all right."

David nodded.

Isabelle turned and walked off.

He returned to his stallion, untied him, and led him to where the two men were still standing. "Y'all know where I might find Miss Isabelle's young'uns?" he asked earnestly.

Hubert grinned. "Now what do you want with two li'l nigger babies?"

"I made a promise that I'd make sure they're all right. If you please, I'd like to know where to locate them." David clenched his jaw and stared hard at the young man, who looked away.

215

"They're at the Primrose Plantation, ten miles southwest of here." Hubert proceeded to tell him the way.

"Much obliged," he responded, tipping his hat. He mounted Renegade.

"Good luck findin' them, though," the older man said. "They could be long gone by now."

David glowered and turned his steed. A tremendous taste of disgust welled up in his throat, so he spat it out. The overseers chortled.

As he rode away, he heard the large man say, "Damned nigger lover!"

The two men chuckled at his expense. David kicked his horse, breaking into a gallop. The large man's accusation, unbeknownst to him, could have been accurate. Bitter memories welled up, compelling David to recall how, not long after Jake died, his comrades had taken him to a brothel, where he'd possibly lost his virginity to a woman of ill repute. He couldn't remember exactly what had happened, since his fellow troopers had liquored him up, and he'd passed out during his encounter with "Miss Charlotte," who had been an octoroon. For all he knew, he could truly be what the man accused him of being. The thought made him sulk with self-loathing. Gritting his teeth, he forcibly directed his focus back to Isabelle. Once he reached the main road, he pulled Renegade to a trot. *Poor Isabelle*, he thought to himself, unconsciously shaking his head. *She doesn't deserve any of this.*

While he was gone, Anna busied herself with housecleaning, and baked a few loaves of apple bread to take to "her boys," the number of which had dwindled significantly, since they had been reassigned to other areas, mostly out west. She rode Ginger bareback to the outpost, and found Ad. He graciously thanked her before inquiring as to whether she'd discussed Kit's situation with her mother-in-law. She informed that, although she was anxious to resolve the issue, she had decided to wait for the most opportune time. After all, two weeks had gone by without incident, so perhaps Kit would behave like a gentleman. Ad shook his head with a grin, and escorted her outside, sending her off with a warning.

"There's no tellin' what he's capable of, Miss Anna, so use precaution."

"Oh, I will, Ad. Thank you."

He gave her a step up. She straddled the mule, gave her a kick, and trotted on her way. After a few minutes, Ginger slowed to a walk. It was late afternoon: Anna wondered if David had returned. She smiled as she thought of him, wanting to search out Isabelle to apologize, because he had a good heart. His involvement with the Klan concerned her, but even with all the turmoil around them, she still felt as though she was lucky to have found him. Suddenly, she heard a loud crack. She pulled back on Ginger and looked behind her.

"Who's there?" she called. She heard nothing but a few distant chirps. An eerie feeling swept over her, like she was being watched. "It's all right, Ginger girl," she said, exemplifying her own confidence. She reached into her dress pocket, and extracted the Derringer pistol. If she was being followed, she was ready to protect herself.

David arrived at the Primrose Plantation, inquired with a woman at the big house as to the whereabouts of Isabelle's children, and was told that they had been sent off to school. He frowned, knowing Lincoln was only three years of age, and far too young to attend. Before the woman had a chance to close the door in his face, he stuck his foot in, preventing her.

"My dear sir!" she exclaimed. "What is the meaning of this?"

"Beggin' your pardon, but I need to know the truth. Their ma requested that I find out."

"Are you fixin' on takin' them back?" she asked.

"No, ma'am. They ain't mine to take."

The woman sighed, and slowly opened the door. She stepped out to join him on the vast terrace. "Mr. Summers, I must confess, I don't rightly know where they are. It's my understandin' that they're stayin' at a children's home in Tuscaloosa, but I have yet to discover the name of the establishment. Heaven sakes, there's likely to be scores of orphanages down there, and who knows if those young'uns are still there. I don't mean to send you on a wild goose chase, but that's jist what it'll be if you try to locate them."

"Oh." David scowled.

The woman turned empathetic, and took his arm. "If I were you, sir, I'd tell their mother what she wants to hear. Your chances of findin' those boys ain't good, and what if you do? There ain't nothin' you can do for them."

He nodded in response. "I hate to have to lie to her, though."

She smiled sympathetically. "You'll be doin' her a favor ... in the long run." With that, she retreated into the house.

David sighed. She was right. It could take weeks, possibly even months, to find Isabelle's sons, and he didn't have the time or resources to pursue it. They might even be split up, which would cause further investigation. He resigned himself to the situation, mounted Renegade, and started for home.

Once she returned, Anna set Ginger free in the pasture, and walked up to the cottage. David wasn't home yet. She wondered what might be keeping him, but shrugged it off, and walked down to the house. She found Caroline in the front room, knitting. Dorie was at her feet, playing with a rag doll.

"Hello, Mother Caroline," she greeted happily, a wide smile spanning her face as Dorie looked up at her, and reached her arms out to her. She picked her up. "How was she?"

"The sweetest li'l angel, jist like always." She smiled at her daughter-in-law, then motioned for her to have a seat.

Anna sat down in a chair beside her. "Where's Josie?" she asked.

"Mr. Lynn came to fetch her. She's gone to spend the night with her friend, Mirabel. She's makin' plans to attend the all-girls seminary in Huntsville, you know."

Anna's eyes lit up. "That's marvelous! I hope she can develop her engineering skills. Wouldn't it be wonderful if she could get a degree?"

Caroline nodded in agreement.

Anna glanced around. "Where is Kit?"

"Don't rightly know. He set off an hour or two ago, and I ain't seen him since."

Anna grimaced. Perhaps it was Kit who was following her on the road. The thought made her shudder.

Caroline took notice, and set the knitting needles in her lap. "You feelin' all right, child?"

Anna nodded, but Caroline could see something was bothering her. "What is it, dear?"

She sighed. "I have some news about Mr. Lawrence that I don't think you'll take very well."

Caroline stared at her, waiting for her to continue.

"I found out why he's been going up to Tennessee all the time, and it isn't to do business with his brother, like he told you."

"Oh?" Caroline's expression eased into a peaceful smile. "He's been busy with other ventures, then."

Anna raised an eyebrow. "Well ... you could say that. He ..."

"Good afternoon!" In burst Kit, as though he'd been listening and had timed his entrance to interrupt her. "What y'all been up to?"

He smirked, glaring at Anna as he did so. She withered under his stare.

"Well, Josie's gone for the evenin', and David ain't yet returned. I'd best be startin' supper. Anna, will you assist?"

"Certainly."

She set Dorie down and led her by the hand. As she passed Kit, she thought she heard him growl, which made her cringe. *He knows*, she thought, but dismissed the idea. *He can't possibly know!* She followed Caroline out to the kitchen.

David returned, unsaddled Renegade, and because he was anxious to eat, left his firearms in the barn. He entered the house just as his family sat down in the dining room for their meal. He said very little, since he didn't want to discuss it in front of Kit, but when the man excused himself and walked outside, David told his wife and mother of the days' events.

"Perhaps we could write letters to the boys homes, and see if we can locate them that way," Anna suggested.

He smiled at her. "That's a right good idea! Ma, do you have pen and paper?"

"I've a pen," she said, "but no paper."

"I'll go up to the cottage and fetch some so we can get started right away," Anna offered.

She lit a candle, walked outside and behind the house, climbed the slope, and entered the dark dwelling. She set the candle on the table, and turned toward the nightstand. As light filled the room, she saw him standing in the doorway, leering at her. She jumped, gasping with fright. He sprang at her, captured her in his arms, and placed a hand over her mouth.

"Don't scream," he gruffly commanded. "You gonna be quiet?"

Petrified with terror, Anna managed a nod.

Tucker removed his hand and spun her around to face him, holding onto her arms. "I know what you're up to. Think you're pretty clever, eh missy?"

"What do you mean?" she asked innocently.

"Don't play coy with me! Pa saw your Injun tracker. Who else did you tell?"

"No one."

"Who else?" he bellowed.

She refused to speak.

"Did you tell Miss Caroline?"

She shook her head, her eyes wide as a doe's.

"Your husband knows, though, don't he?"

Her silence betrayed her.

Tucker's face grew red. He pushed her toward the bed, sending her flailing onto it, pulled back, and slapped her. She shrieked.

"Damn it, girl!" he yelled. "Why couldn't you jist mind your own affairs?" He turned around, clenching his fists.

Anna drew her pistol. She fired, but missed. Tucker whirled back around and came at her. They struggled on the bed until he had her pinned. He pulled the pistol from her grasp, and threw it across the room.

"You won't tell her, will you, girl?"

Anna managed to break free. She ran to the door as David arrived. Realizing what was happening, he nudged her out the door. Tucker lunged at him, but he jumped out of his way. Quickly looking around, David found the only weapon available, and withdrew it from where it hung above the mantle. With one swift swoop, he removed the sheath, and held the saber up in defense, ready to strike, the cold steel glistening in the candlelight.

Tucker laughed. "You think you can whip me with that?" He took a step toward David, who sliced the air before him, the sword making a swooshing sound as he did. "You fixin' to cut me down with that, Summers?"

David stared at him scathingly. "If need be."

Tucker chuckled demonically. "You can't do it and you know it," he provoked.

David's breathing grew rapid.

"You can't take me on when I got this." He withdrew his pistol, and aimed at David's chest. "Too bad you showed up when you did. That li'l ole gal of yours is sweet as sugar."

He glowered. "We all know the kind of man you are, Tucker Lawrence. You're despicable. You're jist as bad as your father."

Tucker chortled. "You found out my uncle didn't sell the farm to Pa."

"You're both liars."

"Least we ain't cowardly, like you."

"If fightin' for my homeland and protectin' my loved ones makes me a coward, then I reckon that's what I am."

"Is that how you see it? You found a Yankee gal to escape from your responsibilities." Tucker cocked the trigger.

"I did what was right, what was morally expected of me, which is more than I can say for you, you son of a bitch. You didn't enlist, and neither did your pa."

Tucker snorted. "Jist 'cause you're a veteran don't make you that tough."

He took a step toward David, who slashed out at him, cutting him across the wrist. He dropped the pistol with a cry, discharging it. The bullet flew into a wall. David coiled and kicked the gun away. He pushed Tucker up against the wall, thrusting the saber to his throat. Tucker let out a groan.

"Now, now, David," he stammered, "let's calm down. We don't need to behave so irrationally." He attempted to grasp the saber, but David pushed it into his flesh, nearly piercing his skin. Tucker winced.

Kit appeared in the doorway. "What's all the ruckus?" He paused, taking in the scene. "What did you tell him, Tucker?"

"Nothin', Pa. I swear! They found out on their own, jist like you thought."

"You need to leave here, old man," David said raucously. "Tonight. And take your despicable son with you."

Kit gulped, his Adams apple waggling. Finally, he agreed.

David released Tucker, who ran out the door into the night. He held his weapon on Kit as he stepped across the room to retrieve the pistol, and followed him to the house, holding him at gunpoint.

"You're makin' a big mistake," Kit said.

"Keep your mouth shut," David barked.

Caroline entered the room. "Anna says your son attacked her," she glared at him. "Is that true?"

Kit said nothing.

"Ma, that ain't all that happened."

David looked over to see Anna leaning against the doorframe. She nodded, coaxing him on.

"Kit's been doin' business with the carpetbag men, and he's got a wife up in Tennessee. That's where he's been runnin' off to."

Caroline's mouth dropped open. "You're married?"

Kit chuckled. "You can't believe what these young'uns are tellin' you. They've been misinformed."

Caroline tore her gaze from Kit and looked at her son.

"He's been playin' us all like a fiddle," remarked David. "His brother didn't sell him his half of their farm, so Kit came up with another plan. He said he wanted to marry you, but I think he jist wanted our land."

"You believed all that I told you?" Kit said with a snicker. "I was jist pullin' your leg, boy!"

Caroline scowled at Kit. "Mr. Lawrence, I don't know what you've been tellin' my son, but you've gotten him into enough trouble. I want you off my premises right now, you hear?"

"He was jist leavin'." David glared at Kit.

"I'll explain it to you later, Caroline," Kit growled.

David escorted him out. Kit climbed up into his wagon and slapped the reins. His wagon barreled down the lane and vanished into the darkness. David waited until the sound of his horse's hooves could no longer be heard, then hurried back in to his wife. She fell into his arms and wept.

Caroline stood beside them, a tear trickling down her cheek. "Why would he do this to us? After bein' such close friends with your pa?" she whimpered.

"Ma." David reached out and hugged her as well. "He was only after our farm, and he couldn't afford to buy it outright. Not like we'd sell, anyways."

Dorie wanted in, so the four of them huddled together.

"Why couldn't he just take some land that has been abandoned?" Anna wondered aloud.

"Because the carpetbaggers have snatched it all up," David explained. "He didn't have money to purchase it from the Yankees, and he's too lazy to make a go of land that's been sittin' idle. He knows how hard I've worked on this place, which would make it all that much easier for him."

"I've a feelin' he didn't really buy us those gifts," Caroline said, wiping her eye with a sniffle.

"Naw. He probably bartered for them, then showed up bearin' gifts to make himself look good." David gave his mother a sympathetic smile. "If it's any consolation, he's likely scammin' his wife up in Tennessee too."

"We're all better off without him, then." Caroline released her son.

"He's gone for good this time," David assured her.

Anna wanted to believe him, but somehow, she had the uncanny feeling that Kit would return, and she didn't want to be there when he did.

On May 13, Jefferson Davis was brought to bail in Richmond, and soon released. Horace Greeley, among several other northerners, including an abolitionist, posted his $100,000 bail. At last, David thought, his president was free, if only for a short time. Then on May 16, President Johnson was acquitted, and his impeachment proceedings came to an end. The South breathed a sigh of relief: at least there was one person in power still concerned for their rights. The Radical Republicans had gained control of the Senate, however, rendering the president ineffective.

One week later, David learned that his hero, Kit Carson, had died. This saddened him deeply. He'd always dreamed of going west and meeting the man who had inspired him in dime novels, but it wasn't meant to be. Eight days after his death, the Navaho Treaty was signed, which was something Carson had worked most of his life to attain: peace between the whites and Indians. David felt sorry he hadn't lived long enough to see his efforts come to fruition. At least they hadn't all been in vain.

With June came the news Anna had been waiting to hear. She kept it a secret, afraid to tell David of her plans, and wanting to see if somehow things would improve. A few days later, she escorted her husband to the Kimball's, where they found Mrs. Kimball sipping lemonade with Callie. Invited in, Anna awkwardly complied, and sat with the women while David located Mr. Kimball outside.

Mrs. Kimball lavished attention on the toddler. Dorie responded by squealing with delight.

"She's as purty as a peach," Jake's mother sighed. "Reminds me of Jenny when she was her age."

"Where is Jenny?" inquired Anna.

"Oh, she's up in Huntsville, lookin' for a room. Decided it was too hard bein' apart from Nate all the time."

Anna nodded appreciatively. "I know what that's like," she remarked.

"Pardon me for a moment," Mrs. Kimball excused as she arose. "I have some biscuits bakin' in the oven that I need to tend to."

"By all means." Callie smiled up at her, then turned to face Anna. She sneered at her. "Miss Anna, it's a wonder why you're still here."

Anna frowned at her.

"What I mean is, you're desirin' to go back up north, ain't you?"

"When David can get away, we will."

"Well, what's keepin' y'all?" She lifted the glass to her lips, all the while staring a hole through her.

"Mama! Mama!" Dorie insisted on sitting on Anna's lap.

"Not now, sweetheart." She withdrew Dorie's rag doll from her bag. "Here darling, play with this."

Dorie took the doll and plopped down on the floor. She jabbered to herself as Anna responded.

"We had an issue with Kit Lawrence, but it's resolved now."

"Hope y'all got rid of that tyrant."

Anna smiled slightly. "Yes, we did."

"Y'all hungry?" Mrs. Kimball called from another room.

"No ma'am," Callie responded without asking Anna. She slyly looked her over.

Anna became self-conscious. She cleared her throat. "How is your husband?"

Callie scoffed. "Right fine. But that ain't none of your concern." She stood, looming over Dorie. "Your baby girl looks jist like her daddy.

She's grown considerably since I last saw her." She bent down to pick up the child, but Dorie protested. She bit Callie on the hand. Callie reacted by slapping Dorie's cheek. Immediately, the toddler wailed as Anna pounced to her rescue.

"Callie!" She picked Dorie up and cradled her.

"What happened?" Mrs. Kimball asked as she swiftly returned.

"She slapped my child!" Anna exclaimed, nearly hysterical.

"I did no such thing," Callie cooed. "I was merely disciplinin' the child. Somethin' she doesn't git from you, I reckon." She turned to Jake's mother. "Li'l Dorie tried to take a bite out of me!"

Mrs. Kimball laughed, but Anna didn't think it was funny.

"You had no right hitting my child," she said, her eyes welling up with tears. "Mrs. Kimball, thank you very much for the lemonade, but I need to be going now."

Mrs. Kimball said nothing. Anna rushed out of the house. She found David conversing with Mr. Kimball.

"Anna, what's wrong?" he asked as she approached.

"I'll tell you on the way home," she snapped.

Taking his cue, he said, "Let me know if there's anything I can do."

"I'll talk to you when I git back," replied Mr. Kimball.

David escorted his wife to the wagon and helped her aboard. On the way home, she described Callie's outburst.

"And Mrs. Kimball did nothing!" she added emphatically.

"Could be she didn't know what to do."

Anna shook her head. "No one likes me here, David, because I'm a Northerner. I've felt that sentiment ever since we came here."

"Don't you think you're overreactin'?"

She glared at him, then glanced at her daughter. Dorie's little cheek was still red where Callie had hit her. "I am certainly not overreacting. Even your mother lets it slip now and again how she can't quite accept me, because I'm a 'Yankee'!" Anna couldn't help it: she started to weep.

"Darlin', don't git yourself all worked up." He reached over to take her hand, but she yanked it away.

"I hate it here," she sobbed. "I don't belong here."

"You belong with me, honey."

He gave her a wry grin as she wiped her tears away. But later that evening, she cried herself to sleep, and in the morning, made a resolution.

She was tired of crying all the time, tired of being miserable and afraid, tired of being told she could go home when things were better, just plain tired. She felt like she was about to lose her mind, like everyone was out to get her and no one believed her. She was out of her element, like a fish out of water, and she'd had enough.

With what little money she'd saved, she rode to Morgan City alone the following afternoon, sent a telegram, and returned home. She knew what was about to transpire, but felt as though she was left with no other recourse. As a last resort, she confronted her husband that evening, and found him sitting at the table, fretting over bills.

"I don't see how we can make our commitment, what with the high cost of taxes and all."

"Darling, it's time we departed for home," she said as she sat on the bed, brushing Dorie's soft blonde hair.

He looked over at her. Raising an eyebrow, he asked, "Now?"

"Yes, now."

He shook his head with a smirk. "Anna, as much as I'd like to, I can't right now. Josie's headed off for school. I can't leave Ma here by herself."

"Your mother's a grown woman. I'm sure she can take care of herself."

"It ain't that." He slowly stood, walked across the room, and sat beside her. Placing his hand on her knee, he said, "Kit or Tucker could come back at any time. I have to be here."

Anna threw a glance at him. "There isn't going to be a 'right time', is there, David?"

He scoffed. "Why sure there is. Jist not yet."

"I want to go, Pa!" Dorie exclaimed. "I want to go see Aunt Maggie and Aunt Abigail!"

David hesitated. "You taught her to say that," he mumbled.

"I did no such thing." Anna stood, turned, and glared at him. "David, I've listened to your excuses long enough. Are we going, or aren't we?"

"Anna ..."

"Well?" She crossed her arms in front of her.

"I told you. Not yet."

"Fine!" She picked Dorie up off the bed and set her down on the floor. Taking the child's hand, she screeched, "Then we're going without you!" She started for the door. Dorie began to whine.

"You don't mean that." He stood, and ambled toward her.

She looked over her shoulder at him, then opened the door and left.

He sighed. *She's jist spoutin' off steam*, he reasoned to himself. *She'll simmer down soon enough.*

Two days later, Mr. Kimball arrived to notify David that he'd secured the amount Percy had deposited in his bank account in Huntsville, all $180 of it. This was no small feat, as most depositors had lost all their money to greedy investors. Mr. Kimball intended delivering it to Isabelle in the morning. He invited David along, but he declined. The last thing he wanted to see was that poor woman in her state of hardship, her children taken from her, her hope dissolved. The guilt was already more than he could bear, and he frequently had reoccurring nightmares about Percy's lynching. He hadn't received a single response from any of the sixteen orphanages he'd sent letters to, either. His hope was waning as well. Understandably, Mr. Kimball said he'd offer Isabelle David's best wishes, and then he was off.

Several days went by. On June 12th, a Friday, before David rode to the blacksmith's for Renegade's monthly inspection, Anna approached him as he was saddling his steed.

"Where are you off to?" she asked.

He noticed that she was dressed up more than usual, but the thought quickly departed his mind. "John Moss's shop."

"Oh."

Her utterance was like a whimper. He smiled at her.

"David, give me your hand."

He did as she asked. She produced a piece of yarn and a pair of scissors from her dress pocket, wrapped the yarn around his ring finger, cut it, and stuffed both back into her pocket.

"What's this for?" he asked, cinching up the saddle.

"We're leaving. You're aware, aren't you? I told you about this."

He barely heard a word. "Renie's in need of new shoes, and that li'l filly'll be next." He ran through his list of chores aloud, not paying much attention to whether she was listening or not.

"I love you." She kissed him gently on the cheek.

He grinned at her. "I love you too, m'lady."

She pulled a wad of bills from her pocket. Taking his hand, she turned his palm upright, and set the money in. "I managed to save up enough for your train ticket home. Please don't spend it on anything else."

"Where'd you git this?"

"From selling pies," she replied.

He hesitated for a moment, then absentmindedly shoved the money into his pocket, and stepped up into the saddle. "See y'all later!" Giving Renegade a slight kick, he rode off.

When he returned that afternoon, he sauntered into the house to discover his mother sitting at the dining room table with a somber expression on her face. When she saw David, she rose to her feet.

"David, Anna's gone," she stated bluntly.

"Oh? Where'd she go off to?" He smiled, but it vanished as he realized his mother's seriousness.

"She took Dorie to the train station in Arab. If you hurry, you might be able to catch them. They're takin' the four o'clock train."

He stared at her, dumbfounded. Suddenly, he bolted for the door, but remembered, and turned back to ask, "Will you be all right while I'm gone?"

"I got the shotgun loaded, and Josie's here."

He ran out to where he'd left Renegade, sprang into the saddle, and kicked his heels into the stallion's sides. Renegade reacted by thundering down the road. He pulled the horse to a trot, allowing him to catch his breath. Even if he galloped Renegade the entire distance, it would take several hours, and he knew he wouldn't reach them in time. Still, he persisted. He thought she had been bluffing, but now knew she'd been serious. Over three hours later, he arrived at the depot. A train was just about to pull away. He threw himself off his horse, ran down the length of the platform, and anxiously gazed in the windows. At last, he saw Anna, and frantically waved to attract her attention. She looked over at him, her continence turning to surprise. David watched as she spoke to a woman across from her, who nodded. She left Dorie and made her way down the aisle, then emerged at the door.

"David!" She jumped off as he caught her.

"Anna, what are you doin'?" He set her down.

"I told you. We have to go, sweetie. We can't stay here any longer."

"You're really leavin' me?" His eyes grew wide with disbelief.

She bit her lip and nodded.

"How did y'all git here?"

"I had a friend deliver us," she replied.

"A friend?"

"He's a Federal soldier."

David glared at her. "You trusted riffraff to transport you?"

"Not all the soldiers left here are riffraff, David." She stopped, seeing the pain in his eyes. "Come with us."

He expelled an exasperated sigh. "You know I can't do that!"

"Please, darling."

"Anna, you're puttin' me in a hell of a bind."

Unexpectedly, the locomotive's shrieking whistle sliced through the air like a dagger. David felt as though it had slashed through his heart.

"Honey, please don't leave," he begged fervently.

"I have to. It isn't safe for me, or for Dorie. My family is expecting us, and Stephen's waiting in Knoxville. He will escort us from there."

"What?" he screamed, attracting attention from the conductor, who was standing nearby. "Stephen? After everything he did, you ..."

"Darling, please." She clutched the locket around her neck. It was the one he'd given her after his release from Elmira prison, the one with an angel embossed on the front of it, the one that encased his portrait. "It's you who has my heart."

He stared at her, horrified. All he could do was shake his head in shock. She threw her arms around his neck, and kissed him deeply. The train lurched as it began to roll. He didn't want their kiss to end. He didn't want to let her go.

"I love you," she whispered in his left ear, forgetting.

He didn't hear, for the shell that had exploded beside him on the field at Gettysburg had left him all but deaf in that ear. She pulled away, seeing the dark clouds form in his eyes.

"Come home as soon as you can."

She moved onto the step, and threw him a kiss. He mimicked catching it, then put his hand to his lips. *This can't be happening*, he thought. He walked alongside the moving passenger car and watched his wife take her seat. She held Dorie up to the window. The little girl waved, speaking to him, although he couldn't hear her words. He gazed at Anna, and she back at him, until the platform ended, and he was left standing at the edge of it. He watched as the train rumbled away, vanishing around a curve.

He considered chasing it, but knew it would be to no avail. Anna had made up her mind. The only resolution was to go with her, but his mother's safety was at stake. The timing wasn't right, and he was caught in-between.

Slowly, he dragged himself back to his waiting stallion and mounted. He sat there for a few minutes, collecting himself, trying to come to terms, but didn't want to realize what was really transpiring. He gave Renegade a nudge, so the horse started to walk. As he rode out of Arab, he remembered that, because of his hasty departure, he'd forgotten to bring provisions, which immediately made him very thirsty. He stopped at a house on the town's outskirts, tapped on the door, and asked for a drink.

"You fight in the war?" the elderly, balding gentleman asked.

"Yessir, under Jeb Stuart."

The man slapped his knee with a loud guffaw. "Ole Jeb! He was quite a character, wasn't he?"

"Yessir."

"Too bad he lost the war for us."

David frowned in response.

The man went inside, and soon reappeared with a large glass of water. David swigged it down, handed the glass back, thanked the man, and climbed onto his horse. As he rode out of town, he knew he'd be lucky to return by sundown.

His head was in a fog: he knew she was gone, but it didn't seem real. He kept imagining that she'd be there waiting for him when he got home. The hurt was too intense for him to grasp.

He kept his mind busy by dreaming up ways to reunite with her, and whistling "Bonnie Blue Flag." He remembered a song he'd heard before the war, and started singing softly. Renegade pricked his ears back to listen.

> "Down in some lone valley, in a lonesome place,
> Where the wild birds do whistle, and their notes do increase,
> Farewell pretty Saro, I bid you adieu,
> But I'll dream of pretty Saro wherever I go.

"My love, she won't have me, so I understand,
She wants a freeholder who owns house and land.
I cannot maintain her with silver and gold,
Nor buy all the fine things that a big house can hold.

"If I were a merchant and could write a fine hand,
I'd write my love a letter that she'd understand.
I'd write it by the river where the waters o'er-flow,
And I'll dream of pretty Saro wherever I go."

David sang through the lyrics again, this time substituting Anna's name. By the time he reached the end, he was too choked up to continue. He rode in silence, occasionally offering Renegade praise and pausing to let him rest, until he reached the familiar saddlebag house.

Once he arrived, he found his mother, who embraced him as she offered words of comfort and encouragement, but she couldn't take away his acute heartache. He excused himself, turning down her offer of food, and walked back to the cottage. As he entered, he realized how small and empty the room was without her, without them both. He pulled his boots off and sat on the edge of the bed in the dark, but before long, sorrow overcame him. A tear trickled down his cheek. He let his body fall against the bed. Covering his eyes with his arm, he immersed himself in sobs. She really was gone, and there was nothing he could do about it. His beloved wife and daughter had abandoned him. He imagined seeing the train pull away from the station again, becoming smaller and smaller until it was gone. His heart had gone with that train. He felt nothing but emptiness.

"If I ever disown, repudiate, or apologize for the Cause for which Lee fought and Jackson died, let the lightnings of Heaven rend me, and the scorn of all good men and true women be my portion. Sun, Moon, Stars, all fall on me when I cease to love the Confederacy. 'Tis the Cause, not the fate of the Cause, that is glorious!"

- Maj. R.E. Wilson, CSA

Chapter Ten

A day went by, and another, until a week had passed. Each day was agony for him; without her, he was lost. He wracked his brain, trying to invent schemes that would enable him to reunite with her, but to no avail. At first, he was angry with her, irritated that she'd been surreptitious about her whereabouts, and how she'd acquired money for train fare. But after a while, he came to understand her intentions. She thought telling him would rile him, which it would have, and he'd left her no alternative. With this, he began to deride himself for letting her go, for not chasing after her, and for chasing her away.

He received a telegram informing him she'd arrived safely, and that she and Dorie were happy. This caused him to break down in private, because more than anything, he wanted to provide their happiness. He considered himself a failure, and loathed himself for his inadequacy. She sent word about changes to the farm, that Patrick and Briana had wed a year ago, and how her mother's friend, Grace, still insisted she could provide him with a job once he got there. Hearing news from home, albeit her home, made him even more heartsick, and the yearning for her was immeasurable. She gave no mention of her love for him, which further dispirited him.

Spending long afternoons in the fields, he returned home after sunset, ate quick meals with his mother and sister, who he knew pitied him, and dragged himself up to the cottage, where he sat on the edge of the bed, alone in the dark until sleep finally took him. His sadness was insufferable, but he still held onto a glimmer of hope that somehow, someday, he would be with her again.

He wrote to his comrade, Sherwood Richardson, whom he'd been imprisoned with in Elmira, as well as John Chase's family, but received no replies. Although his mother and Josie were there, he felt completely alone, and his self-inflicted solitude only made it worse.

Caroline greeted him as he entered for supper one evening in late June, and read aloud the letter she'd received from Rena.

"Dear Ma, David, Anna, and Josie. I take this opportunity to write so you may know that Michael and I have moved from New York to Washin'ton City."

"I wonder why," David said.

His mother shook her head as her hazel eyes scanned over the page. "Don't say."

"Well, I for one am glad they did. Never liked New York much."

She smiled compassionately at him, knowing he was referring to his stint in prison. "Michael has secured employment with the treasury department, and we have set up housekeepin' in a one-room apartment."

"Treasury department? He's the wrong man for that job. He'll steal those Yankees blind if he gets half a chance!"

Caroline and Josie snickered at his remark.

"We are both very happy here. There is plenty to do and see. We miss y'all very much, and hope to be with y'all again soon. All our love, Rena."

"Is that it?" Josie asked.

"P.S. Please give my favorite niece a hug and kiss for me."

He grimaced, then expelled a tormented sigh. "I wish I could," he muttered.

Caroline folded the paper and slid it into her dress pocket. She patted her son reassuringly on the arm before departing.

He sat at the table, watching his little sister scratch a pencil across the surface of a drawing pad, creating a new project.

"What's that one?" he asked half-heartedly.

"This here's my rendition of what a new dam will do for the Tennessee River." She held it up to him, displaying it proudly as she grinned. Seeing his disinterest, her smile faded. "Oh, David, I know you're hurtin', but Anna's the one who left you."

"I don't want to talk about it, Josie," he said.

"All right then, let's change the subject." She set the pad down on the table and took his hand. "Miss Callie's invited us to her place again this year for the Fourth of July."

He scoffed. "I ain't gonna go."

"Yes you are. I need you to be my escort." He protested, but she squeezed his hand. "Please, David. You can be my dance partner. It'll help git your mind off of … things."

"I won't be very amiable company."

"I don't care. I won't leave you here alone to sulk."

He looked over at her, seeing her smile return.

"Good! Then it's settled! Next Saturday, we'll be attendin' a barbeque, and we'll dance till our feet ache!" She arose, kissed his cheek, and skipped out the door.

They can't hurt any worse than my heart does, he wearily thought to himself.

Two days later, a notice was posted in the mercantile, requesting a meeting of the Knights of Peace. David entered the wooden structure to see "Uncle" Dock Gibson, a noted old-time fiddler who lived near Tucker's Point, playing his fiddle in the corner. He was accompanying an ex-soldier who was still wearing his tattered gray Confederate uniform. The soldier sang mournfully:

> "Oh, I'm a good old rebel, now that's just what I am,
>   And for this Yankee nation, I do not give a damn.
>   I'm glad I fought against her, I only wish we'd won.
>   And I ain't asked no pardon for anything I've done.
>
> "I hates the Yankee nation and everything they do.
>   I hates the Declaration of Independence too.
>   I hates the glorious Union, 'tis drippin' with our blood.
>   I hates the striped banner, and fought it all I could."

Ben Johnson drew David's attention to the notice, then asked when the customers had drifted away to observe the sundries, "You plan on attendin', don't you?"

He frowned. "I don't know, Ben. After what happened the last time, I've been feelin' somewhat under the weather."

Ben glared at him. "The whole county knows how that li'l Yankee gal of yours left to go up north, but you best be re-thinkin' your stance. They'll consider you a traitor if you don't show up, and they might even come after you. You don't want that, do you?"

After hesitating, he relented. "No, sir. I don't want that."

"Tonight at eight sharp," the shopkeeper said before acknowledging a customer who approached the counter with his purchase.

Reluctantly, David rode out that evening for the designated meeting place, a stage stop called Mulberry Tavern, where he found his den. The raiders were already mounted up and masked when he arrived. One of them tossed a whistle at him.

"We're ridin' over to the Strom place," he growled. David recognized the voice to be that of Wes McGrath. "There's been trouble with one of the darkies makin' advances at Mr. Garrison's daughters."

David quickly dismounted to camouflage Renegade, then slid the white mask over his head, setting his slouch hat on top. "Strom? You mean ole Matthew Strom?"

"No, one of his sons," came the reply from another Knight.

The men thundered off in a cloud of dust. Once they arrived at their destination, they dismounted. Nightfall had just settled in, and candlelight flickered from behind thin cotton sheets serving as the cabin's curtains. The Knights burst in, taking their victims by surprise.

One hooded man approached the cowering brothers. Raising his gun, he pistol whipped a brother in the face. The other cried out, as if being inflicted himself.

"Heed this warnin', sons of Matthew," the ghostly presence threatened in a low, ominous voice. "Stay away from our women!"

"We will rise up from the bowels of Hell to slit your throats if you so much as whisper their names," said another.

"We will not tolerate interracial relations," said a third, "and inappropriate behavior on your part."

A fourth masked man rattled cow bones from under his robe. The two brothers stared wide-eyed in fright, speechless.

"Consider this your final warnin'."

The men departed, leaving the door wide open. Matthew's sons watched in horror as the disguised Kluxes mounted and rode away.

As they returned to Mulberry Tavern, the men removed their hoods.

Charlie Abbott chuckled. "Reckon we shook them coons up good enough. They won't be leerin' at our womenfolk anymore."

Callie will be glad to hear of it, David thought to himself. He remembered how she'd requested his assistance, but he'd disregarded it at the time, thinking she was being inequitable. But now, because other women in the area had made similar complaints, he knew she was truthfully concerned. The men went inside and partook of cordials, courtesy of the tavern's owner, Mr. Wilber.

After parting ways, David rode alone down the dark road, humming "O Lemuel" softly to himself. His thoughts were immersed in Anna, and he was resolute to be with her, however improbable it seemed. Suddenly, a strange noise rose up from the underbrush, like an escalating growl. His heart leaped into his throat as he pulled his pistol, staring into the darkness. Poised to defend himself, he continued riding Renegade at a walk. Another rumble arose, as if someone was chuckling from behind the trees. David felt his skin rash into goose bumps. A loud pop startled him. Renegade whinnied. David whirled around on his horse, looking for the source of the explosion. The underbrush rustled. He fired into the darkness, the powder from his gun flashing like lightning. He breathed heavily for a moment, listening. There was no sound but that of crickets. David turned Renegade and fled.

As he rode at a slow canter, rampant thoughts invaded his mind. Was it Kit? Or Tucker? Had one of them returned? Who had taken a pot shot at him, hiding like a coward, unseen in the woods? Had someone intentionally tried to kill him, or was that person just trying to give him a scare? A wave of dread flooded over him. His mother had a shotgun, so he knew she was safe, but for how long? He gave Renegade an indication, and the stallion picked up speed. He could almost hear Kit's gravelly voice prodding him into fury.

"What's eatin' you, boy? Where's that Yankee wife of yours?"

David shook the thought from his mind. Reining back on Renegade, he withdrew his pistol and fired a few shots into the trees, releasing his anxiety. He rode at a trot the rest of the way home, coming to the realization that he was a hypocrite, married to an abolitionist, or the next best thing to one, and here he was, a member of the Ku Klux, whose ambition was white supremacy. Although he'd been raised in that atmosphere, after knowing Anna, he wasn't so sure it was the right way of thinking. He made a resolution to quit attending night rides in order to ease his conscience, and as he rode up the lane to the house, he noticed the hurricane lamp burning inside. His mother stood to greet him from her rocker on the front porch, and a peaceful calm swept over him. His family was secure.

When Saturday arrived, David, Josie, and Caroline boarded the buckboard wagon and prompted Ginger to the Copeland's residence. Various vehicles sat aligned in front of the house. David sighed as he pulled the jennie mule to a halt. Anna had been with him the last time the Copeland's held a party. She was his guiding light, but now she was gone. He was sure there would be questions and curious stares thrown his way.

"Why don't you two go on in," he stated. "I reckon I'll jist wait here."

Josie laughed. "That's the dumbest thing I ever heard!"

David frowned at her.

"Come on!" She pulled his arm until he felt obligated to obey.

Fay Copeland welcomed them at the door, and directed them to the party in the garden behind the house. David immediately noticed Callie, who saw him enter at the same time. She was a vision of beauty in a red velvet gown.

As she made her way across the yard, Josie said, "I'll go fetch us some sweet tea." She and Caroline left him there, vulnerable to Callie's approach.

"Why, Mr. Summers." She held her hand out for him to kiss the back of it. "It's a pleasure seein' you again."

"Likewise, Miss Callie," he muttered, forcing a slight smile.

She jutted out her bottom lip in a mock pout. "Now, now. No need to look so downtrodden. You're a good Southern gentleman, I've known it all along. If Miss Anna decides she doesn't want you any longer, then I'm sure you can find someone who does." She batted her eyelashes at him.

"Pardon me."

He sought refuge by rushing across the yard to where his mother was immersed in conversation with the neighbors. Awkwardly, he stood by her side in the shade of a large elm, saying nothing, until Mr. Skidmore called him over. As he made his way to the group of men standing nearby, he noticed his surroundings. A large area had been cleared for dancing, and around it, tables of victuals and drinks were set out with guests mingling before them. Strings of paper lanterns were laced overhead, and a small platform was erected off to the side for musicians. The guests were dressed in finery, an indication that their poverty had eased somewhat. Some ladies waved fans, temporarily relieving themselves from the humid heat. Callie's husband was absent, but obviously, she was enjoying the financial stability and class his money provided.

"The carpetbag men are takin' control of the state," grumbled Mr. Forman. "It's my prediction that they'll be installed in the state legislature this comin' fall."

"And Alabama will soon be readmitted to the Union," informed Mr. Draper. He puffed on his cigar before continuing. "It will provide us with representation in Congress once more, which can only empower us as a people."

"It's for certain Ulysses Grant will represent the Republican Party for presidential candidacy," remarked Mr. McAnnally. "Have the Democrats chosen a man yet?"

"No word yet," responded Mr. Kimball. "But the convention's bein' held this week up in New York City."

David bristled. There it was again: New York. He knew he'd have to get past his apprehension if he was ever to fulfill his promise to Anna by taking her there.

Callie approached from behind and took hold of his arm, startling him.

"Gentlemen, help yourselves to the viands. Mr. Summers, please come with me."

He wanted to avoid her, but couldn't think of a reason to resist, so he relented. She led him into the house to the parlor, sat down on the sofa, and motioned for him to sit beside her.

"Miss Callie, I really should be ..."

"Hush, now. My li'l ole heart desires to have a word with you in private."

He wavered. "What about?"

"About the fact that Miss Anna has left you all alone."

He snorted and tried to stand, but she prevented it. "I plan on reunitin' with her, jist as soon as I can."

"Oh? And how do you propose to do that?" Her penetrating blue eyes drew him in.

"I ... haven't quite figured that out yet," he stammered.

To his chagrin, she moved closer, still clamped onto his arm. "Now darlin', I brought you in here because, well, I have a proposition for you."

He raised his eyebrows. "A proposition?"

She smiled, so radiantly that he felt himself weakening, and was glad to be sitting down. Glancing around the room, he struggled to contain his composure. "That's a new picture, ain't it?" he asked, noticing the print on the far wall of the parlor.

It's called *The Burial of Latañe*," she responded. "I saw it and jist had to have it. It's symbolic of our Southern sufferin'. But don't you change the subject now. As I was sayin', I have a proposition."

He glanced over at her, feeling his face flush.

"I'm in need of someone to oversee my affairs. Here, at the farm."

"Well, can't your husband do that?"

Her smiled faded. "No. He's away nearly all the time." She stroked the back of his hand, causing him unease.

"What kind of affairs?"

"Jist comin' by every now and then, to keep me company." She smiled again, making his heart melt. "You see, my Ambrose could never replace Jake. Or you, for that matter."

"Miss Callie. What are you gettin' at?" He grew increasingly uncomfortable.

"Why, we could keep each other company, you and I. We're both lonely, and we've been friends for such a long time that, well, it would only be natural."

His eyes grew wide. She was seducing him! "Miss Callie!" He brushed her off and clambered to his feet. "I don't know what you're implyin', but I told you before, my heart belongs to Anna!"

She snickered. "Even if she ain't here?" She asked, rising.

"I have a daughter!" he exclaimed, his voice cracking. "I can't believe ..."

Callie burst into laughter, making him pause.

"What's so darned funny?"

"Oh, you are!" She slapped her thighs as she chortled at him. "Do you really think I would consider committin' adultery with you, David Summers?"

"But ... but ... you said ..."

She managed to contain her laughter. "I truly had you goin', didn't I?"

He scowled. "I'm goin' outside." He started to leave, but she pulled him back.

"David, don't be angry. I was merely funnin' with you."

"Well, now ain't a very good time to be doin' that."

She heard the anguish in his voice. "Darlin', I'm sorry. I was only teasin'. I didn't mean to sadden you."

He clenched his teeth. "Miss Callie, you've always enjoyed playin' games with me, but like I said, this ain't the time." He turned to leave.

"Let me make it up to you. I'll find a way to make your wish come true."

"What do you mean?"

"You want to be with Miss Anna. Well, I can make it happen."

He raised a suspicious eyebrow at her. "What do you have in mind?"

"You'll find out soon enough. Jist promise me one thing."

"What's that?"

"That as repayment, you'll do me the honor of dancin' the first dance with me."

He grinned sheepishly at her, and knew he could never resist her charms. "Fair enough."

He held his bent arm to her, inviting her to take it. They went outside to see that the band had congregated and was tuning up. David recognized "Uncle" Dock Gibson. The other five men, Callie informed, were traveling minstrels.

"You should have brought your guitar along to jine in!" she said.

He smiled. The music started, so he took her hand and led her out into the middle of the yard. They began waltzing to the surprise of everyone else in attendance.

"Tell me, Miss Callie, what you have in mind," he insisted softly as they whirled.

"I told you, dear David, you'll find out soon enough." She giggled as he spun her.

"Why the big secret?" He grinned in response.

"Because I'd like for it to be a pleasant surprise."

"I'm sorry I doubted you," he apologized.

She beamed. "Not to worry, darlin'. We're two peas in a pod, you and I." She held onto him as the song ended, whispering in his ear, "And Jake's the glue that binds us together." Releasing him, she added, "Miss Anna has your heart, and Jake will always have mine."

He nodded, swallowing down the lump in his throat.

Josie approached him. "You're supposed to be *my* dance partner!" she complained.

David snickered. "Miss Callie, I believe you're bein' cut in on!" He glanced around at the spectators, seeing all eyes were on them.

Seizing the opportunity to entertain, Callie exclaimed, "Oh, woe is me! I feel I'm about to swoon!" She collapsed as he caught her.

Feeling his face flush, he said, "Miss Callie, are you all right?"

She winked at him. "Of course, darlin'. I'm feelin' much better now." She stood on her own two feet, laughing, amused with herself and his reaction.

"Perhaps you should go sit down for a spell," Josie suggested.

"Yes, Miss Josie, I do believe I'll do jist that." She walked off to join the ladies, who were gawking at her.

A few couples mingled to the center of the yard as the musicians burst into melody.

"Way down souf' in de state of Alabam-a-rum,
state of Alabam-a-rum,
State of Alabam-a-rum,
If you don't pick de cotton you'll surely get a hammerum
Down in Alabama!
I'm so glad dat I come out de wilderness, come out de wilderness,
Come out de wilderness, I'm so glad dat I come out of de wilderness
Down in Alabama!"

The band of merry musicians frolicked through another song, entitled "Oh! Lud Gals!" before playing "Keemo Kimo."

Josie and David danced for nearly an hour, then decided to rest. Throughout the evening, he was asked to dance by nearly every single female in attendance. The thought occurred to him how ironic it was: when he and Jake were together, Jake had attracted all the girls. Now he was the one receiving their attention, even though it was undeserved, since he was married. They all knew it, but their loneliness for a man their age prodded them into his arms. He wondered if they would still be interested in him if he was single and the war hadn't taken away their beaus.

As twilight diminished, the guests partied under the illuminating lanterns with fireflies glittering around them. Later in the evening, fireworks were even provided. It was a spectacle to behold, and although many observers had empty holes in their hearts from losing loved ones, they managed to enjoy themselves. Still, their reluctance to celebrate the nation's birth was fueled by bitter memories of Gettysburg and Vicksburg, so they justified the celebration by referring to it as the "annual neighborhood picnic."

On the ride home, David listened while his mother and Josie raved about Callie's garden party. His heart ached for Anna and Adora, and he felt each day apart from them was more profoundly painful than the last. If only he could come up with some way to reunite with them, his world would be bright again. The South he'd left as a boy wasn't the same one he'd returned to. Escalating violence alarmed him, the country was topsy-turvy, and men he disliked immensely were in power. The voting situation was getting out of hand, and no doubt the Ku Klux Klan would come down harder on the freedmen, attempting to sway their votes. He knew he didn't want to be a part of that horrendousness. One thing he did know for certain: he didn't belong in the South any longer.

Two weeks later, he stood in the field, hoeing rows of sorghum. He looked up through the midsummer heat to see dust billowing up behind an approaching rider. The courier dismounted, delivered something to his mother, and rode off. David sauntered to the house, his curiosity spurring him. When he arrived, he saw Caroline with a letter in her hand, and a broad smile on her face.

"Ma? What is it?"

"Darlin', our prayers have been answered!"

He took the telegram she handed to him, and read:

My dearest sister,

I take pen in hand to inform you that my farm has sold. We would like to come up to your place and stay for a spell. We are very anxious to see you all, and hope our stay will ease your plight. If we don't hear otherwise, expect our arrival in three weeks time.

Your loving brother,
Edward

David looked at her, puzzled. "Uncle Ed's comin' here?"

"I invited him, David. Ever since your Aunt Rachel died, he's been strugglin', and Lord knows it ain't been any easier without his servants. So I thought he could stay with us, but it was contingent on him sellin' his property. Now it seems he's done so." She smiled happily. "I haven't seen my brother in ... nine years!"

"I know, Ma." He was stunned by the realization. Sinking down onto a chair, he equated the situation aloud. "Uncle Ed can help you out here, and I can go up to Pennsylvania."

"That's been my intention."

He looked up at her and grinned. "Thanks, Ma." Standing, he hugged her.

"Now go tell your sister. We have three weeks to git this place fixed up!"

As he walked outside to find Josie, he understood that, with his uncle's arrival, his mother would be safe from marauders. He sighed heavily with relief. He only hoped his uncle didn't back out of the arrangement, leaving him stranded.

Three weeks later as promised, however, Caroline's brother arrived with David's four cousins. They hugged and kissed, exchanged compliments and exclamations of how they'd all grown, then settled down for a picnic under the flowering eastern redbuds.

"After dinner, I want to see a picture of your wife, David," Uncle Edward said.

"Me too!" said his cousin, Mildred, all of twelve years old.

"And your li'l girl!" cried Tessa, the youngest. She had been a baby herself when he last saw her.

"Let him eat," bellowed David's sixteen-year-old cousin, Ira. Turning to David, he asked, "When are you fixin' to leave?"

"Don't rightly know," he replied, throwing a glance at his mother, who looked down at her plate. "Soon as I can."

"What's it like up there in Pennsylvania?" asked Ira's younger brother, Saul, the only blond in the family.

"Hot in the summer, and cold in the winter. Mighty cold!"

The family laughed.

"Ira wanted to jine up, but Ma wouldn't let him," Mildred proclaimed.

"Said I was too young," Ira explained. "Reckon she was right. Now I know it would've been pointless, anyhow."

David glared at him.

"Didn't see any reason for goin'," he elaborated. "I knew we'd lose the fight. It was jist a matter of time."

"Too many of them and not enough of us," interjected Saul.

The family grew solemn for a moment.

"After dinner, let's have us a fine game of horseshoes!" Caroline suggested.

They all agreed. Once Josie had beaten them all, they retired to the parlor. David had moved into his old bedroom, freeing up the cottage for his uncle and male cousins. The girls would sleep together in Josie's room. The family sat on the porch, chatting. One by one, they drifted off until all that remained was mother and son.

Caroline lit her pipe, the pungent smell of burning tobacco floating up around them. She rocked back and forth for a few minutes, then asked, "Have you given any thought to when you'll be leavin', son?"

He knew by the word she used to reference him that it was a difficult subject for her. She'd had to endure her grandchild's absence already.

"I'll show Uncle Ed around, and then take my leave next week sometime."

"I see."

They sat quietly, relishing each other's company, not knowing what to say, but comfortable in their silence.

"Ma."

She looked over at him, his large eyes twinkling in the moonlight. "No need to say it, honey. No need 't all." She reached over and held tightly onto his hand.

In the morning after church, he showed his uncle the workings of the farm, including his still. Relaying instructions on how to operate it, he felt he was leaving it in dependable hands. That evening, he announced his departure date was set for August 12, which was in three days. He noticed his mother's sad glances, but through it, she wore a smile.

The next day, he rode around the county to visit his friends, stopping first at Callie's. He found her out back in the garden, clipping roses.

"Miss Callie," he said as she turned to receive him.

"Why darlin' David. What brings you by?"

"I'm leavin' day after tomorrow."

"To be with your Anna? I do declare, she is the luckiest girl alive!" They chuckled.

"Aw," he uttered embarrassingly.

"Bless her heart," Callie said with a sly grin.

David couldn't tell if she meant it, or if she was being sarcastic.

"Now tell me, how did all this come about?"

He proceeded to explain the situation, all the while noticing the tremendous smile on her delicate face. She looked like she was the cat who had eaten the canary, and suddenly, it dawned on him.

"You know somethin'."

She chuckled. "I'm the one who bought your uncle's farm."

"You?"

Callie nodded. "Your mother informed me of what was happenin', and I felt it was my place to assist."

His mouth dropped open. All he could do was stare at her in disbelief. "So that was your big surprise?"

She nodded. "I'm jist tryin' to make you happy, David. You know how dear to my heart you are."

They grinned at each other, and embraced. Without further thought, their lips met in a kiss. It was then that David knew for certain. They could never be anything more than beloved friends.

Callie stepped back, pulled the chain of her Chatelaine from her pocket, and revealed Jake's pocket watch attached. She gazed down repentantly at it.

"I keep this with me always," she whispered, "to remind me of my one true love."

David didn't know what to say. He merely nodded in acknowledgment, considered embracing her again, but opted against it. She gave him a rueful smile and placed the watch back in her pocket.

Once they had shared their goodbyes, he rode to the mercantile, explained the situation to Ben, and asked that he relay it to his fellow Knights. The shopkeeper consented with well wishes, sending him off with a bag of jerky for the trip.

In the morning, David rode to the blacksmith's to have Renegade re-shod before their departure. John Moss notified him that his stallion was in grand form, and should make the trip easily. After their visit, David went to see Bud Samuels, who admitted his envy, wishing he was well enough to go on adventures, but his stump of a leg was giving him trouble. His wife wasn't faring much better. David expressed his commiseration, asked that he stop by to visit his mother when he got the chance, and departed. He rode by what was left of Percy's old place, sorrow overcoming him as he remembered that horrible night. After muttering a quiet prayer for Percy and his family, he kissed his fist in a gesture of finality. He somberly traveled to the Kimball's house, where he saw the buckeye tree had grown another foot. Jake's mother welcomed him, took him in with open arms, sat him down, gave him a cool drink, and upon his request, found her husband. Once he'd told them of his plans, they smiled understandably.

"We will miss you, dear," Mrs. Kimball said. "But we certainly know how you must want to be with your wife and child."

"Yes'm," David replied shyly. He exchanged conversation with them for nearly an hour before it was time to leave.

"You'll visit Jake before you go," Mr. Kimball said, more as a question than a command.

"Yessir, I surely will."

He mounted and rode away. Deciding now was as good a time as any, he directed Renegade to the churchyard, and walked to Jake's headstone. He dismounted, removed his hat, and sadly gazed down at the grassed-over grave as he numbly held onto his horse's reins.

He stood in the hot sun, sweat trickling down his temples, but he didn't notice. Absorbed in all the things he could recollect experiencing with his best friend, from childhood up until the end, he squinted as his sentimentalism welled up to take him. After several minutes had gone by, he finally uttered, "Jake." It was all he could say, waiting until his emotions died down. He stroked Renegade's muzzle, attempting to calm himself.

"Jake, I've got to be leavin' now. I have to git up to Anna. You understand." He paused, knowing he'd receive no response, but waited anyway. He heard cattle lowing in the distance. "I'll think of you fondly, always." He drew a deep, sad sigh. "There'll be no one to replace you." He forced himself to smile, sniffing back tears.

Slowly turning away, he noticed a bluebird on a nearby fencepost. The bird chirped before flying off to the north.

He could almost hear Jake say, "If you see a bluebird land and it flies off, follow it. Follow your heart."

David frowned. He looked back at Jake's grave over his shoulder. All was as it had been, but for some reason, he was overcome with tranquility. He smiled, stepped into the saddle, waved his hat in Jake's direction, donned it, and galloped off.

That evening, he packed his few belongings. He kept the bookmark Josie had made for him, but opted to leave the Henry rifle Kit had gifted him for his family to use. He also decided to leave mementos he'd collected from the war: his CSA belt buckle, the $100 Confederate note he'd won racing Renegade, and the swords Michael had given him. After giving them to his mother for safekeeping, he lingered near her, feeling awkward and under foot, but she appreciated his gesture, smiled, and hugged him frequently. When the house was quiet, she found him in his room.

"Air's nice and cool outside," she said. "Come on out with me."

He followed her onto the porch, and sat beside her as she rocked and lit her pipe. A show of shooting stars sporadically, silently streaked overhead. He grinned, knowing he'd miss his mother's astute insight and happy outlook. She'd nearly seen and been through it all, but still, she remained optimistic.

"I love you, Ma."

She looked over at him, releasing a puff of smoke. "Now don't you start. I'll git all teary-eyed, and we don't want that."

"Why not?"

"Oh, David! Sometimes you exasperate me so!" He saw a tear fall from her eye.

"I'm sorry."

She puffed again, rocking as she contemplated. "Ain't no love greater than that twixt a mother and her son."

He felt his throat tighten, and could only nod. After regaining his composure, he said, "We'll be expectin' you for Christmas."

She chuckled. "Honey, that ain't likely to happen. I have no desire to travel up north. Besides, I'll be busy here, tendin' to your cousins, and sendin' Josie off."

He fell silent.

As if reading his thoughts, she said, "Life gits hard sometimes. It makes us stronger, though." She extinguished her pipe, stood, and took his hands. He arose, and she embraced him. Releasing him, she added, "Reckon I won't see you again for a spell. Write when you git there."

"I will, Ma."

She gazed at him silently for a moment. "You'll always be my boy, and now here you are, a grown man with a family of your own. I'm so proud of you." She gave him a hug and released him. "I love you too, my precious son," she whispered, and tenderly gave him a quick kiss on the cheek. She shuffled into the house, leaving him alone.

He glanced around the dark yard. *She'll be all right*, he thought to himself. *They'll all be all right.* He went inside and attempted to sleep.

Early the following morning, he said his goodbyes, gave his mother and sister a kiss, and set off for Arab. It was all too reminiscent of the day he and Jake had enlisted, but this time, he rode alone. After several hours, he reached the depot, boarded his stallion, and sat quietly in a passenger car. He stared out the window, waiting for departure. Soon, the locomotive lurched from the station, belching, clanking, and churning in a haze of steam and smoke. It occurred to him that he was leaving home nearly three years to the day that he and Anna had arrived. He considered the notion that he might not see his family again, remembering the same thought had crossed his mind when he'd left for the army. He shook his head, attracting the attention of a young boy who sat across from him. No, he vowed to himself, he would make sure he saw them again.

As the train rumbled along, he stared out at the rolling landscape, the coral and orange-red flowers of Cumberland azaleas blooming along the tracks. It wasn't long before he found himself dozing off.

"Hey mister."

The boy startled him. David straightened with a snort.

"You from these parts?"

David rubbed his hand across his face, glancing at the boy's mother, who was seated beside him. She smiled, sympathetic that her son had wakened him.

"Yeah."

"Where you headed?"

"Up north Pennsylvania way."

"What's up there?"

"My wife and daughter."

He smiled cordially at the woman, but didn't feel like elaborating, so he stood and made his way down the aisle, opened the passenger car's door, and stood out on the landing. His emotions made his head ache; he thought he might become nauseous, but the fresh air eased his discomfort. Momentarily, he reentered, taking an empty seat. Before long, he dozed off again.

The train arrived in Huntsville, where it rested at the depot before continuing on. It weaved its way through the Appalachians, making stops to refuel. At one such stop, he learned Alabama had been readmitted to the Union, which felt like a tremendous burden had been lifted.

After a few days, the train reached Richmond. David led Renegade from his box car into the bright mid-afternoon sun. He had several hours to kill before the train left for Baltimore, so he decided to mount up and ride into town. To his satisfaction, he discovered the city had begun to rebuild, although he reasoned it would take years to establish what had been lost. He'd read about how his commander, Jeb Stuart, was buried in Hollywood Cemetery, so he obtained directions and rode over.

Dismounting, he tied Renegade, and entered the large cemetery with granite and marble markers and statues. He wandered through until he found the stone, and stood solemnly with his hat in his hand, gazing at the grave. His months with the cavalry rushed into his mind, and he recalled his beloved commander with affection. He bit his lower lip, thinking about his general's demise, and the loss of a nation, the

Southern Nation. Sobs escaped him: he squeezed his eyes shut in an attempt to hold back his tears. Other people in the cemetery glanced his way, but seeing his remorse, quietly walked away. After sucking in a few large gulps of air to collect himself, he placed his slouch hat upon his head, retrieved Renegade, and returned to the depot.

As the iron horse tugged away from the Richmond depot, David could only stare out the window, his grief still prevalent, and watch as the Blue Ridge Mountains rolled by. This time, there were no freedmen lining the tracks, vagrants without a home. Three years had changed everything, but the Virginia countryside was still as beautiful as he remembered. It was as though battles fought here had never occurred.

"Monsieur?"

He looked up to see a young woman sitting across from him, seated beside an older gentleman in a dark wool suit.

"Pouvons nous être utiles à vous?" The concern on her face expressed her compassion.

He realized he must look a sight. His long, dark brown hair was ruffled, his homespun clothes were rumpled, and his hazel eyes sported dark rings beneath them. Trying to remember what little French he'd learned in prison, he understood her offer to help.

"Aucun Merci."

She smiled at him.

It was too awkward, so he pardoned himself, stood, and walked down the aisle as the conductor approached.

"Sir, ticket please?"

He handed his ticket to the man, who took the piece of paper from him and punched it. Looking up at him, he asked, "How tall are you, son?"

"Six feet," he replied.

The conductor grinned. "Watch your head then!" He meandered down the aisle.

David considered standing out on the landing again, but decided to remain inside instead, for the August heat was oppressive. He returned to his seat and pulled the window shade, attempting to sleep. *Only a few more hours till I see them again*, he repeated to himself.

Feeling like someone was watching him, he opened his eyes to see the French woman's companion staring at him. He frowned, considered placing his hat over his face, but decided it would be too rude.

"Are you all right, young man?" The gentleman's tone was smooth and reassuring.

"I beg your pardon?" he asked, his voice hoarse.

"You seem saddened. I'm a minister. Is there anything I can do to assist?"

David glanced at the French woman, who had fallen asleep on his shoulder. He paused, but the man's kindness showed in his eyes. "Well, sir, I've been without my wife for two months, and my li'l daughter to boot. I know I shouldn't doubt her, but when she left, we weren't on the best of terms."

"Oh. I see."

"She was writin' to an old friend of hers, who arranged her passage back to Pennsylvania. The thing is, this feller tried to kill me."

The minister raised his gray, bushy eyebrows, provoking David to elaborate.

"I reckon I'm jist upset 'cause she went behind my back. I love her, and I'm purty sure she still loves me too. But with this other feller in the picture, it's hard to say what influence he's havin' on her."

The man nodded. He withdrew a Bible from his coat pocket. Thumbing through the scriptures, he stopped. "Perhaps this will calm your spirit." He began reading. "Love is patient and kind; love is not jealous or boastful; it is not arrogant or rude. Love does not insist on its own way; it is not irritable or resentful; it does not rejoice at wrong, but rejoices in the right. Love bears all things, believes all things, hopes all things, endures all things." He closed the Holy Book and set it on the seat beside him. "I can't say for certain what awaits you, my boy, but if she loves you, she will be anticipating your arrival."

"That's another thing. She doesn't know I'm comin'."

The minister frowned. "Oh. Well, I'm sure she will be thrilled, just the same."

"I hope so," he grumbled in response before closing his eyes and submitting to slumber.

It was dark outside when the train reached Baltimore. He exited the passenger car, retrieved Renegade, and stood staring at the paintings on the station's walls, which depicted the Rocky Mountains in all their splendor, and beneath, the words screamed, "Go West, young man!" He felt as though the paintings were speaking to him directly. The idea of adventure was still attractive. He expelled a forlorn sigh as he walked outside. Seating himself on a bench, he chewed on what was left of the jerky Ben had given him, grasping a rein while Renegade grazed, recalling how he'd been given jerky upon his release from Elmira. It hadn't lasted long, though, because a dog had managed to run off with it while he lay sleeping in a ditch on his way back to Anna.

Two Federal soldiers noticed him and walked toward him. He winced at the thought of confrontation, and rose to his feet.

"Son, we learned that you're a southern boy, way up here from the South."

The man was obviously drunk by the slur of his words.

"Did you fight in the war?" asked the younger one, swaying a bit.

"I ain't lookin' for trouble," David responded. "Pardon me." He pulled Renegade's head up and started away.

"We ain't pickin' on you!" the younger soldier hollered.

"Damned Rebel got what he deserved!" barked the other.

They burst into laughter as David walked to the opposite end of the platform, struggling to control his outrage.

Within the hour, the train to York was ready.

"All aboard!" a conductor yelled as a bell clanked above him.

David boarded his horse and found his seat. Annoyed with himself, he hadn't taken into consideration when his train would be arriving, and realized he'd be riding to Dover in the dark. It was Saturday night. He considered staying in York overnight, but had spent all his money, and his stomach growled incessantly as a reminder.

Once his train arrived, he clicked open his pocket watch, and saw Anna's face looking out at him. He smiled at her likeness. It was nearly midnight. According to his recollection, her farm was about an hour away, but because it was dark, the journey would take longer. Still, he was resolute to persist, and retrieved Renegade as he saw a Yankee soldier come toward him.

"Fine lookin' horse you got there," the Federal said.

"Thank you, sir." David clucked to his stallion, prompting him down the ramp.

"How much you want for him?"

David glared at the stranger. "He ain't for sale." He started away, but the soldier stepped in front of him, blocking his path.

"Where is it you're headed?"

Exasperated, David replied, "Well, sir, it ain't really none of your business, but since you asked, I'm headed up near Dover."

"Dover?"

"Yessir. My wife and daughter are there."

The soldier looked him up and down for a moment, then glanced over Renegade, noticing David's sparse belongings and encased guitar strapped to the horse's saddle. He reached into his haversack. David feared he might withdraw a weapon, and realized they were the only two left on the platform. The depot had shut down, and the engineer was gone for the night. "If you're fixin' to kill me, I got a ..."

He laughed. "I ain't gonna kill you!" The young man pulled a paper-wrapped package from his sack, and handed it to him. "You look half-starved. Take this with my blessing."

David hesitated.

"It's a pound cake my mother sent yesterday. Still fresh." He gestured, insisting that David take it, so he did.

"Thank you kindly, uh, what'd you say your name was?"

"McEllroy. Corporal McEllroy to be exact."

"I appreciate it, Corporal."

"Did you fight?"

David frowned. "Yessir. It's somethin' I'd rather not discuss at present."

"Then you likely outrank me."

He chuckled. "Naw, I was only a private when the war ended."

McEllroy looked upon him sadly for a moment. "I don't have much use for this, either." He pulled a twenty-dollar liberty head gold coin from his trouser pocket, and handed it to him.

"I don't want your charity."

David tried to return the coin, but the corporal refused.

"Take it as a gesture of good will." He grinned. Before David had a chance to protest further, he said, "Have a nice ride," and walked off.

Looking down at the coin, he slid it into his pocket, then ravenously devoured the cake, muttering to his horse, "Sure could go for a cup of coffee with this, ole Pard," between bites. He mounted up, gained his bearings, and rode off into the darkness.

He gauged himself by familiar landmarks on the roadside, although they were few and far between. The night was muggy and quiet, except for crickets chirping in the ditches. Wondering repeatedly if he was heading in the right direction, he talked to Renegade, and sang "Bonnie Blue Flag" and songs he made up for reassurance. Finally, he reached the town of Dover, and recognized some of the buildings. He considered sleeping on Grace's stoop, but decided against it, and pressed onward.

Weariness rapidly overpowered him. He felt himself sway in the saddle. Still, he forced himself to keep going. Renegade stumbled, which only created further worry and guilt for causing the poor beast such trouble. At long last, he came over a hill, and recognized the place immediately. He grinned widely, his heart fluttering, and spurred Renegade to a trot. As he approached, he saw there were no lights shining inside; no one was there to welcome him. Two of the Brady's dogs, Floyd and Colby, emerged from the side of the barn. The collie attempted a lackadaisical bark, but David called his name, quieting him. Their little terrier, Buster, was nowhere to be found. He presumed it must be inside the house. Reining back, he walked his stallion to the barn, dismounted, and led him inside, noticing the smell of musty, fragrant, freshly cut hay. He looked around to see the same two cows he remembered, looking at him, as well as the Brady's horse.

"Hello, Alphie, ole boy," he said softly.

The bay draft horse blew before turning back to his fodder.

David led Renegade into an empty stall beside him. "You two are old friends. Y'all should git along fine for tonight."

He went over to where he knew bales were piled, and carried one back to his steed. Removing his saddle as Renegade crunched, he quickly brushed him down. Once he felt satisfied with his horse's care, he patted the wagging dogs, and walked outside.

Inhaling a deep breath, he took in the familiar, nearly forgotten scent of the Pennsylvania countryside. Memories rushed into his conscience: the great battle at Gettysburg, Renegade's run to the farm, his courtship with Anna. He considered it strange how it had all come full circle, and here he was back again. He looked at the house, up at the window to the room he knew she occupied. Wanting more than anything to lie by her side, he opted to sleep on the front porch instead, so as not to wake them, and that way, he would be the first one to ward off encroaching intruders. He glanced at his pocket watch again. It was two-thirty. He nodded, agreeing with himself that it was the right decision.

Sprawled out on the floor of the front porch, he considered Stephen. If he made an appearance in the morning, David would be there to intercept him. A dreadful notion crossed his mind. What if he was already in the house? What if he had manipulated his way into Anna's bed? The thought made him glower. He clenched his teeth, straining to contain himself. *No,* he thought, *she wouldn't allow that.*

He considered moving to the back porch, but reasoned it wouldn't be any more comfortable, and he might be afforded a little more sleep where he was. His mind wandered back to Stephen. That rascal! After all he'd done, how could she trust him again? He decided it was useless to fume about it; he'd never get any sleep that way. His mind came to a resolution, the only conclusion possible. If Stephen caused any problems, any trouble whatsoever, this time, he would kill him.

"Strange, (is it not?) that battles, martyrs, blood, even assassination should so condense – perhaps only really, lastingly condense – a Nationality."

- Walt Whitman

Chapter Eleven

"David. David! Wake up."

Roused awake, he sat upright to see someone standing over him. It was too dark to distinguish the features, but momentarily, he recognized who it was.

"Miss Abigail?"

She knelt down beside him, hugged him, and gave him a kiss on the cheek. "I knew you were coming home tonight," she stated matter-of-factly.

He glanced around in confusion. "What time is it?"

"About half past three."

"Oh," he moaned, realizing he'd only been asleep for an hour.

"Come inside." She arose and took him by the arm. As they quietly entered the house, she whispered, "Why were you sleeping on the front porch?"

"I didn't want to wake y'all," he whispered back. "I'll jist sleep here on the sofa." He fumbled his way into the parlor, found the piece of furniture, and sat down.

"Are you sure you don't want to go upstairs?" she asked, referring to the bedroom Anna was occupying.

"Naw, I'll be fine here. Go on back to bed."

She sat down beside him, and hugged him again. "I'm so glad you're here!" she whispered. He detected the excitement in her words. "My brother has come home at last!" A giggle escaped her. She clamped her hand over her mouth, stood, and shuffled off.

He lay back on the sofa, his feet hanging off the end, and understood its purpose was definitely not for sleeping. After listening to the mantle clock tick for several minutes, he finally fell asleep.

"There's my beautiful dreamer."

At first, he thought he was dreaming, but as his eyes reluctantly opened, he discovered the love of his life hovering over him.

"Anna." He sat up, propping on one elbow, embracing her with his free arm as they met in a kiss. "I missed you, darlin'."

"And I you," she replied, smiling.

He set his feet on the floor, still in his boots. The pale light of early dawn filtered into the room through lace curtains. "Is everyone else up?"

"No, not yet. Abigail woke me a few minutes ago. She said she knew you were coming."

"Yeah. She told me that too."

"What time did you arrive?"

David attempted to rub the sleep from his eyes, but it was still early, and he'd only acquired a few hours. "Late."

Noticing his weariness, she said, "Oh, darling. Why don't you go upstairs for a while?"

"Not without you." He kissed her again.

Smiling, she stood, took his hand, and led him through the house to the stairs. He followed her up, and they climbed into bed together, quiet so as not to wake the other members of the household.

"Where's Dorie?" he asked in a hushed tone.

"She's with Abigail. How did you get here?"

"I took the train, and rode Renie over from York."

She smiled. "How were you able to leave Alabama?"

He proceeded to explain the circumstances surrounding his uncle's arrival. "And he's stayin' indefinitely."

"Oh. I see."

Her greenish-blue eyes made his heart flutter. He kissed her. Their kisses turned fervent, and soon, they were making love. Tenderly embraced in each other's arms, both reveled in each other's familiar feel, scent, and taste. Two months of separation was nearly unbearable, but the flame of their undying love was reignited, the thrill of each other's touch renewed, and their marriage re-consummated.

As she lay snuggled against him, she listened to the slow, steady rhythm of his breathing. Softly, she kissed the scar on his left shoulder, slid out of bed, enwrapped herself in a robe, and went downstairs. Her aunt was in the kitchen, drying breakfast dishes, dressed for church.

Glancing up from her chore as Anna descended, she asked, "Are you feeling all right?"

She nodded in response, an enormous smile spreading across her face. "He's here, Aunt Sarah."

"Who is?" She paused. "David?"

"Yes. I think I'll stay here this morning, if it's all right."

"Of course, dear!" Her aunt walked across the kitchen and hugged her. "I'm happy he's here. I'm so happy for the both of you!" She smiled. "I'll see you after church." She walked outside to the waiting landau.

Anna returned upstairs and fell asleep beside him. Wakened by his gentle touch, she wrapped herself around him. Their passion unfurled in fury; they made love even more ardently. Coming together in ecstasy, they intertwined like vines, and when it was over, fell upon the bed beside each other, panting until they'd both caught their breath. She reached up, stroked his jaw line, and ran her fingertips over his Adam's apple, then rolled onto her side, kissed him deeply, and lay back exhausted as she expelled a contented sigh.

He softly chuckled. "I'm glad to know you still love me."

She laughed. "Of course, I do, silly!" She turned to look at him, her smile fading as she read his expression. "You're serious. You have the same doubts as before. David, don't you trust me?"

"Sure, I do. It ain't you I don't trust."

She glared at him, staring intensely into his brownish-hazel eyes until he thought she might see into the very depths of his soul.

"You mean Stephen."

"How could I trust him, Anna?" He stroked her long blonde hair.

"You know why I had to go."

He nodded. "Although it saddened me a heap. Don't ever leave me again, you hear?"

"I won't." She hesitated. "You understand why I sought out his help."

He frowned, closing his eyes.

Aware that he didn't care, but saying it anyway, she told him, "He's been promoted to captain."

He snorted. Clenching his jaw, he replied, "Well, that's the Yankee government for you." He turned to her, the creases in his forehead deep with anguish.

Reading his thoughts, she soothed, "David. You are my one true love. The only man I will ever love. There is no one else in my heart now, nor shall there ever be." She kissed him. Suddenly, she sat up, pulling the sheet to her. He opened his eyes to look at her. "Do you believe me?"

He grinned. "Yes, darlin', I believe you."

"Good! Now, we'd better get up before everyone returns." She stood, letting the sheet fall away. He stared, taking in the wondrous beauty of her, aware of how immensely lucky he was.

After they'd both dressed, they went downstairs to the kitchen. While Anna fried eggs, he gulped down a cup of lukewarm coffee, savoring every swallow. He kissed her, excused himself, and went out to the barn. Renegade had already been turned out with Alphie and the cows. He retrieved his guitar and saddlebags from the corner where he'd stashed them, set them on the back porch, extracted clean clothing from one bag, and walked down to the pond, where he quickly bathed. Hurriedly pulling on his clothes, he shook the excess water from his locks, feeling refreshed. As he sauntered back to the two-story farmhouse, he smiled, a sense of ease coming over him. Renegade nickered to him upon his approach. A flurry of dust billowed up from the road as someone turned onto the lane. Renegade bolted along the fence line toward the incoming intruder. David squinted to see it was a lone rider, who rode into the barnyard, pulling his steed to an immediate halt.

"How do," David hollered as the man dismounted.

"Sir." He walked up to him, sizing him up. "I'm here to see Maggie." David raised an eyebrow at him, so the young man continued. "Pardon me. My name is Kenton Price. And you are?"

"David Summers," he replied. "I'm Maggie's brother-in-law."

Kenton's continence changed to a scowl. "Oh. You're that Rebel."

David snickered. "Yeah, reckon I am at that. Why don't you come on inside and make yourself comfortable. She should be back any ..."

"I'll wait out here, if you don't mind."

Kenton appeared perturbed that David would even offer. Picking up on his disdain, he said, "All right. Suit yourself," and walked to the house. He went inside, staring out the kitchen window at Maggie's suitor until Anna noticed.

"What are you looking at?"

"Kenton Price is here. Said he won't come inside. Referred to me as 'that Rebel'."

She smiled as she set two plates on the table. "Sit down and eat, darling. I'll go have a word with Mr. Price."

He caught her hand before she could leave. "Stay here with me, Anna. He can wait outside in the heat."

"That isn't very Christian-like."

He sat. Clutching his fork, he said, "I don't care for his attitude," and took a bite.

Anna sat beside him, insisted that they recite a quick prayer of thanks, and ate breakfast with him. Soon after, her family arrived. They entered the house and greeted David with affection. Contrary to his worry that Dorie might have forgotten him, she ran into his arms, shrieking "Papa" as he embraced her. He shook hands with Anna's uncle, Bill, then gave Sarah and Anna's sisters a hug. Kenton stood back, glaring odiously at David all the while. The womenfolk went about preparing Sunday dinner while Bill and David went outside to gaze at the crops. The topic swiftly changed, however, and David found himself curious about the newcomer, and the events he'd missed. Mostly, he wanted information about Stephen, and what Bill thought his intentions were.

"The Burrows have been doing well with their business, expanding it threefold since you left," Bill was saying. "They've invited you to work under their employ."

"I'll surely consider it," he responded. "You've made a nice go of it here."

Bill agreed. Scratching his thick, bushy beard, he said, "I heard crops didn't fare too well down south."

"Had a rough couple of years, but things are comin' around now."

"Glad to hear it."

The men paused, staring out at the sprawling field, until David could resist no longer. "What has Montgomery been up to? Has he been around?"

Bill shook his head. "Nope. Haven't seen him. Anna says he's up in Washington City. As far as I know, Stephen's been too busy to pay us any mind."

"Thank God," David muttered under his breath. "What do you think of Mr. Price?"

"Nice enough fellow. He's twenty-two. Thinks he's seen it all." David equated that he was two years older than Maggie, and only a year younger than himself.

Sarah called them in for dinner, so they went inside, finding the dining room table covered with victuals. David took a seat beside his daughter, grinning at Anna as they assisted Dorie, who sat between them, balanced atop a stack of books.

"Lord, thank you for this food, which we are about to receive," said Bill as all bowed their heads. "And thank you for bringing us together on this glorious day. Especially David, who we are all happy to see. Amen."

"Amen." The family began chatting as they passed bowls amid clanking china and silverware.

"Tell us about your trip, David!" Abigail prodded, sitting across from him.

"Not much to tell. I met a French lady and her minister friend." He shrugged, and forked in a mouthful.

"Renegade appears healthy," remarked Sarah.

"Yes'm," he replied shyly. "He's fine."

"How is your family?"

"They're all fine. Anna might've told you. My sister, Rena, married one of my comrades from the war."

"Yes, she did," said Maggie.

Kenton glared at him.

"They're in Washin'ton now. And my younger sister, Josie, will be headed off to college in Huntsville. Ma's busy tendin' to my cousins. I'm jist glad Uncle Ed is there."

"We all are, sweetheart," said Anna.

She smiled at him, and he grinned back.

"David, I'm not sure if Anna told you," Maggie said. A huge smile spanned across her face as she said, "Kenton has proposed marriage. We're engaged!"

His eyes grew wide with astonishment. "Congratulations!" he exclaimed.

"Thank you," Maggie replied, glowing.

Kenton cleared his throat. "Who did you fight with, David? Besides the turncoats, that is."

He raised an eyebrow, and replied, "I fought under General Stuart."

"He was in the cavalry," added Anna.

"You?" David asked, trying to avoid confrontation.

"I was under Grant. Spent most of my time in Petersburg." He continued to glare. "Did you take the Oath of Allegiance?"

David glanced at Bill, who furrowed his eyebrows. "Yessir, in prison, and I'd rather not discuss it at the dinner table." He shoved a forkful of potatoes into his mouth.

"It seems the South has started to recover," said Sarah.

"No, ma'am. It'll be a long time before the South recovers, if it ever does." David suddenly lost his appetite. He set his fork down on the table.

"It's God's divine will," said Maggie.

David and Anna stared at her.

"That the war ended, I mean."

"And that the slaves are free," stated Abigail.

David thought of Percy hanging from a tree. If only she knew. They weren't really free.

"They've decided on a candidate to represent the Democratic party," Bill informed, attempting to change the subject. "Horatio Seymour, who's governor of New York."

New York! David felt his heart skip a beat at the words.

"Well, Grant has my vote," declared Kenton. "Johnson has been far too lenient, and all the Democrats want to go easy on them."

David knew who he was referring to. "You're a Radical, sir?"

Kenton snorted. "I just don't feel like we should do them any favors. After all, it was the Confederates who committed treason."

David couldn't tolerate any more. He'd heard enough. Rising, he said, "If it's all right with y'all, I'd like to take my leave now. I'm still tuckered out from my trip."

Kenton sniggered at David's southern inflection.

"Of course, dear," Sarah excused him as she stood and began collecting dishes.

Without hesitation, he rushed from the dining room, strode down the hall, and bounded up the steps. He closed the door and plopped down on the bed, covering his eyes with his arm. He was too close to exploding. It was all he could do to contain his anger, but after counting to one hundred, he gained his composure. Looking around the room, he saw that Anna had set their wedding and family portraits side by side on her dressing table. The furnishings were as they had been three years previously. He had hidden his Colt .44, and Anna's derringer as well, in the secret compartment inside the armoire, keeping them from Dorie's reach. Hearing a soft rap on the door, he looked over to see his wife enter.

"He's gone," she notified him.

David sat up. "I don't care for that feller," he declared.

"I'm not sure why he was so hostile to you. He knows all about you. About us. I told him."

"Well, if I don't see him again, it'll be too soon."

"You'll see him again, darling. Maggie's wedding is set to take place in three weeks."

"Why didn't you tell me this sooner?"

"I sent you a letter, but you must not have received it."

He sighed.

Later that evening as they gathered in the parlor, David showed Abigail his new guitar, and the two commenced to play a duet. She soon opted for the piano, however, and entertained with a new song she'd learned: "The Man on the Flying Trapeze," before embarking on a performance of several more. Maggie spoke constantly about her upcoming wedding, the dress she'd sewn to wear, and how wonderful she thought Kenton was.

Tired of hearing her biased opinion of the man, David blurted, "How's he fixin' to support you, Miss Maggie?"

She glared at him. "Well ... he has secured employment with a harness shop in Dover. In fact, Grace's husband has already co-signed for our apartment."

David and Anna exchanged glances.

"I don't really see how it's any of your affair, anyway," Maggie went on. "After all, what are your plans? Are you going to live here for the rest of your life?"

"Maggie!" Anna scolded. "There's no need to get snippy."

David understood he'd injured her feelings by indirectly attacking Kenton. "I'm sorry, Miss Maggie. I know the two of you will be right happy together. And if I do live out my life here, well, I can think of worse things."

"I didn't mean … Oh, David." She looked as though she might cry. "I've missed you so."

He walked across the room and took her hand. "If you ask me, ole Kenton's a mighty lucky man."

He grinned, causing her to smile.

A week of hot, humid weather drifted by. The younger members of Anna's family spent as much time swimming in the pond as possible. David worked in the fields with Bill by day, and lollygagged around the house in the evenings, playing his guitar, and dreaming of an adventurous life somewhere else. He had written to his mother, but knew mail delivery was still virtually nonexistent in Morgan County. He'd be fortunate to hear from her at all, but hoped Mr. Ford, the postmaster, would assist once again.

On Saturday, the 22nd, David was called to the house, and walked up to the back porch to see his dear friend waiting for him.

"Well, there ye be!" Patrick walked down the steps and sauntered toward him.

"Patrick!" The men patted each other on the back and hugged. "Good to see you again!"

"Aye! And you!" He chuckled. "Three years gone by and you're here where you started!"

David laughed. "Not quite. I have a daughter now."

"'Tis a bonnie young lass too! And I've acquired me entire family!"

"So I heard!"

"Congratulations!" they both exclaimed in unison, and burst into laughter.

Upon Patrick's request, David rode over to the Meyers' farm with him, where he was greeted with affection. Briana and her two children, Keegan and Kathleen, were there, along with their little beagle, Shannon. Keegan remembered him right away, and pretended to shoot him.

"Take that, Rebel!" he exclaimed, firing imaginary bullets at him with a pointed finger.

"Enough of your shenanigans, young man!" Briana scolded, and sent him and his sister outside.

"You missed za most beautiful weddink!" Mrs. Meyers said, reminding David of her heavy German accent.

"I wish we could've been here to see y'all git hitched!" he replied, smiling at Briana, whose face blushed to nearly the same auburn color as her hair. "What happened to your place up north of Harrisburg, Miss Briana?" he asked.

She smiled, crinkling her nose as she rubbed her cheeks. "Sure'n I decided to sell it. Patrick felt obligated to stay on here, and give the Meyers a year's worth of labor."

"Ja, zat is right," said Mr. Meyers. "We are movink to za city in October."

"What city?"

"Philadelphia."

David stared in surprise.

"Ja," said Mrs. Meyers. "My niece vants us to live with her. Zis place has become such a burden."

"We're stayin' here through the winter," Patrick explained. "And then we're off to Nebraska!"

David gaped at him, starstruck. "How did you convince Miss Briana to do that?"

"Patrick and I discussed it," she said, "and decided it would be a fine opportunity. They're givin' land away, you know."

"Aye," said Patrick. "If we find the weather too harsh, we'll continue on to Colorado territory. Rumor has it there's gold in the mountains there too." His emerald eyes sparkled as he said it.

David grinned, disguising his jealousy.

"What ah your plans, David?" asked Mrs. Meyers.

He slowly shook his head. "I don't rightly know at present. I'll wait till the crops are harvested, I reckon, and decide then." He smiled, but a twinge of envy persisted.

After graciously turning down an offer of supper, he and Patrick walked out to where Renegade stood under the shade of an apple tree, balanced on three hooves.

"You heard of Miss Maggie's upcomin' nuptials?" David asked as he untied his stallion and mounted.

"Aye, that I have."

"Did Anna tell you why she left Alabama?"

267

"Kit Lawrence and his son frightened the lass."

David nodded. "She wasn't comfortable there, and I wasn't comfortable without her," he explained.

"She said Stephen the scoundrel escorted her from Knoxville."

"Bill claims he ain't been around."

Patrick frowned. "Bill hasn't seen him, but I have."

David stared down at him, provoking him to elaborate.

"He's met up with Anna now and then. 'Twas like he was courtin' her."

David's heart sank.

"She's sent him on his way, but he's been lurkin' round. I believe he's chasin' the dragon."

"What makes you think that?"

"I saw him partake of the laudanum on more than one occasion. He said it was for his ailin' hand, the one you shot a hole through, but if you ask me, Stephen is addicted." Patrick shook his head in disgust. "One other thing, lad. The Montgomery's have purchased the Meyers' place."

David scowled. "Thank the Meyers for their hospitality. I'll see y'all soon."

He kicked his horse and galloped down the road, fuming. If the Montgomery's had their way, they would soon own the entire county.

During the next two weeks, David waited for Stephen to materialize, but he remained unseen. Knowing he would encounter him again at Maggie's wedding, he readied himself, and promised Anna he wouldn't make a scene.

The evening before the wedding, he went out to the pond to bathe, and upon returning, noticed Maggie sitting alone on the edge of the well, gazing down into it.

"Penny for your thoughts, Miss Maggie," he said upon approach.

She looked up at him.

"Then you can toss it in and make a wish."

She smiled, taking the penny he handed her. "I don't know that my wish will ever come true." She tossed the coin, which fell silently for a second before plunking in.

"That sounds mighty downtrodden," he remarked. "You're gettin' married tomorrow." He took her hand, assisting her down.

"I know." A sad expression crossed her face.

"Don't you love him, Miss Maggie?"

She nodded, wiping a tear from her eye. "At least, I think I do. It's just that ..."

"What?" he coaxed softly.

"When I see what you and Anna have, I want the same thing."

David snickered. "It hasn't all been a bed of roses, you know."

Maggie smiled. "Sometimes I wish it would have been me, instead of her."

He looked at her quizzically.

"Who you fell in love with."

Embarrassed and flattered by her confession, he gave her a rueful smile. "Miss Maggie, darlin', you'll always have a special place in my heart. But if you don't think ole Kenton's the right one, then you'd better call it off."

She shook her head slowly. "I can't do that. He loves me. I know he does. I also know that I can never have you." She hiccupped a laugh. "I sometimes wish Stephen had married Anna, so that I could have you for myself."

He clenched his teeth. She was admitting far more than he cared to hear, which he found disconcerting. "I don't know what to say," he muttered.

"Say that you'll take good care of Anna and Dorie, and that you'll think of me fondly always."

He grinned. "Of course, I will."

"And now I have a favor to ask." She hesitated. "Would you walk me down the aisle tomorrow?"

He chuckled. "I'd be honored."

She gave him a tender kiss, turned and walked inside, leaving him stunned.

The morning of September 6 was warm and sunny. Anna's family attended church, returned home, prepared for the wedding, and drove back to the little white clapboard building. It was the same chapel where David and Anna had exchanged their vows, only now, it took on a different appearance, because the pews were filled with friends and neighbors. David grew bored waiting in the pastor's house for Maggie to primp, so he ambled up to the church's front doors and peered inside. As he glanced around at the familiar faces that he hadn't seen for quite some time, he noticed Stephen with his family, sitting on the bride's side.

Mrs. Tully emerged from a side door. Her shoes clunked across the floorboards as she made her way to the piano. She perched herself on the bench and began to play. Pastor Tully and Kenton entered behind her, along with four other men in Union blue, and stood at the front. From the main entrance, Abigail emerged, leading Dorie by the hand as she attempted to throw rose petals along the aisle. Maggie's friends, Nelly Dalton and Lila Fairfax, followed in one by one.

Anna appeared, smiling at David as she passed him. "Go fetch Maggie!" she whispered before making her way down the aisle to the front.

He was so distracted that he'd nearly forgotten, and started to run toward the Tully's house, but saw Maggie waiting nearby, so he took her by the arm and escorted her to the entrance.

"You look breathtakin'," he said.

She smiled at him as they stood in the doorway. Mrs. Tully pounded a chord several times in crescendo, inspiring the congregation to stand while Maggie, escorted on David's arm, entered. They walked down the aisle to the "Bridal Chorus" until they reached the pulpit, where he took her hand and gave it to Kenton. David sat in the front pew, and Dorie, who had already grown impatient, ran over and sat beside him.

"Dearly beloved, we are gathered here today ..."

Pastor Tully's voice droned on as the ceremony proceeded. Bride and groom exchanged vows and rings, and before long, the wedding was over. David waited for the bridal party to exit, then picked up his daughter and followed them out. Finding Anna, he smiled as he gave Dorie to her.

"I forgot to tell you, I have a surprise for you," Anna said.

He grinned. "What?"

She turned away to greet Grace and Theodore Burrows, who in turn hugged David.

"We heard you'd returned!" exclaimed Grace.

"Happy to see you, my boy," said Theodore. After talking briefly, he stated, "We would like it very much if you'd come work for us. Your artisanship would be much appreciated and put to good use."

"This autumn after the crops are harvested, I'll be happy to start," replied David.

The Burrows smiled at him, and moved on to congratulate the bride and groom. From the corner of his eye, David saw Stephen approach.

"Hello, my dear." He kissed Anna's cheek, making David's blood boil. "Summers, old boy." He extended his hand, and David felt compelled to take it. "Still sporting that long crop of hair, I see."

Tempted to make an untrue remark about Stephen's flawless beard, David stifled his infuriation. "Always a pleasure," he grumbled.

To his relief, Stephen was whisked away by his sister, Mary, who gave David a snide look before walking off. Patrick and Briana congratulated the newlyweds, who climbed aboard the Brady's landau in a hail of rice. The party departed for home, where a reception was held. The day had grown hot, but no one seemed to notice, although the ladies walked about batting fans. After opening gifts and indulging in cake, Maggie and her groom rode off in his carriage, waving behind them as they disappeared down the lane.

Anna stood waving and crying at the same time. "My little sister's married!" she kept repeating. "I can't believe it!"

David gave her a gentle squeeze, and the two walked back inside. He saw Stephen standing in the corner beside his father, both smoking cigars. Anna mingled away as Stephen approached him.

"How's it feel to be a father?" he asked cynically.

"Nothin' else like it in the world. If you'll excuse me ..."

Stephen blocked his path. "I've been waiting to have a word with you. Shall we?"

He motioned toward the front door, so reluctantly, David walked outside and around to the side of the house. Turning on him, he asked, "What's this all about?"

"You're still distraught over your arrest, aren't you?"

"Distraught ain't the word I'd use," David growled, feeling his temper rise.

"You should just accept what happened to you as the fortunes of war, old boy."

He huffed and started away, but Stephen prevented him.

"Anna felt betrayed by the way you led her on."

"That ain't your business."

"She means the world to me, making it my business."

David bristled. "It's all worked out now."

Stephen burst into laughter. David noticed the pupils of his blue eyes were dilated. "She nearly gave up on your marriage."

"What are you talkin' about?"

Stephen was obviously finding enjoyment in emotionally wounding him. "She said that if you didn't return by your wedding anniversary, she would divorce you."

"You're lyin'." David leered at the man.

Suddenly, Stephen lunged at him, pinning him against the side of the house. His face within inches, David could smell his smoky breath. "Anna should have been mine. I love her, and I had grand plans for us until you came along, you damned Rebel."

"She loves me." David stared into Stephen's eyes, refusing to back down. He pushed the man off. "Ain't nothin' you can do or say to change that." He walked back into the house, hearing Stephen holler after him.

"Oh no? We'll see about that!"

Some of the guests who had collected on the porch turned and gasped, staring at David as he stomped past them. Gritting his teeth, he found Patrick inside, and pulled him out to the backyard for a few shots of whiskey. Once he'd told him about the confrontation he'd had with Stephen, Patrick handed him the bottle.

"You're in for a fight, lad," he proclaimed. "He's changed into a wild man since you last saw him."

David shook his head in loathing. "That might be a fact. But I'm quicker on the trigger." He took another swig.

After the guests had gone, he went about his chores before returning to the house. Exhausted, he tromped upstairs and lay down on the bed, hoping to get a quick nap in before supper. His plans were nixed, however, when Dorie ran in and climbed up beside him, followed by Anna.

"There you are," she said. "I wanted to give you your surprise."

He sat up.

"But if you're too tired, I suppose it can wait."

His curiosity aroused, he said, "No. I'm all right. What is it?"

She smiled, walked to her dressing table, pulled open a drawer, and withdrew a tiny satchel. Handing it to him, she said, "I thought of waiting until our anniversary, but I'll give it to you now instead."

He recalled what Stephen had said about Anna wanting a divorce, but pushed it out of his mind, knowing it had to have been a lie. Carefully pulling the drawstring open, he poured the contents into the palm of his hand. "It's a ring."

"It's your wedding band, David." She sat beside him, took the ring, and slid it onto his finger. "Now everyone will know that you belong to me."

He grinned at her, and gave her a kiss. Showing the ring to his daughter, he remarked, "It fits right nice too."

"And it matches mine. See?" She placed her hand on top of his so that both rings were visible. Like Anna's, his had tiny diamonds imbedded into the yellow gold.

"How much was it?"

She stood. "I'm not telling. It's an early anniversary gift."

"Okay, darlin'. Thank you." He pulled her down onto his lap and kissed her before Dorie pried them apart.

In September, the cotton tax was discontinued on all crops raised that year. Although it didn't affect him directly, David was glad for the farmers down south, since it afforded them some relief. As the weeks progressed, he found he rarely had any time to spend with his wife and daughter, because he and Bill were occupied nearly every waking moment with harvest. On October 3, in *Harper's Weekly*, a cartoon by Thomas Nast appeared, titled "The Modern Samson." Nathan Bedford Forrest was depicted with supporters of the Democratic party, touting a sign that read "slavery," Fort Pillow," "mob law," and "the Ku Klux Klan." The Democrats were portrayed stripping the freedman of his right to vote. David shook his head at the sight of it. The Northern press was obviously attempting to portray ex-Confederates in an ill light, making them seem almost demonic in their intentions. The grand leaders of the

Confederacy were now subjected to ridicule and scorn, and the worst thing was, people in the north believed it.

In mid-October, the Meyers moved as promised, so David watched after their farm while Patrick and Briana helped with their relocation. A week later, to his amazement, he received a letter from home, tore it open, and read it aloud to Anna.

"Dear Son and Daughter. That's you."

"David, keep reading!"

"You will be glad to know that everything is fine here. We have had some rain, and the crops are comin' in nicely." He glanced at his wife and grinned before continuing. "Josie has gone off to school, and I git letters from her every now and then. She left Belle here, and your cousin Mildred is lookin' after her. Josie raced her before she left, and guess who won?"

"Belle!" exclaimed Anna.

David smiled. "She's jist like her sire. We haven't had much trouble around here lately. It has been mighty calm. Edward sold your ruckus juice recipe to a nice feller up in Lynchburg, Tennessee. Your uncle and cousins have been a big help. They built a springhouse, where we like to go and sit on hot days. I hope everyone there is well. Give my love to my sweet granddaughter. Love, your ma."

He bit his lip, frowning. "I should've thought of buildin' a springhouse," he mumbled.

Anna took his hand and kissed him. "Everything will be all right, for all of us," she encouraged, and hugged him.

In November, the presidential election was held. David happily participated, and decided to cast his vote for the governor from New York. Three former Confederate states, Texas, Mississippi, and Virginia, were excluded, as they had yet to be readmitted. In the *York Daily Record* the following morning, Grant was proclaimed the victor. David's heart sank. *We're really in for it now*, he thought desperately.

He took a job in Grace and Theodore's carpentry shop in Dover, handcrafting fine pieces of oak, cherry, and maple furniture. After giving it much thought, he invented a signature mark, which he branded into the bottom of each piece. It represented Anna and Adora, the angels of his heart.

The family upheld their tradition of celebrating Thanksgiving with the Montgomery's. This year, to David's chagrin, it was the Brady's turn to host. He had hoped otherwise, so he could make up an excuse not to attend. Now he had no recourse but to participate. Anna had warned that, although Stephen's parents were told of his Confederate affiliation, his sister, Mary, was still in the dark.

When the Montgomery's arrived, he made himself sparse by going out to the barn, but the chilly weather soon prompted him to return to the warm house. His stint in prison had made him that much more sensitive to the cold, and he hurried inside, shivering as he shed his coat. He entered the kitchen, where Sarah and Dorie were assisting Anna with dinner preparations.

"David!" Anna exclaimed, looking up from the potatoes she was mashing. "Where have you been? We have guests, you know!"

Before he could speak, Mary appeared. "Mr. Summers. It is a pleasure to see you again." She held her hand out, and as always, he kissed the back of it, causing her to titter.

"Miss Montgomery. The feelin' is mutual."

She grinned. "It's missus now. I'm married. Come, let me introduce you."

She led him by the arm. He looked to Anna for rescue, but she returned to her chore. They entered the parlor to see Bill, Mr. and Mrs. Montgomery, and Abigail, who was tinkering on the keys. Stephen and a young man sat conversing in the corner. Mary led him over.

"Dear, this is David Summers. Anna's husband."

The clean-shaven man stood, as did Stephen. He extended his hand. "Summers, I've heard plenty about you!"

"Reckon I'll take that as a compliment," he replied. He shook the gentleman's hand. "And you are?"

"Oh, I beg your pardon," Mary apologized. "This is my husband, Asa Brown."

"No relation to ole John Brown, I hope!" David laughed, but Asa stared at him, making him regret his words.

"As a matter of fact, he was a relative of mine," stated Asa.

"I'd shake your hand," Stephen interjected, "but it's crippled." He glared angrily at David, who decided to quickly change the subject.

"How long have y'all been married?"

"Two years," answered Asa. "I feel quite fortunate to have found a girl as wonderful as Mary. I'm forever grateful she bypassed all others to wait for me."

David and Mary looked at each other, both recalling their awkward encounter. Asa reached around her waist, causing her to giggle. "We're expecting."

David's mouth dropped open slightly. "Well, congratulations!" he said.

"That's right, I'm going to be an uncle," Stephen remarked flatly, and threw back his scotch.

David heard the front door open and voices converse, recognizing them as Maggie and Kenton. He breathed a sigh of relief at the interruption. Upon seeing him, Maggie walked over and hugged him. Kenton shook his hand. The thought crossed his mind that Maggie must have had a talk with him about his rude behavior, since he was now as cordial as could be.

Sarah announced dinner was served, so the family and guests moved into the dining room where Anna directed as each took a seat. The presentation included a roast duck and pheasant, various dishes containing home-grown garden vegetables, Irish potatoes, and candied yams. She sat between Dorie and her husband, smiling at him before they bowed to recite the *Lord's Prayer* in unison. The delectable aroma made David's mouth water, and he anxiously passed bowls and plates, taking heaping helpings from each one.

"This looks mighty tasty!" he remarked before stuffing in a mouthful of yams.

"We've been blessed with our bounty again this year," said Sarah, smiling with amusement as she watched David devour his portion.

"Darling, you should slow down a bit," Anna whispered. He looked up from his plate to see Stephen, Asa, and Kenton staring at him.

"Oh, beggin' your pardon," he said, wiping his mouth with a napkin.

Mary chuckled. "David, where did you and Anna go for so long?" she asked.

He stared at her as Anna gave him a sidelong glance. "Oh. Um, down to Alabama. I ... have cousins down there."

"Well, visiting your relations down south seems to have rubbed off on you," she remarked.

David looked at her questioningly.

"You sound as though you're one of them!"

Mr. and Mrs. Montgomery chuckled. Stephen and Kenton glared at David. Maggie scoffed, throwing a glance at Anna.

"It looks as though Grant will be our next president," bellowed Mr. Montgomery, and sipped his sherry. "Bully for him!"

"He is definitely the right man for the position," added Stephen.

"I don't have a problem with him, as long as he does a good job," David remarked.

"Oh, that's surprising, coming from you," Stephen snarled.

Sarah quickly blurted, "Now gentlemen, let us not discuss politics at the table." She looked at David and said, "Mr. Summers has secured a position with the Burrows' cabinetry shop, and I must say, he does fine work."

"He made me a beautiful oak writing table for our anniversary," Anna reported.

"And I'm makin' you somethin' even more special for Christmas," David said, flashing a grin at her.

"Must be nice, having two hands to work with," muttered Stephen.

The air was growing thicker by the moment. David wasn't sure if it was the heat from the fireplace, but he broke into a sweat. Wiping his brow, he said softly, "Miss Abigail would like to play us some fine music after dinner. Wouldn't you, darlin'?"

She laughed. "No, but you would!" She glanced at Mary, and said, "David plays guitar beautifully."

"To match his wondrous voice, I expect." Mary smiled, catching him off guard.

He blushed at the compliment.

Stephen's distraction from his craving and irritation about the topic got the best of him. Suddenly, he sprang to his feet. "Please pardon me for a moment." He exited through the front door.

Sarah looked at Bill and sighed.

A few minutes later, Stephen returned, took his seat, and smiled at his mother with a noticeable difference in his demeanor, for now he was calm instead of annoyingly intrusive. David saw through him. He was the only other person at the table who knew Stephen's secret.

"If it's all right with everyone," Sarah said, "we will clean up the dishes before we serve dessert."

"What are we having?" asked Kenton.

"Pumpkin pie."

Abigail gasped. "I love pumpkin pie!"

"Me too!" Dorie chimed in, causing everyone to laugh.

After she had devoured two small pieces of pie, the first pumpkin pie she'd ever tasted, Anna took her upstairs to ready her for bed. The women congregated in the kitchen, and David was left with the men in the parlor. Asa excused himself, claiming he'd overeaten, and went outside.

"So, tell me, David," said Mr. Montgomery, clipping a stogie and offering it to him, "what are your plans in, say, five years?"

He grinned. "I don't rightly know. I'll admit I haven't thought that far ahead."

"Oh, well," he said, lighting David's cigar. "You're young. We never seem to run out of a workload."

David nodded in retrospect. "I had my work cut out for me down home. The place is shapin' up, though."

Mr. Montgomery took a thoughtful puff. "The people in the south have suffered immeasurably, I'm certain."

"Yessir. I only hope they had as fine a celebration as we had here today."

Stephen meandered over, interrupting the conversation. "Father, I'd like to propose a toast."

"Whatever for?" asked Mr. Montgomery.

"In celebration of this country's reunification, of course." He raised his glass, prompting the others to follow suit. "To the United States."

"Here, here," said Kenton.

They all partook in a sip of wine.

"You might have heard that I purchased the Meyers' farm," said Mr. Montgomery.

David replied, "Yessir, I have."

"That will keep us busy for a while. Although Patrick has done a fine job, the place still needs some attention."

"How much would it take to inspire you to sell, Mr. Matthews?" Stephen asked blatantly.

Bill furrowed his bushy eyebrows at him. "That's between my niece and me."

"Oh. Anna still has a say in the property?"

"She does."

David detected the wheels turning in Stephen's head. A sinister expression crossed his face. He stepped toward him, out of the others' earshot. "Every man has his price," he said, as though thinking out loud. "And a widow with a child would be in need of financial assistance."

Glaring at him, David watched him step back, thinking he should step further into the shadows from whence he came. He was tempted to laugh in defiance, but somehow, the humor, the ridiculousness of Stephen's comment dissipated. He silently sipped his wine, contemplating Stephen's veiled threat.

Accommodating Abigail's wishes, he serenaded the crowd with one his favorite songs, "Cindy," and then invited her to entertain their guests on the piano. When the Montgomery's had at last departed, he walked outside, standing on the cold porch, gazing up at the stars, his breath vaporizing into the darkness. There was no way he could protect himself. Hell, the bastard could be staring down the barrel of a shotgun at him right now. He sighed.

"I'll be damned if I'll let that son of a bitch take my place," he vowed aloud.

Somehow, he had to find a way to protect Anna and his precious little girl. Then again, he could be overreacting, he decided. Still, Stephen had changed, and his unpredictability deeply concerned him. It was all coming into view. Stephen was plotting something diabolical, and it didn't look favorable for David in the least.

"The attempt to place the white population under the domination of persons of color in the South has impaired, if not destroyed, the friendly relations that had previously existed between them; and mutual distrust has engendered a feeling of animosity which, leading in some instances to collision and bloodshed, has prevented the cooperation between the two races so essential to the success of industrial enterprise in the Southern States."

- Andrew Johnson, speech to Congress,
December 25, 1868

Chapter Twelve

David went outside the following morning to discover a thin layer of pristine snow blanketing the entire landscape. He stood gazing across the empty fields, his breath frosting out before him. The pure, glistening, crystallized void was awe-inspiring, but unavoidably, his mind drifted, and he remembered his horrific experiences at Elmira. Anna called his name, snapping him back to the present, so he returned to her, warm and unscathed.

With only a few weeks until Christmas, he spent long days at the cabinetry shop, working fervently to fill orders and complete his personal task of creating gifts for his family. By December 6, he nearly accomplished his goal, with the exception of Anna's. Unable to conceive the perfect gift for her, he saved that project for last.

He read about the Battle of Washita River. General George Custer, the ostentatious man whom he had met on the battlefield at Gettysburg, led an attack on a band of Cheyenne Indians living with Chief Black Kettle on reservation land, and killed 103 of them. War had swept westward, but still, David yearned to be a part of it.

Two days later, he entered the house to discover the post had arrived. Surprised to receive a letter from his sister, he eagerly tore open the envelope and withdrew a folded piece of paper.

"Dearest David and Anna," he read aloud to his spouse as Sarah stood by, "Michael and I are well here in Washin'ton. The reason for my letter is that we are sendin' you a formal invitation to attend my debut." He frowned, unsure of the meaning.

"Keep reading," Anna coaxed.

"I will be performin' in an opera at the National Theatre on Saturday evenin' the nineteenth of December. I have already placed your names on the admittance list. Please send a telegram to let me know if y'all are fixin' to come. Love, Rena."

He looked up from the letter, his large hazel eyes wide with amazement. "She's gonna sing."

Anna smiled and took his hand.

He laughed. "In front of an audience! It's what she's always wanted."

"And she wants you to be a part of it," Sarah said.

David winced. "But it's too close to Christmas. I still have work to do."

"Is it anything Mr. Burrows can't manage himself?" asked Anna.

"No. I reckon not."

"Then we should go!" Anna smiled widely at the prospect. He could detect her excitement by the flicker in her blue-green eyes.

"I don't know."

"Please, David? Aunt Sarah will watch Dorie for us." She glanced at her aunt, raising her eyebrows as if pleading, and Sarah nodded in agreement.

"We can't really afford it."

"I've been putting some money aside. And who knows when we'll get the chance to do this again," Anna persisted.

Still reluctant, he stammered, "I ... I don't have all my gifts done."

"Well, what do you have left?"

"Jist yours."

"Davie, honey. It's only for a weekend. We'll be back before Christmas."

He shrugged.

"All right then, sweetie, it's settled." She wrapped her arm around his. "We're going to Washington City!" She pecked him on the cheek.

"Now hold on jist a cotton pickin' minute. I didn't agree ..."

"Sorry, Mr. Summers, but you have no choice." She released him, snatching the letter from his hand before he could react. "I'm riding into town to send my sister-in-law a telegram!" she proclaimed, and off she went.

David stood in the parlor, unable to resist, because he wanted to go too, but his impending duties concerned him. After a few moments, he saw the landau drive out with Anna and Abigail aboard.

"What's really troubling you, dear?" Sarah asked as she ran a feather duster around the room.

"I'm afraid it might be an imposition, us expectin' you to look after Dorie."

"Nonsense! We love that little girl. You needn't fret about that."

"Thank you, Miss Sarah." He paused, sinking down upon a velvet chair. "Do you have any idea what Anna might like for Christmas?"

She smiled at him as though she knew his question was the true heart of the matter. "No, I don't. But I'm certain you'll think of something lovely. You always do."

He forced a feeble grin. Standing, he said, "Well, I've got a week and a half," and walked out to retrieve Renegade.

The day before Rena was to perform, David and Anna were deposited at the depot in York by her uncle, where they boarded the train destined for Washington, and arrived a few hours later. As they stepped down from their passenger car, David looked over to see his sister running toward them through the crowd. He caught her in an embrace, and they laughed and kissed each other. Michael, who was right behind her, shook David's hand while Rena and Anna hugged.

"I'm so happy to see y'all!" Rena exclaimed. "We have today and all day tomorrow to show y'all the sights!"

"All I care about is seein' you, li'l sister," David replied, grinning. "Reckon you're a starlet now!"

Rena giggled. "Not quite yet. Wait until tomorrow night to tell me that!"

She took Anna by the arm, and they started off, leaving David to struggle with the trunk they'd brought along containing their personal effects. Michael assisted, and the two followed their ladies, chuckling and making small talk along the way. When they reached a carriage, the driver took the trunk and set it in back while his passengers boarded.

"My company has arranged accommodation for y'all to stay in the nicest hotel in Washin'ton!" exclaimed Rena as Anna gazed wide-eyed at the bustling city passing by.

"We'd invite y'all to our place, but it's mighty small for the four of us," Michael explained.

Rena smiled widely across at her brother, and squeezed Michael's arm, who was seated beside her. "I jist can't believe y'all are really here!"

David chuckled. "Oh, we're here, all right. Y'all will be tired of seein' us by the time this weekend's over."

Her mouth dropped open. "I very much doubt that! Now tell me, how is my beautiful niece?"

As they traveled through the city, David caught up with his sister and brother-in-law while Anna contributed little, staring out the window like a cat watching songbirds. Enormous buildings bragged fanciful architecture, the streets were paved with cobblestone, and people were dressed in fine suits, dresses, and hats. As he spoke, David glanced at prancing, well-fed horses leading polished, shining, brass-adorned coaches, and pushed back his revulsion until he could further digest the sight. It was more than obvious how Northerners had prospered from the war by the way their capital boasted its wealth. Soon, their driver pulled to the curb, stopping his carriage.

"We're here!" Rena announced.

She stepped out as the driver assisted her. David glanced up at the tremendous, six-story brick building his family had entered. He followed, noticing a doorman patiently waiting for him. Once inside, the hotel lobby nearly flabbergasted him. He had never been in a place so immaculate, enormous, or daunting before. It boasted grand marble columns, colossal crystal chandeliers, mosaic floors, luxurious rugs, elaborately carved ceilings, heavy green velvet tasseled curtains, and a spectacular staircase. Lavish guests fluttered about, most of which were attired in fine fashion.

"This is the Willard Hotel," Rena informed. "Truth be told that Julia Ward Howe wrote "The Battle Hymn of the Republic" here. And President Lincoln stayed upstairs in one of the suites with his family before they moved into the Executive Mansion."

David meekly followed his sister to the desk, and stood enthralled while she secured their room. They walked across the lobby to a fenced off door in the wall. Suddenly, another door dropped down behind, and the two doors opened at once, revealing a decorated box with a man inside, who was manning a lever. David stood mystified.

"It's an elevator," Rena said. She pulled on his arm, cajoling him to enter.

"I'd rather take the stairs," he admitted softly, but Michael took his other arm, compelling him.

The cage door closed with a clank, and the man asked for their floor. The box lurched upward, passing other doors until it slowed abruptly, shimmied up and down, and finally stopped. David anxiously strode out.

"Jist wait till the ride down!" Rena teased.

They emerged into a long hallway lined with doors. Passing by an open doorway, Rena stopped abruptly.

"Oh, come in here! I have to show y'all somethin'!"

They followed her in, where David discovered a lavatory.

"Rena! We shouldn't be in here in mixed company," he scolded.

"Jist wait! I want to show you this here contraption." She reached up and pulled a chain, causing the toilet tank attached to the ceiling to flush.

"Well, I'll be …" David sighed in awe. He noticed the ornate footed bathtub and the marble sink with brass fixtures standing beside the toilet.

"Each hallway has a bathroom for y'all to use," stated Michael.

Rena motioned for them to follow her out. Upon finding their room number, she extracted a key, unlocked the door, and disappeared into the dark room. David glanced at Anna before following her in. The room quickly brightened as Rena opened the Damask drapes to reveal the magnificent splendor. Michael whistled at the sight. Embellished, thickly carved oak furniture adorned the room, which was complete with a four-poster bed, two bed tables, two dressers, three green velvet armchairs, a floor-length mirror, a long clock, and a candle stand. Currier and Ives paintings decorated the walls, and a tapestry covered the floor.

"Reckon we'll be stayin' here with y'all!" Michael exclaimed.

Rena snickered. "We'll leave you two to git settled, and return at five for supper." She walked across the room, and hugged them both again. "I'm jist so happy y'all are here!" she squealed before departing with her husband.

Anna closed the door behind them. Turning to David, she asked, "Can you believe this place?" She walked across the room, and sat down on the bed.

He sat beside her. "It's somethin', all right. And I can't wait to try out this here bed!"

She laughed as he engulfed her in his arms. "Thank you for bringing me here," she whispered.

"The pleasure's all mine, darlin'," he said, and gently kissed her.

That evening, the foursome enjoyed a fine meal of roasted brisket, oysters, and stuffing in the hotel's dining room, then embarked on an adventure around the city. Rena and Michael took turns explaining landmarks. Gaslights along the thoroughfare emitted subdued light, and with the half moon, gave off enough illumination to provide visibility. They rode by carriage through the streets, where Rena pointed out Frederick Douglas' home, Ford's Theatre, and the White House. They rode past the Arsenal Penitentiary, where Lincoln's conspirators were hung. The excursion continued on to the red sandstone Smithsonian Castle. Their beloved president, Jefferson Davis, had initiated construction of the bastion of knowledge during his time in the Senate before the war. As they traveled past the Capitol Building, Rena explained that it was also Davis who envisioned building its dome, and topping it off with the "Goddess of Freedom Triumphant." David and Michael proceeded to tell of their exploits in the cavalry, how they had chased a wagon train to the outskirts of Washington, and gazed upon the unfinished Capitol from a hilltop. The white dome had since been completed, and rose high above them into the night sky. Their tour concluded with a view of the Aqueduct Bridge, which spanned across the frozen Potomac River.

"I have a surprise for y'all!" Rena jumped out and motioned for the rest to follow. They climbed down as she preceded to hand ice skates to each one.

"Come on!" She prompted, starting off.

"Where are we goin'?" asked David.

"Down to the river. It's frozen over."

Anna clasped her husband's hand as he led her to the riverbank. Other couples were visible, skating in the pale moonlight. She and David sat upon logs to put on their skates, laughing and teasing all the while. Michael led Rena out onto the ice, where they glided away, making it apparent they'd skated before. David struggled to stand atop the thin blades, his ankles threatening to buckle. Cautiously, he made his way to the edge, took Anna's hand, and pushed off. She let go just in time as he lost his balance and fell. He found his footing, only to have it slip out from under him again, repeatedly landing on his backside. Rena and Michael skated up.

"You look like you could use a hand," Michael said, grinning. He assisted David while Anna skated out.

"Look at me!" she hollered. "Look what I can do!" She twirled around several times before taking a tumble, landing sprawl-legged on her rear. David couldn't help but laugh, which caused her to retaliate. "I could have laughed at you too, you know!"

He slipped and slid, trying to get out to her until Michael came to her rescue instead. Rena assisted her brother back to the bank.

"That was fine for a first try!" she complimented.

"Pshaw," David grumbled. "I'm too inept."

Anna giggled. "It was still fun. I wish Dorie could've seen us making fools of ourselves!"

"Reckon she could skate circles around us," David said with a snicker and shook his head as he pulled on the laces of his skates.

The evening advanced rapidly. David brought his sister up on what had occurred in Alabama before he'd left four months previously, informing her of Kit's riddance, and their uncle's arrival, of which she was already aware, since she'd received a letter from their mother. It wasn't long before reflections about the war and politics came up. Michael and David both agreed that Grant would be the worst thing to happen to the South. He seemed to display very little sympathy for ex-Confederates, and his cohort, General Sherman, was even worse, although his despicable colonization plan, with all the vindictiveness of Cromwell, fortunately hadn't materialized. The South's immeasurable suffering had gone on long enough.

"The Ku Klux has taken over," David stated. "After Percy was strung up, Miss Isabelle was separated from her young'uns, and most likely, she'll have to work in the cotton fields for the rest of her life. Everyone is jist so sad. Folks have even tossed out tintypes they had of their soldiers, and donated the glass to greenhouses. That's how bad they want to forget."

"We're all tryin' to move on," remarked Michael, "but times are hard. My kin still haven't rebuilt down in Savannah, and I doubt they ever will."

"That's enough melancholy talk," Rena said. "Tomorrow's my big day, and I won't have y'all spoilin' it!"

She said it jokingly, but David knew she meant it. Changing the subject, he delved into Dorie's two-year-old exploits, which immediately got Anna involved.

At one point in the evening, Rena and Anna left the hotel room momentarily.

"Did you git a chance to talk to my kinfolk, the Ryan's, afore you left?" Michael asked.

David shook his head. "I reckoned they'd hear of my departure soon enough."

"There's one thing I wanted to tell you, but I didn't git the chance to sooner." Michael threw a flitting glance at the closed hallway door. "You recall the gold that went missin'?"

"Gold? What gold?"

"The Confederate gold that was in the treasury in Richmond. It disappeared when ole Jeff Davis was captured. Everyone thought the Yankees took it. But they didn't git it all, if'n they got any."

"How do you know that?"

"Because when I went back to Georgia to see my relations, they had some of it. They said various fellers are keepin' it hid, and there are hidin' places all across the South, over to Arkansas, and even further west."

"Is that a fact?" David asked in awe.

"Sure is. These fellers are callin' themselves the Knights of the Golden Circle. It's a big secret, so you can't tell a soul. Not even Anna."

"Okay," David agreed.

"My kinfolk had me bring some of the gold back to Alabama, and it's bein' watched over by the Ryan's. Jist in case the South rises again, there'll be money to advance the cause."

The ladies reentered before David had a chance to comment. What Michael had told him certainly made him ponder. He hoped Kit wouldn't discover the Ryan's treasure and steal it all for himself. But if he did, David reckoned the entire South would hunt Kit down with a vengeance.

After a few hours of conversation, Rena bid them good night, kissing each one before departing, and the men shook hands. David closed the door behind them, walked across the room to the window, and forced himself to look down from the towering heights of his perch until he saw them board a carriage and ride off. Closing the curtain, he turned to Anna, sauntered to her, picked her up, and lay her upon the bed. They embraced, laughing, the excitement of their adventure shining in each other's eyes. He passionately kissed her, rolled over, and extinguished the lamp.

In the morning, Michael and Rena returned. She presented Anna with a newspaper, saying, "I thought you might appreciate this," as she handed it to her.

"The Revolution," Anna read aloud from the front page.

"It's a weekly journal published in New York City," explained Rena.

"The true republic," Anna continued, "men, their rights and nothing more; women, their rights and nothing less."

"It's written by Susan B. Anthony. She's strivin' for women's suffrage."

Anna smiled at her. "Why, thank you very much!"

"It also discusses more liberal divorce laws, equal pay for equal work, and the church's position on women's issues and abortion."

Michael and David glanced at each other skeptically, but knowing what they were up against, kept quiet and followed their ladies out of the room. They partook in breakfast downstairs, then waved down a surrey. The city was as active as it had been the previous night, but things were easier to distinguish in the sunshine. Horses' hooves clopped through crowded streets, and every nationality of humanity was apparent. David observed one man riding a contraption he'd never seen before: a peddled vehicle with one very large wheel on the front and a small one on the back. Rena informed him that it was a velocipede. Storefronts came into view, with the Capitol Building sitting on a hilltop overlooking the colossal buildings. David noticed many freedmen lining the streets, looking for handouts. It hadn't snowed, but the air was still cold, and he felt sympathy for the homeless families gathered in clusters around bonfires. Their driver pulled his surrey to a stop.

"Let's git out and have us a look see!" said Michael with a smile.

They emerged onto the busy intersection, and walked across the street to where people had gathered. A piping melody grew louder, and upon closer review, they saw that it was an organ grinder dressed like a Zouave. On his shoulder sat a spider monkey wearing a tiny red vest and hat. One man offered the monkey a penny. The little primate ran down his owner's arm, retrieved the coin, dropped it with a clink into the tin cup the man was holding, and ran back up to his position. Anna laughed with delight. She turned to her husband, who relented, dug a penny from his pocket, and handed it to her. She held the coin out as the organ grinder with a fez on his head and a dark moustache on his face winked at her. The monkey ran down, snatched the coin from Anna's fingertips, and dropped it into the cup before returning to his master's shoulder.

"What's his name?" she asked.

"His name is-a Dancy," the man said with a smile and an Italian accent as he churned out more music, "because he-a likes to dance-a!"

The little monkey grinned, causing Anna to giggle.

"Let's go in here!" Rena exclaimed.

She entered a tall brick building with lead glass doors on the front. David managed to make his way through as people exited, and looked up. Above the main floor, the building opened so that each floor was visible all the way to the ceiling, and each floor was lined with white wrought-iron framework, resembling balconies. The store reached three stories; its ornamental corners gilded in gold. Christmas decorations filled the store: tinseled evergreens stood in corners, colorful blown-glass ornaments were displayed in jars on countertops, and candles flickering from brass and tiffany stained-glass fixtures hung around the perimeter of the main floor. Like the mercantile back home, various items were displayed on tables and within glass cases in different areas, but much more sumptuously, and the wares themselves were more opulent. David gazed around, taking in chattering customers, bells dinging from cash registers, and piano music coming from the other end of the store. He recognized it was playing "Joy to the World." Once his family had made their way through the store, they spilled back out onto the street, chuckling with amusement.

Suddenly, Rena gasped. Looking at her husband, she asked, "Honey, what time is it?"

Michael withdrew a pocket watch. "Nearly three," he replied.

"Oh! I have to git to the theatre for rehearsal!"

She flagged down a coach, and they quickly boarded. Once they reached the theatre, Rena climbed out.

"Be here at half past seven. The opera starts at eight." She closed the door, and the coach pulled away as she ran inside.

For the remainder of the afternoon, Michael entertained them at his tiny apartment, where he and David indulged in a few shots of whiskey while Anna sipped tea.

"This is mighty good," David commented after his third shot.

"Yeah, reckon it is," Michael said. "Too bad we couldn't bottle up our still and bring it up here!"

David snickered. "We could start up our own business again."

"No!" Anna said. "You are *not* making a still!"

David grinned at his comrade. "Even though now ain't the right time."

After indulging in a few more shots of whiskey, they decided to return to the hotel, where David and Anna changed into their nicest clothing. They dined, then rode down Pennsylvania Avenue to the National Theatre, observing other vehicles parked in front, and Washingtonians flowing in. As they exited their vehicle and started for the front doors, an eerie feeling came over David. He glanced around at the faces, and back over his shoulder, but saw nothing out of the ordinary, so he went inside the lobby.

A man at the ticket office asked their names, glanced down a long list, and said, "Enjoy the performance," as he doled out their tickets. People near the theatre entrance distributed programs. David was handed one, whereby he read the title: *Roméo et Juliette*.

Directed to their seats, he sat between Michael and Anna, four rows from the stage. He glanced over the program, and found his sister's name listed next to the character named Gertrude. Looking around, he watched as ladies in elegant gowns and gentlemen in fine suits took their seats. Still, the feeling that he was being watched persisted, causing the hairs on the back of his neck to stand on end. He glanced behind him, but becoming self-conscious, quickly turned around.

A few moments passed, and the lights dimmed. The audience came to a hush as the large, red velvet curtain was raised, revealing an exquisite set: a grand hall within a palace. The choir burst into song, and it wasn't long before Rena appeared. David's heart swelled with pride. He beamed at the sight of her, and held back emotion when she began to sing, hearing the familiar, lilting voice he'd known nearly all his life.

After five acts, the opera came to an end. The curtain dropped, only to be raised again as the performers reappeared onstage to take their final bows to thunderous applause. The houselights came back on, and the audience rose from their seats. Michael led the way through the throng to the lobby, where the singers had congregated. He found his wife, kissed her, and gave her the bouquet he'd brought along. Anna hugged her, as did David.

"Sis, you made me right proud," he said, smiling. "I had to bite my lip to keep from cryin'!"

Rena laughed.

"But they should give you the lead role," David added. "You have a purtier voice than ole what's-her-name."

"She's a well-known star, David," responded Rena.

"Well, now, so are you." He kissed her on the cheek. "I only wish Ma and Josie could've been here to see this."

Others flooded in, pouring between them, showering her with compliments. As he stood by the wayside, David slid his hand around Anna's waist, and grinned at her. Strangely, the eerie feeling returned, and he glanced up at the stairs leading to the balcony, but saw nothing except shadows.

He turned back to see Michael shaking hands with Ulysses S. Grant, who moved on to congratulate Rena.

"Splendid performance, my dear," Grant said to his sister. "Your voice is like that of an angel."

"Thank you very much, sir," replied Rena.

David thought she might not realize who she was talking to. He made his way around several admirers so he could stand beside her. Without acknowledging him, Grant took his hand and shook it, all the while gazing at Rena, and took a puff on his cigar, blowing smoke into David's face. The haze temporarily made his eyes and infuriation burn, but he managed not to cough.

"I look forward to seeing you again, Miss Tailor," Grant said before walking off to join his wife.

William T. Sherman congratulated Rena as well, then offered Michael his hand, but he refused to take it. Noticing the hostility, Sherman nodded at David, and mingled into the crowd. Other men surrounded the generals, which David assumed were bodyguards.

"Do you know who that was?" he asked Rena.

"Of course. That was General Grant, and the man behind him was General Sherman." She grinned at David. "At first, I considered askin' why they belittled us so, but I decided that, when he becomes president, perhaps I can pay him a visit, and persuade him to assist the South."

"I jist couldn't force myself to take Sherman's hand," admitted Michael.

Glad Sherman hadn't extended a hand to him, David nodded in agreement.

Later that evening, the family shared bottles of champagne in celebration while Rena described her audition, her struggles to learn French, and her upcoming performance in another opera next spring. After a few hours, they parted ways until morning. David lay beside his wife, so excited that he couldn't stop gushing about how proud he was, until she finally lost patience and shushed him. At last, he dozed off.

Early the following morning, they met up for church, then returned to the hotel, where they exchanged Christmas gifts. All too soon, it was time to leave for the depot. With tears in her eyes, Rena thanked them both for coming, kissed and hugged each one lovingly, and accepted their offer to visit Pennsylvania. Michael gave them a hug, wished them a merry Christmas, and stood on the platform with his arm around Rena's shoulders, watching the locomotive pull away while David and Anna waved from their window.

As the train rumbled along the tracks, David recalled the peculiar feeling he'd had at the theatre, and wondered if it was unfounded. He brushed it aside.

Taking Anna's hand, he said, "Rena and Michael will do jist fine," and smiled at her.

They arrived home later that evening, and after tucking in Dorie, climbed into bed, exhausted from their trip. As they lay in each other's arms, Anna rolled over to look at him.

"I think it's wonderful that Michael and Rena are doing so well," she sighed.

"Me too," he replied.

"And Maggie and Kenton. And Aunt Sarah and Uncle Bill. And ..."

"All the couples meet your satisfaction, then?"

"Yes." She reached up and kissed him. "Especially us."

"We've been through enough, I reckon."

"And we must vow to always be honest with each other, because I wasn't completely honest with you, saving money back and leaving the way I did. But you have to understand, darling, I had to do it. Next time, though, I won't keep secrets."

"Next time? I hope there ain't a next time!"

"We must promise each other, no more secrets."

"I promise."

Without forethought, he frowned. Anna saw his reaction in the flickering firelight. "Is there something you want to tell me?" she asked.

"No. I mean, I don't want to. But there's somethin' that's been eatin' away at me."

She waited patiently for his continuance.

"After you left, I went over to Miss Callie's, and well, um, we kissed."

The hurt crossed her face like a shockwave. "What?"

"It didn't mean nothin', honey."

"Why would you let that happen?" She pulled away.

Instantly, he regretted his decision to be honest. "I don't know why. It jist happened. I'm sincerely sorry, Anna. I never want to hurt you." He reached over to her, but she flinched, and pulled away. "It felt like kissin' a sister," he said, attempting to justify his rash action. "There are no feelin's between us, other than friendship."

She sat up. "Did you know this before you kissed her, or after?"

"Well ... I ..."

His hesitation was her answer. "I'm going to sleep with Dorie," she said, springing from bed to leave him alone.

Guilt ridden, he rolled on his side, staring into the glowing fire, unable to sleep.

In the morning, Anna refused to speak to him, although he repeatedly apologized. Realizing she wouldn't forgive him for his weakness and stupidity, he delved into his projects at the cabinetry shop, and with only five days until Christmas, worked furiously to complete them, as well as Anna's gift.

By Christmas Eve, he had managed to successfully finish them all. He was so exhausted from staying up late every night that he fell asleep upstairs while the Montgomery's and Mulligan's celebrated downstairs with Anna's family. Noticing his absence, Patrick stomped up after an hour and awoke him with a start.

"David, lad, the party's laggin' without ye." He sat on the bed as David propped himself on his elbow, rubbing his eyes.

"Oh, I must've dozed off," he said groggily.

"Aye. Have some hair o' the dog. It'll put a spark in ye."

He handed his friend a bottle. David obliged by taking a sip. The whiskey was so strong that it made the insides of his nostrils burn. Coughing, he handed it back.

"Special blend," said Patrick, "for the occasion!"

He let out a chuckle, and swaggered out of the room.

David followed him downstairs. *This is fixin' to be a very long evenin'*, he thought to himself.

He entered the parlor to see Mr. Montgomery engaging in a lively discussion about politics with Asa and Kenton. Turning to see David, they scowled at him. Mr. Montgomery offered him a cheroot, of which he graciously declined.

"Tomorrow, President Johnson is granting amnesty for all Confederates. What do you think of that, Mr. Summers?" Stephen's father puffed vigorously on the small cigar, causing the end of it to glow bright umber.

"Long overdue," he grunted.

Wishing to avoid confrontation, he walked across the parlor to where Briana was having a conversation with Maggie. Soon, he felt out of place, and went to search for his wife. As he approached the kitchen, he heard her giggling, and entered to see Stephen standing too closely to her. David's indignation rose.

"Darlin'." He walked over to her and kissed her on the cheek.

"Did you have a nice nap?" she asked, handing him a plate of cookies to distribute to the guests as Stephen slithered out surreptitiously.

He frowned. "What were you talkin' to him for?"

She smiled. "He's a dear friend, sweetie. You know that."

"Yeah, but after everything he did, why are y'all still friends?"

"Now, darling, let's not get into it. After all, it is Christmas Eve."

"I don't like it, Anna. I told you that. I don't trust him."

She glared at him. "Trust is an issue I'd prefer not to discuss with you at present." Quickly, she left the room. Expelling a sigh, he returned to the parlor with the plate, and set it on a small table while he glowered at Stephen. As he straightened, Patrick caught his eye, motioning for him to follow, so the two walked out onto the front porch. Offering him the bottle once again, David took a swig, which immediately affected him, since he hadn't recently eaten.

"I can't wait for this to be over," he half-whispered.

Patrick sniggered. "Might as well get used to it, David. Sure'n the Montgomery's plan on makin' themselves larger than life around here."

He shook his head, gritting his teeth. "I'll be damned if they git a hold of this place."

Patrick smiled as David handed him the bottle. "You and Anna should come out west with us, and leave these troubles to her uncle."

He grinned. "I'm fixin' to, but I have to convince her first. She doesn't want to take Dorie away, and now she's mighty riled with me."

Patrick raised his eyebrows. "Oh? And why is that?"

"I told her I kissed Miss Callie."

He snorted. "What on God's green earth would possess ye to do that?"

"I felt too guilty, and somehow, she knew. I had to tell her."

Patrick shook his head, handing his friend the bottle. "If I've learned one thing about women, it's never to confess your true feelin's for another, no matter how much she riddles ye."

David shrugged. "It's too late now, anyways."

He chuckled. "Well, don't fret, lad. She might forgive ye … someday."

Stephen emerged from inside, followed by his sister, brother-in-law, and parents.

"Leavin', are ye?" asked Patrick.

"We've got an early day tomorrow," said Mrs. Montgomery. "We're going to Philadelphia for the weekend to stay with my brother."

"Have a nice time," David said.

"Merry Christmas, Mr. Summers!" Mary said from inside the carriage as her husband, Asa, climbed in next to her.

"And to you, Miss Mary," he replied.

Stephen whisked past him, smirked, paused, and backed up, growling, "Your sister, Rena, has a magnificent voice." He smiled, his perfect white teeth glistening.

"Why, thank y—"

David's heart leaped. His hunch had been right: someone had been watching him. Stephen had been there after all! He started to confront him, but Stephen climbed into his carriage and closed the door. The vehicle started away. David felt a rush of anger surge through him.

"You all right, lad?" asked Patrick.

"Jist a chill is all," he replied.

Patrick handed him the bottle, so he took a deep swig.

That evening, after the stockings were hung above the mantle, David retired, remembering Christmases past. The last time he'd celebrated in the Brady household, Abigail had been only eight, and still believed in Santa Claus. Now she was putting her faith in spiritualism, and he wasn't quite sure how to take it. Anna came into the room and wilted into bed. He bit his lip, then decided to approach her, even though she had avoided him since his confession.

"I love you, Anna."

She said nothing, but whimpered softly.

"I always have, and I always will. No one can replace you in my heart. No one," he emphasized.

She let out a sigh, slowly rolled over, and hugged him. He wrapped his arms around her. Their lips met in a gentle kiss.

"I love you too," she whispered.

Softly, he kissed her forehead, and took a deep breath; the weight inflicted on his heart had finally been lifted. He would never let her go again, nor do anything so foolish as to risk losing her.

In the morning, the family exchanged gifts, much as they'd done in years gone by. Waiting until last, David presented his wife with an astounding engraved chest constructed of cedar. For Dorie, he built a child's dresser, and for the remainder of his family, he gifted wood-carved creations, each one unique to its owner. He'd even found enough vigor to make presents for his mother and Josie, and devotedly sent them, although he knew that delivery was dilatory, and they wouldn't arrive in time for Christmas. Still, the holiday was a joyous one, and he felt happy to be where he was.

President Johnson delivered as promised, granting unconditional amnesty to all Confederates. The heavy weight hanging over ex-Rebels had been lifted, but Grant would soon take office, and because of it, the future seemed frightening and unstable for the South.

December gave way to January. David was once again reminded of how cold winter in the north could be. He remained by the fire as much as possible, because he knew that he'd suffered a mild case of frostbite while in prison, and if he allowed himself to get too cold, the pain became excruciating, nearly crippling. He considered on numerous occasions to ride over to the Montgomery's and confront Stephen, but repeatedly decided against it. As long as Stephen stayed away, David was content to let it be.

When February finally arrived, the winter already seemed dreadfully long. To kill time, David and Anna visited the Mulligan's, or Grace and Theodore, if the weather permitted. David noticed articles belonging to their daughter, Claudia, were still on display above the fireplace. Sometimes, he could almost hear the child's laughter, making his heart ache for the loss of her. Now that he had his own daughter, he wondered how the Burrows could tolerate their anguish, and hoped he would never have to experience such a loss.

One ray of hope emerged for the South, however, when Jefferson Davis was finally released from prison. The papers reported that he received an enthusiastic reception in Richmond, of which David was sure the man must have been relieved. His people had not abandoned him in his time of need. In fact, just the opposite had occurred: Southerners embraced their president with open arms. He was their martyr, their only president, and their connection to the lost cause they still held so dear. Perhaps, if what Michael had told him about the Knights of the Golden Circle was true, there was still a flickering hope of resurrection for the old South.

President Grant was inaugurated on March 4. Newspapers reported that he refused to ride by carriage to the event at the Capitol with President Johnson, who in response, didn't attend the ceremony. Eight divisions of the army marched in the inaugural parade, and a ball was held in the Treasury Building that evening. David shook his head in despair as he read of the extravagance. *Only God can help us now*, he thought.

One afternoon in late March, he decided to ride into Davidsburg, and stopped to collect Patrick. On the way, they discussed Patrick's upcoming departure. David didn't want to disclose it, but he was indeed jealous, and struggled to conceal his envy. He promised to stop by the

Meyers' every Saturday morning after his chores were completed, around ten o'clock, to check on the place until Mary and her husband moved in. When the men reached town, they tied Alphie to a rail and went into a harness shop, whereby David purchased one. They weaved in and out of stores until they reached a hotel, and went inside. Seating themselves at the bar, they toasted to a prosperous year, and threw back several shots of whiskey.

As they staggered out, giggling, David looked across the street. His heart jumped. "Did you see that?" he asked Patrick.

"See what, lad?"

"I thought I saw Stephen standin' across the street."

Patrick snorted. "Well, let's go and have us a talk with him. Shall we?" He took David by the arm and led him across, dodging oncoming traffic as he did so. "Where did he vanish to?"

"Into that store," David replied.

They walked in, discovering it was a ladies' clothing store. The female patrons gawked at them.

"Oh, beggin' your pardon, ladies," Patrick said. "We were lookin' for a man."

A young woman giggled, causing David to chuckle. He looked at Patrick, who blushed.

"We'll be on our way." He doffed his cap, and dragged David outside as the ladies reacted, some disgusted, others amused. "If that was Stephen," Patrick said, slurring, "I didn't see him in there."

"Reckon it was jist my imagination," said David as he climbed up onto the wagon seat. "But I could've sworn it was him. And it looked like he was holding a pistol."

Patrick managed to climb up as well. "You're gettin' a wee bit apprehensive, lad. If Stephen's goal is killin' ye, no doubt he would've done it by now."

David frowned. Perhaps Patrick was right.

As they rode home, dusk rapidly set in. Patrick rambled on about David's trepidation, and then started talking about Irish folklore.

"In the old country," he said, "we have all sorts of demons and superstitions, ye know."

"Yeah, you mentioned a few before," he responded.

"Did I tell ye about the elemental?"

"No, I don't recall that one."

Patrick's voice grew low. "It's a short, neutral creature, and it only interacts if ye provoke it."

"What's it look like?"

"It's the size of a sheep, but it has no eyes. It's corpselike, and smells o' sulfur."

"Sounds disgustin'."

"Oh, 'tis, lad, 'tis. And ye never want to be approached by one."

"Why? 'Cause it'll make you fall down dead from the stench?"

Patrick guffawed, even though David didn't think it was that funny.

"And have ye ever heard of the will-o'-the-wisp?"

"Um, is that the same as a willow switch?"

"No. 'Tis what the bloody Brits call a ghost light. They believe it to be a death omen."

David glared at Patrick. "What's that got to do with anything?"

"Dear David, I probably shouldn't be tellin' ye this." He grinned at him.

Noticing how rapidly the sky was darkening, David gently slapped the reins on Alphie's withers, provoking him to walk a little faster. The air was suddenly very chilly. "Tell me what?"

"I had a dream the other night, and in me dream was a fetch."

"A what?"

"A fetch." Patrick paused. "'Tis an apparition of a livin' person, and it means that person will soon meet his demise. 'Tis bad luck."

"I thought the Irish only had good luck." David forced a laugh.

"I'm tryin' to be serious, lad. If someone dreams of a fetch at night, 'tis a death omen."

"And did you?"

"Did I what?"

"Did you dream about it at night?"

"Aye. That I did. But it wasn't the worst part, lad."

"What was?"

"'Tis what I've been tryin' to tell ye. The fetch I dreamt of was you."

David's grin melted from his face. He shuddered at the revelation.

On April 12, Patrick packed up his family, and David delivered them to the train station in Dover. After thanking him and showering him with kisses, Briana, Keegan, and Kathleen boarded with their little beagle, Shannon, leaving Patrick and David standing on the platform. The bell clanked, and steam from the engine hissed and swirled around their feet.

"Well, 'tis a sorry day indeed, havin' to leave ye," Patrick said with a wink. "But 'tis a grand day, for we're off on new adventure!" He withdrew a bottle of whiskey from his inner coat pocket and handed it to him. "Me thanks, for bringin' us here."

David nodded. "Best of luck to you, Patrick," he said.

"And to you, lad. Convince our darlin' Anna to come out. 'Tis Manifest Destiny, you know. God's will is for us all to move west!"

He took David's hand. The two men shook, and embraced.

"And don't fret about Stephen. He won't follow you to Denver City."

"All aboard!" the conductor bellowed.

"Is that where you're headed? I thought it was Nebraska."

"Aye, we're Omaha bound, till the Transcontinental Railroad's complete. Then we'll be goin' further west."

"Oh, replied David. "Denver City, huh?"

Patrick grinned. "There's plenty o' gold that has yet to be discovered, and 'tis waitin' for the two of us to find!"

He jumped onto the step as the locomotive pulled away, doffed his cap, and scrambled inside. David watched as the train disappeared into the early morning fog. He felt his heart sink. Another friend had left him, and he was abandoned to tediously toil in the fields.

When he returned home, he approached Anna, again asking if she'd consider going out west, but she gave the same response. She didn't want to uproot Dorie from her family, which was understandable. Still, the thought of remaining in Pennsylvania, stagnating in an occupation he only tolerated, didn't appeal to him at all. He wanted something more: he wanted adventure too.

A week of wet, rainy weather went by, discouraging him even more. He wished for the sun, so he could at least keep himself occupied with planting. Instead, he was confined to the house, where he read every newspaper that became available, as well as books and dime novels about the American frontier Sarah purchased for him. He also took an interest in the macabre, reading Mary Shelley's *Frankenstein*, which he never would have been interested in before the war. He'd encountered his own ghouls, and reading of horrors, in some morbid way, fascinated him.

On Friday evening, four days after Patrick had gone, Abigail arranged to have her friend, Dolly, stay over, so they established themselves in her room. Restless as usual, David came downstairs to see the Brady's black cat, Tabby, staring up at him from the foot of the stairs with golden eyes. The feline uncharacteristically hissed sinisterly, exposed a white flash of fangs, and slinked off into the shadows. David saw the two girls sitting at the kitchen table with only a flickering candle between them. Upon his appearance, they hid something behind their backs.

"What y'all doin' down here?" he asked in a low, threatening voice.

"Nothing!" they replied in unison, disguising their clandestine ceremony.

He pulled up a chair, and sat beside his sister-in-law. "You both look mighty suspicious to me."

"Can you keep a secret?" Abigail asked.

"Depends on what it is," he replied.

She extracted what she'd hidden. It was a triangular shaped, wooden object. Dolly withdrew a board from behind her back.

"What is that?" he asked.

"It's a planchette," explained Abigail. "If we place our fingers on it and ask it questions, it'll tell us the answer."

"Y'all think some li'l ole piece of wood will provide the answers to all of life's questions?" David chuckled, and sat back in his chair.

"Don't laugh. It truly works." Abigail set the triangle on top of the board, and the girls touched two sides of it. "You shouldn't be skeptical unless you can prove it wrong."

He grunted. "All right." Placing his fingertips on the available side, he asked, "Is it gonna rain tomorrow?"

The triangle moved slowly, sliding across the board, which had painted words and symbols on it.

"Yes," Abigail read once it had stopped.

He snickered, unimpressed with the necromancer. "That ain't so unusual. It rains every day!"

"I'll ask it a question," Dolly volunteered. "What's the name of my uncle, who was killed in the war?"

The triangle slid, coming to rest on various letters, until it spelled out a name. Dolly quickly backed from the board, her eyes wide. "My uncle's name really was Horace," she declared.

David scoffed. "Y'all are makin' it move to the letters you want it to spell out."

"No, we're not!" Abigail protested. "You ask it a question. Ask it a deep, dark secret, and see what you receive for an answer."

"I ain't doin' that." He pushed his chair back to stand, but Abigail grabbed hold of his wrist. "Okay," he relented. Scooting back to the table, he placed his fingers on one side, and said, "Mirror, mirror, on the wall, who's the fairest of them all?"

Dolly burst into laughter.

"That's not funny!" Abigail growled.

She started to withdraw the instrument, but David decided to humor her.

"I'm sorry, Miss Abigail. I'll be serious."

The three placed their hands on each side.

"Oh, mystical triangle, grant me this answer," he said in as spooky a voice as he could muster. "Tell me, oh triangle, will I convince Anna to go west?"

The planchette moved slowly as they watched in silence. It stopped over a question mark. Inexplicably, the candle flickered more vivaciously.

"What does that mean?" he asked.

"Ask it another question," Abigail suggested.

He sighed. "Will Stephen be a thorn in my side forever?"

The planchette slid.

"No," the trio said together.

"Will I be rid of him?"

"No."

David frowned. "Will he be rid of me?"

The wooden triangle slid over the letters. "Yes."

David and Abigail glared at one another.

"Burn that damned thing," he commanded in aggravation as he abruptly stood, and went upstairs.

That night, he tossed and turned, hearing imaginary sounds coming from outside the bedroom window. Too many unknowns had left his head throbbing. Finally, he submitted to slumber.

A dark, shadowy, overgrown sunken road sprawled out before him. He thought he was riding Renegade. As he came to a hillock, he heard another rider thunder toward him. Over the crest appeared a headless Union soldier on a black steed wielding a glistening sword of steel. The Yankee rode straight at him. David jerked as the blade whooshed toward him, jolting him awake. He sat up with a start, grasping his throat.

"Sweetie?" Anna asked groggily. "What is it?"

"Nothin', darlin'. Go back to sleep."

He panted to catch his breath, sweat beading on his forehead. It was the Yankee soldier he'd killed at Brandy Station. He hadn't dreamt about him since before he'd gone to hear President Lincoln dedicate the National Cemetery in Gettysburg. He lay back down and closed his eyes, wondering if it was a premonition, but the dread it instilled kept him from sleeping. If it did represent something, one thing seemed certain: something profound was about to happen, and he feared it wouldn't be good.

"Now that war comes home to you, you feel very different. You deprecate its horrors, but did not feel them when you sent car-loads of soldiers and ammunition, and molded shells and shot, to carry war into Kentucky and Tennessee, to desolate the homes of hundreds and thousands of good people who only asked to live in peace at their old homes, and under the Government of their inheritance. But these comparisons are idle."

- W.T. Sherman, Major-General commanding
Memoirs of General William T. Sherman

Chapter Thirteen

The following morning, David decided to ride over to the Meyers' farmstead, ensuring that it was secure. As he rode, the morning sun warmed his shoulders. He noticed how wildflowers in the ditches were starting to bloom, trees were beginning to bud out, and the fresh air smelled clean. Once he'd reached his destination, he dismounted, peered into the empty house, walked around the outbuildings, and went into the barn. A few swallows flew out as he entered. He glanced up into the rafters, detecting their nest. Content that everything was in order, he returned home.

Several weeks passed, and he forgot about the dream he'd had, occupying his time with Bill instead, tilling and planting from sunup to sundown. By the time the month was over, they had successfully sown one hundred and thirty acres of corn, wheat, barley, potatoes, and beans. During this time, David learned the Transcontinental Railroad had indeed been completed on May 10. Five days later, Susan B. Anthony began the National Women's Suffrage Association, and he shared the information with Anna, who he knew was strongly in favor of women's voting rights. Rena sent word that her performance company had been asked to tour Europe, so she and Michael would be overseas for several months. He felt a twinge of jealously upon receiving the news, but was happy for her, nevertheless.

Through Kenton, the family was invited to the Dalton's annual spring dance, so on the afternoon of Saturday, June 5, Sarah, Anna, and Abigail primped, then honed Dorie for her presentation. By late afternoon, they boarded the landau, and rode for a few miles until they reached the Dalton farm. Bill parked their vehicle alongside several others that were lined under shade trees. Assisting his wife and daughter down, David followed them to where their neighbors had congregated, realizing the scene was reminiscent of the dance he'd attended here five years ago. He had confessed his love to Anna at that dance, but she had rejected him. He smiled to himself. *Things have certainly changed since then*, he thought.

As they neared the gathering, some people turned to acknowledge them. Others scowled at David, which made him question why. It wasn't long before he discovered the answer.

"There's Johnny Reb now!" One of the Dalton brothers hollered.

The other brother turned to gawk along with their friends, who chuckled as they passed around a bottle.

David frowned. "Looks like the jig is up," he said to Anna while he escorted her through the crowd to the food table. "Someone told them I'm a Confederate."

"Who would have done that?" she asked, but the answer struck her as she spoke.

"I'll wager it was Stephen," David grumbled, confirming her thoughts.

They took their place in line at the end of a long table displaying pulled pork, various spring vegetables, breads, fruit pies, coffee, tea, and lemonade.

"Hello, Anna." The couple looked over to see Nellie Dalton standing beside them. "This must be your lovely daughter!"

"Say hello to Nellie, sweetheart," Anna coaxed.

"Hello," Dorie responded.

Nellie chortled. "She's adorable!" Stepping closer to Anna, she said, "I'm expecting too."

Anna's eyes grew wide. "You are? When?"

"Around Christmastime. It's our second." She looked over at a young man standing several feet away. "That's my husband, Elbert."

David recognized him as one of the fellows who had laughed at him upon his arrival.

"We have a boy, but I hope the next one's a girl, especially after seeing your little sweetheart." Nellie smiled at Dorie, who ducked behind her mother's skirts, and peered out around them.

"Our congratulations to you both," said Anna. "How is Lauren?"

David recalled Nellie's sister, who he'd met at the last shindig the Dalton's had thrown.

"She's fine. Married too. They live in Delaware now."

"Well, the next time you write to her, tell her I said hello."

"I most certainly will. It's been a pleasure visiting with you both again." She smirked at David before walking off to join her husband.

He shrugged it off. "I don't know about y'all, but I'm starvin'!"

Taking a plate, he started piling on victuals as Anna assisted their daughter.

"Mr. Summers," Mary said, approaching him.

She held out her hand. He took it, and gently kissed the back of it. Straightening, he grinned at her.

"Now I understand the source of your gesture," she remarked, sneering. "It's been inbred into you."

"How did you know?" he asked innocently, albeit stealthily so he could find out the true culprit.

Asa walked up and took Mary's arm. "My brother told us," she replied.

"It seems he told everyone in attendance," quipped Anna.

Mary glared at her. "You had to have known all along, didn't you, Anna?"

Stunned momentarily, Anna replied, "I'm certain I don't know what you mean." She walked off, holding her plate, and led Dorie to an empty table.

It was just as David had suspected: Stephen was the perpetrator. "Well, Miss Mary, I hope there are no bad feelin's."

"Of course not. The war's long over. I only hope you will have more integrity the next time, instead of pretending to be someone you're not."

She sashayed off to converse with Lila Fairfax. David wasn't sure what she meant, if she knew he'd been an imposter when he pretended to be Anna's cousin, or if she was referring to the fact that he'd lied about being from New York in order to hide his Confederate affiliation. Deciding it didn't matter either way, he filled his plate. As he made his way over to Anna, he was stopped by Abigail.

"David, come with me."

"But I was just about to eat!"

She took his plate from him and set it down. "Come now."

She grasped his arm, pulling him away, so he reluctantly followed.

"What's the matter, Miss Abigail?" he asked. "Ain't you havin' fun at this here wing ding?"

She walked around to the side of the barn, stopping once she thought she was out of earshot. "I heard a rumor, and I want you to be on your lookout."

"What did you hear?"

"Some of the younger gentlemen don't like your being here. I overheard them talking about it."

"What'd they say?"

"That Anna shouldn't have married you, and that they want to avenge Stephen."

"Avenge Stephen? How?"

"I don't know, but I've a feeling he told them he proposed to her, and she turned him down to marry you." She took his hand. "Anyway, I thought you should know. Please be careful." She quickly hugged him, then started back toward the party.

David followed her, and once he neared, saw that Maggie had arrived with Kenton. He offered his hand, and Kenton unenthusiastically took it.

"My cousins surely know how to have a barbeque," he remarked after taking a bite. "Is it as good as they have down south, Summers?"

He wasn't sure where the conversation was leading, but decided to remain jovial. "Jist as good, and then some," he answered.

Maggie and Anna chuckled.

"The word is out," Anna informed her sister. "Stephen told everyone here that David was a Rebel."

"Was? He's always been quite rebellious in my opinion!" Maggie laughed, her blue eyes twinkling at him from under her bonnet.

"Jist for that remark, Miss Maggie, you owe me the first dance!" David said.

She giggled. "Why, I'd be honored, kind sir."

After supper, the congregation mingled as twilight set in. Upon the Dalton's request, they moved into the barn, where the floor had been cleared for dancing. Like before, bales were set around the perimeters, and a small stage was erected for the musicians. Chinese lanterns hung from the rafters, and the musty smell of hay lingered in the air. Two fiddle players, a banjo player, drummer, and pianist stepped onto the platform to take their places. One of the fiddlers hollered, "Are you ready to dance?"

"Huzzah!" the crowd roared.

The musicians burst into melody, playing "Hawks and Eagles."

"May I have this dance, m'lady?" David asked Maggie, offering her his arm.

She smiled, took it, glanced back at Anna with a grin on her face, and set off for the dance floor as others did the same.

"Are you havin' a good time, Miss Maggie?" he asked.

"I am. Are you?" she inquired back.

"I'd have a better time if those fellers over there weren't starin' at us." He motioned toward a group of young men standing off to the side who were leering at him.

"Why do you think they're staring?"

"I ain't sure, but I reckon it's because they don't like it that Anna married me. They think she should've married Stephen."

As he said it, he glanced over at his wife. Seeing Stephen advance toward her, attired in his Yankee uniform, he squinted in loathing. He'd known as soon as Stephen saw the opportunity, he'd swoop down on her like a ravenous vulture. Once they were on the dance floor, Stephen sneered at him every time he passed.

David felt his anger flare, but managed to contain it, dousing it with humility. The song ended, so he released Maggie to her spouse. Observing Stephen's refusal to let Anna go, he asked Abigail to dance. She complied happily, and the two stepped out to "De Blue Tail Fly."

"They've been staring at you ever since we came in here," Abigail half-whispered with concern, referring to the Dalton brothers and their friends.

"I know, Miss Abigail. Don't fret. They won't try nothin'."

"How do you know?"

"I jist do." He grinned at her, and gave her a wink to ease her anxiety.

She frowned before forcing a smile while they made their way around the dance floor.

With only a brief pause between songs, the musicians played nonstop for an hour, commencing through "Liza Jane," "Cripple Creek," "Granny Will Your Dog Bite," and a few new songs; "Shew Fly Don't Bother Me," and "Little Brown Jug." The last song of their set was a new one as well, titled "Blue Danube Waltz."

"Oh, I'll be damned if I let him dance with her on this one!" he exclaimed to Abigail. Releasing her, he stomped across the floor to where Anna and Stephen were standing. "Darlin', this dance is mine," he said, grinning as he extended his hand.

Stephen glared at him, snorted, hesitated for a moment, and tromped off while Anna took her husband's hand. They walked back out, noticing people stare as they began to waltz.

"I see you haven't forgotten how to dance," she remarked teasingly.

"Honey, dancin' with you makes me light on my feet!" They smiled at each other, twirling around the floor until the music ended, and the audience broke into applause. He was tempted to kiss her in front of everyone just to make a point, but opted against it, sparing her any embarrassment. Instead, he said, "Come with me," and led her toward the open double doors.

"What about Adora?" she asked.

"She's with Abigail. She'll be fine for a spell."

They ambled outside into the cool evening air, making their way down the dark lane to a path that led to a foot bridge. As they stood upon it, he turned to face her, taking her hand.

"Do you remember this place?" he asked sheepishly.

"Of course, I do, silly. It's where you first confessed your love for me."

"And you refused it."

They both chuckled.

Anna placed her hands on his cheeks. He bent down, and tenderly kissed her.

"We've come a long way since then," she said with a smile.

They stared into each other's eyes, and kissed again.

"I love you," she said, making his heart melt.

"I love you too ..."

"Hope we're not interrupting you two lovebirds!"

Anna tore away from his embrace, seeing four young men approach. One of them said, "Anna, go back to the dance."

"I will do no such thing!" she insisted. "Henry Dalton, what is this about?"

"We just want a word with your husband," answered Nellie's spouse, Elbert.

"Whatever it is, you can say it in front of me," she replied.

"Anna, go on ahead," David said reassuringly.

She looked up at him, her eyes filled with dread, but he grinned and gave her an encouraging nod. Slowly, she walked across the bridge, and burst into a sprint toward the barn.

"What can I do for you fellers?" asked David. He intentionally made his way off the bridge onto solid ground.

"We don't take to your kind 'round here," said Elbert.

"What's that supposed to mean?" David responded.

"It means," said Henry, "that you should've stayed down in Alabama instead of coming back up here."

"Well, that ain't none of your business, is it?" David started to walk away, but the younger Dalton brother stepped in front of him.

"You took something that don't belong to you, and that makes it our business," said Elbert.

"Oh? And what would that be?"

"Anna. She belongs to Stephen. Everybody 'round here knows it. You came along and stole her away from him, and we don't think that's right."

"Hold your horses," David said, "Anna's never been betrothed to Stephen."

Suddenly, the other man who had remained speechless grabbed David from behind, his breath reeking of liquor.

"What the hell is this?" David yelled.

"We aim on teaching you a lesson, Reb," said Henry. "You should go on back to Alabama, and leave things the way they're supposed to be, 'cause you ain't welcome here." He slammed his fist into his palm, and stepped toward David.

Henry's brother sinisterly chuckled.

"Now wait jist a cotton pickin' minute! Anna can make up her own mind!"

"David? What's going on over there?"

Turning to see Bill and Kenton heading toward them, the speechless man released David. The four ruffians walked away, slinking off into the shadows as Bill and Kenton approached.

"Are you all right?" Bill asked.

"Yessir. I'm ready to head on home, though."

He sauntered off while Bill and Kenton followed, struggling to control his rage. *How dare Stephen send his attack dogs*, he thought. *First chance I git, I'll make him pay for that confrontation.* As he neared the barn, Anna ran toward him.

"What happened?" she asked.

"I'll tell you later, darlin'," David replied. "Go fetch Sarah, Dorie and your sister. We're leavin'."

She returned to the barn. He saw dancers inside moving to the music, and wished he could remain, frustrated that he'd only gotten one dance with his beloved.

"I'll bid you both good evening, then," Kenton said.

He went inside the barn while Bill and David walked to their vehicle. Hearing loud voices behind them, they turned to see Elbert screaming at his wife. He lashed out and struck her, sending Nellie staggering. David started toward them, but Bill caught him by the arm.

"Best to leave them to their own troubles," he said, "or it'll become yours, and I think you've gotten into enough tonight." He patted him on the back.

They watched Nellie run into the house. Elbert swaggered into the barn. A few minutes later, Anna, Dorie, Sarah, and Abigail emerged from the dance, and joined them at their landau. Bill sat in the driver's seat while the rest of the family rode inside.

"Is everything all right, dear?" Sarah asked him.

"Yes'm. Jist a little misunderstandin' is all."

"The Dalton's and two of their friends were giving David a difficult time," explained Abigail.

"Why?" inquired Sarah.

David glanced at Anna and sighed. "They said I ain't welcome here, that I 'stole' Anna away from Stephen, and they wanted to defend him. Lucky for me, Bill and Kenton showed up when they did."

Anna clutched onto his arm. He faintly smiled at her.

"Why would Stephen tell everybody you fought for the South?" Sarah asked.

"It seems everyone at the dance knows David is … I mean, was, a Confederate," explained Abigail. "I'm certain Stephen told them David stole Anna away from him in order to gain sympathy."

"Why would he do such a thing?" Sarah asked.

David explained, "Because the threat of Anna's bein' arrested for treason is gone, and he wants to smear my name, even though plenty of folks around here supported or fought for the Confederacy."

"Yes, darling," Anna said, "but none of them hid the fact. None of them lied about it."

"I didn't lie! I jist didn't tell the truth is all." He scowled. "I did it for you, Anna."

"I know, and I love you for it. I will always love you for it." She kissed his cheek.

Following suit, Dorie kissed him on the other cheek. "I always love you, Papa," she said. She gave him a hug.

Sarah reached across to pat David's hand. "Why would he want to tarnish your name, David?" she wondered aloud. "Why would he want to hurt Anna in that way?"

"The answer's plain, Miss Sarah," David replied. "He wants to git hold of the farm. He always has. I reckon he's tryin' to break me and Anna up so's he can take my place."

Slowly shaking her head, Sarah sat back. Her face creased with concern as shadows danced across it.

When the family arrived home, they readied themselves for bed. Once David was finally lying beside his wife in the dark, he took her into his arms, and kissed her tenderly.

"I wish we could've had more than one dance," he whispered.

"So do I, but there will be other dances."

"I don't know, Anna. Seems like everyone around here wants me gone."

She rolled over, and snuggled into him. "Let's talk about it tomorrow." Falling silent for a moment, she whispered, "I really do love you, you know."

He smiled in the dark. "I love you too, darlin', with all my heart." He heard her sigh before he fell asleep.

In the morning, he arose early, tended to his chores, and then returned inside to eat a quick breakfast. Anna descended the stairs. Seeing him sitting alone at the kitchen table, she sat beside him.

"I could fry you some eggs," she offered, rubbing the sleep from her eyes.

He grinned. "No thanks, honey."

She reached over, taking his hand. "I'm sorry about what happened last night."

David lifted her hand to his lips. "It wasn't your fault," he said. "Stephen's to blame. He hates me for lovin' you, and he's convinced his friends that his way of thinkin' is right. It's like I told you last night, Anna. They all want me gone."

"Not everyone does," she replied.

He smiled at her assurance. "As long as Stephen's around, there'll be trouble. I wish he'd jist go on back to Washin'ton and stay there."

"Oh, well in that case, this should make you happy."

She gently squeezed his hand. He looked at her quizzically, waiting for her to continue.

"He asked me what I'd be doing today, so I told him Abigail and I were planning to visit Maggie. He said he would be leaving early this morning, and wouldn't return for several days. And then he gave me the address where he can be reached."

"Well, that is good news." He kissed her. "I have a few errands to run. First, I'm checkin' on the Meyers' place, and then I'm ridin' to the blacksmith's to have Renie re-shod, 'cause he's got a loose shoe. I won't be back for a while."

Rising to her feet, she said, "Perhaps when you're finished, you can meet us at Maggie's later, and we can visit the mercantile. I have a few things I'd like to purchase."

"I might find me a new pair of boots too," he added. "Li'l ole Buster keeps chewin' mine up!" He lifted his left foot to display the teeth marks in his boot.

Anna snickered.

He smiled, stood, and turned to leave, but abruptly stopped, stepped toward her, and embraced her. He gave her a quick kiss, then walked out the door while placing his slouch hat upon his head.

As he sauntered to the pasture, he detected how the humidity had thickened in the past few days. Summer was near, which made him yearn to be off on adventure, wherever that might be. He walked to the gate, and let out a shrill whistle. Renegade's head popped up. He looked at David with his ears erect, then burst into a gallop across the field toward him. Alphie tried to keep up, but soon fell behind, so he went back to grazing.

"Hey, ole pard," he said, stroking his horse's neck. "We're gittin' that shoe fixed today."

He led him to the barn, saddled him, and mounted. As he rode past the house, he saw Sarah emerge with a basket on her way to collect eggs. She waved merrily. David returned the gesture before prompting Renegade down the lane at an easy trot.

Once he reached the road, he slowed, allowing his stallion to casually walk to the Meyers' farm. He dismounted and meandered around the deserted outbuildings like he did on every weekly visit. He went into the house. His boots clomped across the floorboards, echoing through the empty rooms. Recalling Patrick's contagious laughter, he chuckled, and wondered if the Mulligan's were still in Omaha, or if they had traveled westward. He wished Patrick would send word of their whereabouts. *At least I can live out his escapades vicariously through him*, he thought with a forlorn sigh. He left the empty house, walked to the barn, entered, and discovered the baby swallows had hatched, their chirps radiating loudly from the rafters. Considering David to be a threat, the parent birds dived at him. He snickered while turning around to watch them fly out the door. Taken by surprise, he jumped at the sight.

"What're you doing here?" Stephen growled like a rabid dog. "You're trespassing. This is private property."

David noticed he was wearing civilian clothing. "I told Patrick I'd keep an eye on the place until your sister moves in."

Stephen withdrew a treen from his pocket, opened the lid, and took a snort of snuff. "Once a Rebel, always a Rebel," he muttered.

"What?" David asked.

"You're always coming around where you're not welcome." He glared at him.

"I thought you were headed for Washin'ton today." Stephen merely smirked in response, making him uncomfortable, so he raised an eyebrow at him, and said, "Well, it looks like everything is in order. Reckon I'll take my leave." Hesitating, he remembered. "Oh, and by the way, I don't appreciate it that you sent your boys after me last evenin'." He walked past Stephen, who bumped into him, nearly causing him to lose his balance.

David bristled. "I've had jist about all I can take of you. Is it a fight you're lookin' for?"

Stephen snorted. "Well now, that wouldn't be fair, would it? I'd have to shoot with my left hand because, thanks to you, my right hand is crippled."

"I ain't armed, anyways," David retorted, "and I don't want any trouble."

"Trouble? You've been nothing but trouble since the day you arrived here. You've ruined everything, Summers. You never should have interfered. I love Anna. She should be MY wife!"

Straightening to accentuate his height, David postured himself to appear more ominous. "She doesn't love you, savvy?"

"You even talked her into selling that sapphire necklace I gave her. Do you know how much that was worth? It belonged to my grandmother!"

"She decided to sell it herself," he replied in defense. "I had nothin' to do with it."

"I don't believe you." Stephen seethed. "I wish I would have been there at Fredericksburg to kill your father personally."

"What?" David glared at him, stunned by his infliction. "How do you know about my pa?" he asked, comprehending the answer as soon as he spoke it.

"From Anna. She tells me everything."

David realized by his inflection that he was delirious.

"She tells me every detail. How inadequate you are." He sinisterly chuckled.

Shaking his head, he clenched his jaw, disgusted with Stephen's attempt to hurt him. "This conversation's over."

"I wish I had been at Gettysburg. I would have done you in myself."

David scoffed. "I wish you had too. I would have whipped you first."

He walked outside, but Stephen tailed him. Stepping in front of him, he growled, "I've been waiting for the opportunity to present itself, and you just provided it ... with your hostility."

He produced a pistol and pointed it at David, who angrily frowned at the sight.

"I've wanted to do this for a long while now. I should've done it before you had the opportunity to take my Anna away." He grinned sardonically. "I'm going to do away with you, just like I did her aunt and uncle." His too-white teeth glistened.

David's eyes grew wide, changing from hazel to brown as the revelation sank in. "What are you talkin' about?" he snarled, gawking at him in disbelief.

Stephen broke into hysterical laughter. "I waited until Anna left with her sister and child, and then I went inside, and did what I had to do." The smile vanished from his face.

David stared at him, aghast with what he was insinuating. Panic rose within him. A sick feeling culminated in the pit of his stomach. It was as though Stephen had physically punched him. "You're a liar," he accused with conviction.

"Am I?" Stephen cocked the trigger. "Abigail will be sent away to live with Maggie, and I'll have Anna all to myself. She's been thinking twice about your marriage because of your involvement with the Ku Klux Klan, and wonders if you can ever fulfill her desires."

"You're insane."

"Yes, well, I'll always have that to fall back on. I'll claim temporary insanity, just like General Sickles did. Hell, if he can get away with it, so can I." He contemptuously smiled. "Oh, and that bastard child of yours will have to go. She reminds me too much of you." He swaggered toward David, holding the pistol on him.

"She ain't a bastard," David said in his daughter's defense, enraged by the misnomer.

"It doesn't matter. She's a goner, either way." He sniggered. "I'm going to shoot you, drag your sorry carcass to the house, and make it look like you did it."

He circled around David, who stood seething, waiting for his chance to attack.

"You had an argument with Anna's aunt and uncle, and killed them both before turning the gun on yourself." He giggled. "Don't you see? I've got it all figured out. I even have an alibi. Anna will come home, see the mess you made, and seek me out for solace. It's the perfect crime."

"You're stark ravin' mad."

"Oh, I'm mad, all right. You ruined my career. I can't even write with this!" He waved his crippled hand in the air, then came toward David like he was going to strike him, but instead, grumbled into his left ear, "Any last requests? Do you want me to tell her anything on your behalf?"

Unable to hear him due to the incessant ringing in his ear, David scowled at him.

"No, I didn't think so."

He stepped back, but nearly stumbled, and glanced down for a second. Quickly, David placed his thumb and forefinger into his mouth to let out a piercing whistle. Renegade responded by cantering toward him. Stephen whirled around, saw the approaching equine, and took aim. David lunged at him and punched him as hard as he could in the face, but still, Stephen wouldn't relent. He pulled the trigger, sending a shot whizzing past David's head. Infuriated, he tried to hit him again, but Stephen was stronger than he'd anticipated. They threw each other onto the ground, dust rising as they scuffled. Stephen fired another shot into the dirt, which ricocheted off a rock, barely missing Renegade's flank. He whinnied, reared, and bolted. David pulled free, and threw himself onto his horse's back.

"I'm gonna kill you, Rebel!" Stephen screamed behind him.

Glancing over his shoulder, he saw the crazed man galloping toward him on his steed. Renegade leapt over a fence, and ran across the field as another bullet whizzed past them.

"Come back here, you coward!" Stephen screeched.

David almost retaliated with a profanity, but restrained himself. *If wantin' to protect my family makes me a coward*, he thought, *then so be it.*

Suddenly, Renegade tripped. The loose shoe had given way, and flew off into the field. His stallion continued to run full-speed, but faltered on his bare foot, and stumbled. David looked back. Stephen was gaining. Another shot zinged past, taking his hat with it.

"Good God!" he exclaimed, whipping Renegade with the reins.

He had to get back to the house for a weapon, even if a sanguinary scene awaited him.

Stephen's mount thundered closer. He caught up, galloping beside Renegade as the two equines ran neck and neck. Stephen fired: his pistol popped. The bullet entered into David's right forearm with a thud. He cried out in pain, grasping at the blood that poured from his affliction.

"You son of a bitch!" David screamed.

Stephen smiled sadistically, and raised the gun to fire once more.

They stared at each other while they heatedly rode on: one waiting to be shot, the other savoring his target's discomfort. Stephen turned his mount, reining him even closer, so close that they nearly collided. Suddenly, Renegade bolted, sprang, and cleared a ditch. Stephen's horse plummeted into it. David heard a loud snap, followed by the horse's scream. The gelding rolled, sent Stephen up over his head, and landed on top of him. He shrieked in excruciating pain, as did his horse.

David pulled Renegade back. The screams rising up from the earth were like those on the horrific battlefields he'd encountered in the cavalry. He trotted up to the gelding to see him writhing in pain, his mouth gaping open, his eyes wide with terror, and a bone protruding out from his pastern, which was bleeding profusely. David dismounted. He walked around the heaving animal. Stephen's legs were pinned beneath the mighty beast, his pistol still grasped in his hand.

"Get away!" he cried, pointing the gun at him.

"Stephen, let me help you."

"No!" He squeezed his eyes shut, releasing the pistol from his grasp as he sobbed in anguish.

David seized his opportunity, and snatched it up. He struggled to steady the pistol in his trembling left hand, poised at the loathsome being who lay before him. Glancing back at his stallion, he saw Renegade frothing at the mouth, favoring his injured foot.

"There's only one bullet left," groaned Stephen, gasping for air. "I pray that you use it on me."

Watching him grovel, David only felt sympathy. "Your horse is done for," he responded. "He's got a broken leg."

"I don't care! Use the damn thing on me!"

David panted from the anxiety coursing through his veins. The sight was all too familiar and overwhelming. Memories flooded into his conscience: Jake's death, his decapitating a Yankee, his comrade, John Chase's bloody demise at Gettysburg. He'd heard horses scream like this before, and the memory was more than he could bear. Slowly, he let his arm fall to his side, immune to the pain he felt in the other. The gelding continued to shriek, and tried to rise, but was unable to stand on its fractured leg. Traumatized, David could only stare.

"Summers!"

Hearing his name jolted him back to the present.

"Just get it over with!"

David frowned at his foe. Stephen had caused more problems in his life than he'd ever thought possible. He was a conniving liar, and had tried to convince Anna that she should pursue divorce. David gritted his teeth. Wiping the sweat from his brow, he was reminded of the wound in his right forearm, and moaned.

"Do it now!"

It was the right thing to do. The only solution. He lifted the pistol, taking aim as the gelding shrieked in agony.

"This is what you asked for," he spat venomously. "You said I should jist accept your sendin' me to prison as the 'fortunes of war'. Well, this is residue of all that war is, and it can never be erased. Reckon you'll jist have to accept that."

Pulling the trigger, he fired the last remaining shot in the chamber. It echoed desolately across the field.

"Always bear in mind that your own resolution to succeed is more important than any one thing."

- Abraham Lincoln

Chapter Fourteen

"You're lucky it missed the bone," Doctor Spencer remarked seriously, "or you might have lost this arm." He finished wrapping David's lower right arm with gauze, collected his bag, and motioned to the jailer, who pulled open the barred cell door, allowing him to pass. The guard slammed the door shut and locked it.

David arose. "Have they set a trial date?" he asked.

Doc Spencer turned to face him. "They're waiting until he's well enough to testify."

"When will that be?"

"Three or four weeks. Try to get some rest."

The doctor walked to his black buggy, climbed aboard, and slapped the reins, prompting his horse. David sighed as he watched him ride down the lane. The cell confining him was enclosed in a fieldstone building no larger than a shed, with four small windows and a wooden door. His arm throbbed incessantly, but he tried to ignore it, wishing he had something to distract himself. Instead, he was forced to relive what had happened during the past three days.

Several hours passed. He heard a wagon pull up in front of the small one-room jailhouse, so wearily, he went to the window to see who it was. Anna and Abigail stepped down and walked to the entrance. A guard emerged from a small adjacent building.

"Kind sir, I'd like a word with my husband, if you please," she stated to the guard.

"We brought you some food, David." Abigail held up a napkin-covered basket. She looked to the jailer, who reluctantly complied by extracting a skeleton key from his pocket.

"All right," he said, rubbing his thumb and forefinger over his chin, "but there had better not be a file in there."

Abigail giggled. Seeing his glare, she quickly stifled it.

He turned the key in the lock, which clacked open. The sisters entered. They waited for him as he closed the door, locked it, and moved out of earshot as he returned to his wood slat chair behind his desk, which was piled high with paperwork.

Anna gently hugged her husband. He moaned slightly from the pain it caused his injured arm.

"Please tell me again what happened, so that I may understand it," she requested.

He glanced at Abigail, who smiled sympathetically.

"I rode over to the Meyers', and Stephen showed up. He was angry, because he said you should be married to him. We got into an argument, he pulled a gun, and shot me. Oh, and he said he murdered Bill and Sarah, and that he would kill Dorie too."

Anna gaped at him, tears welling in her eyes. "That isn't at all what he claims."

David scoffed. "Well, I can jist imagine." He took Anna's hand, and kissed the back of it. "Anyways, I'm tellin' the truth, darlin'. You believe me, don't you?"

She hesitated.

His eyes grew wide. "Anna?"

The guard glanced over from his desk. Retrieving his pocket watch, he clicked it open. "You have one more minute," he sternly informed before returning to his duties.

Abigail handed David the basket.

"Thank you, kindly, Miss Abigail," he softly said, setting it on the cot.

She smiled at his gratitude. "David, I want you to know I've been reading the signs, and they all indicate one thing. That Stephen has been lying, and you are telling the truth." She glanced at her older sister, who looked away.

"I don't want Dorie to have to witness any of this," Anna said, weeping. "Doctor Spencer doesn't know if Stephen will survive. If he contracts pneumonia, he could very well die." She looked at him accusingly.

He slowly shook his head. "He brought it on himself, honey."

"The sight of you in here saddens me deeply," she admitted.

Taking her hand, he said, "I don't like it any more than you do. I never thought I'd be in a cage again." He winked at her, causing her to smile through her tears. "It's only temporary, 'cause I'm an innocent man," he insisted. "Have you found an attorney to represent me yet?"

"No, but Theodore said he knows one, and he'll go over to visit with the gentleman today."

"Time's up," the jailer announced.

Anna couldn't hold back her emotions any longer. She burst into sobs, throwing her arms around him. They kissed.

"I can't believe this is happening," she whimpered.

"Me neither," he replied.

He kissed her again. The guard approached, opened the cell door, and stood beside her sister, waiting patiently for Anna and David to end their embrace. Dolefully, Anna walked outside. The two lovers gazed at each other as the cell door clanked shut to separate them.

"I'll be back to see you tomorrow." She gasped, quickly covered her face, and returned to the wagon.

"Perhaps I'll pay Stephen a visit," Abigail said, a grin spreading across her face, "appeal to his better angels, and make him confess."

"Good luck," he responded cynically. "How's Renie doin'?"

Abigail's smile faded. "Well, the hoof wall was torn a bit when the clenched nails ripped off, and he's got a bruised sole."

David frowned as he watched her join her sister. Anna glanced sorrowfully at him before the wagon rumbled away. *Reckon we all have bruised souls*, he thought wearily to himself, sinking down upon the cot. He pulled back the cotton napkin to see what the basket contained, and started indulging in cold chicken, buttered bread, and strawberries. Once he'd finished eating, he glanced back into the basket, noticing a book still inside. He withdrew it, realizing it was a Bible with a note attached.

> *My Darling,*
> *Pastor Tully and I chose a few verses*
> *which we thought would provide comfort for you.*
> > *All my love,*
> > *Anna*

Thumbing through, he saw her notations, and honored her wishes by reading aloud. "Be strong and of good courage, do not fear nor be in dread of them: for it is the Lord your God who goes with you; he will not fail you or forsake you." He sighed, feeling forsaken, all the same. Finding another passage, he read: "Out of the depths I cry to thee, O Lord! Lord, hear my voice! Let thy ears be attentive to the voice of my supplications!" He was finding Anna's choices discomforting, but decided to read another. "Not that I complain of want; for I have learned, in whatever state I am, to be content. I know how to be abased, and I know how to abound; in any and all circumstances I have learned the secret of facing plenty and hunger, abundance and want. I can do all things in him who strengthens me." Setting the Bible down, he lay back on the uncomfortable, straw-stuffed mattress to contemplate the last scripture. Soon, he became drowsy, his eyelids grew heavy, and he drifted off to sleep.

Waking suddenly, he looked out the windows to see night had fallen. Disoriented at first, he remembered what had happened to land him in jail, and suddenly felt the throbbing pain in his arm caused from Stephen's bullet. He heard men softly talking outside his cell.

"Word is, that Rebel attacked Captain Montgomery in cold blood," one of them said.

"I heard he set out to kill his entire family, but Captain Montgomery stopped him," remarked the other. "And now the captain's a cripple because of it."

David turned his head to get a good look at them. The guard who had previously been there was gone, replaced by another, who spoke and smoked with a uniformed soldier. The two men noticed, stopped their conversation, and stared at him. He rolled over and closed his eyes, wanting to forget everything that was happening, but compelled himself to remember every last detail. He tossed and turned until his head ached from thinking, and finally fell back to sleep.

In the morning, he was startled awake by the sound of several vehicles. Bolting upright, he sat still for a moment, allowing his lightheadedness to subside, then looked outside to see who it was. Three men emerged and came toward the jailhouse, followed by two women in bonnets. They entered, and conversed briefly with the guard, who nodded. He opened the cell door, allowing David's visitors inside.

The older man removed his top hat, and the rest of the party followed suit, removing their headwear. David saw it was Anna's aunt and uncle, as well as her family's friends, the Burrows, and an elderly man he didn't recognize.

"Governor Geary has full authority in this matter," said the gray-haired man. "We shan't be long." He turned to David, smiled, and extended his hand. "Mr. Summers, I'm Thaddeus Cleveland, and I'll be representing you."

The two shook.

David glanced at Theodore, who stood beside his wife, Grace. "Anna said you'd find me a lawyer," he said to him awkwardly. "The best one in the state."

Thaddeus laughed heartily. "Yes! Well, I don't know about that, but I'll certainly do my best. I've only lost five cases in my twenty years of practice, you know."

"That's right good to hear," replied David, forcing a smile.

"It seems you've gotten yourself into quite a pickle, my dear," Sarah observed, "and we're all here to help you get out of it."

"Thanks, Miss Sarah. I'm jist glad y'all are okay."

Bill stepped over and patted his shoulder. "Because there are no witnesses other than us, it's going to boil down to your word against his."

"And if my prediction is accurate," said Thaddeus, "you will be acquitted."

"I hope so," David responded. "But what if I'm found guilty?"

Grace and Sarah exchanged glances.

"They'll hang you," Theodore blurted.

Grace elbowed her husband.

"We needn't concern ourselves with that remote possibility, because it isn't about to happen," Thaddeus stated confidently. "Your court date has been set for July sixth. We will need your testimony, character witnesses, anything that might sway the jury into understanding how Captain Montgomery's demeanor has changed over the past few months."

"It's been longer than that," David remarked. "I'd say the trouble started for certain, back in sixty-five."

"Once the war ended, I noticed how he behaved peculiarly on several occasions," Sarah added.

"We have four weeks to prepare," said Thaddeus, "which isn't much time. Mr. Montgomery has specifically requested the rush, and it is my opinion that he's trying to impair your case by not allowing us adequate time to prepare, so we will have our work cut out for us. Because of Captain Montgomery's high profile, his family most certainly has hired attorneys from Philadelphia to represent him."

"If we play our cards right," said Bill, "they won't have a leg to stand on."

David nodded, ready to do battle. This was one fight he intended on winning: his life depended on it.

During the following afternoon, it occurred to him that the great battle at Brandy Station had taken place on that very day, six years ago. So much had changed since then. The fight he'd participated in for duty and honor of his Southern heritage was lost to history now. He'd buried his best friend, visited the grave of his commander, and now sat rotting in a country jail. His glory days were behind him; only dismal days remained.

Three long weeks went by. His visitors dwindled to just Anna and Thaddeus. To occupy his time, he wrote long narrations about how Stephen had flown into jealous rages more than once. He listed people who could testify on his behalf, wrote love letters to his wife, and drew pictures of castles and carriages being pulled by fine horses for Dorie. Because Anna preferred to protect her, he hadn't seen her since his incarceration, and missed her terribly.

The Saturday before his trial was to take place, Maggie visited him, telling him she was sorry for not coming sooner.

"I know it's inexcusable," she apologized, "since you're right here in Dover, and I'm only a short distance away. But I had to come over when Kenton didn't suspect. He's very disgruntled with you."

"What's he got to be upset about? I'm the one who's locked up!"

Maggie glanced at the guard. "He and Stephen have become friends. Everyone assumes you tried to kill him."

"Miss Maggie, you know that ain't true." He threw himself down on the wooden cot, which complained with a groan. "I wouldn't be surprised if Montgomery persuaded Kenton to be his friend jist so he could induce him into hatin' me."

Maggie snickered. "Oh, David, don't be ridiculous." She sat beside him.

"Am I bein' ridiculous? Don't you reckon Stephen can manipulate people to say and do jist about anything he wants?"

She reflected on his question momentarily. "He is quite convincing, I'll admit that."

"I hope Mr. Cleveland can persuade the jury as effectively," he mused. "If everyone thinks I tried to kill him, it's fixin' to be a hard sell, swayin' them to think otherwise."

"Don't fret, David," she assured, rising to her feet. "Anna won't testify, but Abigail and I will do our very best to portray you as an honest, upstanding citizen."

He raised an eyebrow in skepticism. "You make it sound like you have to force a lie."

Maggie giggled. "No! That's not at all what I meant." She threw a gesture at the jailer, who advanced with the key. "Anyway, I have to go. I don't want him to know I've been here." She kissed his cheek. "My prayers are with you, dear heart. I know you'll win this." She walked out as the guard permitted her exit.

Sinking back onto the cot, he looked down at his bandaged arm. However optimistic his friends and relatives remained, the gnawing feeling still persisted in the pit of his stomach. There was too much at stake, he had to think of something profound that would leave no question as to Stephen's intentions. He lay back on the soiled, striped pillow, wracking his brain for a solution.

The following day was the Fourth of July. Anna paid him a visit, attempting to console him, as well as herself. She sat beside him while he ate the sandwich she'd brought him, then took his hand.

"I received a letter from Patrick today," she informed.

"Oh? What did it say?"

"That he and Briana have moved to Denver City. They plan on traveling further into the mountains later this summer, to a town called Breckenridge. He said that even if he doesn't strike it rich, the scenery is breathtaking, and he wants us to join them."

He grunted. "I don't see how that's possible, bein's I'll likely be swingin' from a rope by this time next week."

"David! How dare you say such nonsense!" She squeezed his hand. "We will get through this," she stated, with such conviction that he believed her, and nodded in response. After a few moments of silence went by, she said, almost in a whisper, "I went to see Stephen the other day."

His eyes grew wide at the admission. "You what?"

"Shhh!" She placed her fingers on his lips, lest he attract the guard's attention. "I went over to see him on Sunday."

"Well, how's the ole scoundrel doin'?" he asked uncaringly.

"He's getting around. One of his legs was badly broken, so now he has to walk with a cane."

David winced. "Oh. Sorry to hear that." His genuine concern soon dissipated. "Did you ask him why he had me arrested after I saved his life?"

Anna struggled to contain her emotions. "I asked him why he shot you, and he said you drew first."

"That's a lie!" David sprang to his feet. "I didn't have a gun!"

"Is there any way you can prove it?"

He shook his head. "No … I have no witnesses." He sank back down beside her. "I wish Renegade could talk."

She smiled. "I want to protect you, darling, but I won't get up on the witness stand to testify, because I'm your wife. You understand."

"Yeah. Who would believe you, anyways." He gave her a kiss before the jailer announced their deadline.

"We'll see what the next few days bring," she said. Walking toward the door, she turned, blew him a kiss, and departed.

That evening, David listened to fireworks being set off, and wished for his freedom. The thought occurred to him that Callie was most likely having her party. His heart grew heavy with the realization, and in a way, he wanted to be there, but instead, he was held captive like a caged animal.

In the morning, a covered wagon arrived at the jail. David was told he was being moved to York before he was bound in handcuffs, led outside, and forced to climb aboard. He sat between two armed guards clad in Union blue, with a third seated across from him. The men rode in silence. Every time he looked up, the guards stared accusingly at him, so David kept his eyes downturned. Regardless, he was thankful to be released from the little jailhouse and out into the fresh air. For nearly eight miles, the wagon rocked and bumped down a dirt road until it reached York. The draft horses were pulled to a stop, whereby David was ordered to climb out. He did so, gazing at his surroundings to see that they had parked in front of the county courthouse.

"My trial's not till tomorrow," he said.

"Just preliminaries," one guard grumbled.

He gave his captive a nudge with the point of his barrel, so David walked inside. To his relief, he saw Thaddeus waiting for him.

"Hello, Mr. Summers," he greeted. He motioned for the guard to remove his handcuffs. Taking David by the arm, he said, "There is absolutely nothing to worry about. You are going to face the judge and enter your plea."

"That's it?" he asked, allowing himself to be led toward the double doors.

"Yes. Tomorrow, the trial shall begin."

Half expecting to see the judge sitting atop an enormous, elevated pedestal, adorned in a white wig and wielding an anvil, he entered. Once inside the courtroom, they took a seat, waiting for David's name to be called.

"All rise for the honorable Judge Madson," said the bailiff.

David glanced at his attorney, who nodded in encouragement. The two men stood. Judge Madson, wearing a black robe, entered, and sat at his bench like a ruler upon the throne. David and Thaddeus approached him.

"Mr. Summers," the judge said, glancing over the tops of his round spectacles as he read from a piece of paper. "You are charged with attempted murder. How do you plead?"

"Not guilty, your honor."

The judge lifted his gavel. "You are hereby ordered to appear in this courtroom tomorrow morning at eight o'clock." He let the hammer fall, producing a resonating bang. "Adjourned."

Turning to his client, Thaddeus said, "All right, David. I've contacted everyone on your list, and they have assured me they will be here to represent you in the morning. I know it's difficult, but try to get some sleep. We want you to be alert tomorrow."

"Yessir," he responded as a guard escorted him through the double doors.

David was taken downstairs to the county jail, where he was incarcerated until morning. As he lay upon his cot, waiting for the minutes to pass, he thought of Anna, and what her reaction would be upon learning he'd been moved. More than anything, he wanted to spare her anguish, but the situation was unavoidable. He clenched his teeth, wishing Stephen would expire.

He tried to sleep, but his nerves kept him awake, so he constantly got up, looked out into the black night through the barred window, and returned to the cot. His head swam with possible outcomes, and he struggled for the one piece of evidence that would clench his case, but came up empty. Frustrated, he covered his eyes with his left arm, hoping for sleep. He wished Patrick was there, because he would know what to say, and how to produce the proof. David felt his heart racing. After hours of unrest, he saw dawn break. A guard entered from another room to deliver his breakfast. When David had finished, he was taken to a bath, and given clean attire to make himself look presentable. The garments smelled stale, like they'd been taken off a dead man. He grimaced at the thought, but pulled them on anyway.

He was directed upstairs to the courtroom. As he reached the main floor, he saw a mob, which drew closer once they noticed him.

"There he is!" exclaimed one man. "There's the murderer!"

David gawked at him. "I didn't ..."

"You're not allowed to talk," groused the guard, poking him with his rifle. "Go on inside."

The crowd grew louder, asking him questions. "Why did you do it?"

"Are you still fighting the war?"

"Were you seeking revenge?"

Annoyed that he couldn't speak in his own defense, he walked toward the courtroom, seeing his family near the doors. Anna rushed to him.

"Darling! I was so worried when I went to the Dover jail and you ..."

"Back away, ma'am."

One of the guards shoved her aside. He led his prisoner through the throng as David gazed sorrowfully back at Anna. Thaddeus appeared, and escorted him into the courtroom. They walked down the aisle, tolerating stares from strangers and recognizable faces alike.

Taking their seat at a table near the front, David said, "Those folks out there were askin' me all sorts of rude questions."

"Most likely the press," responded Thaddeus. "Hungry piranhas, looking for a tasty bite." He glanced at his client. "A good story," he elaborated.

David's unease heightened. They were going to make a mockery of him if they could.

Momentarily, he heard hushed whispers, and turned to see Mr. Montgomery enter, pushing his son in a wicker wheelchair. David knew Stephen was able to walk on his own.

It's all for show, he thought to himself.

Attired in his Federal uniform, Stephen's legs were covered with a plaid blanket. He glared at David without blinking, his penetrating blue eyes frigid as ice. Tempted to hold his gaze, David decided to look away, and glanced outside, where he saw several spectators peering in through the windows. He wanted to crawl into a hole and hide.

After being told to rise by the bailiff, Judge Madson entered, appearing much as he had the previous day. Instructed to take their seats, the circus began. Thaddeus was called upon to utter a few words in David's defense, and then the Montgomery's lawyer, Mr. Sullivan, introduced the jury to all the wrongs his client, the plaintiff, had suffered. He stopped just short of accusing David outright, which made him wonder if Mr. Sullivan also knew he was innocent of the charges. Once the prosecutors had delivered their orations, the parade of witnesses commenced.

"I call to the stand Mary Brown," declared Mr. Sullivan.

Stephen's sister stood, made her way to the front, pledged to tell the whole truth as she placed her right hand on the Bible, and took a seat on the witness stand.

"Now, Mrs. Brown, what can you tell us about Mr. Summers over there?" Mr. Sullivan gestured in David's general direction. "How did you first meet him?"

"I met him through Anna, who was Stephen's fiancé at the time."

"That's a lie," David whispered.

Thaddeus immediately hushed him.

"And he claimed to be a cousin, is that correct?"

"Yes," Mary answered.

"Was Mr. Summers, in fact, a cousin?"

"No. I found out later that he was a Confederate, hiding in the Brady's house, and he pretended to be a cousin."

David clenched his jaw, bracing himself.

"To your knowledge, were the Brady's aware of this fact?"

"No, sir. Not that I'm aware of."

David breathed a slight sigh of relief. At least Anna wouldn't be dragged into this.

"What is your opinion of this young man seated before you?"

"I would consider him a liar, sir." Her glance flitted in David's direction, but she avoided eye contact.

"On what basis, my dear?"

"On the basis that he intentionally deceived us all."

"This ain't goin' well," David mumbled to his attorney.

"Thank you, Mrs. Brown. Your witness." Mr. Sullivan took a seat beside Stephen as Thaddeus walked toward the bench.

"Mrs. Brown, is it true that you were attracted to my client, well before you knew he had feelings for your brother's so called 'fiancé'?"

"Objection!" Mr. Sullivan cried out.

"Sustained," grumbled the judge with a slam of his gavel.

"Your honor, I am trying to establish a pattern here. The young lady claims that my client was deceptive, when in fact, she was deceptive herself."

"Get on with it, counselor," ordered the judge.

"Mrs. Brown, wasn't it you who approached my client on several occasions, in a flirtatious manner, so that you might attract his attention?"

"What does this have to do with anything?" bellowed the judge.

"When all the while, you, in fact, were engaged to your present husband?"

David's eyes flew open wide. The audience gasped.

"That ... that's not how it transpired at all!" Mary exclaimed.

"And wasn't it your own brother who provoked you into such shameful behavior? Because you both believed the defendant was a relative, and the rightful heir to the Brady's property?" Thaddeus' voice grew louder. "Therefore, you thought you could entice Mr. Summers into a fraudulent marriage, and thus convince him to sell the Brady farm to your family. Is that correct?"

"Objection!" Mr. Sullivan hollered.

"Overruled!" Judge Madson responded. "Answer the question, please, Mrs. Brown."

"Well, I ..." Mary's voice trailed off as the room grew silent. "Yes," she admitted. The audience grew louder with discourse. "Yes, it's true!" She cupped her face in her hands.

"That is all, your honor," Thaddeus stated. He took his seat while Mrs. Montgomery ran up to collect her daughter.

"How did you know all that?" David asked, containing a grin.

Thaddeus nodded. "On to the next witness," he said, taking pen in hand to scribble notations.

From there, the procession of witnesses proceeded. Stephen's father took the stand, and when asked if he knew of David's Confederate affiliation, became agitated.

"That confounded boy had us all believing he was a true compatriot, bound to the Union cause!" he stated enthusiastically. "It wasn't until after the war that we learned the truth! He went back to his real home in Alabama, and took our Anna with him!"

The crowd grew excited.

The judge banged his gavel. "Order! Order in the court!"

Mrs. Montgomery was called to the stand, and reiterated what her husband had declared. Following her testimony, and a break for lunch, a string of Stephen's friends followed: the Dalton brothers, their sister, Nellie, Lila Fairfax, and two soldiers David hadn't seen since his arrest; Corporal Hunter and Lieutenant Marks, who were dressed in full uniform. Each one proclaimed David had lied to disguise his identity, thus trying to instill upon the jury his questionable integrity. Mr. Sullivan showed no scruples when he called Pastor Tully's wife to the stand. Reluctantly, she described David and Anna's secret wedding, which caused his heart to break. He sat with his head bowed. Now the jury would verify Anna's knowledge that he was a Rebel, but she'd hidden the fact anyway, betraying her fellow countrymen.

Mrs. Tully was asked to step down. She walked over to David, and said, "I'm sorry," before being led back to her seat beside the pastor.

David looked up at the oak wall clock. It was now 4:00 p.m. The judge clapped his gavel to attract everyone's attention.

"This court is adjourned until eight o'clock tomorrow morning, when we will hear witnesses for the defense. Counselors, please see me in my chambers." He arose, and whisked out through a side door.

As the audience stood, a guard immediately swooped in to detain his prisoner.

"It all went quite well, in my opinion," Thaddeus reassured.

David glared at him, wanting to disagree.

"I'll visit you once I've finished with the judge." He walked across the room, shook hands with Mr. Sullivan, and disappeared with him behind the side door.

"Can I talk to my wife?" he asked the guard, as he was led away.

"She'll be allowed to visit in an hour."

David caught sight of Anna, her forehead wrinkled with worry, and smiled at her. Upon exiting through the double doors, the reporters attacked again, throwing barbs of ruthless questions at him. Strangely, he wanted to be back in his cell, away from the spectators, alone. Finding the thought ironic, he faintly chuckled.

Released to his confines, he impatiently waited for visitors. Thaddeus was the first to arrive. The guard allowed David to leave his cell and take a seat at a table with his attorney.

After discussing the day's events, David mumbled, "I don't reckon it went well at all."

"Now, don't be discouraged, my boy. Tomorrow is another day." Thaddeus arose. Placing his top hat on his head, he said, "Please pardon me, but I have a dinner reservation with my wife. Oh, has Anna been by to see you?"

"No, sir, not yet."

"Well, when you do see her, tell her that everything is moving along splendidly." He motioned to the guard, who escorted David back to his cell while the counselor departed.

David sat upon his cot, contemplating. He wanted to be as optimistic, but the hand of dread grasped his heart. At long last, his beloved appeared.

"Anna," he said as the guard opened his cell. They fell into each other's arms.

"Tell me everything will be all right," she sighed into his right ear.

"Mr. Cleveland seems to think so," he replied. Unconcerned that the guard was standing by with a grin on his face, David kissed her deeply. He took hold of her hands. "Tomorrow, they'll put your kinfolk on the witness stand, and I reckon they're fixin' to push the issue about my bein' a deserted Confederate."

"I understand. When we arrive home, we'll have a discussion about the best way to approach it."

"Jist know that, once y'all are cross-examined, Mr. Sullivan will try to find a way to tear apart your testimony."

"Time's up, you two," the guard announced.

"I love you, David." Her aqua eyes glistened; a tear ran down her cheek.

He gently wiped it away. "I love you too." He kissed her again while the guard opened the door and extracted an impatient sigh.

She released him, walked along the dark hallway, and disappeared up the stairs.

He sank down upon the cot as his heart sank. Another sleepless night lay before him: his exhaustion was immeasurable.

In the morning, the jury reassembled, the crowd gathered, and David was led through the horde again, feeling like a sideshow freak. His eyes burned, and his head throbbed from lack of sleep. After rising for the judge, Bill was called to the stand. Thaddeus asked him about his niece's husband, and Bill stated that David was loyal, honest, devoted, and hardworking. Once Thaddeus had established David's integrity, it was Mr. Sullivan's turn to interrogate the witness.

"Did you know Mr. Summers was a Confederate, hiding in your niece's home?" asked Mr. Sullivan, throwing a sidelong glance at David.

"No. I found out after I returned from the war. By then, it didn't matter, and he took good care of the place ..."

"Thank you, sir. You may step down," Mr. Sullivan abruptly interrupted.

Bill did as he was told, giving David a wink as he walked by. Next, Grace presented her testimony, followed by Theodore and Sarah. All three echoed what Bill had stated previously: that even though David had pretended to be a northerner, he was of admirable character. Sarah explained the course of events in which Stephen grew increasingly agitated. This, she thought, was because he was covetous. Mr. Sullivan, however, dismissed it as "here say."

After court recessed for lunch, the trial resumed, with Abigail taking the stand. She gave her oath on the Bible, and took a seat.

"Please state your name," prompted Thaddeus.

"Abigail Brady."

"Miss Brady, please tell us about the defendant in your own words."

"Well, I believe David is kind and gentle, and wouldn't intentionally hurt anybody."

"Have you ever seen him behave aggressively toward anyone?"

"No sir. Just the opposite."

"What do you mean, young lady?"

"Well, he saved my life once."

"Objection!" Mr. Sullivan shrieked.

"Overruled. Go on, counselor," the judge said to Thaddeus.

"How did he save your life?" Thaddeus asked.

"I fell into Conewago Creek, and he jumped in, and pulled me out. I nearly drowned."

"Here say, your honor!" bellowed Mr. Sullivan.

The judge banged his gavel. "Do you have anything else, Mr. Cleveland?"

"No, your honor." He turned to face his opponent. "Your witness," he said.

Mr. Sullivan approached Abigail, whose blue eyes grew large in apprehension. "Miss Brady, were you aware of your brother-in-law's political affiliations when you met?"

She frowned at him.

"Were you aware that he was a Confederate?"

"Oh! Yessir."

The audience whispered amongst themselves, the whir of their voices resembling an approaching tornado.

"Whose idea was it to keep his identity a secret, and not turn him in?"

Abigail threw a glance at her oldest sister. "It was my idea."

The crowd buzzed like swarming bees. Judge Madson tapped his gavel several times.

"Your idea?" Mr. Sullivan asked. He bent over Abigail, sticking his long nose in her face. "Are you certain?"

She nodded.

"Please answer the question, Miss Brady," requested the judge.

"Yes. I mean, it was all of us. We wanted him to stay, so he could protect us."

Mr. Sullivan straightened. "Protect you from what? Other Rebels?"

"No, sir. From Stephen."

The audience gasped in unison.

"Your honor, I call for a recess ..."

"Objection, your honor!" Thaddeus rose to his feet.

"Wait your turn, Mr. Cleveland! Mr. Sullivan, please continue."

Stephen's attorney appeared shaken, and David guessed he was displeased with the direction Abigail's testimony was taking.

"Why would the defendant need to protect you from my client, Miss Brady?"

"Because he can be scary sometimes. He used to be nice, but after Father died, he changed. I think it's because he got greedy, and he wanted to take our farm from us."

"How do you know this?"

"Because he tried to seduce Anna." She pointed a finger at her sister, who gave her a slight smile. "He told her our two farms would be combined."

"I'm sorry, Miss Brady, but I'm afraid I don't understand." Mr. Sullivan walked toward the jury. "How did this make Captain Montgomery 'scary'?"

"He attacked Anna, and tried to kidnap her. He attacked David, and tried to kill him. He wanted to take our farm away from us, and keep it for himself!" She suddenly burst into tears.

"Did you witness these actions?" asked Mr. Sullivan.

She shook her head. "No!"

Some of the women in the audience whimpered.

"All right, Miss Brady, you may step down."

Abigail jumped to her feet, and ran into Anna's open arms.

Upon the judge's suggestion, the court took a brief recess. David sat beside his lawyer, wondering whether Abigail's testimony had been helpful or harmful. Soon, the judge returned, and Maggie was called to the stand. She resonated what Abigail had conveyed to the jury, adding that she'd witnessed Stephen's brutal treatment of her sister, and exemplified David as a hero for staying with them, when he could have left at any time.

"Was it because he didn't want to risk capture?" asked Mr. Sullivan.

"More than that, I believe it was because he felt obligated for our saving his life, and he wanted to protect us. As it was, he was captured anyway. By Stephen." Maggie glared at him unsympathetically.

"So, your brother-in-law had reason to hate the plaintiff, because he had him sent to prison?"

"I didn't say that!"

"Objection!"

"Sustained."

"Thank you, Mrs. Price. You may step down."

Watching her make her way past the bar, David expelled a heavy sigh. *At least she didn't mention I had to stay because Renegade had been lame*, he thought.

Kenton was requested to testify. He took his oath, then answered a few questions tersely. "I really don't know the man well enough to say," he kept repeating. Out of frustration, both attorneys released him.

Doc Spencer was next. Taking the stand, he stated his name and relationship to the defendant. He explained how he had been introduced once David had returned from prison, whereby he treated him for dysentery. Most recently, he tended to his wounded right arm. When asked if he could determine the weapon which caused David's injury, Doc Spencer stated with certainty that it was Stephen's.

"I assisted the county sheriff, and we found no evidence of any other weapons, other than that used by the plaintiff," he affirmed.

The sheriff followed, endorsing the doctor's statements. Finally, after nine hours of grueling testimony, the jury was released for the day. David was allowed to give his wife a hug before being returned to his cell. Lying back on his cot, his head grew heavy on the pillow, and soon, he fell asleep.

Court was set to resume at eleven o'clock, thus allowing the jurors and the defendant time to rest. It didn't matter much to David, though. He was bored to tears inside his 6 x 6 cell, thankful he at least had a street level window to peer out of, and wanted to get the whole thing over with. So far, he couldn't tell who was winning, but he knew the day's events might be the deciding factor, depending on how convincing his testimony was. Preparing himself, he sat on the edge of his cot, running possible questions and responses through his mind, considering every angle he could imagine. Two armed soldiers appeared to take him upstairs, and escorted him to the courtroom. Once inside, Thaddeus asked him to take the stand.

Answering his questions, David depicted what had happened on the day he'd been shot, how Stephen's hostility had alarmed him, and how he'd lied about killing Anna's aunt and uncle. He explained that Stephen threatened him, drew on him, and fired. David told the jury about his attempt to gallop away in avoidance, and Stephen's own negligence, which caused his accident. Responding to his attorney's queries, he described Stephen's reaction upon learning he'd returned from Elmira.

"He tried to kill me then too," David testified, glancing down at his bandaged arm, "but as y'all can see, he didn't succeed."

A few members of the all-male jury chuckled.

Mr. Sullivan proceeded to cross-examine him. David answered all of his questions honestly, and even admitted that he had wanted to protect Anna because he'd fallen in love with her. Several jury members wore smiles on their faces while he timorously described their love affair. David kept a sober demeanor, although he was amused the prosecution could find no nails with which to hammer into his coffin. Testifying for over an hour, he finished by saying he indeed saw Stephen hit Anna, and was deeply concerned for her safety.

"If you were so worried, why did you take her down south with you?"

"Because, at the time, I didn't know any better. As far as I knew, it was safe."

"Is it true she left you because of the torrential climate down there?"

"Yessir."

"And you failed to go after her, because of your involvement with the Ku Klux Klan?"

The audience whispered in hushed tones. Judge Madson tapped his gavel to quiet them.

"I left as soon as I could, and it didn't have anything to do with the Klan. I felt responsible for my ma and sister. I knew Anna would be safe in Pennsylvania, but it upset me that Stephen was escortin' her."

"Why is that?"

"Because I don't trust him. I never have."

"Mr. Summers, is it true you're still fighting the war, and that is why you attacked Mr. Montgomery?"

David frowned. "No sir. I took my oath of allegiance before I was released from Elmira. And I did not attack Mr. Montgomery."

David and Stephen glared at each other. The tension it caused reverberated around the room.

"Order," the judge said, slamming his gavel, even though all was quiet. "Counselor, may we move on to the next witness?"

David clenched his jaw. He couldn't stop leering at Stephen, and wished he'd stumble over his testimony so everyone would know he was lying.

"That will be all, Mr. Summers. You may step down."

Rising to his feet, David walked over to the table where his attorney was seated, all the while staring at his adversary.

"I would like to call Stephen Montgomery to the stand."

Mr. Montgomery wheeled his son to the front of the room and parked him in front of the judge's bench.

The bailiff requested his oath upon the Bible. Stephen's attorney came forward as his father walked back to his seat.

"Now then, Captain Montgomery, we've heard from the defendant. Please state, in your own words, what happened on that fateful day four weeks ago."

Stephen looked down at the blanket on his lap, obviously distraught. David winced, knowing he was behaving that way to acquire the jury's compassion.

"I went over to the Meyers' farmstead, which my family purchased last summer, and encountered Mr. Summers, who was trespassing." He glared at David with a nod, directing the jury's attention toward him. "When I asked what he was doing there, he said it wasn't my business, and accused me of letting the place fall to ruin."

David frowned. "He's makin' this up," he whispered to Thaddeus, who raised his hand to quiet him.

"When I objected, he became agitated. He said he was going to ride back to the Brady's to fetch a torch so he could set the Meyers' place on fire. And he said that if I got in his way, he'd shoot me."

"He's lyin'!" David hissed quietly to his attorney. Thaddeus gave him a side glance and slightly nodded.

"Why, in your opinion, would he behave so irrationally?" asked Mr. Sullivan.

"He's always wanted me dead. He knows I've loved Anna all my life, and when I did my duty as a soldier of the U.S. Army by having him arrested, he hated me for it." Stephen's steely blue eyes turned to Anna.

She looked away.

"Well," he continued, "that's when we got into a tussle. He attacked me, so I pulled my iron and fired, shooting him in the arm. I told him I was going for help, but he jumped on his horse and chased after me. He screamed he was going to kill me. He forced his horse into mine, and my mount stumbled, sending me down under him. Because of him, now I have one ruined leg."

David's mouth dropped open. Stunned, he couldn't believe what he was hearing. Stephen twisted the truth so proficiently he nearly believed it himself.

"That ain't what happened," he whispered to his attorney. "He's committin' perjury!"

Thaddeus patted him on the wrist. Called by the judge to conduct his cross-examination, he arose from his hardwood chair, and approached the plaintiff.

"Captain Montgomery, is it true that you attempted to abduct the defendant's wife against her will?"

"Well, I ..."

"Objection!" Mr. Sullivan called out.

"And you told him you had murdered his wife's relatives, when in fact, that was not the case?"

"I don't recall telling him such poppycock," Stephen smugly replied.

"Is it true that you claim my client instigated the fight at the Meyers' farm, when in actuality, it was you?"

"State your case, counselor," Judge Madson growled.

"Your honor, I would like to present to the jury, Exhibit A." He motioned to his attendant, who brought forth a slouch hat. Grasping it, he held it up to each jury member as he strutted past them. Sweeping it in David's direction, he asked, "Does this hat belong to you, Mr. Summers?"

"Yessir."

Spinning on his heels to face the plaintiff, Thaddeus inquired, "Could you please explain to us, Captain, how this bullet hole could have gotten here?"

He put his index finger in the hole, and waved it at the jury. A few members chuckled.

"I have no idea," muttered Stephen.

"I understand. Is it difficult to recall between doses of laudanum?"

"Objection!"

"I take it for the pain," Stephen replied coolly. "For the wound Mr. Summers inflicted on my hand ..." He held up his right hand, exposing the scar to the jury, "... and now for my leg, which Mr. Summers also inflicted upon me." He put his left hand to his face, and let go a sob.

David grimaced in repulsion. The man was an excellent liar, and should have been performing with the best of them. John Wilkes Booth sprang to mind.

"Because of the angle in which the bullet entered, and the freshness of the puncture, which is exactly the same width as the bullets your weapon holds, isn't it apparent that this was made by your pistol?"

"Speculation, your honor," said Mr. Sullivan.

"Sustained."

David's heart thumped in his ears. His attorney, like Napoleon at Waterloo, had been beaten in defeat. Thaddeus' attempt to sway the jury backfired. He let his arm fall to his side, still grasping onto David's hat.

"No further questions, your honor," he muttered.

Following a brief recess, the courtroom refilled to capacity.

"The counsel will now present closing arguments," announced the judge.

David's lawyer went first. He pleaded with the jury to understand his client's intentions, and implored them to search their souls, finding him not guilty of the charges. David, he reasoned, was merely at the wrong place at the wrong time, originally escaping from Union forces only to become entangled in a stranger's deceitful lies. This situation, he explained, had escalated over the years, and now was at fruition. Because of Stephen's addiction, he was incapable of reasoning, and therefore, reacted with violence.

Mr. Sullivan followed up Thaddeus' statement by claiming Stephen was the injured party, not David, whom he maintained was the perpetrator. Seemingly as clever at manipulation as his client, he declared David knew of Stephen's relationship with Anna, yet wormed his way between them. According to Mr. Sullivan, David had initiated all aggression, including the episode that played out four weeks prior. It was only right, he said, for the jury to find him guilty, and instill the maximum sentence: death.

David was led back to his cell. After nearly an hour, his attorney appeared. He apologized for the end result, but still held out hope that the jury would see the light of truth. Once he'd gone, David sat on his cot, feeling empty inside. The situation seemed hopeless.

Anna was allowed to visit for a few minutes. He hugged her tightly, not wanting to let her go. After listening to her assurances, she departed, leaving him alone with his doubt. Although weary, he found himself unable to sleep, and lay awake, listening to the drone of the guards' voices.

"Summers! Get up! You've been called to appear in court."

David startled awake. A guard stood at the open door of his cell.

"Come on! We ain't got all day."

He motioned for David to come toward him, so slowly, he arose on stiff legs, and followed the guard upstairs. There was no media circus this time. Apparently, the press was unaware of the change in plans. Led to his place at a table, David was released to his attorney.

"What's goin' on?" he asked, attempting to smooth his ruffled hair.

Thaddeus smiled at him like a fox who had escaped the hounds.

The judge entered. After seating himself at the bench, he grumbled, "Mr. Cleveland, this is highly unorthodox. Why have you assembled us all here?"

345

David looked at Stephen, who was scowling, then threw a glance over his shoulder to see that Anna, Abigail, Sarah, and Bill were present, as was Stephen's family, and several spectators who had wandered in off the street.

"Your honor," said Thaddeus, "I'd like to call Ida Meyers to the stand."

David glared at his attorney before turning around to observe Mrs. Meyers enter. The bailiff escorted her to the front of the courtroom, where she took her oath and a seat.

"Please state your name."

"Ida Meyers."

"Mrs. Meyers, tell the jury what you witnessed on June the twelfth."

She slightly smiled at David. "Vell, I vas goink to za old house, because I missed za place, and decided to see it von last time. And zat's when I saw zem."

"Saw who?" Thaddeus asked.

"David and Stephen."

"Please describe to us what you saw."

"I saw Stephen chase after David and shoot at him. I saw Stephen drive his horse into David's, and zat's ven Stephen lost control of his beast. His horse fell on top of him. David rode back to help him, and shot the poor animal in za head. Zen he rode to za Brady's for help. Zat's when I left."

"Why didn't you assist Captain Montgomery?"

Mrs. Meyers' demeanor changed drastically. She seemed reluctant to look in Stephen's direction, and instead, glanced at her husband, who coaxed her on with a nod. "Because I vanted him to die."

The audience groaned.

"Why would you want such a dreadful thing to happen?" inquired Thaddeus.

Mrs. Meyers' lower lip quivered. For the first time since he'd known her, David witnessed her display apprehension.

"Because Captain Montgomery threatened me."

"Objection," Mr. Sullivan said.

"Overruled. Please continue, Mrs. Meyers." Judge Madson gazed down at her kindheartedly.

She squeezed her eyes shut for a moment to gain composure. "Last summer, he paid us a visit, but Carl, my husband, vas out in za field, and I vas alone." She hesitated, so Thaddeus prompted her. "Stephen said he vanted to speak wis my husband, but ven I told him he vas out, he came at me. He said he vanted to buy za farm, and he vouldn't take no fo an answer. And zen, he hit me."

"He hit you?"

"Ja. He slapped me, and said zat I needed to convince Carl zat we should move, or bad tinks vould happen to us."

"He threatened you."

"Ja, zat he did." Finally finding the courage, she stared at Stephen.

He sprang to his feet from his wheelchair. The blanket that had covered his legs fell to the floor. "That's a lie!" he shrieked. "It's all a damn lie!"

"Sit down, Mr. Montgomery!" the judge ordered with a bang of his gavel. "Or I will find you in contempt of this court!"

Stephen complied, his face turning beet red.

"Thank you, Mrs. Meyers," Thaddeus said. "Your witness."

Mr. Sullivan approached her, obviously unprepared. "Mrs. Meyers, it's rather coincidental that you happened to be at your previous residence just as the event in question was transpiring. How do you explain that?"

"Vell, I was dere because I got a letter from our hired hand, Patrick, and he told me zat David checks za farm every Saturday mornink around ten o'clock. I vanted to go dere ven I knew I vouldn't be alone, but I didn't vant to tell Carl, because I knew he vouldn't vant me trespassink."

Mr. Sullivan managed to come up with a few more questions, but could find no flaws in her testimony. Like a dog with its tail between its legs, he slinked back to his seat.

"The jury is dismissed to deliberate," announced the judge. "And hopefully this won't take all weekend," he mumbled before descending.

David was escorted to his cell. Astounded by what Mrs. Meyers had just confessed, his head throbbed, compelling him to lay back against the pillow. Momentarily, he was requested to return to court. He was taken upstairs, where a horde of newly arrived reporters lurked, firing questions at him, but he didn't have any answers. A guard pushed his way through the media while leading him by the arm into the courtroom.

"The jury has taken less than an hour," Thaddeus informed as he took his seat.

"Is that a good sign?" he asked, just as the jury shuffled in through the side door. They took their places within the box. Judge Madson entered, and made his way to the bench.

"Members of the jury, have you reached a verdict?" he asked.

An elderly man with gray sideburns stood. "Yes, your honor, we have."

He extracted a piece of paper from a pocket of his waistcoat, and gave it to the bailiff, who in return handed it to the judge.

"What say you?" Judge Madson asked after unfolding the paper, reading it, and folding it again.

"We the jury, find the defendant, David Summers ..."

Without blinking, David felt a lump get caught in his throat, which caused him to catch his breath.

"... Not guilty."

A cry from the crowd went up as the judge banged his gavel.

"This court is adjourned!" he proclaimed, and hurriedly exited.

David jumped to his feet, emphatically shook Thaddeus' hand, and turned to receive hugs from his wife and family. After accepting their congratulations with an amiable smile, he took Anna's hand while she led him outside, but not without looking at Stephen first, his vanquished foe, who avoided eye contact by surrounding himself with his own people. A sudden sentiment of pity swept over David, but he quickly forgot it, distracted by what awaited on the other side of the double doors as he emerged into the limelight.

"Mr. Summers! You've been vindicated. How does it feel to be a free man?" inquired one reporter.

David chuckled. "Right nice, I reckon."

"Have you anything to say to the plaintiff?" asked another.

"Jist that I'm sorry about the way things turned out ... for Captain Montgomery, that is."

"What are your plans now, sir?"

He stopped, glanced around, noticed several artists drawing his likeness, and grinned. "I plan to head on home to my wife and young'un."

"And after that?"

He shrugged. Looking at Anna, he said, "We'll see what tomorrow brings."

They went outside to the waiting landau and boarded. As Bill drove them out of town, Abigail, Sarah, and Anna chattered excitedly. David sat gazing at them with a contented continence on his face. The ladies soon fell quiet, and Anna laid her head on his shoulder. He was so exhausted that his eyes began to drift shut.

"I knew you'd escape them."

He opened his eyes to see Abigail smiling at him. "I'd ask how you knew, but I reckon I already know the answer."

She giggled.

A week went by, and summer grew hotter. David worked obediently in the cabinetry shop when he wasn't toiling in the fields, but the situation grew increasingly discomforting for him. He repeatedly overheard people comment in hushed tones about his trial and verdict. Deep in his heart, he knew the locals would always blame him for what had happened to Stephen, and they would never let him forget. It occurred to him that he didn't belong up north, or down south either, for that matter. There were only two directions left, and going east to Europe was far beyond his means.

On Monday the 19th, he decided to confront Anna with his decision. Entering the kitchen to find her there with her aunt and younger sister, he announced, "We're goin' out west."

She looked at him, but showed no surprise. "When were you planning on departing?" she asked nonchalantly.

He glared at her, taken aback. "I ... dunno," he stammered.

Sarah chortled at his reaction. "David, dear, have a seat."

He did as she requested.

Glancing at her older niece, she asked, "Would you like to tell him, or should I?"

"I'd be more than happy to, if you'll assist me with the details," Anna replied.

David raised a questioning eyebrow at her.

"Sweetie, I've already had a deed drawn up. Uncle Bill has agreed to sign it under pretense. He's also agreed to foresee the farm, and allow Abigail to remain, of course. We expected this, in fact."

"So what took you so long?" Abigail asked him, grinning.

David gaped at her, then looked at his wife. "I was afraid to bring it up, 'cause I know you don't want to leave your kinfolk." He frowned. "But you're okay with this?"

Anna nodded with a smile.

He stood, and took her in his arms. "Thank you, darlin'." Tempted to kiss her, she reacted by deflecting his affection.

"Go wash up. Supper's almost ready."

Mildly embarrassed, he went outside to the well. Abigail followed him. She ogled him while he scrubbed.

Becoming self-conscious, he asked, "Miss Abigail, is there somethin' I can do for you?"

"No." She sat at the edge of the well, watching him.

Her silence made him nervous. "What is it?" he inquired, growing impatient.

"Oh, I was just remembering the night Dolly and I showed you the planchette. Do you remember what it said?"

Drying his hands, he stated, "Yeah, sort of."

"Don't you see, David? It all makes sense. Stephen will be rid of you because you're leaving, but you'll never be rid of him. Do you know why?"

"Because he's fixin' to haunt me for the rest of my life?" He grinned, but seeing her nod in agreement, turned sober. "Come on, Miss Abigail. Let's go eat."

They set their departure date for July 31, a Saturday. This allowed them two weeks to finalize paperwork, get all of their effects in order, and say their goodbyes. It also gave Renegade time to heal, which concerned David as much as his family's safe travel. Anna wrote a letter to Patrick and Briana, informing them of their plans, while David assisted Bill with farm work.

In the meantime, Sarah ran across Mrs. Montgomery at the dry goods store, who notified that she and Mr. Montgomery had decided to have their son committed to an asylum for a short time. "For observation" is how she put it, making Sarah wonder if the court had ordered it instead. Mrs. Montgomery apologized for her son's erratic behavior and requested that Sarah express her regrets to her family. After learning of Stephen's plight, David felt sorry for him, but considered that, once he was released, Stephen might seek revenge. Therefore, he wanted to be as far away as possible when it happened.

At last, Friday the 30th arrived. David started the day by testing his stallion's sole, and finding it sound, breathed a sigh of relief. He searched out Bill, who requested his assistance with loading bales of hay into the barn loft. By early afternoon, he was exhausted from the heat, but promised to take Anna to Dover to see her sister, so he kept his word, and borrowed Alphie to pull the wagon into town. They sent a telegram to David's mother, informing her of their plans, and another to Patrick, notifying him of their anticipated arrival to Denver in several days. Once they arrived at Maggie's, he stood by the wayside, watching her hug Dorie and Anna repeatedly. Both women wept uncontrollably. Maggie turned her affections toward David, who embraced her fondly while she sobbed into his shoulder. After bidding bittersweet farewells, the Summers rode over to visit Grace, who invited them in, gave them a cup of tea, and told David that if things didn't go according to plan out west, his occupation with the Burrows was always secure. After graciously thanking her, they set off for home.

"That was right nice of Mrs. Burrows to say I'd always have a job here," he remarked as they rode down the dusty road. Dusk was rapidly approaching; he slapped the reins on Alphie's withers to get him to trot. "You know, darlin', if for some odd reason I don't strike it rich in Colorado, I can always fall back on my cabinetry skills ... out there."

She took his hand. "I know. We'll see what life has to offer."

Dorie laid her little hand atop her mother's, so that all three were stacked up. Amused, she burst into hysterical giggles, which caused her parents to chuckle.

That evening after supper, David walked out to the barn for a last-minute check to look over his tack, and to feed the livestock. A thunderstorm was rolling in, and he wanted to ensure that Renegade wasn't alarmed by the thunder, although his horse had heard many a cannon go off. He entered to find Abigail, who had already fed him his oats.

"Now you be a good boy, and take care of everyone for me," she was saying to him as she stroked his cheek.

David softly cleared his throat. She looked over to see him standing near the stall, and smiled.

"I was just telling Renegade that he …"

"I heard." He entered the stall. "We'll be jist fine, Miss Abigail." He let out a snicker. "Why, next time I see you, reckon you'll be all grown up and married with young'uns of your own!"

Her eyes glistened. Quickly, she turned to leave, but he caught her by the arm. A tear rolled down her cheek.

"I'm sorry, darlin'," he apologized. "I didn't mean to upset you."

"You didn't. I know why you want to leave, and I don't blame you, but I'll miss you terribly." A whimper escaped her.

"We'll miss y'all too. But you can always write. And if, for some reason, you decide you don't want to stay here, you're always welcome to come out west and settle in with us."

Abigail beamed. "Really?"

"Of course."

She threw herself on him, and held him tightly. "Thank you," she replied.

"You're welcome," he bashfully responded, releasing her. Why don't you go on in. We've got an early start in the mornin'."

"Okay." She grinned as she wiped her cheek, and sauntered off.

David watched her go, remembering a similar promise he'd made to her before he and Anna had gone to Alabama. Relieved she was spared possible exposure to peril, he was glad she had never made the trip down there, after all.

He turned back to Renegade. Calmly running his hand along the horse's neck, he said, "Another adventure's awaitin' us, ole pard, and it's jist around the corner."

He began whistling "The Bonnie Blue Flag" while checking his tack, and when he'd finished, walked back to the house. He went upstairs to see Anna sitting on the edge of the bed, crying, her long blonde hair undone and hanging loosely.

Hastening to her side, he asked, "Darlin', what's wrong?"

She wiped her eyes. "It's starting to sink in that I might never see my sisters again."

Softly caressing her shoulder, he said, "Aw, honey, don't fret. You don't know that to be true."

Anna arose, and looked out the window at the torrential rain pouring down. "David, could you please light a fire? It's somewhat chilly in here."

He did as she requested, and when he'd finished, he sat back upon the bed. Pulling her down beside him, he took her hands in his. "You know, Anna, we don't have to go. If it means that much to you, we can stay. I wouldn't want to sadden you that way."

She smiled, but seeing he was serious, her bluish green eyes grew wide. "Do you truly mean it?"

David nodded, and bit his lower lip. He didn't really mean it, but he couldn't drag her away to some unknown place and make her suffer. He'd already done that.

Springing to her feet, she giggled. "Oh, David!" She kissed him, straightened, and said again, "Oh, David! I'll go tell the others!" Before he had a chance to respond, she flounced out of the room.

For a few moments, he sat listening to the rain pelt down upon the roof, feeling his heart sink. He rose to his feet, walked over to the armoire, opened the door, and reached back to the hidden compartment inside. Withdrawing a piece of paper, he unfolded it, gazing at the script etched upon it. He heaved a weighted sigh, stepped toward the fire, and prepared to cast it in. A hand grasped his suddenly. Startled, he reeled to see Anna.

"No," she said, gently taking the document from him. "I won't let you destroy it."

"But I thought this is what you wanted," he replied, confused.

"What I want, darling, is what you want. I want you to be happy. I couldn't ask you to remain here when I know how difficult it is for you." She walked over to her dressing table, and set the bill of sale receipt on top. "I love you with all my heart, and I will follow you to the ends of the earth if need be."

He glowered. "But what about Dorie?" he asked. "And your sisters?"

She returned to him. "I realized on the way downstairs that we are all destined to live our own lives. My sisters could just as easily move away from me. But I made a promise to you. We are bound to each other by our vow." She took his hands in hers. "We both know the bill of sale Uncle Bill signed is merely a way to deter Stephen, should he try to obtain the farm. I still own it, and it would rightfully go to Maggie if I decide to decline ownership. Stephen can never obtain our farm."

"Anna," he said, "are you absolutely sure this is what your li'l ole heart desires? 'Cause Lord knows, the last thing I want is for you to git out there, decide you don't like it, and run away from me like you did before."

She chuckled. "I won't run away from you, darling. Not ever again." She stepped toward him. They consumed each other in a passionate kiss.

"I have a suggestion," he said.

She looked at him curiously. "What?"

"How's about, if things don't work out in a year's time, we come back here to stay?"

She smiled happily. "That sounds like a splendid idea." She tenderly kissed him. "We'd better get some sleep," she advised. "Tomorrow will arrive far too soon."

He agreed, shed his clothing while she changed into her nightdress, and climbed into bed with her. As they lay next to each other, basking in the warm firelight, his mind began racing, the exhilaration of his prospects thumping within his chest, and he wondered if he'd ever get any sleep. Anna rolled over, and lovingly kissed him. Lying back beside him, she quietly dozed off.

Forcing his eyes shut, he soon found himself submitting to slumber. His dreams were becoming a reality, nearly within reach; he could almost grasp them. What lay in store was a mystery, but an exciting one at that. The future awaited, and he couldn't wait to pursue it. Tomorrow was the beginning of a new life for them; a new episode. Tomorrow morning, they would start anew ... unless Anna changed her mind again. Smiling to himself, he blissfully fell asleep in her arms.

The rooster's crow awoke him. He rolled over to see that Anna had already risen. Climbing out of bed, he dressed, gathered his things, and went downstairs. On the way down, he glanced out the window and noticed something he hadn't before. A small peach tree had sprouted under the window. It struck him as odd how a peach tree could be growing in such a strange place, but then it dawned on him. He remembered how he had eaten a peach and thrown the pit out the window directly prior to the last time he and Anna had departed. It all seemed too reminiscent of the last time he'd left Pennsylvania. He smiled to himself as he entered the kitchen, took a ripe peach from a bowl on the counter, and quickly ate it. Tossing the pit out into the yard, he wondered if another tree would be there to greet him once he returned. The thought of it warmed his heart.

Like before, the family boarded the landau and rode to the train station. David and Anna shared their goodbyes with Sarah, Bill, and Abigail, who managed to hold a grin this time. Once onboard, the couple secured Dorie between them and settled in for a long ride.

David learned their journey would start by riding the B & O Railroad line to Chicago. They would then travel across Iowa on the Chicago and Northwestern, and board the Union Pacific Railroad in Council Bluffs. From there, they would take the newly constructed Transcontinental Railroad to Cheyenne, Wyoming, and then ride the Denver Pacific Railway down to Denver. The prospect of such a trip thrilled him. Like before, he was encountering the unknown. But last time, it was different. He had been returning to his Southland, and although he hadn't known what exactly awaited him, it was still home. This time, it was all new, undiscovered territory, full of excitement, Indians, outlaws, and wilderness. He couldn't wait to get there. He only hoped Anna would find it as exciting as he did. If not, in a year's time, they would return to Pennsylvania. Taking her hand, he smiled at her. She returned the gesture.

This time, things will be different, he thought to himself. *This time, we'll find happiness, and I'll strike it rich.* He glanced at her again and knew he was already a wealthy man. *Things can only git better from here.* His heart leaped with exhilaration as the locomotive lurched forward. Another grand adventure was about to begin.

The Last Will and Testament of J. Reb

I, J. Reb, being of unsound mind and bitter memory, and aware that I am dead, do make public and declare the following to be my political last will and testament.

I give, device, and bequeath all my slaves to Harriet Beecher Stowe.

I direct that all my shares in the venture of secession shall be cancelled, provided I am released from my unpaid subscription to the stock of said enterprise.

My interest in the civil government of the Confederacy I bequeath to any freak museum that may hereafter be established.

My sword, my veneration for General Robert E. Lee, his subordinate commanders and his peerless soldiers, and my undying love for my old comrades, living and dead, I set apart as the best I have, or shall ever have to bequeath to my heirs forever.

And now, being dead, having experienced a death to Confederate ideas and anew birth unto allegiance to the Union, I depart, with a vague but not definite hope of joyful resurrection and of a new life, upon lines somewhat different from those of the last eighteen years. I see what has been pulled down very clearly. What is to be built up in its place I know not. It is a mystery; but death is always mysterious. Amen.

- John Wise

Figures released by the U.S. Government in 1866:
Of the 270,000 Federals in Confederate prisons, 22,576 died (8.3%)
Of the 220,000 Rebels held in Federal prisons, 25,436 died (12%)
The death rate of Confederates was almost 50% higher.

According to **Governor Parsons'** inaugural proclamation on July 20, 1865:
Alabama's male population, 15-60 years of age, in 1860 was 126,587
Soldiers enlisted – 122,000
Died in service – 35,000
Disabled – 35,000

Colonel W. H. Fowler, superintendent of army records:
Had a list of nearly 20,000 dead, and believed that was only half the number.
Alabama troops lost more heavily than any other troops.
He asserted that of the 30,000 Alabama troops in the Army of Northern Virginia, over 9,000 died in service, and of those who were retired, discharged, or who resigned, about half were either dead or permanently disabled.

Alabama's 1866 census:
8,957 soldiers killed in battle
13,534 died of disease or wounds
2,629 disabled for life

Governor Patton's statement in his address to Congress on May 11, 1866:
Alabama property losses totaled $500,000,000, including the value of slaves ($500 each)

1860, 1866 and 1870 Alabama State Census:

White	Black
1860 – 526,271	1860 – 437,770
1866 – 522,799	1866 – 423,445
1870 – 521,384	1870 – 475,510

References

Civil War and Reconstruction in Alabama, by Walter L. Fleming, Ph. D., © 1949, Columbia University Press

Death at Cross Plains: An Alabama Reconstruction Tragedy, by Gene L. Howard, © 1984, University of Alabama Press

How to Think Like a Horse, by Cherry Hill, © 2006, Storey Publishing

Neither Carpetbaggers nor Scalawags: Black Officeholders during the Reconstruction of Alabama, 1867-1878, by Richard Bailey, © 1991, Richard Bailey Publishers